D0952050

Lies

we tell

ourselves

Robin Talley

Lies
we tell
ourselves

HARLEQUIN® TEEN

ISBN-13: 978-0-373-21133-3

LIES WE TELL OURSELVES

HARLEQUIN®TEEN
www.HarlequinTEEN.com

Printed in U.S.A.

To the Norfolk 17:

Delores Johnson Brown
LaVera Forbes Brown
Louis Cousins
Alveraze Frederick Gonsouland
Andrew Heidelberg
Geraldine Talley Hobby
Edward Jordan
Betty Jean Reed Kea
Olivia Driver Lindsay
Lolita Portis-Jones
Johnnie Rouse
James Turner Jr.
Patricia Turner
Carol Wellington
Claudia Wellington
Patricia Godbolt White
Reginald Young

May your courage resonate with every generation.

part 1

Rock of Ages

Sarah

LIE #1

There's no need to be afraid.

THE WHITE PEOPLE are waiting for us.

Chuck sees them first. He's gone out ahead of our group to peer around the corner by the hardware store. From there you can see all of Jefferson High.

The gleaming redbrick walls run forty feet high. The building is a block wide, and the windowpanes are spotless. A heavy concrete arch hangs over the two-story wood-and-glass doors at the front entrance.

The only thing between us and the school is the parking lot. And the white people.

We've all walked past Jefferson a thousand times before, but this will be the first time any of us steps inside. Until today, those big wooden doors might as well have been triple-locked, and we didn't have the key.

Our school, on the other side of town, is only one story. It's narrow—no wider than the Food Town. Our teachers put boards in the windows to cover the cracks in the glass, but that's not enough to stop the wind from whistling past us at our desks.

Our old school, anyway. Jefferson is supposed to be our school now.

If we can make it through those big brown doors.

"They're out there all right," Chuck says when he comes back. He's trying to smile, but he just looks frozen. "Somebody sent out the welcome committee."

No one laughs. We can hear the white people. They're shouting, but the sound is too disjointed for us to make out the words.

I'm glad. I don't want to hear. I don't want my little sister Ruth to hear it, either. I try to pull her closer to me, but she jerks away. Ruth will be fifteen in two weeks, and she already thinks she's too old to need help from her big sister.

"If anything happens, you come find me, all right?" I whisper. "Don't trust the teachers or the white people. Come straight to me."

"I can take care of myself," Ruth whispers back. She steps away from me and links arms with Yvonne, one of the other freshmen.

"What are you gonna do if they try something?" Chuck asks Ennis. He keeps his voice low, trying to blend in with the dull roar coming from the school, so the younger kids won't hear him. Chuck, Ennis and I are the only three seniors in our group. Most of the others are freshmen and sophomores. "They've got some big guys on that football team."

"Never mind that," Ennis says, raising his voice so the others can hear. "They won't try anything, not in school. All they'll do is call us names, and we'll just ignore them and keep walking. Isn't that right, Sarah?"

"That's right," I echo. I want to sound in charge, like Mrs. Mullins, but my voice wobbles.

Ennis holds my eye. His face looks like Daddy's did this morning, when he watched Ruth and me climb into the carpool station wagon. Like he's taking a good, long look, in case he doesn't get another chance.

Ennis sounds like Daddy, too. My father and Mrs. Mullins and the rest of the NAACP leaders have been coaching us on the rules since the summer, when the court first said the school board had to let us into the white school. Rule One: Ignore anything the white people say to you and keep walking. Rule Two: Always sit at the front of the classroom, near the door, so you can make a quick getaway if you need to. And Rule Three: Stay together whenever you possibly can.

"What if they spit on us?" one of the freshmen boys whispers. The ten of us are walking so tightly together down the narrow sidewalk we can't help but hear each other now, but none of us makes any move to separate. "We're supposed to stand there and take it?"

"You take it unless you want to get something worse after school lets out," Chuck says.

There's a glint in Chuck's eye. I don't think he'll take anything he doesn't want to take.

I wonder what he thinks is going to happen today. I wonder if he's ready.

I thought I was. Now I'm not so sure.

"Listen up, everybody, this is important." Ennis sounds serious and official, like the NAACP men. "Remember what they told us. Look straight ahead and act like you don't hear the white people. If a teacher says something to you, you don't talk back. Don't let anybody get you alone in the bathroom or on the stairs. And no matter what happens, you just keep walking."

"What if somebody tries to hang us from the flagpole?" the freshman says. "Do we just keep walking then, too?"

"You watch your mouth," Chuck tells him. "You'll scare the girls."

I want to tell him the girls are plenty scared already.

Instead I straighten my shoulders and lift my head. The younger kids are watching me. I can't let them see how my stomach is dropping to my feet. How the fear is buzzing in my ear like a mosquito that won't be swatted away.

We round the corner. Across the street, Jefferson High School sweeps into view. The white people are spread out across the front steps and the massive parking lot. Now I know why we could hear the crowd so well. There must be hundreds of them. The whole student body, all standing there. Waiting.

"Just like I said," Chuck says. He lets out a low whistle. "Our very own personal welcome wagon."

Ahead of me, Ruth shivers, despite her bulky winter coat. Under it she's wearing her favorite blue plaid dress with the crinoline slip and brand-new saddle shoes. I'm in my best white blouse, starched stiff. Our hair is done so nice it might as well be Easter Sunday. Mama fixed it last night, heating the hot combs on the stove and yanking each strand smooth. Everything's topsy-turvy with school starting in February instead of September, but we're all in our best clothes anyway. No one wants the white people to think we can't afford things as nice as theirs.

I try to catch Chuck's eye, but he isn't paying attention to me. He's looking at the crowd.

They're watching us.

They're shouting.

Each new voice is sharper and angrier than the last.

I still can't make out what they're saying, but we're not far now.

I want to cover Ruth's ears. She'd never let me. Besides, she'll hear it soon enough no matter what I do.

Our group has gone quiet. The boys are done blustering. Ruth lets go of Yvonne and steps back toward me. Behind us, a girl hiccups.

What if one of them starts crying? If the white people see

us in tears, they'll laugh. They'll think they've beaten us before we've begun. We have to look strong.

I close my eyes, take a long breath and recite in my clearest voice. *"The Lord is my shepherd. I shall not want."*

Ruth joins in. *"He maketh me to lie down in green pastures. He leadeth me beside the still waters."*

Then, all ten of us, in the same breath. *"He restoreth my soul."*

Some of them have spotted us from across the street. The white boys at the front of the crowd are pushing past each other to get the first look at us.

Police officers line the school's sidewalks in front of the boys. They're watching us, too.

I don't bother looking back at them. The police aren't here to help us. Their shiny badges are all that's stopping them from yelling with the other white people. For all we know they trade in those badges for white sheets at night.

Then reporters are running toward us. A flashbulb goes off in my face. The heat singes my eyes. All I see is bright white pain.

Yea, though I walk through the valley of the shadow of death, I will fear no evil.

I want to reach for Ruth, but my hands are shaking. It's all I can do to hold on to my books.

"Are you afraid?" a reporter shouts, shoving a microphone at my chin. "If you succeed, you'll be the first Negroes to set foot in a white school in this state. What do you think will happen once you get inside?"

I step around him. Ruth is holding her head high. I lift mine, too.

Thou preparest a table before me in the presence of mine enemies.

We're almost at the parking lot now. We can hear the shouts.

"Here come the niggers!" yells a boy on the steps. "The niggers are coming!"

The rest of the crowd takes up his chant, as if they rehearsed it. "The niggers! The niggers! The niggers!"

I try to take Ruth's hand. She shakes me away, but her shoulders are quivering.

I wish she wasn't here with us. I wish she didn't have to do this.

I wish I didn't have to do this.

I think about what the white reporter said. *If you succeed...*

And if we don't?

"It will be all right," I tell Ruth.

But my words are drowned out in the shouting.

"Mau maus!"

"Tar babies!"

"Coons!"

And "nigger." Over and over.

"Nigger! Nigger! Nigger! Nigger! Nigger!"

I've never been called a nigger in my life. Not until today.

We step over the curb. The white people jostle us, bumping up against us, trying to shove us back. We keep pushing forward, slowly, but it's hard. The crowd isn't moving, so we have to slide between them. Ennis and Chuck go in front, clearing a path, ignoring the elbows to their sides and shoves at their chests.

I want to put Ruth behind me, but then I couldn't see her, and what if we got separated? What would I tell Mama and Daddy?

I grab her arm too tight, my fingers digging in. Ruth doesn't complain. She leans in closer to me.

"Go back to Africa!" someone shouts by my ear. "We don't want niggers in our school!"

Just walk. Get inside. Get Ruth inside. When the reporters go away everyone will calm down. If we can get through this part it will be all right.

My cup runneth over.

Ruth's arm jerks away from me. I almost fall, my legs swaying dangerously under me, but I catch myself before I collapse.

I turn toward Ruth, or where she should be. Three older boys, their backs to me, are standing around my little sister, towering over her. One of them steps close to her. Too close. He knocks the books out of her arms, into the dirt.

I lunge toward them, but Ennis is faster. He dodges through a gap between the boys—he doesn't shove them; we're not allowed to touch any of them, no matter what they do to us—and pulls Ruth back toward me, leaving her books where they fell. He nods at me in a way that almost makes me believe he's got everything under control.

He doesn't. He can't. If the boys do anything to him, Ennis doesn't stand a chance, not with three against one. But they let him go, snarling, "We're gonna make your life Hell, black boy."

Ruth's still holding her chin high, but she's shaking harder than ever. I wrap my hand back around her arm. My knuckles go pale. I swallow. Once, twice, three times. Enough to keep my eyes steady and my cheeks dry.

"What about my books?" Ruth asks me.

"We'll get you new books." The blood is rushing in my ears. I remember I should've thanked Ennis. I look for him, but he's surrounded by another group of white boys.

I can't help him. I can't stop walking.

Two girls, their faces all twisted up, start a new chant. *"Two, four, six, eight! We don't want to integrate!"*

Others join in. The whole world is a sea of angry white faces and bright white flashbulbs. *"Two, four, six, eight! We don't want to—"*

"Is the NAACP paying you to go to school here?" a reporter shouts. "Why are you doing this?"

A girl pushes past the reporter to yell in my ear. Her voice is so shrill I'm sure my eardrum will burst. "Niggers go home! Dirty niggers go home!"

Ennis is back in front, pushing through the crowd with Chuck. Ennis is very tall, so he's easy to spot. People always ask if he plays basketball. He hates it because he's terrible at basketball. He's the best player on the football and baseball teams, though.

He was at our old school, anyway. That's all done now that he's coming to Jefferson. No sports for the boys, no choir for me, no cheerleading for Ruth. No dances or plays for any of us. No extracurriculars, that's what Mrs. Mullins said, not this year.

Something flies through the air toward Ennis. I shout for him to duck, but I'm too late. Whatever it is bounces off his head. Ennis keeps moving like he didn't even feel it.

I look for the police. They're standing on the curb, watching us. One sees me looking and points toward the main entrance. Telling me to keep moving.

He's looking right at us. He must have seen Ennis get hit.

He doesn't care. None of them do.

I bet they'd care if we threw things back.

"Nigger!" The girl is still shrieking at me. "Nigger! Nigger! You're nothing but a filthy, stinking nigger!"

We're almost there. The door is only a few yards away, but the crowd of white people in front of it is too thick. And the shouts are getting louder.

We'll never make it. We were stupid to think this could ever work.

I wonder if they knew that. The police. The judge. Mrs. Mullins. Daddy. Mama. Did they think we'd even get this far? Did they think this was enough?

Maybe next year. Maybe the year after that. Someday, they'll let us through, but not today.

Please, God, let this be over.

Someone shrieks behind me. I glance back.

Yvonne is clutching her neck. I can't tell if she's bleeding.

"Yvonne!" Ruth tries to turn back, but I hold her arm. We can worry about Yvonne later.

"Nigger!" The white girl at my shoulder is so close I can feel her hot breath on my face. "Coon digger! Stinking nigger!"

"Oh!" Ruth stumbles. I reach to catch her before she falls, but she finds her footing quickly. She's wiping something off her face.

The boy who spat on her is grinning. I want to hit him, hard, shove him back into the group of boys behind him. See how he likes it when he's not the one with the power.

Instead I keep walking, propelling my sister forward. We're inching closer to the doors.

We're not so far now. Maybe we can get inside. Inside, it will be better.

"You know you ain't going in there, nigger!" the girl screeches in my ear. "You turn around and go home if you know what's good for you! We don't want no niggers in our school!"

Ennis and Chuck are on the steps, almost at the front entrance. The doors are propped open. Behind them more white students are yelling and jostling. Two boys in letterman's sweaters have their fists raised.

We just have to get past them. Inside the school, the teachers will keep everyone under control. The people who are shouting will start acting like regular people again. The entire school can't be made up of monsters.

Chuck and Ennis have stopped to wait for the others to catch up. Ruth and I are right behind them, so we stop, too.

Now that we're not moving, the crowd around us gets even thicker. The shouts get louder. The girl who's been following me has been joined by two of her friends.

"Who's that other nigger girl, huh?" she yells. "Is that your baby sister? Your tar baby sister?"

The girls screech in laughter. Ruth looks straight ahead, but her chin isn't quite as high anymore.

I want to take Daddy's pocketknife and slice the white girl's tongue in two.

"Keep the niggers out!" A group of boys chants in the doorway. "Stop the niggers! Don't let the niggers in!"

But they have to let us in. This is Virginia, not Mississippi. They'll let us in, and they'll see that having us here doesn't make any difference. Then things will settle down.

That's what Daddy said. And Mama. And Mrs. Mullins, and Mr. Stern, and everyone else at the NAACP. It'll be hard at first, but then things will go back to normal. We'll just be going to school. A better school, with solid windows and real lab equipment and a choir that travels all over the state.

Everything will be easier when we get inside that big brick building.

I turn toward the police. They'll make sure we get inside. That's their job, isn't it? To enforce the court ruling?

But the police are so far away, and the crowd is so thick. I can't see them anymore.

We're together now, all ten of us, surrounded by hundreds of white people who are shouting louder than ever. Chuck and Ennis press forward, and the rest of us follow. We're so tightly packed I can smell the detergent Ennis's mother used on his pressed white shirt. It's the same kind my mother uses. I try to imagine I'm back at home on laundry day, helping Mama hang sheets on the line. My little brother playing by the porch steps. Ruth turning cartwheels in the yard while Mama calls for her to go inside and finish her homework.

"It's gonna be open season on coons when y'all get inside," a boy shouts behind me. "Just you wait."

Ennis pushes past the boys blocking the doors. Ruth and I stumble after him.

We're inside.

It's done. We did it. We're in the school.

But the white people are still staring at us. Shouting at us.

They're all around me. And they still look hungry.

Someone shoves into my right side. From behind, someone else's elbow juts into my lower back. Another tall boy with blond hair is right in front of me. All I can see is the thick white wool of his letterman's sweater.

Someone pushes into me from behind. My face is crushed against the blond boy's sweater, but he doesn't move. I can't breathe.

"Hey!" I hear Ennis shout, but he sounds far away. I don't know where Ruth is. My chest feels too tight.

Someone is ramming me hard from the left, but I can't move. There are too many white people. There's nowhere to go.

I can't do this. I can't stay here. I can't breathe.

A tight grip closes around my right arm above the elbow, cutting off my circulation. Fingers dig into my flesh. They're going to drag me out of here.

I've just made it through, and already it's all going to be over. But I don't care, because all I want is to breathe again.

The hand on my arm tugs harder, pulling me through the thick knot of people. This is it. They're going to take me away. I don't know what they'll do to me, and I don't care, because I just want to breathe. I just want this to be over.

That's when the screaming starts.

LIE #2

I'm sure I'm doing the right thing.

MY ARM FEELS as if it's being wrenched from its socket as I stumble through the crush of white people. The pain rockets through me, and my eyes flood with tears.

The grip on my arm lets go. I clutch at my chest as the breath floods back into my lungs.

Then I remember where I am. I turn to run.

"Sarah!" It's Chuck. It's only Chuck.

Ruth is next to him, staring at me with her forehead creased. The rest of the group is gathered behind them.

"Sarah, you all right?" Chuck says.

I nod. I can breathe again, at least. But we're not safe yet.

The shouts are louder here than they were outside. They echo off the walls and high ceilings of the school vestibule, pressing in on us from all sides. More shouts come from deep inside the building. All around us, white people press in, shoving at our backs and glaring at our faces. The building looks huge from the outside, but the vestibule feels tiny with all these people packed so tightly into it, every one of them turned toward us.

Where are the teachers? The principal?

"Where do we go?" Ruth asks. I don't know what to tell her.

"Mrs. Mullins gave me the list," Ennis says. "Seniors go to the auditorium, juniors, the atrium, sophomores, the gym, freshmen—"

"The cafeteria," Paulie cuts in.

"No way." I'm not letting go of Ruth. Not again.

She pulls out of my grip anyway. She's holding her head up again. Back to her old self.

"What are you going to do, babysit me all day?" she asks me.

"I'll walk the freshmen over," Chuck says. He nods toward Yvonne, who's still rubbing her neck. There's a red mark near her collarbone, but no blood. "I'll watch out for them."

I'm not sure about that. I don't want my sister out of my sight.

But I don't know what else to do. Ruth is right. I can't be with her all day.

Plus, I don't know where the cafeteria is. Or the auditorium, or anything else. I've never set foot in this building before, but Chuck is looking up and down the halls as if he knows his way around. I'll have to trust him.

My heart thuds as I watch Ruth go to Chuck's side, turn her back and walk away. All I can do is pray she'll be safe.

Yesterday I would've thought prayer was enough. Today I'm not so sure.

"Come on," Ennis says. "We've got to go. If we're late we'll get detention."

I've never had detention before, but Mrs. Mullins told us the white teachers would look for any excuse to send us there. We can never be late to class, no matter what.

But if we have to deal with shouting crowds every day, won't we always be late?

No. The crowd was only for today. Tomorrow things will go back to normal.

Whatever "normal" is at this huge, looming school, with the shining glass trophy cases lining every hallway and the brand-new books everyone is carrying. And the huge white boys in letterman's sweaters lurking around every corner.

Somehow Ennis already knows his way around Jefferson, too, so I follow him. The auditorium isn't far from the front doors, but it takes us a long time to get there because the white people are still swarming.

They're still shouting, too. And throwing balls of paper. And sticking out their feet to trip us. One catches Ennis's ankle and he falls hard, catching himself with his hands before his face hits the ground. It takes all my strength not to cry out when I see him going down.

The white people howl laughter as I help him up. Ennis is biting his lip and cradling his wrist. I pray it isn't broken. If one of us comes home with a broken bone, the courts could say they were wrong and integration was too dangerous after all. They could send us all back to our old school. Daddy would be furious.

"Hey, you look real pretty today," a girl says in my direction.

I turn around. Did one of the white people really say something nice to me?

No. Of course not.

The girl laughs at me and draws back. I can see what's going to happen but there's nothing I can do about it. The crowd is too thick for me to get away before the girl spits on the yellow flowered skirt Mama made for my sixteenth birthday.

I'm shaking again. Ennis looks at my skirt, then at me. He's still holding his wrist.

"Come on," he says. "We're almost there."

It's getting hard to breathe.

Chuck will have to leave Ruth to come join us. It'll be my

sister and two other freshmen alone with all these angry white people. What if someone trips her like they did Ennis? What if she gets hurt, and she needs me?

Somehow Ennis knows what I'm thinking.

"You'll only make it worse if you try to go back, Sarah," he says, giving me that serious look again. "You've got to have faith it will be all right."

I'm trying to have faith. It's so hard. It's the hardest thing I've ever had to do.

Chuck catches up with us at the auditorium doors. It's too loud for us to hear each other, but he nods to tell me Ruth is all right.

She was all right when he left her, anyway. Who knows what might have happened since then.

A group of boys sings as we walk through the doors. The tune is a song that's been playing on the radio lately, "Charlie Brown." I used to like that song, but the boys have changed the words. *"Fee fee, fi fi, fo fo, fum! I smell niggers in the auditorium!"*

They howl with laughter at their own joke. Other boys and girls join in, snickering at Ennis and Chuck and me as we try to find seats. This room must be built to hold a thousand people. All the seniors are running back and forth between the rows, shouting, laughing, pointing at us. Teachers are standing around, too, but they're talking to each other, looking at their watches, as if they haven't even noticed we're here.

"Two, four, six, eight!" The chant continues as the three of us move toward the front of the room. "We don't want to integrate!"

Posters for school activities hang on the walls. Basketball practice. Science club meetings. Ticket sales for the prom. My eyes linger on a poster for Glee Club auditions before I remember we aren't welcome at the clubs and teams and dances at this school. We aren't even welcome to breathe the same air.

We find three seats together in the front row. I sit between Chuck and Ennis, trying to fold my coat so the spit on my skirt doesn't show. Normally I'd feel uncomfortable sitting with two boys, but everything about today already feels strange.

We haven't been sitting ten seconds when everyone else who was sitting on the front row stands up, all in one smooth motion, and files out.

For the second time this morning, I wonder if the white people rehearsed that.

"Boy, does it ever stink in here all of a sudden," one girl says. Her friends laugh and pinch their noses.

Now that we're alone in the front row, the chanting starts up again behind us. At first it's just a few people, but then the rest of them join in. The voices get very loud very fast.

"Niggers go home! Niggers go home! Niggers go home!"

I look straight ahead. Ennis and Chuck are doing the same thing. I want to meet Chuck's eyes but I'm afraid he'll only try to make some awful joke, and instead of laughing I'll burst into tears.

There is only one thing in this world right now that I want.

I want to get out of here. I want to get up, go find my sister and drag her out the front door. I don't want either of us to ever set foot in this place again.

I'm starting to think things aren't going to get better after this. I'm starting to think they're going to get worse.

"All right now," comes a voice. A teacher is on the stage, holding a clipboard. I wait for her to tell everyone to stop yelling and be polite and respectful, the way the teachers at my old school would have, but she just says, "All right," again. Slowly, the chanting dies down.

The teacher looks bored. As if it's any other first day of school. As if we aren't starting five months late because the governor closed the whole school last semester to stop ten Negroes from walking through the front doors. As if there wasn't almost a riot in the parking lot five minutes ago.

"Your senior class president will lead us in prayer," the teacher says. She nods toward yet another boy with blond hair and blue eyes and a varsity letterman's sweater.

"Let's all bow our heads," the boy says.

Automatically, my head goes down, my eyes shut and my hands fold in my lap. Before the prayer has even started, I feel something pushing on my lower back. Then the pressure gets sharper. Digging into my flesh through my thin cotton blouse.

Is it a knife? Am I going to die right now, right here? Before I've been to a single class in this godforsaken school? What will happen to Ruth if I die?

I'm about to leap out of my seat when I realize it can't be a knife. A blade would be slicing into my skin, not just pressing.

This isn't a knife. It's a sharpened pencil point.

But it still hurts. A lot.

I ignore it and breathe deeply, trying not to let the pain distract me from my prayer as the blond-haired boy intones, "Our Heavenly Father."

A second pencil joins the first, twin points drilling into me. I move forward in my seat, but the pencils move with me. They're pushing deeper now. I wonder if I'm bleeding.

"You best pray hard, nigger bitch," a boy's voice says, low in my ear. "We're gonna tear you to pieces first chance we get."

That makes me shiver, but I don't let the boy see. I move my lips along with my own prayer. *Please, Father, watch out for Ruth today. And for me, and for all of us. Please watch over us and protect us and let us make it through safely. In Your holy name.*

"Amen," I say with the blond boy and the rest of the senior class. I open my eyes.

The stabbing pain is gone.

Even though I know better—and I'd have killed Ruth if she'd done this—I turn around. I want to see who gave me the bruises forming on my back. I want to meet his eyes.

There's no one there. The seat behind me is empty. So are the seats on either side of it. The rest of the auditorium is a blur of identical-looking white faces.

Then I see a pretty girl with red hair and a stylish white Villager blouse a few rows back. She's looking at me. But this girl isn't sneering, or pinching her nose, or getting ready to throw something at me. She's just looking.

She nudges her friend, another white girl with frizzy brown hair. The brown-haired girl sees me looking at them and puts her hand up in front of her cheek as if she's embarrassed, but the red-haired girl isn't shy about staring.

It takes me too long to realize I'm staring back at the red-haired girl.

I drop my head, but it's too late.

Did she notice? Could she tell?

This hasn't happened to me in a long time. Noticing a girl like that, and letting her see it. I've learned how to force it down when I feel those things. To act as if I'm normal.

But sometimes I can't stop it. I can't stop it now.

My cheeks are flushed. I feel off balance, even though I'm still sitting down. I grip the armrest to steady myself.

My mind is running to scary places. The images come too fast for me to stop them.

I imagine what it would be like if I were alone with the red-haired girl. How it would feel if she smiled at me with her pretty smile, and I smiled back, and—

No. I know better than to think this way.

I can't take any risks. Especially not at this school. If anyone found out the truth about me it would mean—I don't even know what it would mean. I only know it would be horrible. It would be a hundred times worse than what happened in the parking lot this morning. A thousand times.

Then I realize I've got another problem altogether.

The other white people have noticed I'm turned around. They're whispering to each other and pointing at me.

The boys leer. The girls scrunch up their faces. One boy rolls a spitball.

I turn back around fast. I can't make that mistake again.

I'd thought some of the white people at Jefferson might be all right. But if they were, they'd be helping us, wouldn't they? They'd be telling the other white people to leave us alone. They'd have held the doors open so we could get through.

No one's helped us yet.

The teacher is back at the front of the stage, still looking bored. "All right, seniors. It's time to distribute your schedules and locker assignments for the year. When your name is called, go to Mr. Lewis or Mrs. Gruber to pick yours up. Then go straight to your first period class. There will be no dawdling in the halls. Tardiness will result in detention."

"Want to bet she said that just for us?" Chuck mutters.

The spitball hits my back. The surprise of it makes me catch my breath, but I don't let the white people see me flinch. Instead I reach back and pull the spitball off my blouse. It's cold and slimy. It makes my stomach churn, but I tell myself it's no worse than changing my little brother's diapers, and I did that for two and a half years.

"Donna Abner?" calls a man standing in the aisle to our left. Mr. Lewis. His name was on the Glee Club poster, so he must be the Music teacher. A white girl moves up the aisle toward him.

"It's alphabetical," Ennis whispers as Mrs. Gruber calls for Leonard Anderson from the opposite aisle. "Sarah, you'll be first, but come back here and wait for us after you get your schedule. We'll all go to first period together."

"What if we're not in the same class?" Chuck asks.

Mrs. Mullins said the school might put us in different classes. If we were separated, the school officials thought, there'd be less risk of violence. I guess they thought two or three Negroes to-gether would try to take on an entire classroom full of whites. As if any of us wanted to get killed.

"We'll walk together anyway," Ennis says. "The longer we're together the safer we are. That's more important than detention."

But when the teachers reach the *D*'s, they skip right over where my last name, Dunbar, should be and go straight from Thomas Dillard to Nancy Duncan.

Should I say something? I look at Ennis.

"Let's wait," he whispers.

When they get to the *M*'s, when Ennis should be called, the teachers skip over him, too. The same thing happens with Chuck when they get to the *T*'s.

Maybe this was all a big mistake.

We were told we'd been admitted to the school, and that we should come in today along with the white people, but maybe the courts have issued a new ruling. Maybe the police will troop in to pull us out of here. The white people will line the halls and cheer as we're escorted from the building.

The auditorium is almost empty now. Somehow it's scarier seeing just a few angry white faces staring us down instead of a hundred. If they got one of us alone they could do anything they wanted and it would be their word against ours.

Finally the last name, Susan Young, is called. Mr. Lewis gives Susan her schedule. Once her back is turned he comes over to stand in front of Ennis, Chuck and me.

The rest of the teachers have left. Mr. Lewis leans back and rests his elbow on the stage, looking us over.

My heartbeat speeds up. Mr. Lewis is a teacher, but that doesn't mean he supports integration. Would he do something to us if it meant risking his job? Not that anyone would believe three colored children telling stories about a grown white man.

Then Mr. Lewis smiles.

I tilt my head, confused. It looks like a real smile, not a sneer.

"Hello," he says. "Welcome to Jefferson High School."

Is this a trick? Next to me, Chuck shifts in his seat. There's suspicion in his eyes.

Mr. Lewis looks at each of us in turn, still smiling. "I'm told you three will be the first Negroes to graduate from a white school in Davisburg County. All I can say is, it's about time."

Oh.

It's the first kind thing anyone has said to us.

I try to smile back at Mr. Lewis. Mama would want me to be polite.

"Let's get you some schedules." Mr. Lewis pulls three rumpled papers from his pocket. "Sorry we didn't have them with the others. Apparently someone in the office didn't think you'd be here today, so your schedules had to be assembled rather hastily."

He chuckles. I don't. We might very well not have been here today. Some of the white parents tried to file an emergency petition at the courthouse just yesterday to stop us from getting into Jefferson.

The white parents, and the school board, and Senator Byrd and Governor Almond fought this with everything they had. It's been five years since the Supreme Court said integration had to happen, but for five years, the white people kept fighting, and our schools stayed segregated. Until last week, when the courts put out their final ruling: the white parents, and the governor and the rest of the segregationists had lost.

Here we are. Whether they like it or not.

Whether we like it or not, too.

"Miss Dunbar." Mr. Lewis hands me a paper.

No one ever calls me "Miss." Usually it's just "Sarah." Or, if it's a white person talking, "Girl."

He hands Chuck and Ennis their schedules, too. I try to read the scrawled handwriting on mine.

Sara Dunbar, Integ.

Period	Course	Room
	Homeroom	252
1	Math-12 R	218
2	Typing B	20
3	Am. History-R	149
4	French II	207
B	Lunch	
5	Home Econ.-12 B	12
6	Study Hall	127
7	English-12 R	116

Typing? I took Typing at my old school. And I've already had two years of French. Plus there's no music class on my schedule at all. At my old school, Johns High, I was going to take Advanced Music Performance this year.

"What do these *R*'s after the course names mean?" Chuck whispers. I look at his schedule. He has the same first-period Math class I do. Other than that, we don't have any classes together.

I don't know what the *R*'s mean, either. I want to ask Mr. Lewis, but Ennis is already standing up.

"Come on," he says. "We don't want to be late. Thank you, sir."

"Go straight to your first-period classes," Mr. Lewis says. "There's no Homeroom today. Good luck."

Good luck? I wonder if he's joking.

We file out of the auditorium in silence. Someone has shut the doors, even though the assembly only just ended. Ennis pushes them open and steps out into the hall.

"There they are!" The cries are coming from all around us. At least a dozen boys are gathered, most in letterman's sweaters. "There's those coon diggers!"

"You have to go to the second floor?" Ennis mutters to me, not taking his eyes off the boys. They're coming closer. They're smiling.

"Yes," I whisper. "Chuck does, too."

"You go first, Sarah," Chuck says. His voice is low and gravelly. "We'll keep them from following you."

"If we separate they'll only split up and follow us all," I whisper.

I wonder if Mr. Lewis knew this would happen. If that's why he kept us late. I want to trust him, but it's hard to trust anyone in this place.

"What're you doin' here, niggers?" one of the boys says. "You know you don't belong in our school."

"It's our school, too," Chuck says. "So what are *you* doing here?"

That sets the boys off. Two of them run at Chuck.

"Hey!" comes a loud voice behind us. Mr. Lewis. The boys stop in their tracks. "What's this about?"

"That one started it," one of the boys says, pointing at Chuck.

"He didn't," I say. "He wasn't doing anything, he—"

Mr. Lewis raises his eyebrows at me. "Young lady, I think you and Mr. Mack had better get to class. Charles, Bo, Eddie, come with me."

"But—"

Ennis takes my arm and pulls me away before I can finish.

"What will happen to Chuck?" I whisper when we're far enough away. Behind us Mr. Lewis is leading Chuck and the two white boys who charged him toward the front office.

"Probably nothing," Ennis says. "That teacher got there before anything happened. He'll get a lecture, that's all."

"Will anything happen to the white boys?"

"No way."

We're walking up an empty staircase. Ennis is looking around in every direction, and I remember I'm supposed to do the same thing. We have to be extra alert in the stairwells. In Little Rock that's where they set off the firecrackers.

"Keep an eye out for Ruth, will you?" I ask Ennis. "If you see her in the halls, make sure she's all right?"

"I'll try."

Ennis leaves me at my classroom door, walking as fast as he can down the hall. I hope he doesn't run into any other white boys.

I hadn't thought much about Ennis before this morning. Chuck was in my group of friends back at Johns, but Ennis mostly kept to himself. After the way he helped Ruth in the parking lot, though, I'm going to be watching out for him, too.

The door to room 218 is closed. I'm scared to push it open, but if I don't I'll get a tardy slip. So I take a long breath, say a quick prayer and open the door.

Inside the room it's dead silent. Then, as one, twenty heads jerk up. Twenty white faces gaze up at me. The door latches closed behind me like a gunshot.

I want to drop my eyes. Instead I look out into the sea of faces. Every one is looking back at me.

First come the stares.

Next, the pointing and the whispers.

Last, and most frightening, are the grins.

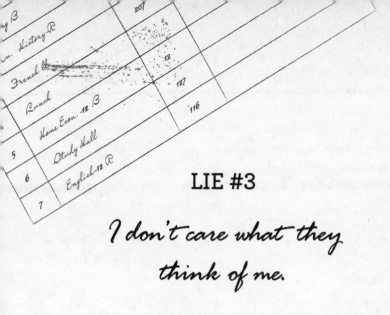

LIE #3

I don't care what they think of me.

ALL THE GRINNERS are boys. They're looking at me as if it's Christmas morning and I'm the biggest present under the tree.

My legs are so weak I'm sure they'll give way. I'll wind up sprawled out across the floor on my backside while the white people laugh.

I keep my chin up as I move toward an empty seat in the front row.

"Who are you?" a woman asks. She's tall, with gray-streaked hair, a sour look on her face and a stack of textbooks in her arms. She was the other teacher handing out schedules in the auditorium. Mrs. Gruber.

We have to be polite to the teachers, no matter what. We can't do anything they could discipline us for. Especially not today.

That's easy for me. I'm always polite to adults. I don't know how to be any other way.

"My name is Sarah Dunbar, ma'am. My schedule says room 218."

Mrs. Gruber dumps the stack of books on an empty desk and snatches my schedule out of my hand. She frowns at it. "Did you write this yourself? How do I know you're supposed to be here?"

After Mr. Lewis, I'd thought the teachers might be nice to us. I should've known better. Mr. Lewis is just one white man. This school has plenty more.

"No, ma'am, I didn't write it," I say. "Mr. Lewis gave it to me. He said the office had to write out our schedules by hand at the last minute."

Mrs. Gruber gives the paper back to me. "That doesn't give you an excuse to take until the last minute yourself. Maybe at your school students can show up for class whenever they please, but at Jefferson you get detention when you're tardy."

I bite my lip. Mama and Daddy will be so disappointed in me. "Yes, ma'am."

Mrs. Gruber writes out a detention slip and thrusts it at me. "Take a seat."

I go to the empty desk in the middle of the front row and put down my books. Before I can sit down, the white girl at the desk next to mine bolts out of her chair.

She's moving so fast I don't recognize her at first. She sweeps up her books and her coat and glides to an empty seat on the far side of the room. Her hips swing under her pleated skirt and her lips curl in a smile. Everyone is watching her. And she knows it.

It's the red-haired girl from the auditorium. With the smattering of freckles across her nose and the bright look in her blue eyes.

She's even prettier up close. Except for the hateful look on her face.

Her frizzy-haired friend is in the seat right behind mine. She has a heavy layer of makeup on one side of her face and a stricken look in her eyes.

Only when the boy in the seat on the other side of mine gets up to join the red-haired girl do I understand what's going on.

Everyone sitting within two desks of mine is gone in seconds, scurrying to find other seats. Soon there aren't any empty desks left except the ones near me. The extra white students perch on the radiator at the back.

Mrs. Gruber studies a pile of papers on her desk. To look at her, you'd never know students were running around as though the classroom were under siege.

The seat behind mine is the only one near me that's still occupied. Everyone looks at the frizzy-haired girl.

The girl looks fast from side to side. She meets my eyes for a second. Then she cups her hand over her made-up cheek. The red-haired girl whispers, "Judy, come *on*."

The frizzy-haired girl, Judy, jumps out of her seat, dropping her books in her haste. A few boys laugh as she kneels to gather them up. She goes to the back of the room and sits on the radiator with the others.

I keep my chin high. At least this way I won't have to worry about anyone drilling pencils into my back.

Mrs. Gruber passes out our textbooks as though nothing happened, dropping mine onto my desk with a thud. She's turning toward the blackboard when the door swings open.

Every head in the room jerks up again, mine included.

I should be glad to see Chuck standing there. Instead I wish he'd turn around and walk right back out. I don't want to watch it happen all over again.

"What now?" Mrs. Gruber slams a textbook down.

"I'm sorry I'm late, ma'am," Chuck says in his most polite teacher voice. "I'm Charles Tapscott. I was talking to Mr. Lewis in the office about—"

"Sit down." Mrs. Gruber sighs and writes out another detention slip.

Chuck takes the empty seat next to me. Two boys sitting near him get up and join the others in the back of the room.

Chuck doesn't ignore it the way I did, though. He turns to watch them walk away, his mouth open in an O.

One of the boys in the back of the class opens his mouth wide and makes a face just like Chuck's. Then he squeals like a pig.

Everyone laughs. Mrs. Gruber acts like she didn't notice that, either.

"Hey, this ain't fair," another boy says. "Why we gotta have *two* of 'em in our class? Like one coon's not bad enough."

Some of the others grumble in agreement.

"All right, everyone, settle down," Mrs. Gruber says. She doesn't even look at the boy who spoke. "Who doesn't have a book yet?" Chuck and a few other people raise their hands.

I flip open my new textbook. I've always liked school. Adults always tell me I'm a bright girl with a good future ahead of me. If I can concentrate on my classwork maybe the white people's antics won't bother me so much.

As soon as I open the book I know something's wrong.

I leaf through to the last chapter to make sure. There's no doubt. I raise my hand. Then I put it down again. Mrs. Gruber isn't going to want to help me.

But she saw. She comes to stand right in front of my desk and sighs again, loudly. "Did you want something?"

"No, I—" I start to falter, but I can't show any weakness in front of these people. I meet Mrs. Gruber's eyes. "I was curious as to the name of this course."

One of the white boys laughs. "Nigger shows up, doesn't even know what class she's in!"

Another joins in. "Don't you see the charts on the wall? Can't you tell a Math class? Ain't you ever seen numbers before, nigger?"

"As your schedule clearly states, this is Remedial Math 12," Mrs. Gruber says. Then she turns her back.

"*Remedial?*" Oh. That's what the *R*'s stood for. They were on almost every class on my schedule. Chuck's, too. They've put us in the remedial track.

All the Negroes who came here were in the college prep courses back at Johns. That's why they picked us to integrate Jefferson. We were supposed to be the best of the best. The kind of students who could handle the white school's classes and still have enough smarts left over to put up with the rest of it.

I learned how to do the work in this textbook in ninth grade.

I wonder if they put us in these classes because they think we're stupid or because they wanted to punish us for coming here in the first place. I wonder if my college will still let me in when they see those remedial classes on my transcript.

But I don't have time to worry about that now. I have a bigger problem.

Everyone in this room heard what I said.

They know I think I'm too smart for Remedial. Smarter than they are.

I *am* smarter than they are, but that isn't going to help me now.

The boys start in right away.

"The nigger thinks she's a genius," one says. "Look everybody, we've got Einstein in our class!"

"Hey, girl, if you too good for Remedial, how 'bout you put your smarts to use and come clean my house?"

"Hey, nigger, can you count this high? Two, four, six, eight, we don't wanna integrate!"

Mrs. Gruber keeps her eyes on the chalkboard.

It goes on that way for the rest of the period. The boys leave us alone while Mrs. Gruber is talking, but as soon as she looks away they start in on me, and Chuck, too. Mrs. Gruber hears it, but she doesn't say anything.

I keep looking straight ahead. At first I think I'll get used to it. Instead, the longer it goes on, the more it stings.

"Those niggers need to be put in their place."

"What'd they come here for? Don't they know we don't want to look at their ugly black faces?"

"I bet they got their nigger tails tucked in under those clothes. Let's rip 'em out."

When the bell rings I want to charge out of the classroom. I want to put as much distance between myself and these people as I can.

There's no use. The white people in the hall won't be any better. It'll be worse, in fact, because there will be more of them.

So Chuck and I gather our things and leave with everyone else, ignoring the pushing and shoving until we're out in the hallway. There, the white people gather around us in a circle to shout names until we've separated and made our way to our next classes. Then they follow us down the hall, shouting at us, pushing us, stepping on our heels, jabbing elbows into our sides.

Not much changes the rest of the morning. In every class the students move away from my desk as soon as I sit down. My Typing and History teachers aren't as bad as Mrs. Gruber, but neither of them makes any effort to make me feel welcome. I come to recognize the look in each of my teachers' eyes when I walk through their classroom doors. The look that says they wish I'd turn around and walk right back out. I'm making their jobs harder just by being here.

Fourth-period French is different.

The students look the same as ever. Most of them have been in some of my classes already that day. The red-haired girl and her friend Judy are there, sitting on the far side of the room, scowling at me.

As I come in a boy yells, "Ain't you heard? We don't care what no nigger-loving judge has to say. We don't believe in race mixing in this class. So you best turn around and run back to Africa." The rest of the class move their seats away from mine.

I sit straight in my seat, blinking at the chalkboard, like always. It's a lucky thing I'm good at pretending.

The teacher, Miss Whitson, comes in as the final bell rings. She stands in the doorway for a long minute, gazing around the classroom. I can't tell what she's thinking.

She comes over to my desk and whispers, so low only I can hear, "What's your name?"

"Sarah Dunbar," I whisper back.

She makes a note on her roll and goes to the chalkboard. The room is still quiet. Everyone must already know you don't mess around in Miss Whitson's class.

"This is French II." She gives us all a hard look. "I expect you to have the fundamentals of the language down. We're getting a late start this year and we have a lot of makeup work to do, but I'm not lowering my expectations of how you'll perform on your end-of-year exams. So if you want to pass you'll have to work hard."

Everyone looks worried. Good. If they're nervous about passing the class maybe they won't have time to yell at me.

"We'll start off with a refresher on conversation," Miss Whitson goes on. "I'll pair you off. You and your partner will talk about what you did over Christmas. Then you'll drill each other on the irregular verbs on pages fourteen through eighteen. I'll be listening closely and grading you on your participation. If I hear one word of English it's an automatic failure."

There's low grumbling from the back of the class. A girl raises her hand. "Miss Whitson?"

"Oui?" Miss Whitson says.

The girl replies in English. "Miss Whitson, you're not going to pair anyone with *her,* are you?"

"That's enough," Miss Whitson says in French. She begins to read the pairs off from her roll book. "Abner, Baker."

I suppose it doesn't matter who I'm paired with. None of these people want anything to do with me. My partner will probably go sit as far from me as he can get, even if it means we both get a failing grade. Maybe Miss Whitson will let me do a makeup assignment instead.

"Campbell, Dunbar," Miss Whitson says.

I have no idea who "Campbell" is. No one remembers my last name, either, so there's no reaction until Miss Whitson finishes the list, claps her hands and tells us all to go sit with our partners.

I don't move. I expect everyone to ignore me. So it's a surprise when the frizzy-haired girl from this morning puts her books down on the empty desk next to mine.

"You got the nigger, Judy?" a boy says behind us. He's part of the gang who tried to charge at Chuck in the hall this morning. "You better watch out if you don't want to get any of that black on you! You don't want to wind up even uglier than you already are!"

"You leave Judy alone, Bo!" the red-haired girl says. She looks furious.

"Bo Nash!" Miss Whitson says. "You heard me. One more English word out of anyone in this class and it's an *F*."

I keep my gaze fixed straight ahead. What does this girl Judy think she's doing, sitting down next to me? She moved away from my desk in Math, so I don't know why she thinks it's safe to be near me now. Well, whatever she tries to do to me, I won't give her the satisfaction of reacting.

"Um," Judy says. "Bonjour?"

Oh.

I wasn't expecting *that*.

No white student has said a single sentence to me today that didn't include *nigger, coon* or some other hateful word. Except the girl in the hall who spat on my good skirt.

"Bonjour," I murmur, waiting to see if this is a trick.

"My name is Judy," she says in terribly mangled French.

"My name is Sarah."

We're quiet after that. I suppose Judy thinks she's said enough not to fail. I look at the clock over the blackboard, wondering how many minutes will pass before someone yells something new at me.

"Um," Judy says again. She holds the cover of her French textbook out in front of her, squinting.

Then I see the real problem. "My name is Judy" is the only sentence this girl knows how to say in French.

"How are you?" I ask, hoping a simple sentence like that will be familiar to her.

She stares at me blankly.

This is useless. I turn back to the clock.

"I—" Judy starts to say.

I shake my head to show her she's still speaking English.

Judy shakes her head, too, and half smiles. She raises her eyebrows and shrugs in what looks like an apology.

Maybe this is an act. Part of an elaborate trick she and her friends are pulling. I bet the cruel red-haired girl is the ringleader.

Or maybe I was right before. Maybe not *all* the white people in this school hate us.

Miss Whitson is coming our way. Judy peers up at the bulletin board, which lists some common French words. Colors. Parts of the body. Family members.

"Sister!" Judy says. She struggles to say a complete sentence, butchering the French. My mother, who teaches French and English at the colored junior high, would cringe if she heard. "Um. You have sister?"

What?

The only way this girl could know I have a sister is if she's seen her. Everyone always says Ruth and I look alike.

I haven't seen Ruth all morning.

"Did you see my sister?" I ask Judy in rapid French. "Where? How was she? Was she safe?"

Judy frowns and shrugs helplessly. She doesn't understand.

"Have you seen her?" I repeat in English. "Is she safe?"

Miss Whitson is watching us. I'm sure she heard me speaking English, but she doesn't say anything.

"*Oui,*" Judy says.

"Was anyone hurting her?"

"No," Judy says. "I mean, *non.*"

I close my eyes and breathe in, long and slow. I feel like I haven't breathed all morning.

Maybe we really can do this. Maybe it will be all right.

I'm so relieved I don't even mind practicing French with a girl who can't pronounce bonjour. So we get out our books and take turns conjugating *regarder.*

When the bell rings I grab my books. I try to move straight for the door, but before I'm even out of my desk the red-haired girl is blocking my way.

I wish she wouldn't stand so near. I try again to force that feeling down. The strange buzzing in my chest that comes with being so close to a girl who's this pretty. It doesn't work.

"It's a shame you had to work with *her,* Judy," the girl says, looking right at me. "I'll speak to my father tonight. He'll get us both transferred out of this class. Math, too. We shouldn't have to suffer just because some Northern interloper judge says so."

The girl is right in my face. Her bright blue eyes are narrowed and fixed on mine. I can't let her know she's getting to me. I try to edge around her but she blocks my way with her purse. It's just as fashionable as the rest of her—a cloth bag with round wooden handles covered in the same plaid fabric as her skirt.

There's something about the way this girl talks. Something about the look in her eyes.

She makes me angrier than the others do.

She's not like the girl who screamed at me in the parking lot or the one who spat on me in the hall. This girl doesn't do that sort of thing. She works quietly. Efficiently. Ruthlessly.

I just wish she weren't so pretty. That lovely face sets off a fire inside me that isn't ever supposed to burn.

She frightens me. But she makes me want to stop being polite.

I shouldn't say anything to her. It's against the rules, and the rules are there for a reason.

It only happens because I can't stop myself.

"It's a shame *you* had to have such an awful friend, Judy," I say, looking straight into the red-haired girl's eyes. "I suppose we all have to suffer in our own ways."

The red-haired girl stiffens. Everyone in the classroom is staring at us.

As soon as the words are out of my mouth, my nervousness returns. This girl may be too smart to throw rocks in the parking lot, but that doesn't mean she isn't just as dangerous as the rest of them. Smarts can do more damage than strength.

But if this girl is really so smart, why does she believe in segregation? There's nothing logical about keeping people separated by their skin colors.

She's as bad as the governor. Everyone says he's an intelligent man. He's a lawyer who argued in front of the Supreme Court, saying it would be too dangerous for colored children and white children to go to the same school. Then he got elected to the highest post in the state. Governor Almond has got to be one of the smartest men there is, but he believes in segregation, too.

I should've been smart enough not to talk back to this beautiful, dangerous girl.

It scares me, the way she makes me feel. I need to get away from her.

I slip around the red-haired girl while she's still distracted and leave as quickly as I can. The rest of them spill out behind me. They don't seem to be following me, though. They're talking to Judy and her friend.

"It's true," one of them says. "Those agitators are just awful.

I can't believe that one had the nerve to talk to you that way, Linda."

Linda. That must be the red-haired girl's name. It suits her.

"What was it like speaking French with the nigger?" a boy asks Judy.

"Yeah, did she speak some of that coonjab to ya?" another one says.

"I don't know," Judy says. "I couldn't understand what she said. It was in French."

"No way," a boy says. "You know that nigger don't speak no French. They don't say no '*parlez-vous*' in Africa."

Everyone laughs.

I've still got my back to the group. To be safe, I really should speed up to get away from them, but I want to hear what else Judy says. She's the only white student all day who's seemed like she might be all right.

"Does she stink even harder up close?" a boy asks her. "Man, I bet sitting next to one of them is worse than being on a pig farm in August."

"I didn't smell anything," Judy says.

There's a long pause where all I hear are footsteps. Then one of the boys says, "What's the matter, Judy, you turning into a nigger-lover?"

There's another long pause.

Then Linda speaks up. I'd recognize her voice anywhere.

"Don't feel like you have to protect *her*, Judy," Linda says. "You don't owe her anything. They're the ones who messed up this whole year for all of us, remember?"

There's another pause. Then Judy's voice falters. "Well. She talked real fast. Like how people up North sound."

Some of the boys chuckle.

"I bet she wasn't really saying anything in French," Judy says. "I bet she just making a bunch of noises."

No. *No.*

Everyone's laughing now. One of the boys makes a honking sound.

"Yeah, do that again!" another boy says. "That's what nigger French sounds like."

Soon all the boys are doing it. Their laughter howls down the hall.

But they're getting drowned out now by the other shouts. The usual ones. The circle has started to form around me, the way it always does in the halls. There are too many catcalls of "Nigger!" and "Ugly coon!" to distinguish one voice from another.

In a way, I'm relieved.

When it's this loud it's hard to hear the voice in my head.

The one that's saying I was wrong. That Judy isn't all right.

That every white person in this school is just as bad as every other.

LIE #4

I'm not lonely.

"LOOK AT THAT ugly face." The white girl behind me in the lunch line is talking to her friend, but she's gazing straight at me. "I guess there ain't nothing she can do about it, though. They don't make no black lipstick."

Her friend stares at me, too.

I want to tell the white girl she's uglier than I'll ever be, with her fat ankles and her rat's nest hair.

Instead I keep my eyes on the wall.

I'd expected the name-calling. The spitting. The shoving. I wasn't ready for it, but I'd known it was coming.

What I didn't plan on was the staring.

Everyone stares at me. Boys, girls. Freshmen, seniors. Teachers, secretaries.

Everyone. All day long. If I so much as move my little finger, fifty people watch me do it.

Maybe they think I can't see them. That I'm blind as well as black.

"There she is!" a man's voice booms. "There's our young Miss Sarah Dunbar!"

I start to panic. Then I remember none of the white people know my name.

Mr. Muse is coming toward me, a bucket swinging from his hand and a wide smile on his face.

"Mr. Muse!" I grin up at him. He's the tallest man in our church, nearly a foot taller than Daddy. His wife is in the choir with me, but I'd forgotten he worked at Jefferson. He sets his bucket down on the floor, peels off one of his rubber gloves and holds out his big hand to me. I clasp it, ignoring the looks and snickers from the white people. Mr. Muse's hand is warm in mine.

"Bless you, Sarah," he says, beaming down at me. "You know we're all real, real glad to see you here."

I can't find words to tell Mr. Muse how glad I am to see him, too. His is the first friendly face I've seen in I don't know how long.

"Now you just remember, we're all so proud of you." Mr. Muse drops my hand. He bends down to retrieve his bucket with the mop handle poking out the top. "And you're surely making your mama and daddy proud, too."

"Thank you so much, Mr. Muse, sir," I say.

"*Sir?*" the girl behind me snickers in a high-pitched voice that she probably thinks sounds Northern. Like me. "Leave it to a doggone dirty nigger to call the doggone dirty janitor '*sir.*' You get on out of here with your stinking bucket, *boy.*"

Mr. Muse acts like he didn't hear the girl. He smiles at me again, then turns to leave the cafeteria, whistling that jazz tune they've been playing on the radio all winter.

I wish I could keep clasping Mr. Muse's big warm hand for the rest of the day.

Usually when I see Negroes working as janitors or cleaning women, I get embarrassed. I understand why they're doing it—

it's hard enough to find jobs as it is—but I hate to think of any of us mopping up spilled food we wouldn't be allowed to eat if we were paying customers.

But the food in this cafeteria isn't only for white people anymore. I'm here now.

I smile as I make my way through the lunch line. I take a double helping of green beans, my favorite, from the lunch ladies who pass me a tray without meeting my eyes. I will eat green beans today. The same green beans the white people get to eat. Because that's my right. Mr. Muse and the others are counting on me to prove that it's so.

But when I come out of the line Mr. Muse is long gone. The only black face in the room is mine.

The tables are arranged in long rows. There are almost no empty seats left. I was near the back of the lunch line, since I was late getting to the cafeteria. Groups of boys kept blocking my way in the halls.

One table has a few empty seats at the end. I move toward it, carefully stepping over the feet stuck out in my path, and set my tray on the painted wood surface.

Right away there's a murmur from the white people nearest me. And then everyone sitting at the long table—there must be thirty of them—stands up.

"I can't eat with this stench," one girl says.

"I know. I lost my appetite."

"They're going to have to bleach this whole table to get the smell out."

They leave, squeezing into other tables. Some of the girls are sharing seats. The boys hold their trays in their hands, trying to shove food in their mouths standing up.

I pretend not to notice. I pretend not to hear the laughter all around me. Or the new rounds of taunts that come with it.

I know I don't really smell, but I still want to take about fifty showers when I get home to make sure.

No. I can't think that way. I can't let these white people get to me.

I'm lucky, really. I have a whole table to myself.

But I don't feel lucky.

I take a bite of my green beans. They taste like rubber.

Just then, a girl shrieks near the end of the line and I forget all about my food. What if it's Ruth?

I stand up fast, ignoring the boy behind me who calls me a damn nigger when my chair bumps into his, and crane my neck to see what's going on in the line.

It's not Ruth. The shrieking girl is white and blonde. She's standing with a group of friends, covering her face with her hands.

Ten feet behind her Ennis is backing away slowly, gripping his tray, his eyes surveying the room.

No one else seems to have noticed the girl's shriek. I sit back down. Whatever's going on, I don't need to draw more attention to it.

Ennis sees me and makes his way over, casting looks back at the blonde girl. She's crying. Her friend pats her arm.

Ennis swiftly lifts his tray away from a boy who's trying to knock it over and puts it down on the table across from me.

"What happened?" I nod toward the blonde girl.

Ennis sits down, shrugs and stirs his applesauce. "I don't know. I walked by her, and she took one look at me and started screaming. You'd think she'd never seen a colored man before."

Oh. I hadn't thought about that. I wonder how many other girls at this school are going to scream whenever one of the Negro boys crosses their paths.

For years now, ever since we moved down here, I've been listening to Mama and Daddy talk about integration. Sometimes at night Ruth and I sneak out of our room and sit on the top step in our nightgowns, listening to our parents' voices drift up the staircase. Mostly they talked about the court cases. That part was boring, but sooner or later they'd stop talking about injunctions and petitions and hearing dates and start talking about what integration might really be like for us. Once, when it was so late Ruth had fallen asleep, I heard Mama whisper to Daddy that what worried her most was our Negro boys. The white parents might give a dozen reasons for opposing integration, she'd said, but what they were really worried about deep down was their girls being around our boys. She never said exactly what worried them about that, though. Intermarriage, I suppose. The idea that black boys might get their nice white girls in trouble.

I don't like to think about that sort of thing. It makes me blush. Besides, no Negro boy I know would ever risk going near a white girl. A few years ago a boy down in Mississippi got killed for doing a lot less than that.

"Hey, I saw your sister after second period," Ennis says. "She was all right."

I jerk up in my seat. "You're sure? She wasn't hurt?"

"She looked great. Walking down the hall with her nose in the air. From the way she acted you wouldn't even know there was anyone yelling."

I'm relieved, but at the same time I want to cry. "People were yelling at her?"

"Well, yeah. But no worse than the rest of us."

I nod. "Thanks for helping her this morning. With those boys on the way in. I was so worried."

"Oh. Sure." He shrugs like it was nothing.

"I wish I could see her," I say. "During the class breaks, just to make sure she's all right. Then I wouldn't have to worry all day. But I don't even know where the freshmen classes are."

"They're all mixed together." Ennis opens his notebook and turns to a blank sheet. He sketches out the school's first floor, second floor, third floor and basement. "This is where I saw her this morning. She must have a class near there."

He draws blocks around the Math, English, History and Science sections of the school, then draws in the stairwells and puts stars next to the gym, cafeteria and auditorium.

"How do you know all this?" I ask him.

"Mr. Muse snuck Chuck and me in during one of his shifts last summer. He wanted to make sure we knew our way around in case there was trouble."

Right. Just in case.

"This is the main entrance." Ennis draws a big *X*. "Where we'll never go in again if we can help it."

"You really think it'll make a difference?"

"I think we've got to try."

I can't tell whether Ennis means what he's saying. Whether he really thinks there's any point in hoping things will get better.

But there are only five months left until I graduate. I can do this for five months.

I have to graduate from this school. It means so much to Mama and Daddy.

To me, too. I want to walk across that stage in front of all those white people and get that diploma. Show them there's nothing they can do that I can't.

But once I'm gone, Ruth will still have another three years in this place.

I squeeze my eyes tight against that thought.

A tray clatters down on the table beside mine, making me flinch.

"Sorry I'm late," Chuck says.

"What happened?" Ennis fixes Chuck with a look.

Chuck shrugs. "Some guys hassling me. I got rid of them."

"Got rid of them how?" There's a warning in Ennis's voice.

"It's not important," Chuck says.

I don't want to know how Chuck got rid of them. I wonder if fighting is the sort of thing boys always talk about at lunch.

I've never sat with a boy in the cafeteria before. Girls and boys don't usually do that after elementary school. But everything in my life is different now, so I suppose this might as well be different, too.

I wonder what will happen when word of it gets back to our old school. I wonder if the girls will talk about me. Say the sorts of things that get said about girls sometimes.

I had my first boyfriend last year. His name was Alvin. We went to the movies and held hands and walked around the park. We even kissed a little, but we never French-kissed. Girls aren't supposed to do that until after high school.

I don't mind that. I try not to even think about things like kissing and holding hands. When I do, I get confused and upset, and I have to stop thinking about it fast before I start thinking the wrong things.

I used to think the wrong things all the time. Before I knew they were wrong.

It started back when we lived in Chicago. One day I was walking with Mama and Ruth and we passed a movie theater that had a poster out front for *Gone with the Wind*. The poster showed the girl lying back in the man's arms. Her green dress was cut low. I looked at that picture and it made me feel—

Something. I don't know what, exactly. I just know that feeling was wrong.

But I didn't know that then. And I didn't know it was wrong when I used to take Mama's copies of *Ebony* off the coffee table when she was done with them. I'd take them up to my room and turn straight to the back, where they had the fashion pictures. I'd turn the magazine around to all angles and look at the girls posing. The swimsuit articles were my favorites. I read every word on those pages. Mama was always surprised when she'd take us shopping for swimsuits in June and I knew all about cotton knit Lastex and the new "disciplined" bikinis.

Now that I'm almost grown-up, I know about right and wrong. It was shameful, the things I used to do. That's why I don't like to think about things like kissing.

I still have every one of those magazines in a box under my bed, though.

I try to focus on Chuck and Ennis's conversation. They're talking about their teachers. None of the others were as bad as Mrs. Gruber.

I tell them about what happened in French. Neither of them knows who Judy is, but when I mention Linda, Ennis knows exactly who I'm talking about.

"That's Linda Hairston," he says. "You know about the Hairstons, right?"

I shake my head, but as Ennis starts to explain, I realize I do know.

Linda's father is William Hairston, the editor for the *Davisburg Gazette*. He's the one who writes the editorials opposing integration. He's also Daddy's boss.

Daddy reads his editorials out loud at the breakfast table sometimes. They're mostly about how integration will ruin our state for good. The last one he read us had a section about how Negro children should be taught only by Negro teachers, for our own benefit, because no one else can understand how "uniquely" our brains work.

Daddy says Mr. Hairston is much worse for Negroes than the boys who throw rocks or call us names. People respect Mr. Hairston. Thousands of people read what he writes and think it's the truth.

Daddy is a copy boy for Mr. Hairston's paper. He hates working there, but he doesn't have any choice. He doesn't make enough money just writing for the Negro paper, the way he used to when we lived in Chicago.

Did I put Daddy's job at risk when I talked back to Linda? I need to be more careful from now on.

"What other classes did you have this morning?" Ennis asks me.

"Math, Typing, History and French. Every one was either a repeat or remedial."

"Mine, too," Ennis says. "And I'm in Auto Shop."

"I've got Shop, too," Chuck says. "Next period."

The boys in College Prep at our old school never took Shop. I doubt Chuck and Ennis ever learned how to use tools. Ennis especially. His father is a lawyer, and his mother hires a handyman whenever they need something fixed. I hope Ennis doesn't wind up cutting himself with a saw or anything like that.

"Why can't we take the right classes?" I say. "The ones we were supposed to take at Johns?"

"The white teachers don't know we're going to college," Chuck says. "They just put us in the classes they thought colored kids would take."

That makes sense. Mrs. Gruber seemed surprised I could even read.

"Do you know where you're going to college?" I ask Ennis. I already know Chuck is going to Virginia State College.

"Howard, if I get in," Ennis says.

I sit back, surprised. Ennis's whole family lives here in Davisburg, so I thought he'd go to a school around here. Howard's all the way up in Washington, D.C. I'm going there, too, but it doesn't matter so much for me since my family is spread out. My aunt and uncle and cousins are in Chicago and my grandparents still live in Alabama.

"I'm going to Howard, too," I say. "My uncle's friend works there. He said he's sure I'll get a scholarship."

Ennis nods and looks down at the chili on his plate. Quickly I add, "Of course, I'm sure you'll get one, too. Your marks have always been good."

Good, but not as good as mine. I was first in my class at Johns, and Ennis was only third or fourth.

I don't say that. It would be rude. Besides, it isn't right for girls to talk about being smart around boys.

"That was at Johns," Ennis says. "Who knows what will happen here."

Oh. I hadn't thought about getting lower marks now that we're at a white school. I shift in my seat.

Ennis gets up to dump his tray. I'm still picking at my food. Chuck tries to tell me a joke about Fidel Castro but I'm too anxious to pay much attention.

Chuck cuts himself off halfway through the joke. His eyes are fixed on something over my shoulder. I turn to follow his gaze.

Ennis is twenty feet from our table, frozen in his tracks. Another blonde girl is running up to him, smiling. She speaks to him, but I can't hear what she says. Ennis keeps his eyes on the floor and mumbles a response. The girl smiles as if nothing is wrong.

The room is getting quiet. We're not the only ones watching Ennis and the blonde girl.

This is even worse than the girl who screamed earlier. This time, people are seeing it. A Negro boy who's seen talking to a white girl could be in for very serious trouble.

Ennis backs away from the girl, keeping his head down.

I'm so focused on them I don't even notice the boys coming up behind me until one of them knocks into the back of my chair. The table juts under my rib cage, knocking my breath out of me. Then something cold trickles down the back of my neck.

The table behind me bursts into laughter. "She almost looks white now!" a boy calls out.

I reach around and feel wetness on my hair, my neck, the back of my blouse. I pull my fingers back. They're dripping with milk.

Is it all over me? I jump out of my seat, twisting backward to see my clothes. That only makes them laugh harder. It feels as though I'm soaking wet all over.

"Hey!" Chuck leaps up. His eyes dart around the room, even though the boys who drenched me are long gone. I didn't get a look at them, and I don't think Chuck did, either. "What the

Hell is the matter with you, picking on a girl? You afraid to go for somebody who'll fight back?"

"Didn't nobody do nothing to her," a boy at the next table says. "She must'a spilled it on herself. You coons ain't got no table manners."

Ennis takes my arm. He must've gotten away from the blonde girl somehow. He shakes his head at Chuck and pulls gently on my sleeve. "Come on."

The laughter gets louder as the three of us wind our way toward the exit. The milk drips down into the waistband of my skirt. They must've dumped an entire carton on me.

Accidentally, of course. That's what they'd say if I told a teacher. Which I can't. I didn't even see who did it. And it's not as if any of the white people who saw would say so.

I go straight to the girls' bathroom. Inside, three girls are standing by the mirrors, talking. Their eyes go wide when they see me. I wait for them to call me a nigger or laugh at the milk dripping from my hair. Instead they look at me, look back at each other and rush out the door without a word.

I close my eyes and savor the quiet. It's the first time all day I've been alone.

As badly as I want to clean myself up, I go into a stall first. I've been avoiding the bathroom, afraid of getting trapped inside where I'd have no chance of calling a teacher for help, but I can't wait any longer.

When I reach for the toilet paper, I pull my hand back, surprised. Then I touch it again to make sure.

The toilet paper here is soft. At my old school, our toilet paper was rough and coarse. I'd thought that's how all school toilet paper was.

Just colored-school toilet paper, apparently.

When I go back out to the mirrors, the bathroom is still empty. I wonder if those girls told the others I was in here. There could be a crowd forming outside the door, waiting to get me when I leave, but there's nothing I can do about that now.

I mop up as much of the milk as I can with toilet paper and paper towels. There isn't much use. I can wipe off my neck but I can't reach my back without unbuttoning my blouse, and I am *not* going to do that here, where anyone could walk in. The milk that's soaked into my hair is a lost cause. I can pick some of it out once it dries, but Mama will still have to help me wash it tonight. For now, I'll just have to walk around with milk all over me.

This shouldn't be important. It was just a prank. Boys being boys. I should be able to handle this.

When I look back up into the mirror I'm crying.

I wipe the tears away and stare at my reflection until my face smooths out and my eyes go empty.

This is how they have to see me. If they know I feel things, they'll only try to make me feel worse.

Maybe if I keep trying, I really won't feel anything.

Another tear springs up in the corner of my eye. I scrub it away with the heel of my hand.

I stare into the mirror and wait until there's no more threat of tears.

Everyone is counting on me. I can't be a failure.

I won't.

LIE #5

This can't last forever.

MY AFTERNOON CLASSES are no better than the morning's. In Home Ec the teacher gives me my own set of pans and bowls and silverware to use for the whole semester so the white girls won't have to touch the same things I do. In Study Hall I sing hymns in my head while the boys make honking noises at me and the teacher takes a nap at his desk. In Remedial English our textbook reader doesn't have any stories longer than fifteen pages, except for one by James Joyce that my mother gave me to read when I was twelve.

I'm the only Negro in every class.

Halfway through sixth period I start counting the number of times I hear people call me a nigger. By the time the bell rings at the end of the day I'm up to twenty-five.

Chuck and Paulie, the only junior in our group, are a short way down the hall when I come out of my last class. They're walking so fast they're almost running. Behind them a group of white boys is walking even faster.

I can tell from the looks on their faces that the white boys aren't playing. As soon as we're off school grounds they're going to do whatever they want to us.

"Downstairs, side exit," Chuck mutters when they reach me. "The NAACP's got cars waiting for us."

I struggle to walk as quickly as Chuck and Paulie as we head for the stairs, but my breath is coming fast, and my sweaty feet are sliding in my loafers.

"What about the others?" I ask.

"Everyone knows where to go. Ennis is spreading the word."

I pick up my pace and try not to worry about Ruth. Ennis will make sure she's all right.

All around us, more white people spill out of classrooms. Some of the boys join the group following us. I want to look over my shoulder and see how many are back there, but if they see me looking it will only make things worse.

Besides, I can tell the crowd is growing by the number of *niggers* I hear. My count is already up past forty.

I scan the hallway for a teacher, but there are none in sight. And if I did spot a teacher there's no way to know if she'd help. The stairs are still a long way off.

"They're only trying to scare us," Chuck whispers.

"It's working," Paulie whispers back. He looks paler than I've ever seen him.

"Don't talk that way," I say.

We don't know who might be listening.

Ahead of us, in front of the stairwell there's another, bigger, crowd, also shouting taunts. Strangely, though, this group has their backs to us. They don't even seem to know we're coming. They're gathered around something lying on the floor.

No. Not something. Someone.

I break into a run. Chuck calls out for me to wait, but then he must see what I'm seeing, because the hard soles of his shoes come pounding down the hall behind me.

The boys following us have started running, too.

The shouts coming from the group ahead are the loudest they've been since we made it inside the school. They're so noisy I want to clap my hands over my ears.

I can't. Not until I know who they're shouting at.

"Somebody show that girl this ain't no school for coons!" someone shouts.

"We're gonna teach her a lesson!"

So it's a girl. I want to pray for my sister's safety but my thoughts are racing too fast for prayers.

"Look at her all bent over like that," someone else says. "That nigger's fatter than Aunt Jemima!"

"Go back to the cotton field, you ugly burrhead!" a girl shrieks.

Chuck gets to the crowd first. I'm right behind him as he pushes through the group to the center of the circle. I spot a pink skirt hem crumpled on the floor.

It isn't Ruth. To my shame I breathe a sigh of relief.

It's Yvonne. She's crouched on the ground in the middle of the crowd, facedown, her hands folded over her head and her knees tucked under her.

It takes me a second to piece together what happened. Someone must have tripped her, and she couldn't get up right away in the midst of that huge crowd. Instead she hunched down to protect herself from being kicked. It doesn't look as if she's badly hurt, not yet, but the longer she stays where she is the more likely something is to happen.

She's trapped in the middle of a crowd that's getting bigger with each passing second. The boys who'd been chasing us have merged with it. There must be fifty of them surrounding her, jeering and throwing pennies. There's spit all over Yvonne's dress. Some of the boys are winding their legs back like they're about to kick her.

Chuck reaches the middle of the circle first. He leans down and says something to Yvonne that I can't hear over the shouting. The white boy nearest him, a greaser with slicked-back hair, kicks out at Chuck, but Chuck sees him in time and lunges out of the way.

That only makes the boy angrier. He's backing up to deliver another kick when a woman's voice booms, "Everyone move along, now!"

The shouting dies down fast, but no one moves. Not until the teacher, a gray-haired woman I don't recognize, comes into the middle of the circle. When she sees Yvonne huddled on the floor she recoils.

"One of you, go to the office and call for a doctor!" she says.

The white girls nearest me turn and run. Within seconds, all the other white people have gone as fast as they came. The four of us Negroes and the gray-haired teacher are the only ones left in the hall.

I kneel on the floor. Chuck is still bent down, trying to say something in a low voice, but Yvonne hasn't moved. I catch his eye and whisper, "Let me try."

He shrugs and stands up. The teacher takes him aside to ask a question. I want to talk to the teacher, too, but I need to focus on Yvonne. Ruth could get here any second and I don't want her to see her friend like this.

"They're all gone," I tell Yvonne. "You can get up. I'm here, and Chuck and Paulie, too. You're not by yourself anymore."

After a long second, she turns her head and meets my eyes. Hers are wet.

"They tripped me," she says.

"I know. Are you bleeding at all? Did you get hurt when you fell?"

"I don't think so. My knee hurts a little. There were so many of them. I was afraid to get up. I thought they'd never leave me alone if I—"

"I know," I say. "It's all right. It was smart, what you did. Can you stand?"

Slowly, Yvonne uncurls from her crouch. She lifts her head and looks around the hall. When she sees we really are alone she lets me help her up. Dust and dirt are all over her clothes, and her face is streaked with tears. She winces when she puts her weight on her right leg.

I reach out a hand to help her up. That's when I notice I'm shaking harder than she is.

What if the teacher hadn't gotten there when she did? Yvonne could've really been hurt. Or Chuck could've.

It could have been any of us.

I look around for the others. Paulie is standing against the lockers, pressing his fist into his forehead. Ennis is here, too, talking with Chuck and the teacher. Chuck looks angry. The teacher is nodding at Ennis, who's saying something in a low, serious voice.

"All right," Ennis says to all of us after a minute. "We've got to go fast. The others are waiting for us by the side exit at the bottom of the stairs."

"Are they safe?" I ask.

"They were when I left them."

That doesn't make me feel better.

Yvonne's knee is worse than she'd thought, so we have to move slowly. I want to run ahead to see Ruth, but that wouldn't be right. I'm the only other girl here, so I have to let Yvonne lean on me as we make our way toward the stairs.

At least Ruth isn't alone. I'll see her soon. As soon as I possibly can.

"What did the teacher say?" I ask Chuck as we navigate the stairwell. Yvonne flinches on every step.

"She wanted to call a doctor to come look at Yvonne. Ennis talked her out of it. He said she'd be safer if we could get her to Mrs. Mullins's first."

I think Ennis is right, but from the set of Chuck's jaw I can tell he disagrees.

When we finally get to the side exit Ruth is waiting for us just inside the door with the other freshmen and sophomores. One of the younger girls is crying. Ruth has her arm around her.

I want to gather Ruth into my arms and never let go. Instead I motion for both girls to walk with me and Yvonne.

"That's enough of that, now," I tell the crying girl. "We have to move."

Ruth glares at me. I ignore her.

The four of us will be the first ones outside. Through the narrow window we can see the crowd gathered around the door, waiting for us. We have no choice but to walk right into the middle of it.

"Can you get them to the curb?" Ennis whispers to me. His forehead is creased, but we both know it's better this way. The boys should be at the back of the crowd this time, where the rowdiest white people will be. "The cars are waiting. Get in the first one. It's Mr. Stern driving."

I nod. "What about everyone else?"

"We'll be right behind you."

He says something more, but I can't make out the words. As soon as we step outside the doors the noise from the crowd is deafening.

I can't see any faces now, or hear any voices. It's all a blur of white and hate.

I want to run, but the crowd would just run after us. As soon as we're off school property, they'd catch us. I don't want to think about what would happen then.

So I walk as fast as I can, and I make the others do the same, even though Yvonne is groaning from the pain in her knee. She and I are in front, with Ruth and the other girl behind us. I can see Mr. Stern's car up ahead. Ennis was right—it's probably the safest of the NAACP cars for us to take. No one will think we're aiming to get into a car with a white man.

The white people are swarming us from all sides now. It's as bad as it was this morning.

No. It's worse. This morning the white people just looked furious. Now they look like killers.

"Get the niggers!" A chant starts up. "Get the niggers! Get the niggers! Get them!"

They're right up in our faces. After a full day of this their glares and shouts aren't shocking anymore. I'm used to the feeling of my heart throbbing in my chest, my eyes sharpening, my shoulders quaking with fear.

Police officers line the curb. I don't expect any more help from them than I did this morning.

I glance over my shoulder to see the other girls and almost trip, catching myself at the very last second.

This won't work. I can't walk in front of them and make sure they're safe at the same time.

Ruth catches my eye and nods. It feels like a terrible mistake, but I move behind the others and let Ruth take the lead.

This is the most frightened I've been for her all day, but there's nothing I can do. Ruth marches through the crowd, her head high, her gaze straight ahead. The white people scream at her but they move aside, like she's Moses parting the waters.

This time, when someone spits on her hand, she ignores it and keeps on walking.

It makes me want to cry. Instead I keep my eyes dry and fixed, letting Ruth lead us.

They're still shouting. I sing to myself in my head to drown out their words. An old hymn. The old ones are always the best.

Rock of Ages,
cleft for me,
let me hide
myself in thee.

Something sails over Yvonne's head. A ball of paper with something heavy wrapped inside.

I don't say anything. I don't think she noticed. I can't tell whether the white boy who threw it was only trying to scare us or if he just has bad aim.

The chant has changed now, back to the familiar "Two, four, six, eight, we don't wanna integrate." We're almost at the curb. Mr. Stern is waiting in the car with his engine on.

It's over. Soon we'll be out of this place. We've survived. This day is finally at an end.

Ruth opens the back door and climbs inside, moving over so Yvonne and the other girl can slide in. I get in the front seat with Mr. Stern.

With the windows rolled up we can barely hear the chants. It really is over. Mr. Stern steps on the gas.

But just as he's turning the wheel, the back door on the far side—Ruth's side—jerks open. A grown white man with a wide chest and huge hands is standing by the side of the car, holding on tight to the door frame and looking right at Ruth.

"Get out of the car, niggers, before we drag you out," the man's voice booms. "You, too, you nigger-loving Jew."

LIE #6

I'm not strong enough
for this.

THE MAN'S WORDS slap me in the face, hot and wet and vicious. I slam open my car door. My heart pounds in my ears. I'll go over to where the man is and—I don't know what I'll do. Something. Whatever it takes to get him away from my sister.

Before I can get out of the car Mr. Stern jerks on the wheel and pounds on the gas. The car jolts into the street. The white man loses his grip on Ruth's door and stumbles backward onto the pavement.

Two of our car doors are open, but we're already speeding along the street in front of the school. I lean out to pull my door shut, even though I'm sure I'm going to fall out of the car. In the backseat Ruth does the same thing. She slams the lock down on her door. I should lock mine, too, but I'm shaking too hard.

Two more big white men chase our car down the street, shouting. We outpace them at the next block. The police are nowhere to be seen.

I turn around to make sure Ruth's all right. She's resting her head on the window, gazing outside. Her hands are clasped in her lap. They're trembling.

"Is anyone hurt?" Mr. Stern says when it's quiet enough to hear each other.

"Yvonne is," I say. "She'll need a doctor."

"It's only a bruise on my knee," Yvonne says. "No worse than I used to get roughhousing with my brothers."

I try to meet Yvonne's eyes in the rearview mirror. She won't look at me. I know what happened today was nothing like playing with her brothers. She knows it, too.

"Even so," Mr. Stern says. "We're going to Mrs. Mullins's house. She'll call a doctor if you need one. Ruth, Sarah, your father will be at the Mullins', too."

I can't imagine seeing Daddy now. Not after everything that's happened today. It's hard to believe that I still have parents. That there's a world outside Jefferson High School.

We all know the way to Mrs. Mullins's house by heart—she's in charge of our integration case for the NAACP, and we go to her house a lot—so I notice Mr. Stern is taking the long way. We've been driving almost an hour when we get there. Trying to keep any white people from following us, probably.

We're the last ones to reach the house. Daddy is on the front steps when we pull up. Ruth bolts out of the car and runs up to the porch, her saddle shoes leaving dents behind her in the freshly mown grass. She flings her arms around our father the way she used to when she was little.

"Daddy," Ruth cries, loud enough for the rest of us to hear even though we're still at the curb. "Daddy, Daddy."

Daddy looks at me over her shoulder. I nod to tell him we're both all right. He hugs Ruth back, then unwraps her arms from his waist. He rubs his eye, and I can tell from his bleary look he's skipping his afternoon nap to be here. Daddy works two jobs— days at the Negro newspaper, the *Davisburg Free Press,* where he's a reporter and editor, and nights and weekends at the *Davisburg Gazette*, where he's a copy boy. Whenever he has to miss his nap we all know to stay quiet and let him have his peace.

"All right, Ruthie," he says. "Let's go in the house and you can tell me all about it."

I help Yvonne inside. All the people from the NAACP who've been working on the court case and teaching in the special school they set up for us last semester are gathered in Mrs. Mullins's living room. Their eyes bob from one to the other of us as we walk in and sit down on the rug. They've been waiting to make sure all ten of us are safe.

Ruth comes in last, with Daddy, and only then do Mrs. Mullins and the others cheer.

"Praise the Lord," Mrs. Mullins says. "I knew He'd watch over you and keep you safe."

Oh. Is that what He was doing? Is that what the Lord calls keeping us safe?

That was a sinful thought. I close my eyes to pray for forgiveness.

Praying usually brings warmth and relief. I wait, but I don't feel any different than I did before. I don't feel anything at all.

Mrs. Mullins asks how our day went. The younger kids rush to answer her.

I stretch my legs out in front of me and try to hide the stains on my skirt. I wish we could go home. My house is only a few blocks away. Mr. and Mrs. Mullins live in Morningside, like us. Ennis's family lives here, too. It's the nicest Negro neighborhood in Davisburg. Too nice for us Dunbars, really. Some nights I hear Mama and Daddy arguing about money in the kitchen. Daddy's newspaper work doesn't pay as well as it did when we lived in Chicago, and Mama's always worried his boss at the white paper will fire him once he checks the state registry and finds out we're involved with the NAACP. We could move to Davis Heights—that's where Chuck lives—but Daddy says he wants Ruth and Bobby and me to "associate with the best kind of children," whatever that means. He's probably worried we'll have to move to New Town, where everyone's so poor the whites and Negroes live side by side, but I don't think New Town would be so bad. At least it's not Clayton Mill, the Negro neighborhood way outside of town, where the houses are made of tar paper.

Ennis, Paulie and I reach for the sandwiches Mrs. Mullins has set out for the adults. I barely ate any lunch and now I'm starving.

"You and your sister were leading the pack out there," Ennis says. He's talking quietly, so Mrs. Mullins won't hear us on her side of the room. He pours a cup of coffee and passes it to me. I've never had coffee before, but I take a sip. It burns my tongue. "Looks like you got in the car all right."

"It was awful." I put the coffee down on the floor. I hate to be wasteful, but if I have to keep drinking that after everything else that's happened today I think I really will cry.

"I know it was," he says. "But we all got out safe. That's what matters."

Ennis smiles at me. I don't smile back.

"It'll settle down after a couple of days," Paulie says. "The white people will get used to us. Once they see we aren't going away."

"No they won't!" Chuck shouts.

Everyone in the room stops talking and turns to look behind us. Chuck's standing there with fire in his eyes.

"Did you *see* what they did today?" Chuck says. He's the only one of us who didn't sit on the rug like children at story hour as soon as we came in. He's standing with his back straight, his fists clenched.

"Did you see what they did to Yvonne?" he shouts. "They aren't going to get *used* to us! Or if they do, they'll just get used to calling us niggers and trying to lynch us in the parking lot!"

"Charles Irving Tapscott!" Daddy is on his feet, pointing his finger. Chuck is just as tall as my father, but he steps back. "You know better than to say something like that in front of these children. I'll be placing a call to your father tonight."

Chuck bites his lip and drops his head. "I'm sorry, sir." He sits down next to Ennis and me on the rug.

Chuck is usually a jokester. The sort of boy everyone likes because he's funny and nice to everyone. The boy trembling next to me now is somebody else altogether.

Yvonne's lip quivers. For a minute, we're all quiet. Then the younger kids start whispering.

"I saw somebody in the hall who said he had a knife."

"A girl in Gym said she was going to pour gas on us and set us on fire."

"On TV they said a girl got stabbed in Little Rock."

"That's not true," Mrs. Mullins says. "Anyway, this isn't Little Rock. Those sorts of things won't happen here."

"They were throwing rocks at us," Ruth says.

"And sticks and pencils," a sophomore boy says. "One almost stuck me in the eye."

Mrs. Mullins shakes her head. "It's because today was the first day. It will die down."

"I tried to tell a teacher," the sophomore boy goes on. "She said she couldn't do anything because no adults saw it happen."

"Most of the teachers and the administrators won't be much help, I'm afraid," Mrs. Mullins says. "But if anything serious happens, if you need a doctor, you should certainly tell your parents right away."

"Translation," Chuck mutters so only Ennis, Paulie and I can hear. "Don't tattle, or the judge will send us all back to our old school. Jim Crow is still alive and well in good old Virginia."

"Shush," Ennis tells him.

But I've heard Mama and Daddy say that, too. If there's any sign integration is causing violence, the courts could delay it another year. Then we'd have to go back to Johns High, and the school board lawyers would probably come up with some reason why integration had to be pushed back another year after that. And another, and another. Decades would pass before the next black face showed up at Jefferson High School.

We've already been waiting forever. When we filed our lawsuit, two years had passed since the Supreme Court said all the schools in the country had to be integrated.

My family was still living in Chicago when we first heard what the Supreme Court had done. I was only in seventh grade. We moved to Virginia that summer, and I thought when we got here, we'd be going to school with white people.

That was before I understood how hard the white people in the South would fight us. It wasn't until the next year, when Little Rock integrated its high school and the white people rioted in the streets, that I understood what my family and I had signed on for.

Mama and Daddy signed on to the NAACP's lawsuit, and for three years, Ruth and I and the other colored children waited. We took tests and went to court and watched white lawyers talk about whether colored children were smart enough to keep up with white children. I sat on a bench in the courtroom and watched the superintendent hold up my file and testify in front of a white-haired judge about how, even though I'd scored in the top 5 percent on the aptitude tests, I wasn't fit to go to a white school because I'd have "trouble adapting socially."

Forty Negro kids had applied to transfer to white schools in Davisburg. Some of them changed their minds when they saw what we were up against. Most of the rest got rejected because the school board said they hadn't passed the tests—even though none of us ever saw a grade book. So now it was down to us ten. We'd done so well on the tests they couldn't come up with any more excuses. The judge said "trouble adapting socially" wasn't a good enough reason to keep us at a school where the heaters only worked on the days it wasn't raining.

The white parents tried to get the decision overturned, and

the case went back and forth and back and forth until last summer, when the federal judge ruled Jefferson had to admit us, period.

So the governor shut down all the white schools in Virginia that had been ordered to admit Negroes. He figured if colored people couldn't go to the white schools, it meant he'd won. He didn't seem to care that if the white schools were closed, then white people couldn't go to school, either. The white people called it "Massive Resistance," because they were doing whatever it took to resist the Supreme Court's order. When Daddy first saw that newspaper photo of the big locks on the Jefferson High's front doors he said, "I've got to hand it to the governor. I didn't think he had the nerve."

Starting last September, the white kids had to find a private school to go to or miss school altogether. But the ten of us did all right. The NAACP tutored us at Mrs. Mullins's house for free. We studied so much English and History and French and Math and Science no one could accuse us of not keeping up with the white kids.

When Christmas break came and went and the schools were still closed, we'd started to think we might spend the whole year taking classes in Mrs. Mullins's house. Then, last week, another court said it was illegal for the governor to close the schools just because he felt like it. After five months of sitting empty, Jefferson had to be opened. Even to us.

Daddy says we're lucky. Down in Prince Edward County, they shut down their entire school system—every single white school and every single colored school, from kindergarten up through twelfth grade—so they wouldn't have to integrate. The courts can't do anything about it. So the white parents there used county tax money to set up a private school for their kids to go to, for free. Only the white kids get to go there, though. The Negroes in Prince Edward County don't have any schools at all. Some of their parents could afford to send them to private schools in other districts, but most of them are sitting at home all day, reading whatever books their parents can scrounge up for them and hoping they'll wind up with enough education to get a job someday.

"Sarah, honey, do you want me to help you with your hair?" a quiet voice says behind me.

I turn, startled. Miss Freeman, Mrs. Mullins's younger sister, is smiling at me.

I'd forgotten all about the milk in my hair. After Mama took all that time to wash it last night, too. I must be stinking up the house for Miss Freeman to mention it.

"Thank you, ma'am." I get up and follow her to the bathroom.

"I'm sure looking forward to seeing you sing at church this Sunday," Miss Freeman says as she closes the door behind us and pulls pins out of my hair. Her voice is soft and pleasant. I ignore the way she's yanking at my scalp because it's so nice to hear someone talk about something that's not integration. "What's the anthem this week?"

It takes me a minute to remember. "'Light Rises in the Darkness.'"

"Oh, that'll be real pretty. Do you have a solo?"

I wince at another sharp tug. "Not this time."

"Well, I hope you have one soon. I loved it when you sang on Christmas Eve." There's a pause in the yanking. "You know, why don't I go see if I can find you a clean blouse to wear home. We'll put this one in the wash."

She leaves. The milk stain must be bad. I twist around to see it in the bathroom mirror. Sure enough, a broad swath of yellow runs all the way down the back of my blouse. Revolting. Below it are two holes in the fabric where the boy poked me with pencils in the auditorium. I press my fingers against the spot and feel a tender bruise.

A tear pricks at my eye, but I squeeze my lids shut. I can't give in to tears. If anyone saw, they'd think I was just another weak colored girl. That I couldn't handle this.

The door opens. I try to put on a smile for Miss Freeman, but it's just Ruth.

She gazes at my reflection in the mirror. "What happened?"

"Nothing. Somebody accidentally spilled some milk on me."

Ruth nods, pretending to believe me.

I sit on the toilet seat, facing the wall. Ruth comes up behind me and combs through my hair with her fingers, picking out the flakes of dried milk. Ruth and I are used to fixing each other's hair. She's a lot gentler than Miss Freeman.

We're quiet for a long time. Then, softly, Ruth says, "I didn't think it would be like that."

I want to hug her. Instead I say, "What did you think it would be like?"

"I don't know. I guess I thought— No. It's stupid."

"It's not stupid. Tell me."

I turn to face her. Ruth sighs and looks at the window over my head. "I thought when we got there, they'd see they were wrong. I thought they'd let us join their clubs and come to their football games, like everyone else. And maybe later, when the white people thought about it some more, they'd stop trying to tell us we can't do other things, too."

"What kind of other things?"

Ruth shrugs and looks down. "You know. Other places. Like at the Sugar Castle."

The Sugar Castle is the candy store downtown. We always walk past it when Mama takes us to shop for school clothes and Christmas presents. Through the windows you can see dozens of white children filling little bags with Bazooka gum and Red Hots and candy cigarettes. They dig their dirty little hands right down into the candy bins to pick the best pieces and plop them in their bags.

Bobby always begs to go in. He doesn't read well enough yet

to understand the sign on the door that says White Only. So Mama and Ruth and I always tell him we're running late and can't go in the store. Then we stop by Food Town on the way home and pick him up a Tootsie Roll.

When we first moved down here Ruth would gaze in the Sugar Castle windows, too. She was big enough by then to know the rules. She could read the sign, and besides, she knew no white parents would want their children putting their hands in candy bins where black children's fingers had been. But Chick-O-Sticks were always Ruth's favorites when we lived in Chicago, and the Sugar Castle was the only store in Davisburg where you could get them.

For her eleventh birthday Mama gave Ruth a whole bag of Chick-O-Sticks. I've always wondered how she got them. She must have paid someone to go in the store for her.

"I used to think that, too," I tell Ruth. "When they first started the lawsuit."

"Did you think it would make the white people be nice to us?"

"No." I almost laugh. "I don't think that's ever going to happen."

"Well, maybe some of the white people at school could be—"

"No. They won't."

I think about the girl who smiled at me this morning before she spit on my good skirt. And the one who shrieked at Ennis in the cafeteria. And Judy, who acted nice at first, then got all her friends to make honking noises whenever I passed by.

"No," I say again. "We can't ever trust any of them. We have to stick together, like Mrs. Mullins says."

Ruth bows her head. "All right."

I want to say something to make her feel better, but I don't want to lie. I don't want to do any of this.

All I really want to do is go to sleep. Lie down in my room at home and stay there, and keep Ruth there, too. Forever.

It feels like there's a giant hole opening inside me. My future, sliding into a gaping black pit.

I don't want this to be my life. My sister's, either.

It's too late for that now.

The door behind us opens. I swallow and try to smile again. It doesn't work.

"Sorry, this was all Helen had." Miss Freeman holds out a hideous pink high-collared blouse. "Let's see if it fits."

I take off my stained white blouse.

"Ooh, the milk went all the way through your slip, too," Ruth says. "Mama's going to be so upset."

"No, she won't," Miss Freeman says. "She'll know it wasn't your fault, Sarah."

That's right. Mama will know. Because it's not my fault.

It's hers. And Daddy's. They were the ones who wanted this.

If it hadn't been for them we could've stayed at Johns. I'd be president of the choir and taking college prep classes. I wouldn't have to worry about Howard revoking my scholarship once they hear I'm in Remedial. I wouldn't have to worry about Ruth getting her arm broken on her way to Homeroom.

I shouldn't be thinking this way. It's disrespectful. Besides, it's my own fault. I never said I didn't want this. Our parents asked Ruth and me years ago if we wanted to register at Jefferson—to get the best education we could, and to do our part for the movement. We said yes right away. Why wouldn't we? Adults had been telling us all our lives that it was up to us to make sure we got a good education. Besides, back then, it seemed impossible that integration would ever really happen here.

But I still said yes.

I have no one to blame but myself. Anything that happens now is my own fault.

I close my eyes and say a quick prayer for God to forgive me for thinking disrespectfully. This time, it does make me feel a little better.

Mrs. Mullins's blouse comes close enough to fitting me. I do up the buttons on the sleeves while Ruth finishes picking the biggest white flakes out of my hair.

"Remember what I said," I whisper to her when we're leaving the house an hour later. "The white people aren't like us. They'll turn on you without any warning. You have to be careful, Ruthie. You can't trust them."

"I'll remember." She huffs, the same way she does when I tell her not to mess with the stuff on my desk at home.

I pray she takes this seriously. I pray she really will remember. Not one of us can afford to forget.

LIE #7

They won't really hurt me.

"THIS IS DUMB." Ruth yanks a needle through the old brown skirt she's sewing a patch onto and bites down on a piece of bacon at the same time. "You can't follow me around all day."

"I won't be following you." I'm hunting through Mama's sewing box for gray thread. All I can find is garish pinks and blues. "And stop chewing with your mouth open."

"I'm not a little kid. It's not your job to tell me what to do." Ruth puts down her sewing and grabs the biggest piece of bacon on the plate. She takes a huge bite, chewing with her mouth open so wide pieces of bacon fall out.

"Girls, hush," Mama says. "Your father needs to concentrate."

"Sorry, Daddy," Ruth and I murmur toward where our father is perched on the ledge of the living room window.

There's a loud bang. "Dang it," Daddy says. He hammered his finger again.

"We still need to close the gap on this end, Bob." Mr. Mullins hefts up the other end of the last piece of plywood. It's barely light out yet, but already they've nearly finished covering all the first-floor windows on the front of the house. For the first ten minutes they were working Bobby kept wandering around asking why they were making so much noise, and could he help Daddy play workshop. Mama finally told him to go to his room until it was time for school.

Ruth and I didn't ask why they were putting the boards up. We didn't ask why Mama brought down the basket of old clothes from the attic and told us to mend them, either. We knew we'd be wearing our old clothes to school from now on in case they get ruined. We knew Daddy and Mr. Mullins were putting boards on the windows in case the white people threw rocks when they drove by the house.

There's no use talking about these things. These things just are.

Mama snips a piece of thread, then looks at the map I've laid out on the breakfast table next to our sewing. "You're sure this is necessary, Sarah?" she says.

I look at her. She looks back, then lowers her eyes.

I don't know if this will work, but I've got to try.

School is worse than I thought it would be, but I can survive this. And I'm going to make sure Ruth survives it, too.

As long as I have my dignity, I can do anything.

Last night I took Ennis's sketch of the school and Ruth's class schedule and I drew a map to follow through the day. I've already figured out how I can check in on Ruth after Homeroom and before third period, but our lunch periods are staggered, and I'm having trouble figuring out a way to get from the basement to the second floor and back without being late for Home Ec.

I can't be late to class again. I've already got detention after school today, thanks to Mrs. Gruber. Ruth will have to leave school without me. That's not a risk I ever want to take again.

I barely slept last night. Instead I lay there for hours, listening to Ruth tossing and turning in the next bed, murmuring in her sleep. High-pitched cries, the kind she used to make when we were little and Mama tried to make her take her stomach medicine.

I must've fallen asleep sometime. Because I remember dreaming.

In the dream it was still yesterday morning. I was trying to get across the school parking lot, holding Ruth by her arm, but instead of walking, we were running. A monster as big as a city bus was chasing us. It had deep red scales, a thumping, clubbed tail and glistening huge white eyes. Ruth and I were trying to get inside the school, where we'd be safe, but once we'd finished the sprint across the lot and made it through the front doors, the monster kept coming. Then there were more monsters, and more. Soon a whole herd of them was thundering down the hallway behind us. We kept looking for a way out, but every time we turned a corner it led to another hallway, endless rows of gleaming lockers and polished floors.

Ruth was pulled from my grip. I screamed. When I turned to look for her, Linda Hairston was standing in Ruth's place. She smiled at me, her pretty red hair glistening under the fluorescent lights, just like the monsters' scales. Linda threw back her head and howled. Her laughter was so loud and fierce the monsters stopped chasing us and started laughing with her.

"You be careful today," Mama says after we've changed into our mended clothes and gathered our things to meet the carpool. "Even with the new rule, you make sure and keep a watch out."

"We know, Mama," Ruth says, wiping off her cheek after Mama kisses her.

Mrs. Mullins called us late last night to tell us about the new rule. The principal had just announced it. When the gray-haired teacher reported what happened to Yvonne, the principal decided no one could be punished because no adult saw who'd instigated it. So from now on anyone who got caught fighting—no matter who started the fight—would be expelled.

Ruth whooped when Mama told us the news. Mama and I just frowned at each other. Somehow we didn't think it would be as simple as that.

Mama puts her hand on my shoulder as I'm going to the door.

"Remember what to do when it gets hard," she says. "Take your worries to the Lord. Have faith. He's watching over all of you."

I nod. Mama's right, of course.

But I can't help wondering why the Lord has to watch over us from so far away.

New rule or not, today is no better than yesterday.

We go in the side door this time, like Ennis planned, but there are just as many white people waiting for us there. The police aren't here today, but that doesn't seem to make a difference. The white people throw sticks past our heads and shout as loud as ever. That must not count as fighting, because no one gets expelled that I hear about.

I'm still not used to being called "nigger," but I've stopped keeping track of how many times I hear it. Instead I count the minutes left in the school day. I watch the hands of the classroom clocks wind their way around until I'm free of this place and the people in it.

In Math someone's brought in extra desks for the back of the room. Now everyone has a seat without having to get anywhere near Chuck and me. Chuck draws a picture in his notebook of Mrs. Gruber standing in front of a classroom full of tanks and soldiers firing on each other. The Mrs. Gruber in the picture, who's twice as fat and three times as ugly as the real Mrs. Gruber, has her eyes squeezed shut and fingers stuck in her ears. A comic-book speech balloon has her singing, "LA LA LA I CAN'T HEAR YOU!!!" When Chuck shows it to me I almost smile.

Adults always tell us education is the most important thing in life, but I'm not learning anything at Jefferson. It's supposed to be the best school for miles around, with the best facilities and the best teachers, but none of that is doing me any good. Our science labs at Johns weren't as nice as the ones here, but when I was at Johns I could focus on my schoolwork. I didn't have to spend every moment looking over my shoulder to see what would be thrown at me next.

In History I overhear two girls gossiping about something they heard from their friends. According to their story, one of the Negro girls (only the girl telling the story calls her a "nigger girl," in the giggly whisper of a child who's trying out a naughty word for the first time), went up to a white girl in the locker room this morning and told her she smelled like cow shit and looked worse. The white girl told her boyfriend, and he told his friends. Now the boys are saying they'll "get that nigger back" later today.

The gossip can't be true. None of the Negro girls in our group would ever do such a thing. None of them would use that kind of foul language. Besides, Mrs. Mullins has told us a thousand times not to talk back to the white students. I can't stop remembering what Yvonne looked like yesterday, though, huddled in a pile in the hall. When school lets out today, I'll make sure to keep every single one of these girls someplace I can see them until we get safely home.

When I get to Typing, the teacher points out a typewriter she's set aside in the far corner for me and the Negro girls who take Typing in other periods. The teacher smiles, like she's waiting for me to thank her. And I do it. I grit my teeth, but I still say, "Thank you, ma'am," sweet as sugar.

As I drop my purse on the desk I see something tucked under my typewriter. One of the white girls must have left it there. It's a clipping from the *Davisburg Gazette*. I didn't see the paper this morning—Mama had already put it away somewhere—but this front-page story is headlined Negroes Integrate Jefferson High. Two School Board Members Resign in Protest. Under the headline is a photo of the ten of us. Someone has drawn a circle on the photo in lipstick, right around my face, and put a big red *X* over it. Scrawled black ink in the margins says "DIE UGLY NIGGER."

I swallow, glad I have my back to the rest of the room so the girls can't see my face. I start to crumple up the paper when I see a sidebar with the headline Jefferson Students Speak Out. One of the reporters who blinded me with his flashbulbs yesterday must've talked to some of the white students afterward. The first quote in the story is from Linda Hairston.

"'What about our right to an education?'" Linda's quote reads. "'No one talks about that. The colored people aren't the only ones who should have rights.'"

Yesterday I'd thought Linda Hairston was *smart*.

I crush the paper in my fist, march to the front of the room and throw it in the trash can. On my way back I fold my arms across my chest so no one will see my hands shaking.

During each class break I walk as fast as I can, following the routes I mapped out at breakfast. I see Ruth every time, and every time, she's all right. There's a new ink stain on her blouse that wasn't there this morning, but she isn't hurt. She's just walking down the hall surrounded by a circle of white people, clutching her books and pretending not to hear the chants of "nigger, nigger, nigger" that follow her everywhere.

The white people follow me, too, slowing me down. It doesn't matter what route I take. They walk behind me and in front of me. Trying to trip me, calling out to me, stepping on my heels, blocking my path. It's like walking through quicksand.

When I leave third-period History, trying to forget what that awful Mrs. Johnson said in her lecture about the slave trade, there are still two hundred and thirty-five minutes left in the school day. I speed toward the stairs to get to Ruth, uncertain of how I'll get back to the second floor in time for French.

It isn't the distance that's the problem. I could walk there and back easily if the white people would only leave me alone.

But they won't. In fact, there's a group of white boys following me as I exit the staircase and start down the first-floor hall.

They've been behind me since History. I don't have to look back to know they're still there. The feeling of eyes on my back is familiar by now.

But there's something different about this time. These boys are being quiet. They aren't chanting, or calling me names or joking with each other. Occasionally one of them will snicker, but the others quickly hush him.

When I'm halfway down the hall, they're still following, silent except for their thudding footsteps. From the sound of it there are at least ten of them. People coming the other way wave at the boys as they pass, smiling and calling to them.

The boys are getting closer.

I speed up, but their footsteps get faster, too. There's no way I could outrun them.

They must be planning something. I hope they get it over with soon. I brace myself for the feeling of an object striking my back. A wad of spit, a pencil, a rock they snuck in from outside.

Nothing comes.

Something's wrong.

The voice in my head is certain. I don't know what's happening, but I know it's something new. Something bad.

I speed up, but the shuffling footsteps are louder now. One of the boys is right behind me.

The pain comes with a jolt. I freeze. My breath stops, and my voice catches in my throat. The shock of it is too strong.

The boy is squeezing my breasts, hard.

He lets go as fast as he grabbed on, and then all the boys are running past me at once. Laughing. Trading high fives.

There's no way to know which of them did it.

The crowd coming the other way has stopped moving, too.

They're pointing at me, laughing. The girls are covering their mouths to hide their giggles.

I cross my arms over my chest, but that only makes them laugh harder.

That really just happened.

That boy touched me. I didn't want him to, but he did it anyway. That was *why* he did it. Because he knew I didn't want it.

Nothing is mine anymore.

Even my own body isn't mine. Not if that pack of white boys doesn't want it to be.

Everyone saw what they did.

It's exactly like my dream. The pack of monsters, laughing.

I drop my head so they can't see my face. I would *never* let someone do that to me. I'm not the sort of girl who would ever do anything like that.

The white people at this school don't care what sort of girl I am.

I look down at myself. I don't look any different than I did this morning. What the boy did hadn't left a mark. But nothing will ever undo it.

My dignity was all I had.

Tears well in my eyes. The pack of boys is all the way at the end of the hall now. One of them, a tall brown-haired boy, is still looking back at me, grinning, but the rest are looking at something up ahead.

"That's her," one of them calls. "That's the nigger who talked back to my girl."

"Big Sis still back where we left her?" another boy answers. His voice carries all the way down the hall. They don't care who hears them.

"Yeah," the other boy says. "We scared her off but good."

"Let's go, then."

I recognize the brown dress. The one she was mending this morning.

It's Ruth they're running toward.

She's the one the story was about. The one who talked trash to a white girl.

My shoes feel like lead. I run, my legs pumping as hard as they can, but I'm not fast enough.

"Stop it!" I shout. It comes out as a screech. The white people gathered on the sides of the hall are still and quiet, watching.

The boys have caught up with Ruth. They've got her in a corner where she can't back away. I'm still too far to see her face, but I can picture the fear in her eyes.

"Leave her alone!" I scream, but the crowd has gotten noisy again. No one hears me.

I don't care about the rules anymore. I'm not going to ignore what's happening.

I tear down the hall after them.

But I can already tell I'm going to be too late.

part 2

Onward Christian Soldiers

Linda

LIE #8

None of this has anything to do with me.

THEY CANCELED THE prom today.

Because of the colored people. Everything that happens now is because of the colored people.

If Daddy has to work late at the paper it's because the integrationist teachers are making up stories. If I'm behind in English it's because the NAACP forced the school to close last semester. If I get caught daydreaming in Math it's because the colored girl in the front row distracted me.

But the prom? Why did they have to get that, too?

I was going to the prom with Jack. It was going to be my last date of high school, and the first time Jack and I went to a dance together. Jack is far too old for these sorts of things—he's twenty-two—but he said he'd come anyway. He said I shouldn't have to miss out on my own prom just because my fiancé is an older man who's long past childish stuff like school dances.

"I don't see why they had to cancel in the first place," Judy says. She has to raise her voice for me to hear her. There's noise up ahead. People shouting. There's always shouting in the halls now that the colored people are here.

We're walking down the hall toward the first-floor bathroom near the stairwell. It's the only bathroom Judy ever wants to go in because it's always empty and she can fix her makeup without anyone seeing. The toilets in that bathroom have been stopped up since our freshman year.

"It's obvious," I say patiently. You have to be patient with Judy. She's not slow like people think. She's naive, that's all. "No one wants white people and colored people dancing together."

"Would that really happen?" Judy says. "Was someone going to *force* us to dance with them? Wouldn't the coloreds only dance with each other?"

"*Coloreds* isn't a word," I tell her for the hundredth time. I swerve to step around a group of giggly sophomores. People are so rude, blocking the halls like this. They think just because our school is integrated they all have the right to act like animals.

"Right," Judy says. "Sorry. The Nigras, I meant. But wouldn't they?"

"Who knows what would happen," I say. "No one thought we'd be forced to let them into our school. It's not as if they didn't already have their own. If they weren't happy going to school with each other, why should they be happy dancing with each other?"

"Oh," Judy says. "I hadn't thought about it that way."

I picture the shiny blue dress in my closet. It's strapless, with a matching blue wrap and blue high heels. It looks almost as good as the fancy one from Miller & Rhoads I modeled in the Future Business Leaders of America fashion show last year. Mom took me shopping for it the day they announced the schools were going to reopen. She said it was too bad about the integration, but at least I wouldn't have to miss out on all the fun of my senior year.

Daddy was furious when he found out. He said I wasn't going

to any dance with any colored boys. I told him I wasn't going with a colored boy, I was going with Jack, and besides, it wasn't *my* fault the governor gave up on segregation. Daddy said as long as I was under his roof I would speak to him respectfully, and I said then it was a good thing I wouldn't be under his roof much longer. Then he pulled back his hand. For a second I thought he was going to do it. I think he thought so, too.

I almost wanted him to do it. To prove I still mattered to him even a little bit.

But he didn't. He put his hand down and said I was an ungrateful little girl and he had work to do. Then he went to his study and didn't come out again all night. As though he'd forgotten I was out there.

Mom told me to keep the dress because you never knew. Daddy had been known to change his mind about things. Then she disappeared upstairs with a glass of sherry and I was alone again.

The noise is getting louder as we near the stairwell. "We're gonna shut that nigger up!" a boy yells.

Oh, for heaven's sake. This again?

"That looks like a colored girl they've got there," Judy says. The shouting is so loud I have to strain to hear her.

"A girl?" I say. "Who's got her?"

"Bo and his gang, I think."

I could've guessed. Bo Nash and his friends are a bunch of nobodies. Or they would be, anyway, if Bo hadn't scored two touchdowns back-to-back sophomore year. He went from no-good redneck farm boy to town hero in one night. It only got worse that spring, when he pitched a no-hitter for the baseball team's state championship. Girls stopped joking about Bo's dirty, mismatched socks and started cooing about his dreamy blue eyes. It was enough to make you vomit. Now Bo thinks he owns the school. And everybody else seems to think so, too.

Well, not me. Any boy who wants to beat up on a girl, colored or not, isn't worth the sweat in his undershorts. Bo's a star of the team, so I can't be outright nasty to him—not unless I want to hear everyone whispering about me in the halls all year—but I can take him down a peg or two.

Bo is right up in front of the colored girl when I get there. He and his friends have got her backed into a corner. She's turning her head this way and that, looking for a way out. It's one of the younger ones. Her white blouse has an ink stain on it, and her brown skirt is old and patched.

I stride up to the group and step in neatly between the boys and the girl, facing Bo. He scowls at me. Behind us, people are yelling, and another girl is screaming. I hold out my hands the way Reverend Pierce does when he's trying to get an especially rowdy congregation at Davisburg Baptist to sit down and be at peace already.

"What's the matter, Bo?" I ask, raising my voice so everyone can hear. "You've got everybody all riled up. For a second I thought Elvis came to town."

A bunch of people laugh. I smile, because I know it'll make Bo mad. I haven't forgotten what he said to Judy in French yesterday. If he thinks he can get away with treating my best friend like that, he's even dumber than I thought.

"You best just get on out the way, Linda," Bo says. "We're teaching somebody a lesson."

I look over my shoulder in fake surprise, as if I didn't know the colored girl was there. She's cowering against the lockers. I take my first good look at her. Her eyes are wide and shockingly white around her deep black irises. The sleeves of her blouse have been let out so far the frayed edges are showing. She probably lives in one of those falling-down shacks out in Clayton Mill. My brothers say those places are full of lowlifes and it isn't safe for a girl like me to go near them.

The colored people are all poor as dirt. They look it and smell it, too. Everyone says so.

I turn back toward Bo. "Right," I say. "Because picking on some dumb, dirty little colored girl takes you and twenty of your friends."

There's more laughter behind Bo. The girl who was screaming before has stopped, thank the Lord. Everyone is watching me.

"She talked down to Gary's girl," Bo says, nodding toward the black-haired boy behind him. "She needs to learn her place."

"Gary has a girl?" I'd heard that—Gary started going out with that freshman Carolyn, because everyone says she'll go all the way with anyone who gives her his football pin—but I pretend I haven't. "That's really nice, Gary. Maybe we can double-date sometime."

"Well, sure, Linda," Gary says, smiling as if it's a sunny Sunday afternoon, and there isn't a scared little colored girl hiding behind me in the hallway. All the boys on the team want to go on double dates with Jack and me. "That'd be swell."

Bo isn't smiling.

"I'm not joking around, Linda," he says. "You got to get out of our way. I don't like to push a girl, but—"

Unless she's a colored girl, apparently. I lower my voice so only Bo can hear. "I'm sure you didn't just threaten me, Bo. Because if you did, you know Coach Pollard will hear all about it."

Bo cocks his head to the side. His face slackens. I've won.

I raise my voice again.

"I thought you all might like to know Principal Cole is right around the corner," I lie. "I saw him on my way from English. Maybe you don't care, but I just figured I'd mention it..."

The boys back away. Everyone knows the new rule about fighting. No one's talked about anything else all day.

My father thinks the rule is absurd. He told Mom and me all about it last night. He'll have an editorial out tomorrow about how we need to teach our children personal responsibility, instead of harshly disciplining boys for being boys. Once the people of Davisburg have read what he has to say, he told us, he expects the policy to be reversed promptly.

"Don't you do that again, Linda," Bo says under his breath before he fades away with the rest of his group.

"Aw, Bo, I'm just teasing," I reply, just as low.

I hope he believes me. I don't have a bit of respect for Bo Nash, but he's not someone you want mad at you, either.

When I turn around, the little colored girl is gone. I guess she went to her class. We only have two minutes left before French, but Judy still needs to do up her makeup, so we go into the bathroom.

Judy scrubs her face clean, grabs her compact and gets to work, moving so fast she's going to leave streaks. I'm about to tell her to fix it when the door bursts open and a girl rushes past us and crouches on the floor. It's another colored girl.

Judy drops her compact she's so shocked. I'm surprised, too. We used to come in this bathroom between classes every day last year, and not once did anyone else come in.

"What are you—" Judy says, but I hold up my hand for her to let me handle this.

"You're not welcome here," I tell the girl, who's not looking at us. I'm not sure she even noticed we were in here. It's not the same colored girl Bo was after, so I don't know why she's making such a fuss. "We were here first."

The girl doesn't seem to hear me. She's fallen down on her knees on the tiles, her head bent.

Oh, no. She's *praying*.

I can't interrupt a girl who's praying. Even a colored girl.

Why does she have to pray in the *bathroom?* They have colored churches, don't they?

Why does she have to come where I am in the first place? And why did that other girl have to go where Bo and his friends were waiting? It's utter foolishness. If the school had to let them in, they should've picked some other section of the building where the colored people could go so the rest of us wouldn't have to see them, the way they did at the bus station.

Or smell them. I sniff the air to see if the girl has made the bathroom stink yet. So far it's just the usual smell of disinfectant and old paint, but she hasn't been here long.

Judy looks at me, waiting for me to tell her what to do, but I don't know what to say. When someone's praying, you're supposed to be quiet and respectful. But those are the rules for white people. Are they the same for Negroes? It's so hard to keep track.

There's still another minute until French, and Judy isn't done with her makeup yet. I gesture for her to keep working on her cheek. She turns back to the mirror.

There's something wrong with the colored girl. Her lips are moving quickly but silently, and she's rocking up and down. She's crying. I wonder what's upset her so much.

If Daddy ever finds out I was in a bathroom with one of them, by *choice*, he'll let his hand fly after all.

The girl goes on praying for a long time. She looks familiar. I must've seen her before, but it's hard to tell them all apart.

Then I remember. This girl is the one from French. The one who called me "awful."

She's the worst of the whole lot.

Why did *she* have to run in here, out of all of them? Why do these colored people have to keep making my life harder?

Finally the girl stops rocking. She keeps her head bowed and her eyes shut, but her lips aren't moving anymore.

It's strange seeing a colored person so close up. Her hair is straight, but it looks rough and coarse. Not like my hair or Judy's at all. And her skin is so dark. Much darker than mine gets even after I've been out in the sun for months. Touching her probably feels like touching sandpaper. Not that I'd ever touch colored skin.

It would be all right for us to leave now. God would understand. The truth is, though, I want to know what's wrong with this girl.

I'm just curious. Who wouldn't be?

And it doesn't matter if I'm a tiny bit late to French. None of the teachers ever give me detentions, not if they want to get invited to the Christmas parties. My mother has been president of the Jefferson PTA since my oldest brother was a freshman.

"Are you all right?" Judy asks the girl when she finally opens her eyes.

I glare at Judy. She whispers an "Oh" and looks apologetic.

Judy never remembers you're supposed to act differently around different people. If it weren't for me, she'd talk to this colored girl the same way she talks to Reverend Pierce.

The colored girl doesn't show any sign of having heard Judy. She's looking down at her clothes. I wonder if she's checking for stains. This morning I saw one of the other colored girls get sprayed with ink outside the library. Everyone was laughing. It made me think of the time Eddie Lowe pushed me into a puddle in second grade when I was wearing my new Easter dress. I got so upset Daddy wrote an angry letter and Eddie's father sent us a check for five dollars to buy me a new one.

The girl this morning didn't look upset, though. She just kept walking with her head held up so high I wanted to look around for her puppet strings.

"I'm leaving," this colored girl says, standing up.

"You don't have to," Judy says. "No one ever comes in this bathroom. If you want to be alone—"

Judy stops talking when I shake my head at her. It's one thing to show basic human decency. It's another to go out of your way to accommodate someone who's trying to change our whole way of life.

I wrote an editorial about that for the school newspaper last year. I said if the integrationists won, the rest of us should behave like civilized people, but we shouldn't feel obligated to act happy about things.

Daddy liked that column. Or anyway, Mom told me she thought he probably did.

The colored girl is looking at Judy, her head tilted. Even with her dark skin and old, patched clothes, the colored girl is pretty. She has long hair, longer than the style is now, and her eyes are wide and dark.

It's strange. I've never thought of a colored girl as being pretty before. My friends whisper sometimes about how a few of the colored boys look all right, but everyone says that's because so many of them are tall and muscled from working outside. I don't know what would make a colored girl nice looking, exactly. But then, I'd never seen a colored girl up close before yesterday.

"Do you need—?" the colored girl starts to ask Judy. Then she stops. Judy cups her hand over her cheek, and I realize what the girl is looking at. Judy never finished fixing her makeup. The colored girl saw her birthmark.

Judy takes out her makeup case and hurries to brush more onto her face.

"Never mind," the colored girl says. "I'll be leaving now."

"Good." I tug Judy's elbow. "You can leave the whole school while you're at it, and take your friends with you. Hurry up, Judy, we're already late."

"Are you all right?" Judy asks the girl as she sweeps on more makeup. "You were crying. And—praying."

"Don't talk to her, Judy," I whisper.

The colored girl looks at me, tilting her head to one side. I look back just as fiercely. What gives her the right to stare at me?

She looks like she's thinking hard. Deciding something. Finally, she opens her mouth. When she speaks, it's slow, like she's measuring each word before she says it.

"Since when do *you* care about being polite?" the colored girl says.

Judy gasps. I would, too, except I can hardly breathe at all.

I can't believe she spoke to me that way.

No one speaks to me that way.

No one who's not related to me, anyway. Certainly not a *Negro*.

Who does this girl think she is?

And after I just finished helping that other colored girl, too. If it weren't for me that little girl would be splattered all over the lockers by now.

Daddy was right. The Negro students think they're entitled. They think their own schools—the ones set aside *specifically for them*—aren't enough. They think they have to come to *our* schools, even if it means hundreds of us have to suffer just so a handful of them can be satisfied.

The colored girl smiles. As though she's proud of herself.

"I didn't ask you to come to this school," I tell her.

A corner of the girl's lip turns up.

Is she *laughing* at me?

"I've got you figured out," she says. "You're Linda Hairston, aren't you? Your father is William Hairston."

"Yes," I say. Everyone knows that. I don't know why this girl is acting as if knowing it makes her special.

"You were the one talking to that gang of white boys. You called my sister dumb."

Oh. I try to remember if I heard anything about two of the integrators being sisters, but I don't think the paper said anything except that there were ten of them and they'd all claimed they weren't Communists.

"So why did you get in front of her in the first place?" the girl asks me. "Some sort of stunt to show that your father isn't the monster his editorials make him out to be?"

"My father's no monster," I hiss.

But I do wonder why I got between Bo and that girl. I was mad at Bo, sure, but I could've just made fun of him in the cafeteria or something instead.

I guess it just didn't seem right, what Bo was doing. A whole group of boys, going after a little freshman girl.

And there was something about the little girl's face, too. She looked so afraid. It didn't seem right that she had to be so scared just because she was a Negro. She couldn't help her color.

She *could* help being an agitator, though. She shouldn't have been stirring up trouble at our school. What happened to her was her own fault. I'm too softhearted for my own good.

What bad luck, that I had to run into her older sister right after. I glare at the girl. She glares back at me and shakes her head.

"I've read your father's editorials," the girl says. "Looks as though you both like to tell everybody else what to do. Especially us Negroes."

"Nobody's telling you what to do," I say. "Your people are the ones telling *us* what to do. If you'd just let things be, we'd all be better off, your people and mine both. Your sister wouldn't have gotten in trouble in the hall today and needed my help."

I try to emphasize that last word, *help,* so this girl will know she should be thanking me, not arguing, but she doesn't look especially thankful. When she speaks again, her words are still slow and deliberate.

"All my sister and I are trying to do is go to school," she says. "We should be able to do that without having to worry about people coming at us in the halls."

"You already had a school to go to," I point out. "A school that's been open all year long. *Your* prom didn't get canceled. I bet you're happy to have ruined it all for the rest of us, though."

"You think any of this was *my* idea?" The girl crosses her arms over her chest. Her eyes are turned down but her voice is angry.

I still can't believe she's talking this way. She acted uppity yesterday, too, but it wasn't this bad. Daddy says Negro brains are naturally predisposed to be submissive. Something must've gone wrong in this girl's brain.

"Um, can I say something?" Judy asks. I glare at her, but she's not looking at me. "Since it seems like you're all right now."

The colored girl nods, slowly.

"I'm not sure if you heard us yesterday, but I wanted to say I'm really sorry about what I did," Judy says all in a rush. "What I said to Bo and the others after French. And moving seats in Math. I—I wanted to tell you I don't think that's right."

The colored girl and I both roll our eyes at the same time.

"What are you playing at?" the colored girl says. "If you didn't think it was right you wouldn't have done it."

"And since when do you think it isn't right?" I ask Judy. This is certainly the first time *I'm* hearing any of this.

"Since—I don't know." Judy blinks three times, fast. Like she's trying not to cry. "It all—yesterday was so—"

She turns back to the mirror.

I sigh. "You missed a spot. Far right, near your neck."

Judy nods and gets her makeup sponge back out, still blinking.

"Have you seen a doctor about your face?" the colored girl asks her. I can't believe her nerve.

"Leave Judy alone," I tell her. It's all I can do not to shout. How dare she come where she *knows* she's not wanted, treat me with disrespect and then say something like that to my friend? I wouldn't even let a white girl get away with that. "It's a port wine stain. It's normal. She's not sick."

"Oh, so *my* skin color is the only one you have a problem with?" the colored girl says.

I roll my eyes again. "Come on, Judy. Your makeup's done. Let's go."

The colored girl moves toward the door at the same time we do. I remember we're going to the same class and I hold out my hand to stop her.

"No," I say. "You wait here until we're gone. Someone could see us leaving together."

The girl starts to step back. Then she hesitates and shakes her head.

"No," she says. "I won't let you tell me what to do anymore."

In the end, I give up and let her leave first, but for all that, we reach the door to French at the same time.

Miss Whitson frowns at us when we open the door. The rest of the class is already working on some assignment. I hadn't realized we were so late.

"Mademoiselle Hairston, Mademoiselle Dunbar, Mademoiselle Campbell, welcome," Miss Whitson says quietly, in French. She comes into the hall to talk to us. "You're very late, you know."

The colored girl and I nod. Judy looks blank. I've tried to help her with her French but it just won't take.

"I've been assigning partners for the winter term project," Miss Whitson says, still speaking French.

Judy looks at me with wide eyes. She has no idea what's going on. The colored girl does, though. She looks as nervous as I feel.

"As everyone else has been assigned, that leaves the three of you to work together," Miss Whitson says. "Your assignment is due in April. Instructions are on the board."

"No," the colored girl and I say in the same breath. We lock eyes for a second. Then we both scowl and look away.

"I'd like to do the project alone, please," the colored girl tells Miss Whitson in rapid French. Her accent is better than I would've expected.

"Yes, please, Madame, let her work alone," I say.

Judy is still blinking back and forth between the rest of us, lost.

"This is a team project," Miss Whitson says. "No exceptions. Now take your seats before I go looking for my tardy slips."

Fear leaps in my stomach. If my father finds out I'm going to be doing homework with a colored girl, he'll do worse than hit. I don't even want to know what he'll do.

I can tell from her face the colored girl wants to argue with

Miss Whitson, but she doesn't. The colored people are always polite with teachers, no matter how rudely they treat the rest of us.

This is all her fault. This colored girl, and the others like her, aren't just out to ruin our school. This girl is going to ruin my entire *life*.

I bump her with my elbow as we make our way to our seats. It's childish, I know, but it's nothing compared to what I'll get at home tonight.

"Next time go find yourself a colored bathroom," I hiss when Miss Whitson turns away. "And tell your dumb kid sister to watch out for herself from now on, because I'm certainly not doing *that* ever again."

The girl fixes her dark eyes on me. It's strange to see so much anger on such a pretty face. She raises her eyebrows, then looks away. Dismissing me.

I can't remember the last time I've ever been this mad at someone who wasn't my father.

My father.

My stomach rolls over again. He'll never believe me when I tell him this project was that hateful colored girl's fault, not mine.

But I'll always remember what she did. And I'll make sure she pays for it.

LIE #9

I'm exactly who I want to be.

WHEN I GET home, the ball of fear in my stomach grows bigger and bigger until it swallows me whole.

I'll figure a way to fix this. I always think of something.

They wouldn't really expect me to be partners with a colored girl. Not with my father being who he is.

I have to put a stop to this before he finds out. If I don't—

I shove that thought far away and tighten my grip on Mom's eyeliner pencil. I'm hiding in the bathroom, trying out eye makeup for my date with Jack on Saturday. I want to look like Sophia Loren, but my hand isn't steady enough to pull it off, so I just look like a red-haired raccoon.

"Linda?" Mom knocks on the door. "Are you in there?"

Shoot. I reach for a cloth to wipe off the makeup. "I'm washing my hair," I call.

"You just washed your hair on Sunday." Mom tries the knob,

but I've locked it. She tries again. "Linda Louise Hairston! Come out here right now!"

I scrub my eyes clean and throw Mom's pencil back in the drawer before I swing the door open. Mom rubs her eyes, her dark hair coming loose from her bun. She used to get mad when my brothers and I were little and broke the rules, but ever since I got sick in fifth grade, she's always just looked tired.

"I'm sorry," I say. "I haven't been feeling well. Something awful happened at school today."

Mom softens. "What is it?"

"It's Miss Whitson. You remember, I had her for French last year?"

Mom nods, her jaw set. Mom and Miss Whitson fought all year when they were co-chairing the PTA charity carnival. Miss Whitson kept assigning boys to the cleanup crew, which had always been just girls. Mom kept changing the assignments behind her back because she said the boys would only make a mess of things. By the time the carnival was a week away they were both sending me back and forth every day with nasty notes to pass to each other. Mom's notes said Miss Whitson was too modern in her sensibilities and Miss Whitson's notes said Mom wasn't appropriately charitable.

It's made French class awkward ever since. Which is too bad, because I love French.

I tell Mom what happened today, and her face goes white. She knows as well as I do what would happen if Daddy found out about the colored girl.

"I'll call Sharon Whitson right now," she says. "We'll get this taken care of. Don't worry."

I go to my room to wait. I try to start my homework, but I don't get far. With the school closed, I spent September to January doing all my work through correspondence courses, where all you have to do is read a text and take a quiz through the mail—

easy-peasy. Having actual assignments from actual teachers is a lot more work.

When Mom comes into my room a few minutes later, I give up and shut my textbook. Mom's face is still white.

She sits across from me on the bed and squeezes the bedspread in her fist. "That Sharon Whitson has some nerve."

I sink back into my pillow. "It didn't work?"

Mom shakes her head. "Maybe there's still time to get you into a different class."

My heart is pounding so hard I can hear it. "I can't. She's the only French teacher at Jefferson. Maybe I'll just skip the project."

Mom touches her hand to her forehead. "Apparently this is your main project for the year. If you don't do it, you won't pass the class."

Maybe I could fail French this year. I don't need it to graduate. And it isn't as if I'm going to college.

But that's silly. I'm not going to fail a class over some foolish colored girl.

But if Daddy—

"We can't let your father find out," Mom says. "Or anyone else in town. Can you meet with this Negro, this Sarah Dunbar, in private, somewhere you won't be seen?"

"Yes. I'll think of something."

Mom puts her hand on mine and smiles. I try to smile back at her.

Then the front door slams in the hall.

We both stiffen and close our eyes. After a moment, we get up, smooth our skirts and go down the hall, not looking at each other.

Daddy doesn't look at us, either. Instead he sets his briefcase down by the front door and walks straight past us toward the dining room. The way he always does.

When I was little I used to watch Daddy's eyes when he came home at night to see if it had been a good day or a bad day. If his eyes were heavy with dark circles I knew to stay out of his way. If they were crinkled with the beginnings of a smile, I'd smile back. Then, if I was lucky, he'd pick me up and swing me around and call me his darling girl. I used to live for nights like that.

I never bother to look at Daddy's eyes anymore. All I see now is the shiny bald patch under his thin red hair as he walks away from me. I inherited that thin red hair, and the freckles that came with it. I'd give it all back if I could.

Mom follows Daddy down the hall, going to the cabinet to pour them both a drink.

He doesn't say a word to me. He's not going to, either.

He won't ask me any questions. He never does. He never even glances my way. He's barely looked at me since I was eleven years old. When Daddy decided I was a waste of a daughter. I'm invisible to him now.

Maybe keeping this secret will be easier than I thought.

"Did you hear what Bo and the boys did at lunch?" Donna says. We're in Home Ec, rolling out pizza dough and sneaking bites of cheese out of the bowl when Mrs. Brown isn't looking.

"What did they do?" I ask.

Donna drops her voice. "Snuck up behind the colored seniors' table and spit in their food."

I sigh. When we were younger we used to think Bo and Eddie and their gang of friends were funny. Then we got older and more mature, and they stayed exactly the same.

"They said it was because of prom. You know, to get back at them." Donna passes me a chunk of mozzarella. The cafeteria food is terrible. We always snack in Home Ec to get us through the day.

I wonder if the colored people really minded having their food spit on. They couldn't have wanted to eat it anyway. They might have just as well said thank-you to Bo and Eddie and the other boys. That's what I'd have done if it were me.

"As if that's going to do any good," I say. "If they want prom back, they need to go to court and file another petition. If we can keep the colored people out of our school altogether our parents won't have to worry about the prom being integrated."

"Yes, that does make more sense," Donna says.

"It would be even better if the school board would stop dragging their feet on the Davisburg Academy," I go on. "Then we could have all the proms we wanted."

"When's it supposed to open?" Donna asks.

"Soon. In the next month or so."

Ever since the NAACP's lawsuit started picking up speed, Daddy and the other parents have been talking about opening the Davisburg Academy, a private school where we won't have to listen to the Supreme Court or other agitators in the federal government. I heard Daddy tell one of his friends at church that he'll transfer me there the first day it opens, even though I only have a few months of high school left. Daddy said it's the principle of the thing.

They'd planned to open the academy before the final court rulings came down, but it's taking longer than they thought. They've already borrowed a spare building from the school board and they've got money from the state to pay part of the teachers' salaries, but they still have to raise money to pay the rest of the costs. Daddy complained to his friend about that, too. He said if the teachers were true segregationists they'd be willing to take a salary cut if that was what it took.

"You always know so much about these things," Donna says. "Do you talk with your father about it a lot?"

The only time Daddy talks to me is to deliver an order. Or a lecture. But I tell Donna, "We get advance copies of the paper every day. We always know the news first."

Donna nods. She reaches for the tomato sauce. "Were you going to prom with Coach Pollard?"

"Yes." I swallow.

"I was hoping Leonard might ask me. I think he'll probably take me to a movie that night instead but it isn't the same, you know? Oh, did you hear what happened to Joanie Williams's car this morning?"

I nod. All last year, when people were saying the courts were going to integrate Jefferson any day, Joanie kept talking about how nice she'd be to the colored people when they came, and how she'd set a good example for everyone else to follow. So on Monday, Joanie went up to one of the colored boys at lunch. She tried to talk to him as if he were any other boy she'd run into in the cafeteria. The boy hadn't wanted to talk to her, though. He'd left the first chance he got.

Ever since, people have been shouting "nigger-lover" at Joanie in the halls. This morning a gang of freshmen brought eggs to school and threw them at her mother's car when she pulled up to drop Joanie off. Joanie hasn't talked to any colored people since that first day, and now she never will.

"Joanie's a Quaker," I tell Donna. "What did you expect?"

"You're right, of course." Donna nods. "Hey, do you think the colored people will be allowed at graduation?"

It's been four whole days since the colored people got here. Why do we always have to talk about them? Doesn't anyone at this school think about anything else?

"I suppose so," I say. "Three of them are seniors."

"Oh, that's right. The senior girl is in my History class. Did you hear what happened with her?"

I shake my head, but I listen with interest. She's got to be talking about Sarah Dunbar.

"On Tuesday we were talking about the slave trade out of Africa," Donna says, "and Mrs. Johnson said that girl would've gone for a good price as a house slave. Because she's lighter-skinned than the others, you know, and her face is pretty. The boys were saying some things after *that*, I'll tell you. I heard some of them even followed her out in the hall afterward. Do you think her skin is really that light? All of them look the same color to me."

"Mrs. Johnson said that?" I say. "Really?"

"Yes. Why?"

I shrug. I don't want to tell Donna, but it doesn't seem right for a teacher to single out a student like that. How would it feel if a teacher said that about me? I shiver.

"Well it makes sense, doesn't it?" Donna goes on. "It was a lesson about the slave trade, and here's a former slave sitting right there. Might as well use it for the lesson."

It does make sense, but I wonder if Mrs. Johnson knew how the boys would act after she'd said something like that. And I wonder if it has anything to do with how strange Sarah was acting in the bathroom that day. "Did Sarah say anything about it?"

"Who?"

"The colored girl."

"Oh, is that her name? No, she didn't say anything. She sat straight up and looked at the chalkboard the whole time. You wouldn't have known she even heard. Do you think their hearing is different from ours?"

I'm surprised Mrs. Johnson said anything about Sarah. Daddy said the teachers were all being very careful with what they said to the colored people because they were afraid they'd be hauled into court. He said that was why more teachers weren't speaking out against integration. Most of my teachers just pretend the colored students aren't there.

Donna and I slide our pizza into the oven with the others and sit down to listen to Mrs. Brown's lecture. Today it's Foods of Italy. I doodle in my notebook instead of taking notes on the different types of grapes. It's hard to focus on classes now. School is almost over and I've got my real life ahead of me.

Graduation is June 15. Sometime after that will be the wedding. We haven't set a date yet because Jack says we can't get officially engaged until I'm out of school. I don't see why it matters so much. I'm eighteen, and so many people already know about me and him. Jack says some people won't think it's right, since he's older than me. My parents, for one. The head coach, for another. And that's important, since the head coach is sort of Jack's boss. Jack was the star quarterback of the football team when he was in school, and now he helps out as a part-time assistant coach. He's also the assistant manager at Kiskiack Lake. Last summer he always made sure my friends and I got free French fries at the concession stand. Then he'd kiss me out under the pier where the others couldn't see.

Jack's never tried to do more than kiss. I used to think that meant he didn't like me, because every other boy I've gone out with tried for as much as he could get. One day when we were out on a drive, I was upset enough that Jack finally asked me what was wrong, so I told him. He said it wasn't about that at all. He said it was about respect. He said he didn't want to treat me like he'd treated girls when he was younger. He wanted to treat me like someone special. Like his future wife.

That was the day he gave me his fraternity pin from the year he was in college. He said that pin meant we were engaged to be engaged. He said as soon as I graduated he'd give me a ring instead.

I've worn that pin on my collar every day since. I'll wear it forever. Even once I have a ring. That pin means I belong to someone. It means I don't have to live this way forever.

But I don't see why we can't just tell everyone. Jack's not that much older than me, after all, but he says all the same, we can't do anything that might put his work at the school in jeopardy. He wants to be head coach at Jefferson one day.

Mrs. Brown is standing over me. I slap my arm down over where I've been doodling "Mrs. John Pollard" in the margins of my notebook.

"Linda," she says. I look up at her, pasting on a polite smile. "What city is most known for risotto?"

"Venice, ma'am."

Mrs. Brown nods and steps away to scare someone else.

After class we see one of the colored boys in the hall. It's the good-looking senior who's in Math with me. His name is Charlie, I think, or maybe Chuck. Donna and I give him as wide a berth as we can, which isn't hard because Bo and his gang have him surrounded. They shout names at him the whole way down the hall. The colored boy's shoulders are clenched and he's biting his lip.

"I heard a rumor about that one," Donna whispers once he's gone. "I heard somebody saw him parked beside the road up to Kiskiack last night. With Kathy Shepard."

I shake my head. "People always say such nasty things about girls like that."

Kathy Shepard has never been bright, but even she'd know better than to get mixed up with a colored boy. If her father found out he'd send her off to her grandparents' farm in the country for sure. And who even knows what would happen to the boy.

"Well." Donna doesn't like to argue with me. Most of my friends don't. So she changes the subject. "Are you coming to Deltas after school?"

Our girls' charity group, the Deltas, meets once a week to do service projects and plan fund-raisers. Jefferson is the biggest high school around here, so it has a bunch of Tri-Hi-Y social clubs for girls, but everyone knows Delta is the best, with the prettiest, most popular members. Even though Alpha thinks they're the best just because they're listed first alphabetically in the yearbook.

Today we're putting together gift baskets for the patients down at the hospital. Nancy, Brenda and I went shopping last weekend for the candy, paperback books and cigarettes. Today we're putting them in baskets and tying them with pretty bows and writing note cards with little "get well soon" poems.

"Yes," I say. "I have to go to the *Clarion* office, too. I'm writing an editorial for next week. I'll have to leave early, though. I'm working on a French project with Judy."

I don't tell her I'm working with the colored girl, too. No one is going to find out about that if I can help it. Except Judy, but Judy can keep a secret. That's why we've been friends for so long.

When I leave the school newspaper office that afternoon I don't tell the others where I'm going. And during the walk to Bailey's Drugstore I look over my shoulder every few minutes.

It's not as if there's anything wrong with going to Bailey's. Everyone goes there after school, and on Friday and Saturday nights after the game or the movies. It's part of what's fun about living in a town like Davisburg. You can always count on seeing everyone you know at the same places all the time.

No one ever stays at Bailey's longer than an hour or so in the afternoons. At four o'clock on a school day it'll be empty except for Judy, who works behind the lunch counter. Sarah Dunbar will meet us there. We couldn't think of anywhere else to meet, since none of us wants to be seen together.

I've been trying not to think about what Daddy would say if he knew. He'd pull me out of Jefferson for sure. He didn't want me to come back here this year in the first place. He wanted to keep me out of school until the Davisburg Academy was open. I begged Mom to let me come back, though, and she talked Daddy into it somehow.

I was afraid the academy wouldn't open before the end of the school year. Then I'd have to wait a whole other year before I could graduate and get married. And I couldn't stand another year in that house with Daddy.

Jack's apartment is in Fairland Park. It's not as nice as where I live in Ridgewood, but Mom says Fairland Park is good enough for a young married couple, and at least it's not New Town. I haven't been inside the apartment yet, but it's pretty from the outside. Jack said he'll let me pick out new curtains and things after the wedding, provided I don't spend too much.

Sure enough, Bailey's is almost empty when I push open the front door. An hour ago the store and the lunch counter would've been teeming with kids from school, flirting in the merchandise aisles and belching over milk shakes, but not a single person is shopping now. At the checkout counter at the back of the store the cashier, old Mr. Fairfax, is dozing behind the register. The coffee-stained lunch counter at the front of the store with its neat row of stools and dimly lit booths is deserted.

On the other side of the counter Judy is pulling her dirty gray apron over her head. Standing at the counter's edge—she wouldn't have been allowed to sit on a stool, of course—is Sarah Dunbar.

The colored girl looks me up and down. For a second I wonder if she's jealous of my new green angora sweater. I'd thought it was too tight, but when I wore it to school today, four different girls told me they wanted to get one just like it.

Then Sarah scowls at me. I scowl back before I remember I'm supposed to ignore her.

Judy leads us into the back room, where she takes her afternoon breaks. It's a big closet full of cleaning equipment and food containers, lit by a single lightbulb dangling from a cord in the ceiling. There are no chairs, only boxes and crates.

I enter the room last and sit on the crate farthest away from Sarah. I might have no choice but to spend time with a colored girl, but I don't want her thinking I like it.

Judy's hands tremble as she lights her cigarette. She offers me one. I shake my head. She starts to put the pack back in her pocket, hesitates, then holds it out to Sarah. Sarah recoils as if the cigarettes might bite her. Judy's shaking so hard she drops them. I scoop up the pack, pass it to Judy and say, "Let's get started. We should pick French opera for our topic. My mother has a lot of old magazines I can bring in. Judy, what about you?"

Our assignment is to make a book using typing paper and pictures cut out of magazines about a particular theme—Miss

Whitson suggested "scenes of the Riviera" or "French music and cuisine"—and write a story in French to go with the photos.

"What about me?" Judy says, her forehead wrinkling.

"Do you have magazines at home you can bring in?" I ask her. "Anything with pictures that might look French?"

Judy frowns. "My grandmother used to bring me her old *Reader's Digest*s, but I don't think they've got many—"

"I have a lot of magazines," Sarah interrupts. "My mother never throws anything away, and my sister's been getting *Seventeen* since junior high."

I glare at her. Then I turn back to Judy. "We should start by deciding on a title."

"Oh," Judy says. "Well, um—"

"Maybe the title of a famous French opera," I suggest.

"Um." Judy looks helplessly from me to Sarah.

I try to think of a French opera, but now that I've suggested it I can only think of Italian ones. I'm about to make an excuse for why an opera title isn't a good name anyway when Sarah interrupts.

"That's a terrible idea," she says. She's talking faster than she did in the bathroom that day. Her words don't sound as careful as they did then, either. "Opera names don't work as book titles. *Carmen. Faust. Les Troyens.* They don't make sense on their own."

"No one asked you," I say, even though she's right.

"Well you should've," she says. "I'm doing this project, too, in case you forgot."

I sniff. "As if I *could*."

I expect Sarah's face to crumple. Instead she just gazes at me, her head tilted, her eyes thoughtful.

If I talked to another girl this way, she'd already be getting teary. That's how it's always happened before. It's how I got that freshman last year to stop asking if she could write an editorial for the *Clarion*. It's how I got Donna to drop out of solo auditions for the Balladeers so I don't have to worry about sharing the girls' parts.

But Sarah only says, still talking so fast it's hard to keep up, "Believe me, I don't want to spend any more time with you than I have to, either."

"I *don't* believe you, actually," I say. "I think you're getting exactly what you wanted."

"What I *wanted?*" She shakes her head, then chuckles. Her laugh has a tinkle to it that would sound nice coming from someone else. "You think this is how I want to spend my afternoons?"

"You wanted integration, you got it," I say. "If you're not happy now, then, well. I'm sorry for *us,* because we didn't have a choice in the matter. I'm certainly not sorry for *you.*"

Sarah shakes her head again. "No one *wants* to go to school with someone who hates them."

Judy frowns. "Then why did you—"

I cut her off. Judy never understands things like this.

"No one said anything about *hate,*" I tell Sarah. "We're Christians. Christians don't hate."

Sarah's mouth drops open. For a long moment, she just stares at me.

"Do you really believe that?" she finally says.

"There's a difference between hate and disagreement," I explain. "We don't hate anyone. We simply don't approve of your methods. You're trying to shove integration down our throats instead of letting things happen naturally."

"All we're doing is going to school." Sarah's still watching me closely. It's unnerving. "What's unnatural about that?"

"You went to court and forced it, is what's unnatural." I force myself to stop and take a breath. I'm trying to be patient, but it's not easy. "If you'd just let things happen in their normal course the school board would've figured out a way to make sure everyone was happy with their schools, white and colored both, but that takes time. That's why everyone's so angry now. Before all this happened, whites and Negroes in Davisburg used to get along just fine, but the way your people did this has made everyone hostile. The integration has been so rushed we haven't been able to prepare."

"How did you need to prepare?" Sarah says. "Rehearse new chants and practice tripping us?"

I roll my eyes. Why do integrationists always blame all of us for the actions of a few? Why can't they see that we're talking about bigger issues here than chants and slogans?

"Some people will always behave childishly," I say, "but what matters is—"

"*Some* people?" Sarah interrupts me again. "Try everyone!"

I roll my eyes again. She's so predictable. She probably saw one bratty kid behaving badly and assumed every single white person was doing exactly the same thing.

"Not everyone," I correct her. "*I* wasn't one of those immature people yelling at you in the parking lot."

"You might as well have been." Her eyes are flashing. It would be frightening if she weren't so wrong about everything. "You might let other people do your dirty work, but that doesn't mean you're any different from them."

I shake my head, but I'm thinking about Barbara Points and her friends. We all saw them follow those two colored girls into school on the first day, screaming into their faces the whole way. I didn't know then that the two girls were Sarah and her little sister.

Barbara's a sophomore who lives on one of the tobacco farms outside town. Last year she missed more school than she showed up for. I've certainly never known her to get to school early before. But she still got to school in plenty of time to see the colored people coming in.

Sarah's little sister had looked terrified that morning, but Sarah never once looked scared. Even when we were all sure there was no way the colored people were going to make it inside the school without somebody getting knocked onto the pavement. Or worse.

Is that what Sarah thinks of me? That I'm the same as Barbara Points? And here I'd been starting to think Sarah seemed intelligent.

"That's ridiculous," I say. "Don't lump me in with those girls. They don't have half a brain between them."

"So you think because you have a brain, that makes it all right for you to act the way you do?" Sarah tilts her head back and fixes her eyes on the ceiling. I can't tell if she's tired or frustrated. She's still talking as fast as ever. "It doesn't show much in the way of brains to decide you don't like people you don't even know. All because of their color."

"It's not that I don't *like* colored people," I explain. I want to make sure she understands this part. "This isn't about liking anyone or not liking anyone. It's about right and wrong. And what you're doing—agitating—is wrong."

Sarah looks straight at me. I sit back, startled. Something about that look in her eyes makes me feel dizzy. Like I might fall if I don't work hard to keep steady.

"That might be what you tell yourself," she says. "But that doesn't excuse screaming at us every day, or tripping us in the halls."

"*I* haven't tripped you," I point out. "Neither has Judy. Neither has—"

"The entire school was shouting at us! Hundreds of you!"

"Well, what did you expect? If you'd let things happen gradually, instead of—"

"The Supreme Court ruled five years ago! What do you need, ten more years? Twenty?"

I hate being interrupted more than almost anything. I give Sarah my hardest glare and wait for her to look sheepish. She just glares right back.

"We needed time," I repeat, trying not to let that flashing

look in her eyes throw me off track. "You didn't give us any, so the governor was forced to close *our* school, even though *yours* stayed open. You want to make everything better for *you* no matter what it does to *us*."

"No one forced anything," Sarah says. "It was only last year the governor made that law about closing the white schools so they couldn't be integrated. After *your* father wrote all those editorials about it. If the governor hadn't put up such a fight we could've integrated quietly, without all this hatred and name-calling."

At first I wonder if there could be any truth to that. But then I forget about it. I'm too busy being shocked that Sarah Dunbar had the nerve to talk about my father.

Sarah's father works for my father. I found out from that article about the integrators. I pulled that paper out of the trash and reread it. It said Sarah was the daughter of a junior high school teacher and a copy boy at the *Gazette*. And that she sang in her church choir and wanted to be a teacher herself someday.

The part about her parents and her church choir was strange to read. I'd never thought about what the colored students do when they're not in school. Sarah must have a house somewhere. She must do things like help her mother with dinner or iron her clothes for church. The same kinds of things I do.

"The point is, we didn't force your governor to do anything," Sarah goes on.

"*My* governor?" I say. "He's your governor, too."

Sarah lifts her chin and looks me straight in the eyes again. "He's not my anything if he doesn't treat me the same way he treats you."

My jaw drops.

"That's anarchy," I say quietly. I wait for her to take it back.

Sarah doesn't even blink. "No it's not. If the law is wrong, we have to say the law is wrong."

Daddy was right. The colored students really *are* Communists.

I scoot backward, trying to put as much distance between Sarah and me as I can in the tiny space of the storage room. I turn to Judy for help, but she's looking back and forth between me and Sarah with a lost expression on her face.

"It's anarchy!" I cry. "It's Communist, too!"

"We're not Communists." Sarah sounds much calmer than I feel. "We go to church every week. Not everyone who disagrees with you is a Communist."

When I tell Daddy what Sarah said, he'll get her kicked out of school for sure! Her father fired, too, probably.

My heart thumps. She might not really be a Communist, but with what she said, she's close enough. And if she is, the other colored people must be, too.

I was right about everything.

We're going to win. We'll get the integration overturned, and everyone will know it was me who did it. My father will smile at me the way he used to.

"You're going to wish you never said that," I say. "Wait until my father hears—"

"How's he going to hear?" Sarah says. "I bet he doesn't even know you're doing this project with me. You can't have him knowing you've been associating with one of *us,* can you?"

I sit back onto my crate. My head thunks against the concrete wall behind me.

She's right.

For a second I actually believed I could fix integration.

How stupid could I be? I'm not important enough for that. I'm not anyone special.

Then Sarah Dunbar has the nerve to smile at me.

I *hate* her.

She thinks she can say whatever she wants. She thinks I can't stop her.

Sarah Dunbar isn't afraid of me at all.

What gave her the right to tell us what to do? How can she be so sure she's right when everyone else, from the governor to Reverend Pierce to Daddy, all say she's wrong?

She doesn't even know what she's talking about. She's just saying what the Communists at the NAACP taught her to say.

She *acts* like she knows, though. That's the problem. She sits over there with her pretty smile and her pretty words. Someone who didn't know better might think she was telling the truth.

Someone has to show Sarah she's wrong.

I may not be important enough to fix integration, but I can fix her.

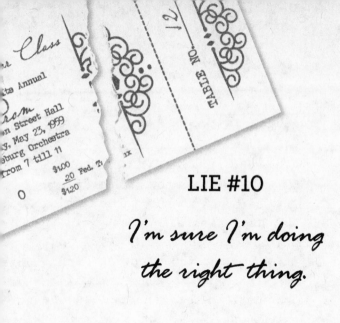

LIE #10

*I'm sure I'm doing
the right thing.*

JEFFERSON HIGH CLARION
Wednesday, February 11, 1959
How Will You Be Remembered?
By Linda Hairston, Editorial Page Editor

We thought it could never happen. Not here in
Virginia. The governor did what he could to stop
it, but even George Washington's hardest fought
battles sometimes ended in defeat.

No matter what may be happening around us,
I implore my fellow Jefferson students to hold
fast. We can't give up yet.

I don't mean giving up the legal battles.
That's for the government to settle. I mean
something much more important: don't give up
the beliefs you hold in your heart.

Your heart is much stronger than any court

ruling or edict from Washington. Your beliefs come from your faith and your heritage. Faith and heritage run deeper than the orders of any politician.

Someday, the history books will write about what's happening to us right now. What do you want them to say about you? That you did nothing while history was happening all around you? Or do you want them to say you stood up for your beliefs, for your culture, for your state?

We all have to stand up for what we know is right. It's up to us as Americans and as the generation who will someday lead this country to set the right path for those who will come after us.

If you believe, deep in your heart, that the way you were raised was right—that the world has always been this way because that was how our Heavenly Father intended it—then you can't simply sit back and wait while agitators from the North try to cram their radical ideas down our throats.

It's up to us to make our voices heard. What we do right now could determine the very future of our state. Please don't make your children, or your grandchildren, hang their heads in shame when they speak of you.

I'm proud of our traditions. I'm proud to be a Southerner and a Virginian. I'm proud to fight to preserve our way of life.

If you're proud, too, then I hope you'll fight alongside me.

"SETTLE DOWN NOW," Mrs. Gruber says, pulling a pack of gum out of Kenneth Cox's hand before he can put another stick in his mouth. He's been chewing gum and spitting it at the junior colored boy in the front row. Two pieces have already hit the boy's arm, but I guess Mrs. Gruber only just got tired of watching it.

"Why can't you all be well behaved in Study Hall, the way these girls are?" Mrs. Gruber says. "Look how hard Linda's studying over there."

Mrs. Gruber smiles at me. I smile back, even though Mrs. Gruber smiles like a weasel. I've had her for Math all four years of high school, and this year I have her for Study Hall, too. She likes me. All my teachers like me because Mom always finds out my teachers' birthdays at the beginning of the year and sends me to school with loaves of fresh-baked banana bread for them. (Fresh-baked by Martha. She's the colored woman who comes to our house three times a week to clean and do our baking.)

After Study Hall I pack up my books and turn to talk to Donna, but Kenneth gets in my way. He's an offensive lineman. Standing in front of me he might as well be a mountain range. I have to tilt my head back to see his face.

"Teacher's pet," he says, but he's smiling. The boys know better than to really tease me. Especially the juniors, like Kenneth, who want to stay on the football team next year.

"Don't blame me," I say. "If you don't want to get in trouble, don't do silly things in class."

Kenneth frowns. "I thought you'd think it was funny. After what you wrote in the paper."

He thought my editorial was about gum-spitting? Now I understand why Daddy's always complaining about his writing being misunderstood.

I wasn't writing about silly, petty things. I was writing about the real issues behind integration. About the federal government telling all the states what to do, since they don't trust us to decide for ourselves.

It gets me fired up again just thinking about it. Why should anyone else tell us how to run our schools? Or tell Judy's boss, Mr. Bailey, what he's allowed to do in his own store? Why should the government tell me I have to use the same bathroom as colored women when I'm doing my shopping? What business is it of theirs?

"I wasn't talking about acting childish," I tell Kenneth, rolling my eyes.

His face twists into an angry frown. I've gone too far. I'm about to apologize when he says, "Well, it shouldn't matter to you anyway. It's not like you're one of those nigger-lovers."

I laugh. It's just so preposterous. Kenneth laughs, too, the tension evaporated.

"Sorry, Kenneth," I say. "You're right. It doesn't matter."

"What was that about?" Donna asks me when Kenneth's gone.

"Nothing," I tell her.

The junior colored boy—I think his name is Paul—is still sitting rigid in the front row. There's some gum left on his arm, as though he tried to pull it off but couldn't get it all. I think about having to touch a wad of gum covered in Kenneth Cox's spit, and I shudder.

I know Kenneth and the other boys in Bo's gang are only trying to protest integration in their own way. I know the colored people should've known better than to come to our school if they didn't want this kind of thing to happen. But I still don't like seeing it happen right in front of me. It's only natural not to want to talk to the colored people, or sit near them, but there's no need for boys like Kenneth to be disgusting in front of all of us.

Everything is so much worse with the colored people here. If they aren't giving the boys reasons to act like idiots, they're driving people to send angry letters to Daddy about his editorials. Those letters make Daddy storm around the house so much I've started reading my books in the laundry room. That's the one place he never goes.

The colored people are ruining my senior year.

And now I have no choice but to spend time with one of them.

I still haven't told anyone about being project partners with Sarah. All I said to Jack was that I had to meet Judy after school a few days a week for a homework assignment. Jack didn't like that—we usually go for drives out to the country on sunny afternoons when he doesn't have to work—but he didn't ask me any more about it.

I've never talked to Jack about integration, but once at a game I overheard him telling Daddy that if he got made head coach, he could promise there wouldn't be any Nigras playing football for Jefferson.

When I walk to Bailey's in the afternoons I always have an excuse prepared in case someone sees me. So far I haven't gotten caught. Sometimes, though, I think getting caught on the way would be better than what I have to deal with when I get there.

Sarah Dunbar is an awful girl.

Not only because she's an NAACP agitator. Simply because she's awful.

She insists on talking when I want to talk. She argues with me even when I'm right. She even makes Judy think I'm wrong sometimes.

Judy and I have been best friends since we were five. She's supposed to listen to *me*.

All my school friends listen to me. School is the one place where what I say and what I think matter.

It's still strange hearing Sarah talk so much in the first place. In school I barely hear her say a word. When she does, she speaks slowly, every sentence precise and deliberate. Most of the time she just walks stiffly down the hallways with her chin in the air, pretending not to hear everyone shouting at her, the way all the colored people at Jefferson do.

I used to think maybe the Negroes really didn't hear those things. That maybe they could tune them out the way I tune out a bad song on the radio, or Eddie making a dumb joke during choir practice about Mr. Lewis's pants being too tight.

But Sarah seems to notice everything. She pays attention to the tiniest moments. The most insignificant comments. I'd be impressed if I didn't find it so tiresome.

One afternoon, when we were arguing over which picture to use on the cover of our report, I said we shouldn't use the picture Sarah had picked out because the model in the picture looked Spanish, not French. Sarah said, "You don't think there's a single person in all of France who's got skin any darker than yours, is that it?"

During our meeting today, while I'm still annoyed about what Kenneth said in Study Hall, the same thing happens. Judy has been telling us about an old lady, Mrs. McCormick, who came into Bailey's and asked the cashier if they have lighter colored Band-Aids because she has "such unusually fair skin." Judy and I always laugh about Mrs. McCormick—how she always wears a hat even when it's cloudy outside and how she wears white gloves every day, even to the dry cleaner, to protect her "such unusually fair skin." Mrs. McCormick's skin is wrinkled so bad you can't tell whether she's as fair as Grace Kelly or as dark as Carmen Miranda. Judy and I are still laughing about it when Sarah interrupts us.

"It's good luck for Mrs. McCormick her skin is white and not black," Sarah says. She's leaning back on a box, one arm stretched over her head, playing with a rubber band. She looks so different than in school. There, her back is always straight and her face is always carefully composed. "Or she couldn't find a Band-Aid to match even that much."

"Why do you have to make everything about color?" I ask her.

"I don't." Sarah rolls her eyes. I still can't believe she has the nerve to do that in front of us. "You're the one who makes everything about color. What's worse is half the time you don't even know you're doing it."

"That's not true at all," I say. "I barely even think about color. Or I didn't until your people forced this on us."

"I know it would've been easier for you if we'd stayed where we were," Sarah says. She yawns, covering her mouth with her hand. "But if our situations were reversed you wouldn't have wanted to stay there, either."

I know better than to egg her on, but I can't help it. "What do you mean?"

"Your Biology class at Jefferson has a microscope at every single lab table," Sarah says. "At my old school we had *one*. For the whole class. We all took turns."

I shake my head. "That's not true. I don't believe you."

"Johns doesn't have enough textbooks for everyone to have their own, either," Sarah goes on as though she didn't even hear me. "We have to share those, too. No one's allowed to take them home."

I never read about that in the paper. And Daddy never mentioned it.

Well, but even if what she's saying *is* true, everyone knows Jefferson is a better school than Johns. Jefferson is a better school than most of the other white schools around here, too. That's just how it is. I'm about to say so when Judy says, "Hey, um, so, I have an idea."

Sarah and I turn to her. I'm not sure which of us is more surprised.

"You do?" Sarah and I say at the same time.

Judy nods vigorously. "For our project. Because it's about French music, right?"

I've never once known Judy to have an idea about homework.

"What is it, Judy?" Sarah says. Then something strange happens.

Sarah smiles at Judy.

I've never seen her *really* smile before. I've seen her smile meanly, or sarcastically, but this smile is different. Genuine.

She looks so different this way. Her face is lighter, somehow. Not whiter, exactly—her skin is just as brown as ever—but it's like a dark shadow has been lifted off her. Her eyes take on a sparkle that makes her brown irises look golden.

When Judy speaks again, I realize I'm staring. I shake my head so fast Sarah cocks an eyebrow at me. I blush like an idiot.

"I spotted some old French records in the secondhand bin in the back," Judy says. "And there's a record player up in the window. It's for display only, but if we just listen to a couple of songs, Mr. Bailey won't find out."

Now I'm staring at Judy. I've never known her to come up with a plan like this.

"That sounds perfect, Judy," Sarah says, still smiling. "I'd love to listen to some French records."

I'm not sure how some old records are going to help us with our project, but when Judy brings in the box and the record player I figure it out. She thinks if Sarah and I are listening to music, we won't be able to argue so much, and she won't have to worry about us getting her in trouble.

It turns out she's right.

"Édith Piaf?" Sarah turns an album over in her hands. "My Music teacher at our old school played this record for us years ago. That was before we knew enough French to understand the words, but it sounded so beautiful. For weeks after that I'd dream about Édith Piaf's voice."

I've never heard Sarah say so many words in a row without once telling me I'm wrong about something.

"Wow." Judy smiles at Sarah, her eyes wide. "I'd love to hear it."

We set up the record player, turn the volume as low as we can and drop the record on the turntable. I haven't heard this record since I was little. My mother used to love Édith Piaf. The song makes me think of my mother smiling down at me while she fixed supper. Or sitting in the living room, her head tilted back, a dreamy look on her face.

Mom doesn't listen to records anymore. I'm the only one in our house who still does. I'll listen to the radio while I do my homework, or to records when I have a concert I need to practice for, but I don't like to practice singing at home much. It's better at school, where I don't have to worry about who can hear me.

I shake off the thought and try to catch Judy's eye, but Judy's watching Sarah. Sarah's eyes are closed, and she's mouthing the words to the song "La Vie en Rose."

"Do you know this song, Sarah?" Judy asks. "You should sing with it."

Sarah opens her eyes and shakes her head. "I couldn't."

"Why not?" Judy says. "You sing with your church choir, right? It would be fun to hear you sing in French."

I wonder how Judy knows Sarah sings with her church choir. Do the two of them talk when I'm not here?

Do they talk about me?

I expect Sarah to tell Judy no again. Instead she closes her eyes, opens her mouth and begins to sing.

I don't know what I was expecting, but it wasn't this.

Sarah's voice is wonderful. She's better than the other girls in the Balladeers. Better than a lot of girls who sing on the radio, even.

She's better than me.

And there's something about the way her face looks when she's singing that makes you want to stare at her forever.

She keeps going, all the way to the end of the song. If anything her voice only gets better. When the song ends, Judy claps.

"That was wonderful!" Judy says. "Linda, wasn't she wonderful!"

"Yes, she—" I start to say. Then I remember myself and stop talking.

"You should join the school choir!" Judy says. "Linda, shouldn't she join?"

I clear my throat. Judy looks at me. I raise my eyebrows at her to be quiet. Judy shakes her head, confused.

Sarah saves me from having to explain.

"Thank you for getting the record player, Judy," she says. She takes the record off the turntable and passes it to me, her hand brushing mine for a moment. My finger tingles. "I love Édith Piaf. You can take it back up front now, if you're worried about getting in trouble with Mr. Bailey."

Judy smiles gratefully and packs up the record player.

My finger is still tingling. For a moment I don't know why. Then I realize it's because my hand brushed Sarah's.

I just touched colored skin.

Everyone used to say if you touched a colored person the black on his skin would rub off onto yours.

In first grade, we played a game during recess called Nigger in the Hole. Whoever was in the hole stood in the middle of a circle with a bandanna tied around his face so he was blind, and then he ran around trying to touch you. If he tagged you, you were the new Nigger in the Hole. Everyone would say "Ew!" when you got near them until your turn was over.

I haven't thought about that game in ten years at least.

When I touched Sarah's hand, it should have felt disgusting. Like playing Nigger in the Hole.

It didn't.

Sarah's skin didn't feel any different than anyone else's. It felt smooth and warm.

Now that I'm thinking about it, she didn't have to brush my hand when she passed me the record. She reached all the way over. Almost like she was *trying* to have us touch.

That's a strange thing for a colored girl to do. Or any girl, really.

When Judy comes back she's smiling. I smile back at her, glad to have something else to focus on.

"Were you in the choir at your old school, Sarah?" Judy asks.

Sarah nods. "We won the county-wide contest last year."

"You did?" I've never seen Sarah at any competition I've been to with the Balladeers.

"Yes," Sarah says. "For the Negro schools. We weren't allowed in the same contests you were."

She doesn't sound angry this time. She's not arguing with me. Just telling me something I didn't know.

"Do you want to be a singer when you grow up?" Judy asks Sarah. Judy's face is earnest, but Sarah laughs. She has a nice laugh.

"No," Sarah says. "I'm going to be a teacher, like my mother. She speaks French and Spanish and she has her master's degree."

She sounds so proud. I wonder if that's what I sound like when I talk about Daddy.

"Why not do Music instead?" I say. "If you like it so much?"

Sarah raises her eyebrows. I remember too late I'm not supposed to be interested in anything about Sarah.

"My parents wouldn't want me taking Music in college," she says. "They'd want me in something practical, where I can find a job."

"But what do *you* want?" I say.

Sarah looks at me, a crease around her eyes I haven't seen before. For once she's actually thinking about something I said.

"I love music," she says after a minute. "Sometimes I think it would be wonderful to study it more, but it's childish to think that way."

"No it's not," I say.

She shakes her head, still giving me that look. "I have to be serious, Linda. I have to think about my future."

"Do you at least want to be a Music teacher?" Judy says.

"I don't know," Sarah says. "I like Math, too. And History."

"You *like* Math?" I can't believe anyone would like Math. Especially Sarah. She spends our Math classes sitting with her arms crossed and her steely gaze fixed on Mrs. Gruber. She always keeps her face blank, but I can tell she's miserable.

"Well, not this year," she says. "It was always my favorite class at Johns, though."

It was? That's too bad, that she can't enjoy her favorite class this year.

Wait. No. She brought this on herself. I don't feel *sorry* for her.

"I don't like Math," I say, so I won't have to think about that anymore. "I like History, though. Last year for World History we did a project on ancient Greece. Did you know a lot of the Renaissance artists were inspired by the Greeks?"

"Ugh, I hate History," Judy said. "I can never remember dates."

"If you like History so much why are you in Remedial?" Sarah asks me. "And Math, too. I've been wondering. You seem too—I mean, I wondered why you're in remedial classes."

I've wondered the same thing about her.

"My parents asked the school to put me in Remedial freshman year," I say. "I missed some school because I was sick when I was younger, and my father didn't think I could handle the work in the harder classes. At least the homework is easier this way."

Sarah nods, frowning. "Well, anyway, I think recent history is more interesting than ancient. It's more relevant to how the world works today."

"That's not true," I say. "Ancient Greece was the foundation of civilization."

"Not of *all* civilization," Sarah says. "The Egyptians were building pyramids two thousand years before the Greeks built the Parthenon."

"Did they really?" That's interesting. Then I remember who I'm talking to and I add, "That can't be right."

"It is," Sarah says. "You can look it up in the encyclopedia."

"Then why does everyone talk about the Greeks so much?"

"Why do you think?"

Sarah points at my wrist, bare under the lace edge on my sleeve. Then she points at her own wrist. She's saying it's because the Greeks were white and the Egyptians were colored.

"That doesn't make sense," I say. "People didn't care about those things back then."

Sarah smiles a little. And I realize what I just said.

This is all her fault. She's twisting my words around, trying to confuse me.

"People have always cared about those things," Sarah says. "They've just cared in different ways. Sometimes it means the history books get written differently. Sometimes it means a war gets fought. Sometimes it means people wind up slaves. That's why I like History so much. It makes you think about those things."

"That's nonsense," I say. "God made white people and colored people different, and he put them on different continents. Everything was fine until the races started to mix. That's what caused all the problems we have today. Everyone knows that."

Sarah just shakes her head.

I know she's wrong, but I still want to hear what she has to say next.

She makes me so angry. But there's something about the way Sarah talks, the way she *is,* that makes me want to talk to her more without all these problems getting in the way.

No. I'm not thinking clearly. This must all be some sort of trick she's pulling.

"Judy, what were you talking about with Tommy Dillard today?" I say. Sarah sits back, surprised. I ignore her. "I saw you two in the hall after fifth period."

Judy's whole face lights up. Even her birthmark is shining

under the makeup. She must've been waiting all afternoon for me to ask her about Tommy.

"He asked me to the dance!" Judy says, holding her fists up in a little cheer.

"Oh, that's wonderful!" I say.

Tommy Dillard is a skinny boy with glasses who plays the French horn in band. He's not someone I'd have ever thought of dating. He should be good for Judy, though.

"So," Judy says, "I know *you* won't be coming to the dance, Linda, because Coach Pollard wouldn't want to. What about you, Sarah? Has one of those colored boys at your lunch table asked you?"

My smile fades. I swallow, but my tongue sticks in my throat.

Judy thinks she's gossiping. She thinks from here we'll launch into talking about dresses and makeup and corsages.

Judy is my best friend, but sometimes she makes huge mistakes.

First of all, she shouldn't have mentioned Jack. From the lack of surprise on Sarah's face, though, I can tell she's already heard about him and me. She's heard about the dance, too.

"I can't go to the dance, Judy," Sarah says gently.

"Why not?" Judy says. I try to catch her eye, but she's looking at Sarah. "You're not engaged, too, are you?"

"Judy!" I snap. For Sarah to hear gossip about Jack and me is one thing, but for Judy to outright tell her we're engaged is completely unacceptable.

But Sarah only shakes her head. She doesn't look shocked at all.

"The dance isn't for me," she says.

"Why not?" Judy says. "Don't you like dancing? Didn't they have dances at your colored school?"

"I love dancing," Sarah says. "But this isn't a school dance. It's a special dance some of the parents are putting on since the school canceled the prom."

Judy's mouth drops open.

"It's a private dance," Sarah goes on. "If it was an official school dance they'd have to let anyone in."

Judy nods. "So you couldn't go—because—"

"Because I'm a Negro," Sarah finishes for her. "It's a white-only dance."

Sarah turns toward me. I drop my eyes.

A month ago I would've been thrilled about the dance. One last time to have fun before the end of high school. A chance to wear my new blue dress.

But yesterday, when we heard David Baker's parents had rented a hall and all the white juniors and seniors were invited, all I felt was a strange emptiness inside.

I bite my lip. Blood rushes to my cheeks. I try to turn my head so Sarah can't see, but she leans over and studies me for a long moment before she speaks again.

"We aren't supposed to do any extracurriculars this year," Sarah says. "That's why I can't join the school choir, either."

"But this is your *last* year," Judy says. "If you aren't in the choir now you never will be."

Sarah shrugs.

Judy turns to me with a searching look. I don't know what she expects me to do about it.

"We're behind on the assignment," I say. "We still have another ten pages before we're done. We should stop wasting time."

I get out my scissors. After a moment, Sarah reaches for a magazine and flips it open.

I wonder what she's thinking.

I've been trying to make her understand. It isn't working. I'm not even close.

I can't give up. That wouldn't be the honorable thing to do. Her path ahead couldn't be clearer. All I have to do is show her the way.

Except that I'm starting to feel a little lost myself.

LIE #11

If I keep pretending, everything will be all right.

"THIS IS EXACTLY what I'm talking about!" Daddy slams the newspaper down on the dining table and fumbles for his lighter. He puffs on his Winston once, twice. He picks the paper back up and slams it down again. "This kind of writing only glorifies the Negro!"

Mom laughs. Daddy glowers at her. "I wasn't joking, Rose."

"I'm sorry," Mom says without looking up from her plate. It used to bother Mom when Daddy talked to her that way, but that was years ago.

"Who wrote it, Daddy?" I ask.

"That knucklehead editor in Norfolk. I told him if he keeps this up he'll never work at another paper in this state again. He doesn't listen. He's a fool."

I nod. Daddy stops to take a few more puffs on his cigarette, but he's not done yet. He's just gotten started.

He puts out his Winston and lights another. "It's dangerous, publishing articles like this. It skews the way readers see the world. It gives no regard for the Negro who is lazy, who is thieving, who is cowardly."

I nod again. We read about those kinds of Negroes in the paper all the time. It's why a lot of my friends' mothers came to the segregation meetings all last year. They were worried about a criminal element coming into our school.

But since only a few Negroes came to Jefferson this year, I suppose we got lucky. None of them have done anything criminal yet. I've never seen them act lazy, either.

Sarah sure doesn't. She works harder than anyone I know. I've seen her doing homework at lunch, her pencil flying across the page. She's got to be solving the problems in her head at lightning speed.

I don't know how she does that. Sometimes, I almost wish I were more like her. I definitely wish I were as brave as she is. I've never stood up to anyone the way she does every day when she walks in those school doors.

She makes it look easy. No matter what people do to her she just walks on, her head high, her skirt swinging. There's something mesmerizing about the way she walks.

But Sarah's unusual in a lot of ways. She's certainly not a normal colored person. She's not naturally predisposed to be submissive, for one thing. People always say *I'm* stubborn, but that's because they've never met Sarah Dunbar.

For weeks now I've been trying to make Sarah understand how things are, but for everything I say, she has an answer ready.

I'll say segregation is the law, and always has been. She'll say laws get changed when they're wrong, and always have.

I'll say God put the races on different continents so we'd each stay with our own. She'll say my people messed that up, then, when we brought her people over here as slaves, and when we came to America even though the Indians were already here.

I'll say she's an agitator, and an infuriating one at that. And she won't even answer. She'll just cock her head and smile. Like I'm one of those monkeys with the windup boxes and I've just done a silly dance for her.

And the day after we've argued, I'll see her in school, looking docilely up at the teachers as though she's never said an unkind word to anyone.

No. The real Sarah Dunbar is reserved for me and Judy alone.

Just for me, really. When she's talking to Judy, Sarah's perfectly nice and polite, but when I try to tell her something, her eyes narrow and her arguments fly.

Worst of all, she seems to enjoy it. Whenever I make a point, something lights up in her eyes, and I can tell she's already planning what she's going to say back. She talks so fast it's difficult to keep up with her, and I have to think harder about what I want to say back. It takes more effort than it used to for me to think through what she's saying and look for places to point out what she's getting wrong, but the arguments all come rapid-fire to Sarah.

It's as though we're back in my tenth-grade Debate class. Except in class, no one ever wanted to debate me because I always won.

It's a good thing Sarah wasn't in that class. One of us might not have made it out alive.

"It's not as if I disagree with Herb's premise, of course." Daddy is still talking, even though Mom isn't listening anymore. "I'd never suggest the Negro isn't *worthy*. Indeed, the majority of Negroes make up a worthy, God-fearing people. It is our obligation as Christians to love the Negro as we love our own children."

I nod again. What's different about Daddy, compared to the other people in town who don't have his education, is that he understands the subtleties of these things. These are complicated principles he's talking about. He knows they need to be handled in complicated ways.

"But to suggest that the white man and the Negro are the

same is dangerous," he goes on. "It only stirs them up. Gives them the idea they're better than us. Why, it's already worked on some of them. This week one of our reporters reviewed the latest lists and found out one of our copy boys works for the NAACP. There's an agitator on my own payroll!"

He's talking about Sarah's father.

"Who hired him?" Mom says. Probably worried if word gets around she'll lose her next PTA election. When she heard my aunt Betty had paid a Puerto Rican woman to teach her Spanish, Mom canceled my spring break trip to visit her in Alexandria. Instead I spent that week sleeping over at Judy's and helping her mom with her laundry orders.

"I don't know," Daddy says. "I intend to find out. I've told them this boy's not to be fired, not yet, but I won't have anything like this happening again. From now on we'll consult the lists before we hire any Negroes."

"Is he a good copy boy?" I ask.

Daddy looks at me for the first time all night. I sit up straight.

"Copy boys get the coffee and run the wire stories to the news room." Daddy taps the ash off his cigarette. "Any idiot could do it. Most of them get run off the job the first year because they aren't tough enough to handle the pressure."

"Is this one tough enough?" I ask.

Daddy scowls at me.

I clamp my mouth shut, but it's too late. He's leaning back in his seat the way he does when he's preparing for a good long yell.

"This isn't about any one copy boy," he shouts. "How many times do I have to tell you?"

I shrink back in my seat, but he isn't waiting for an answer. He isn't even looking at me anymore.

"It isn't about *them* or *us*," he goes on. "It's about right and wrong! It's about the way things are supposed to be, and the people who want to come in from the outside and tell us they know better. Well I've been in this state all my life, and my parents and grandparents and great-grandparents were here before me, and I don't need some agitator coming in and telling me they all had it wrong. We aren't going to sit by and let these outsiders tell us how to run our state!"

He isn't yelling at me this time. He's yelling at the world. All the people who won't just do as he says.

"Just as it's unethical to say nothing when we see a neighbor being robbed, or a dog being beaten," he says, "it's wrong to sit idly by and allow these things to destroy our community."

I nod. I wonder what Daddy would do if he really saw a dog being beaten. Probably join in.

"We must speak out!" He pounds his fist in his hand. Ash dangles from his cigarette and drops onto the tablecloth. "We must take action! When agitators try to steer our country in a direction we know to be wrong, it's up to us to steer it back again. That's why it's important for our children—the ones who suffer the most from this—to be outspoken in their support for our way of life."

I nod some more. Mom takes another sip of sherry and keeps her eyes fixed on the clock over Daddy's head.

When Daddy talks like this he's practicing for his editorials. Soon he'll make these same words prettier and print them in the *Gazette*. The day after that, every white man in town who thinks himself intelligent will be saying these words and pretending they're his own.

Daddy doesn't put everything he thinks in his editorials, though. I know, because I've seen the letters he writes to his friends. Newspapermen who write for papers down South. Georgia, Alabama, Florida. Daddy works on his letters at the kitchen table for days before he posts them. They use words he'd never put in the *Gazette*. "Racial purity." "The sanctity of Southern white womanhood." "The dangers of mongrelization."

No one wants to say it out loud or put it down in newsprint, but we all know the truth.

Colored people aren't the same as whites. They aren't as smart. They haven't accomplished the things we have. They aren't as good as we are.

Everyone knows it. Even the colored people know. It's just not good etiquette to say so. It feels shameful to even think the words.

That's probably why I've never thought about it much. It's just how things have always been.

But I'm thinking about it now. And it feels more shameful than ever.

When I first saw Sarah it was easy to think of her as just another Negro. Now it's getting harder to remember what her dark skin, chocolate eyes and full lips really mean.

Sarah is special. She's smarter than the rest of her people. Better.

Does God do that sometimes? Make one person different? Put her up above the rest of her race?

Daddy says when he was a boy they didn't have these problems. The colored people knew their place and they stayed there. He says he's sorry I have to grow up in trying times like these and can't enjoy my childhood the way he did.

"May I be excused?" I whisper to Mom when Daddy pauses to light another cigarette.

She nods. I go to my room and close the door.

When I first found out about the French project, I used to be terrified every night I might let something slip to Daddy over dinner.

As the weeks went by I stopped worrying. The truth is, I could probably tell Daddy the whole story and he wouldn't even look up from his food. He doesn't listen to what I say. And he only pays attention to the things I do to tell me I'm doing them wrong.

I go to my bedroom mirror and stare at the picture of Jack taped up in the frame. This isn't going to last forever.

I take out my calendar and cross off March 16.

I'm one day closer to getting out of this house for good.

"So I had to tell Leonard I can't very well go to the dance with him since I already told Mom I'd go with Mrs. West's nephew, but the problem is Mrs. West tricked my mom into it. She said yes before we saw a picture of the guy, and it turns out he's short and has pimples and his name is *Barney,* of all things. So now I have to go to a dance with a short boy who'll probably step all over my toes. And I can put up with that because it can't be worse than when I went to Brenda's sweet sixteen with Gary and he spilled punch down my dress because I wouldn't play Seven Minutes in Heaven with him in that gross basement closet where Mr. Green keeps his taxidermy equipment. I mean, really, what if I'd sat on a dead raccoon or something? Can you imagine? But now the problem is, Leonard thinks I didn't *want* to go with him, so how do I get him to find out I don't really like Barney, so I can get Leonard to ask me on a date without seeming too, you know, forward?"

"What?" I blink over at Donna. Our Tri-Hi-Y meeting just ended, and we're sitting with Nancy on a bench in front of the school parking lot, waiting for our rides. Donna frowns at me, but I don't have an answer to give her. I lost track of her story somewhere around Barney's pimples.

Normally I'd have been full of advice for Donna's boy trouble, but I'm preoccupied thinking about my new idea. The next time I see Sarah—which will be an hour from now, at Bailey's—I'll tell her what the colored people should really focus on, if they're so concerned about their schools, is raising money to buy new books so their students won't have to share. I bet the colored churches could raise a lot from their own people if they put their minds to it. Instead of putting all their money into court cases that ruin everything for the rest of us.

Donna repeats her story, telling me all about Leonard and

Mrs. West's trickery. I stifle a yawn and tell her she should spend the dance making eyes at Leonard every time he's nearby. Especially if she gets a chance to do it over Barney's shoulder while they're dancing.

"Leonard will get the message," I tell her. I gaze out across the parking lot, wishing Jack would hurry up and get here. "Trust me."

"That's right, he will." Nancy taps her foot on the pavement. "Hey, I forgot, how long did Bo go steady with Kathy Shepard for?"

Bo asked Nancy to the dance last week. She hasn't let us talk about anything else since.

"A month, sophomore year." Donna waves to three JV cheerleaders crossing the grounds. The cheerleaders always travel in packs.

"You really want to go steady with Bo?" I ask Nancy. I can't imagine wanting to see more of Bo Nash than absolutely necessary.

"Maybe." She shrugs, smiling. "I haven't gone steady yet this year."

Donna must be as tired of talking about Nancy and Bo as I am because she says, "Did you hear about choir?"

"What about choir?" I ask. We're supposed to start rehearsals soon. We've already missed the competitions, thanks to the integration messing up our school year, but the spring concert will be coming up before long.

Donna lowers her voice to a whisper, even though we're the only three people in sight. "I heard that colored girl is joining. Brenda saw her sign up in Mr. Lewis's office this morning."

Colored girl? Do they mean *my* colored girl?

"I thought they weren't allowed to do that," Nancy says. "No activities. I thought that was the rule."

"I'm not sure if it's really a rule or just something everyone agreed on," I say. My hands are getting clammy. Sarah, in the choir? With me? "Either way it's awful. I'm sure Mr. Lewis won't let her in."

"Brenda said he let her sign up," Donna says. "She said he held the pen right out to her. He didn't even put it down on the desk for her to pick up."

"Well, Mr. Lewis has always been a little strange," Nancy says.

I'm bursting to ask. Finally I give in. "Are you talking about Sarah Dunbar?"

"Who's Sarah Dunbar?" Donna says.

"The senior colored girl. She's in our French class. The one with the little sister." I'm exasperated. We've been in classes with these people now for a month and a half. I can't be the only one who's learned their names. "She was wearing a white dress with green ruffles yesterday."

Donna and Nancy are looking at me oddly.

"I'm not sure," Donna says. "I think it was her, maybe."

"We should ask *you*," Nancy says. "You seem to know an awful lot about the colored people."

Shoot. I shouldn't have mentioned Sarah's dress. I just couldn't help but notice it. You wouldn't think dark skin would look good in white, but it does. The pale dress made Sarah's face glow, somehow.

"Can you even imagine, a colored girl singing in the spring concert?" I say. "Our parents would never stand for it."

I can imagine it.

I imagine standing next to Sarah in our Balladeers robes, singing with her. Listening to her hit each note in her clear, shining voice.

I imagine the way her face will look when she sings. How her eyes will light up when she hears how good we sound together. The way she'll smile when the crowd applauds us.

I hope Mr. Lewis will put her in the Balladeers with me. It's the most elite group out of the whole choir—only four boys and four girls—but she's good enough, no question. Last year the Balladeers traveled across the state for competitions. It would've been fun to travel with Sarah. We could stay up late talking on the bus on the way home. Then stop off for hamburgers and Cokes. We'd sit at the counter with our knees knocking together and giggle about how bad the other teams were.

Jack's car pulls up. I'm not as happy to see him as I'd thought I'd be. He rushes over to take my books and smiles hello at my friends. I wave goodbye to them as Jack opens the car door for me. We only have an hour before I have to meet Sarah and Judy, but I'm glad he's ushering me around like a gentleman all the same.

Jack drives us out to the country and we park far out on the edge of town, where we won't have to worry about someone seeing us. I tell him little things about my day, but all I'm thinking about is what it will be like seeing Sarah at choir practice. Will she argue with me even there? Flash her eyes at me the way she does at Bailey's? Whenever she does that, it makes me feel weird in the pit of my stomach.

"Are you all right, honey?" Jack asks when our hour is nearly up. "You're so quiet today."

"Of course I'm all right." I tilt my head and bat my eyes, trying to make my smile extrabright to make up for all the bad things I've been thinking.

"Your ankle isn't still hurting, is it?" he says.

"No, I'm fine."

But my cheeks flush, and I look away. I wish I hadn't told Jack what happened to my ankle. I only brought it up because I was trying to think of things to say so he wouldn't notice how preoccupied I was.

I tripped on my way down the steps today right outside the Shop corridor. I twisted my ankle and nearly fell into a whole group of boys leaving the auto workshop. One of them caught me by the elbow. I said, "Thank you," and grabbed his shirtsleeve to steady myself.

Then I looked up and found myself face-to-face with the biggest of the colored boys. The one who's running around with Kathy Shepard.

I jerked my hand away from him fast, but not fast enough. When I turned around, at least twenty people were looking at where the colored boy's hand had touched me.

I don't know why that boy caught me. If he'd fallen I certainly wouldn't have caught him. Maybe he just wanted an excuse to touch a white girl.

"Good, I'm glad." Jack puts his arm around me. That makes me feel a little better. "You know I don't like it when something's bothering you."

I smile up at him again.

I wish I could feel the way I used to when I was out alone with Jack. Like we were the only two people in the world. It used to be that when Jack and I went out driving I was the happiest I'd ever been.

After I graduate—after the wedding—it will be like that forever. I'll never have to see Daddy's frowning face at the breakfast table again. During the day I'll keep Jack's house, and at night I'll welcome him home with his dinner waiting on the table.

He'll love me and take care of me. He won't have any choice. We'll be married. Once you're married, you're stuck.

I'm lucky I've found a good man already. Other girls have to go all the way to college to do it.

"I like it when you wear your hair that way." Jack runs his fingers through the curls I pinned up last night. It took an hour to do, and it hurt, but it's worth it to see the twinkle in his eye when he looks at me. The one that means he's glad I'm his girl.

"Thank you," I say. "I'll wear it like this more often."

He smiles again. Then he kisses me.

I try to melt into his kisses, the way I did before, but all I can think about is Sarah Dunbar. Why did she sign up for choir, anyway? She knew she wasn't supposed to. Why would she break the rules? Is it more of her agitating?

Maybe she did it because I'm in the choir, too.

No. That's silly to even think. Sarah hates me. She must, after everything I've said to her.

Has she said so? She must have, but I can't remember for sure.

All I remember is how her eyes flash when she argues. It makes me lose my train of thought every time, and I have to start over from the beginning, only to lose my place again the next time she—

"So, all right," Jack says suddenly. He pulls away from me and turns to face straight ahead, his hands gripping the steering wheel. "There's something I've got to tell you."

I swallow. When boys have broken up with me, this was usually how it started. "All right."

"I've decided something." Jack grips the steering wheel tighter. "I don't know how to say this, so I'll just say it. I'm going back to college."

Oh, no. *No.*

I choke out the words. "You're leaving Davisburg?"

"Not right away." He's still looking straight ahead. "I'll stay here and go back to the JC, but when I finish there, I'll head to the new teacher's college in Hopewell. Get my certificate, so I can come back and coach at Jefferson."

I nod, trying not to cry. I hate tears, but I hate this more.

Hopewell. It might as well be the moon.

What am I going to do without Jack? Without a wedding?

I'll have to keep living at home.

No.

I'll find another man. Maybe one of the senior boys at Jefferson. Or someone who graduated last year. A lot of those boys are working on the farms just outside town.

I'll have to start over from scratch. I'll have to flirt my way into a first date, then bait him into going steady, then wait—for months, maybe longer—before he starts thinking about something more.

I don't have months to spare. I don't want to let some boy with dirt under his fingernails paw at me in a backseat.

I was past all that. I was just a few months away from my new life. And now it's gone, just like that.

A tear slides down my cheek. I dab at it with the cuff of my blouse, hoping Jack didn't see.

"Aw, don't look so sad, honey," he says. "This is the right thing, I promise. Once I've got my degree I'll be able to provide for you. It'll be hard for the first few years. You'll have to find a job, and you won't know anyone in Hopewell, but after I'm done we can come back here and get a nice house in a nice neighborhood and you can fix it up however you want."

I'm still crying. I think he said—

"You still want to marry me?" It comes out like I'm begging.

"Of course I do!"

My stomach is doing somersaults. "And we can get married—soon?"

"Well, yeah. As soon as you want to, honey. Once you're done with school and all." He fumbles in his pocket and pulls out something small and shiny. "I was scared you wouldn't think I was serious. Mama said I should give you this so you'd know I meant it. It was my grandma's."

It's a gold ring, with a tiny green stone perched on it.

"I thought—" I swallow. It's hard to breathe. "I thought you said no rings until after I graduate?"

"Well, you probably shouldn't wear it around your parents, but we can tell everybody soon enough. Here, put it on."

He slides it onto my left hand. It's a little tight, but it settles on my finger like that's where it's meant to be.

This is really happening.

This is what I've wanted for as long as I've known what it meant to want something.

My stomach is still turning over.

This is really happening.

I look at the ring on my finger, and at Jack's happy smile.

"I love you," Jack says.

"I love you, too," I echo.

He kisses me again.

Five minutes ago, when I thought this was all being taken away from me, it felt like the end of the world.

But now that I have it back, I'm not so sure.

Being with Jack forever means never being with anyone else. Ever.

It means I don't have to flirt with the immature boys at school. But it also means no one else will ever kiss me. I'll never feel that sizzling feeling in my chest you're supposed to feel when you kiss someone you really love.

I want to kiss someone who really makes me smile. The way Jack smiles when he tells me he loves me. Jack always smiles like he means it.

I've never felt that. Not even with him. I've always wondered what it would be like.

I stare at the gold ring on my finger.

"Shoot, I'm sorry," Jack says. "You're going to be late, aren't you? For your homework project? I'll get you to Bailey's." He starts up the ignition. The engine makes a spurting sound.

"Thank you," I say when he pulls up three blocks from the drugstore. I'm not sure what I'm thanking him for. The ring? The promise?

No. I'm thanking him for taking care of me. Getting me out of where I've been.

That's what I've always wanted. *That's* what really matters.

A few heartbeats, a funny feeling—that means nothing compared to escape.

Jack is all I need. He's more than I deserve.

I climb out of the car. Two women I recognize from church

are across the street. I'm sure they saw us in the car together, but they look away.

When I walk into Bailey's, the front of the store is empty. Judy's already put up the sign on the lunch counter that says Thank You For Your Business, We'll Be Back Shortly! The sign has a drawing of a smiling waitress in a uniform a lot nicer than the stained gray apron Judy wears.

I'm annoyed that she's already gone back. I'm not *that* late.

I'm still twenty feet from the storage room when I hear two voices laughing.

Laughing?

I didn't know Sarah *could* laugh.

The door is half-open. Now that I'm closer I can see Sarah on the other side of it. She's wearing a soft pink dress and a broad smile. Her head is tossed back. Her long hair brushes her shoulder blades. She looks relaxed and happy and beautiful.

I don't want her to look like that. Not when she's alone with Judy.

I want Sarah to look at *me*.

I shove open the door. Judy and Sarah turn toward me, their eyes wide, their smiles falling.

"Linda, what's that on your hand?" Judy asks. "Is that a—"

"It's nothing." Shoot. I should've known Judy would notice right away. She can be quick when she wants to be.

Sarah's eyes dart toward my hand, too. They grow even wider. I fold my arms across my chest so the ring won't show. I've got her full attention now.

"I had an idea," I say. "If you're so worried about your colored schools, your churches should raise money to buy new books. I bet if your people had been doing that all along instead of spending money on court cases, you'd have more books than you could even carry."

I wait for Sarah's eyes to flash with anger. For her to let loose with a speech about how wrong I am.

Instead, she turns back to Judy. Worse, she smiles.

"I agree, Judy," Sarah says. "My little sister and I love *Gun-smoke,* and my brother's always begging my parents to let him stay up late to watch it, but Daddy says he can't until he's older, but my brother says—"

"Did you *hear* me?" I must've spoken loudly, because both girls look alarmed when they turn my way. "I said—"

"I heard you." Sarah shakes her head. She's facing me again, but she still doesn't look angry. Just sad. "Do you ever stop to think about the things you're saying, Linda? Really think about them? Instead of repeating whatever your father last said to you?"

"My father didn't say anything about this!" Now *I'm* angry. "It was my idea!"

"Well, you should try thinking through your own ideas." She shakes her head again. She's wearing a faded but pretty white cardigan with a circle pin on the collar that shimmers as she moves. She never wears makeup, but her face always looks so bright and open anyway. It makes me jealous. "If you had, you'd have realized *your* school doesn't have to raise money to buy books. The state buys as many books as you need. It just doesn't buy as many for the Negro schools."

I frown. "You probably miscounted your students, then. Or else you lost some of the books."

Sarah gives me a piercing look, like she can see right through me.

"I don't think you really believe what you're saying." She's talking fast again. I have to struggle to keep up. "I think you know our schools don't get as much as yours do in the first place. And that that's why we have half as many teachers for the same number of students. It's why you have a brand-new school building with a gym *and* an auditorium *and* a cafeteria when we have to use one room for all three."

"That's not true," I say.

It can't be true. Can it? Surely the paper would have said so.

"Yes it is," Sarah says. "And can I be honest with you, Linda? I think you know I've been telling you the truth all along. I think you just don't like the idea of believing me."

For the first time, I actually want to hit her.

"Is that why you're integrating our school?" Judy asks suddenly. "Because your old school is so bad? Because it seems as though you hate Jefferson."

Sarah doesn't answer at first. She doesn't roll her eyes the way she would have if I'd said something like that, either. Instead she frowns. It's so strange, seeing her look thoughtful instead of angry.

"No," she says. "Johns High is a wonderful school with wonderful teachers, but I've always been taught that it's important to get the very best education I can. That's why I wanted to come to Jefferson."

She's speaking slowly, deliberately. The way she talks in school.

But she's still frowning.

I don't think she believes what she's saying, either. I think she's repeating something someone told her to say.

Then Sarah turns and looks right at me. She still doesn't look angry, but that flashing look is in her eyes.

"You do know, don't you, Linda?" she says. "I really think you do."

I shift in my seat. "I don't know what you're talking about."

It sounds like she's saying I agree with her about integration. That's why she's confusing me, talking about how her school wasn't as good as ours. She's trying to make me feel mixed up. It's working, kind of.

But that doesn't mean I believe in integration. I couldn't. Not with my father being who he is. Not with me being who I am.

She wants me to believe her, though.

She's still looking straight into my eyes.

I stand up. "I have to go."

"But we haven't even started on the project," Judy says. "We were supposed to finish pages eight through ten today."

"I have to go," I repeat. "Sorry. Leave it for me and I'll do it during Study Hall."

I push through the door, yanking at my left hand as I storm down the empty aisles. The ring won't come off. When I get outside I hold my hand up to the light so I can see it better. The green stone glistens.

I have to start being more careful around Sarah.

I need to make sure she knows I haven't changed my mind about integration or any of the rest of it. I never will. She's wrong about everything. I can't let her forget that.

I can't let myself forget, either.

LIE #12

She's wrong.

"THANK YOU, LINDA," says Miss Jones, the school secretary, as she hands me a stamped stack of papers. "Please tell Mr. Farrell we'll need these back from him by tomorrow morning."

"I will," I say. "Thank you, ma'am."

Miss Jones smiles at me. Teachers always send me on errands to the office because they know I can be trusted to go straight there and back. A lot of girls, the ones who aren't engaged, will sneak over to the Shop classrooms on their way to flirt with the boys during their smoke breaks, but I already have my man.

I put Jack's ring under my pillow when I got home from Bailey's that day two weeks ago. I take it out and look at it every night before I go to bed.

That ring means everything to me. It means soon everything that's hard will be over, and my real life—the good one—can start. All I have to do is wait.

I smile at Miss Jones and turn to leave. The door swings open before I can reach for it. I step back in surprise.

Sarah is standing in the doorway. Her eyes go back and forth between me and Miss Jones and the half-dozen freshmen and sophomores waiting to get their excused absence slips signed.

Sarah bites her lip. I've never seen her look this upset.

I open my mouth to ask her if she needs help. Then I close it again.

"Well, are you coming in or not?" Miss Jones asks Sarah. Her smile is long gone.

Sarah comes in and sits in one of the empty chairs, folding her hands in her lap. They're trembling.

She must've been called to see the principal. I wonder why she's so nervous. Whenever I'm called to see Mr. Cole it's because he has a community service project he wants me to have the Deltas do, or a note he wants me to bring home to my father.

"Well come up here, then," Miss Jones says to Sarah. "I'm not going to shout it to you."

Sarah approaches the desk. She glances at me, then looks away fast.

I have the papers for Mr. Farrell. There's no reason for me to be here anymore.

But Sarah's still shaking.

I stay where I am.

"I was told to come see the principal," Sarah says. It's so strange, the way she talks in school. Slowly, demurely, each word calculated to sound polite and obedient.

"No you weren't," Miss Jones snaps. She turns away from both of us and opens a magazine. *Family Circle.* "Your mother called with a message. She said for you to pick up your brother at kindergarten and take him straight to the doctor. He's sick."

"Oh." Sarah's voice is barely a whisper. "Thank you for telling me."

I wonder how sick her little brother must be for Sarah's mother to have called the school. I got sick a lot when I was a kid, and the nurse always called my mother to come get me. One time in fifth grade I fainted, and Mom picked me up and took me straight to the hospital. I stayed there for a month.

"You should tell your mother we aren't a messenger service," Miss Jones says. "This is a school office. We don't have time to get involved in people's family troubles."

Last year Miss Jones called me to the office and asked me to please tell my mother how much she loved the pumpkin bread I brought in for Thanksgiving. She kept me there for ten minutes talking about recipes.

Sarah nods. "Yes, ma'am. Thank you again. I'll tell her after I go over to my brother's school."

"I certainly hope you don't think you're going anywhere." Miss Jones's eyes are still on her magazine. "I don't know how they do things over in your part of town, but here we don't let students cut class whenever they feel like it."

"But my brother—" Sarah's eyes are wide.

"You can go and get your brother after school," Miss Jones says. "I'm sure the teachers at his kindergarten can handle him in the meantime."

She's not going to let Sarah get her little brother?

But he's sick. He might be really sick. And he's only in kindergarten.

He isn't an agitator. He's a little kid. He didn't do anything wrong.

He's sick, the same way I got sick when I was little. Being sick must be harder for him than it was for me, though, because he's colored.

"May I please call my mother and tell her I'll be late getting him, then?" Sarah's hands are trembling harder than ever. She glances around at the other students gathered in the waiting area. They don't bother to drop their eyes when they see her looking.

She doesn't look my way.

"The phones in this office are for faculty use only," Miss Jones says.

There are tears in Sarah's eyes.

"Then could you call for me, please, Miss Jones, ma'am?" she says.

If something like this happened to me, I'd be shouting by now.

I wish I'd left the office after all.

Something aches deep inside me. As if this is somehow my fault.

"Or could you call my brother's school?" Sarah's still being polite even though water is threatening to spill from her eyes. "I can tell you the number—"

"I told you, we aren't a messenger service." Miss Jones slams down her magazine. "Now if I were you I'd get back to class before you get into more trouble."

I think about Sarah's little brother sitting in kindergarten, sick and miserable, waiting another two hours for the school day to end. Wondering where Sarah is. Why there's no one who can help him.

It's as though a switch has flipped over in my brain.

This is wrong.

It's *wrong*.

It's so wrong I almost say it out loud.

I almost tell Miss Jones it doesn't matter if Sarah's little brother is white or colored. What matters is he's a little boy, and he's sick, and someone should help him.

I almost—

But then I remember the six other people in the room, watching raptly as though this is their favorite television show.

It isn't right, what's happening to Sarah's little brother, but that doesn't mean color doesn't matter.

It always has. I've always known that.

I paste a smile back on my face and turn around to leave.

Then I see them through the glass window. They're watching, too.

Bo Nash. Eddie Lowe. Kenneth Cox. And two of the JV cheerleaders. They're lined up against the lockers, looking right at me. Looking at me standing next to Sarah.

I push back from the desk, mumble another thank-you to Miss Jones, and walk out as fast as I can.

It's not fast enough.

"What were you doing in there with that nigger, Linda?" Bo asks before the door's swung shut behind me.

Bo's the only boy at school who talks to me this way, as if I'm any other girl.

Jack doesn't like Bo much. He went to school with one of Bo's older brothers, and he says all the men in that family are all the same. They've worked for the same tobacco farm for more than thirty years. The Nash boys all start work as soon as they're old enough to pull weeds. When they're not in school they work from sunup to sundown. Jack says all that time in the sun has made the whole Nash family wrong in the head.

I heard Bo didn't want to come back to school this year, but Mrs. Nash wanted him to get his high school diploma. He's the first in the family to make it this close to graduating.

I feel bad for her. Imagine, having Bo Nash be the only thing you have to take pride in.

Bo smiles at me, but it isn't a friendly smile.

"Do you need help washing the stink off, Linda?" one of the cheerleaders, Margaret, asks me. Her smile isn't friendly, either.

"No," I tell her. I look back through the window. Miss Jones is still talking to Sarah. It looks like she's writing her a detention slip. To teach Sarah's mother a lesson about not calling the school again, I suppose. Or to teach the whole family a lesson about being colored.

No. Like Daddy says, it's not about us and them. It's about right and wrong.

Except there's nothing right about that fear in Sarah's eyes.

"Which of the niggers is that, anyway?" Kenneth asks. "The superugly one?"

"No, that one's shorter," Bo says. "This is the one with the little sister. The house slave, remember?"

The others laugh. Eddie tells us the story again, about what Mrs. Johnson said in that History class.

"And I said if I had that nigger in my house, I'd put her to work real good, that's for sure," Bo says when Eddie's finished the story. The boys laugh. The girls cover their faces as if that sort of joke makes them blush, even though their cheeks are still lily-white.

"I have to go back to English," I say.

I leave without waiting for anyone to tell me goodbye. I know they'll talk about me when I'm gone, but I don't care.

Something's changing inside my head. I don't like it, but I can't make it stop.

I walk fast down the hall, my skirt whipping between my legs and my loafers squeaking under my feet, mouthing silent prayers for Sarah's little brother to be all right.

I'm still praying as I walk into Bailey's that afternoon.

I'm glad I'll see Sarah soon. She'll tell me whether her brother made it to the doctor all right.

But Sarah isn't here. The store is empty except for Judy behind the lunch counter and Mr. Fairfax dozing at the register. Sarah always gets to Bailey's before I do.

"Where is she?" I ask Judy instead of saying hello.

"She said she might not come today." Judy starts clearing a row of dirty milk shake glasses off the counter. "She left a note in my locker. Her brother's sick."

"Oh."

"She said we should go ahead with page twelve and she'll work on it at home tonight. Do you want to go in the back?"

Sarah's not coming.

That strange feeling is back. The feeling that I'm the one who made this happen.

Which doesn't make sense. I didn't make Sarah's brother get sick. I didn't make Miss Jones act that way.

When I wrote those things in the school paper I was talking about *ideas*. I wasn't talking about any actual colored people in particular. Certainly not Sarah or her kid brother.

Anyway, none of this is my fault. If it weren't for her, if she hadn't come here, I wouldn't be feeling all these strange things.

"It's just like a Negro to do something like this," I tell Judy. "Pushing her work off on someone else. They're known to be lazy and inconsiderate."

Judy frowns. "Well, but—if her brother—"

"You believe that story?" I'm angry. I have a right to be angry. Sarah was supposed to be here, and she isn't. "They're all a bunch of liars."

"But—I mean—Sarah's never lied to us before, has she?"

"You don't know that." I glare at Judy. When did she start contradicting me? That's Sarah's fault, too. She marched into my life and changed everything. "We don't know anything about her. All we know is she's an agitator and an integrationist."

"I thought you didn't mind her so much anymore," Judy says. "When we listened to the music that time you seemed like you were starting to think she was all right."

I drop my purse down on the counter with a bang, making Judy jump. "I've never thought that! Not for one second!"

Where *is* she, anyway? If she did take her brother to the doctor, shouldn't she be back by now? Aren't all the doctors' offices downtown? Maybe the colored doctors practice farther out.

I don't want to talk *about* Sarah. I want to talk *to* her. Why isn't she here?

I step back so fast I bump into one of the counter stools.

"She's awful." I'm talking almost as fast as Sarah does. "She's the worst of the lot. I can't wait for the academy to open so I can get away from her. I mean, from all of them."

"Will you really go to the academy?" Judy says. "We're almost done with school for good. What's the point of changing schools now?"

"There's a huge point! It's about right and wrong! It's about standing up for what we believe in, and—"

"My brother is fine, thank you," Sarah says behind me.

I spin around to face her. Two minutes ago I wanted nothing more than to see her. Now I only want to scream.

But she's giving me that piercing look again. It's hard not to shrink back from her gaze.

"Miss Jones was right, you know," I say. "You can't expect the office to do those kinds of things. Your mother should've gone to get that boy herself. Or your father."

"My mother is a teacher." Sarah's eyes are locked on mine. She sounds calm. Frighteningly so. "My father works two jobs. They can't just leave when they want to. And *I* certainly wasn't doing anything important. Except sitting in Study Hall having pennies thrown at me."

Why would anyone throw things at Sarah? Sarah didn't do anything to anyone. She's not like the others. She's—

No.

Sarah is awful. I can't let myself forget that.

"That's your own fault!" I'm nearly shouting. "You came to our school. You knew we didn't want you here!"

"Can we go in the back, please?" Judy's stopped clearing the glasses. She looks anxiously between Mr. Fairfax and the door. "Someone might come in, and if you're going to yell we shouldn't be—"

"She's the one who's yelling!" I say.

"You're right." There's no trace of a smile on Sarah's face. "Everything is my fault. All of you were perfect, until we came in and ruined your perfect little lives. You can't wait to go off to your perfect all-white school where you won't have to see us anymore. You probably hate every second you have to look at me."

I don't hate every second I have to look at Sarah.

I kind of like looking at Sarah.

"What the Hell is *this?*"

The man's deep voice echoes behind us, making me jump again. It sounds for all the world like the voice of God.

"Sir!" Judy stands up stick straight. It's Mr. Bailey. "I wasn't—"

Mr. Bailey strides up to the counter, right between where Sarah and I are standing, and grabs the two dirty milk shake glasses. He marches behind the counter and slams them into the trash can by the fryer. They shatter, the glass tinkling like music.

Mr. Bailey turns to face Sarah. He points to the back door. "You order at the *back,* girl, like all the others."

"She didn't order, sir." Judy trips over her words, she's trying to get them out so fast. "I didn't serve her. Those glasses were left over from the last customers. She only stopped by to tell me the homework assignment."

Mr. Bailey narrows his eyes at Sarah. "You're one of those Nigras integrating the school?"

Sarah doesn't say anything. Her eyes never leave his face. She's gone paler than I've ever seen her.

I hate seeing her this way.

This isn't like with Bo and Eddie and the others. Those boys might call the colored people names, throw things at them, even hit them. Mr. Bailey, though, is a grown man. And he looks like he just might kill Sarah for standing at his lunch counter.

"What's the matter?" he says. "Can't you talk, nigger?"

Sarah shrinks back. She's shaking again.

I want to grab one of those milk shake glasses and smash it right over Mr. Bailey's head.

"I won't have integration in my store," Mr. Bailey says. "You go on back where you came from. Tell your people not to try anything like this again."

Sarah backs away, not taking her eyes off Mr. Bailey until she's ten paces from the counter. Then she pivots on her heel and walks out of the store so fast I can't catch her eye.

So I follow her.

I shouldn't. Not with Mr. Bailey watching me.

But I want to tell her I'm sorry for what I said before. Even though I know what Daddy would say about me apologizing to a colored girl.

I know what Daddy would say about what Mr. Bailey did. He'd say he doesn't approve of "those sorts of tactics." That he wants us to remain a civil society. Then he'd say Mr. Bailey was right all the same. It's his store and he has the right to serve whom he pleases.

Daddy's right, of course. He's always right.

I catch up to Sarah at the edge of the empty parking lot and grab her arm. She jerks out of my grasp and turns to run out into the street, even though the traffic light is still flashing.

"Sarah! Wait!"

When she hears my voice, she whips around so fast I take a step back and nearly fall off the curb.

"What do you *want?*" For the second time today there are tears in Sarah's eyes. "Why can't you and your *people* just leave me be?"

I swallow.

"I just wanted to make sure you're all right," I mumble. "And your brother, too."

"Did you?" Sarah turns back toward the street. I think she's going to run back into it again. Instead she says, "My brother is fine. He scared me half to death saying he was sick, but when I went over there it turned out he had a fight with a girl over a purple crayon and didn't want to sit next to her anymore."

I say a silent prayer of thanks.

"And as for me?" Sarah turns back to look at me. Her eyes are flashing. "I don't think you care at all if I'm all right."

"Mr. Bailey shouldn't talk to you that way." This is so hard to explain. My thoughts are all jumbled up. "You're not like the others."

"The other what? The other Negroes?" Sarah laughs. She wipes at the corner of her eye. "I'm exactly like them, don't you see? That's why you act the way you do. It's the same with Miss Jones. It's the same with *everyone*. Except it's worse with you, because—"

She closes her mouth. I have to stop myself to keep from grabbing her arm again. "Because what? Why is it worse with me? *Why?*"

A car cruises through the intersection. It's a man and a woman I don't recognize. The woman looks out at Sarah and me. She turns to say something to her husband.

She'll tell someone. She'll tell them she saw me out here, talking to a colored girl in plain view of the whole town.

I shouldn't have done this.

"I have to go," I say.

"Yes, you do." Sarah has already turned away.

That hurts, but I'm too afraid to answer her.

Sarah crosses the street without looking back. I fumble in my purse, looking for a pencil.

I have an editorial to write.

LIE #13

This doesn't change anything.

JEFFERSON HIGH CLARION
Tuesday, April 14, 1959
Southern Pride and Southern Courtesy
By Linda Hairston, Editorial Page Editor

It has been said that it takes a strong man to change his views.

I firmly believe that integration has always been, and will always be, a violation of our most deeply held principles. However, I'm coming to believe that even without embracing such an extreme change in our way of life, there may be certain smaller changes to our current practices that we may consider.

For example, perhaps a few individual Negroes ought to be treated differently from the majority of their kind. Perhaps special consideration should be given to the Negro whose innate talents or achievements make him a credit to his race.

I'm not, of course, suggesting that we make any sort of changes to the decisions made by the wise men in our state government. However, I think we might consider extending certain courtesies to select Negroes on an individual basis. For *example, perhaps young children shouldn't be subject to limitations on their access to certain necessities, such as medical care. Or perhaps Negroes with certain gifts should be offered concessions. For example, the decision to allow the especially skilled baseball player Jackie Robinson to join the Brooklyn Dodgers, while lesser players remained on the Negro teams, was a wise one.*

~~*Perhaps certain well-mannered Negroes should be allowed to sit at lunch counters alongside whites, so that they may have the opportunity to absorb the benefits of white society*~~

I CROSS OUT the last line. Then I draw an *X* through the rest of the page. My pencil tears the paper. The weight of it is too much, since I only have my left palm to bear down on.

I can't print this. I don't know what I was thinking. I can't ever let anyone so much as see this piece of paper.

I crumple it up and stuff it in my skirt pocket. I dart glances at the risers on either side of me, but no one's looking at me, thank the Lord.

When Mr. Bailey yelled at Sarah yesterday, he didn't know who she was. He didn't care. He just looked at her and saw a colored girl. Any colored girl.

I've never known a colored person before. I thought they were all the same. Like the ones Daddy tells us about. The lazy ones who aren't smart enough to go to our schools. The criminals who need to be kept away from white women.

I didn't know there were other kinds of colored people. People like her.

Except for her color, I don't think Sarah is actually all that different from me, but what does that say about either one of us?

I'll have to throw this paper down the toilet the first chance I get. I can't believe I was so stupid as to put my name on it.

For now I need to act normal. Donna's standing next to me, so I smile at her. She smiles back, then snickers at Mr. Lewis, who's directing the Glee Club boys through their third run-through of "When the Saints Go Marching In." It sounds just as dreary as it did the last go-round.

Our joint choir rehearsals have been harder to get through ever since Sarah joined the Girls' Ensemble. In class she always sits at the front of the room, so I don't have to worry about her looking my way, but in choir, I'm always nervous she'll catch me watching her.

Not that she seems to have time for that. She's too busy looking behind her to stop the other girls from putting things down the back of her blouse.

"All right, that's it for today," Mr. Lewis says once the boys have droned out their final chorus. I toss a quick goodbye to Donna and make a beeline for the hallway. I need to get to the first-floor bathroom, the one where no one ever goes.

When I push open the door, I almost trip I'm so startled. Sarah must've been in even more of a hurry than me.

She's sitting on the floor against the far wall, her back straight against the cold tile, her blue wool skirt spread out in front of her. Her eyes are closed, her head tilted back. When the door clicks shut, she looks up, sees me and rolls her eyes.

I try to glare at her, but I feel like crying.

I'm holding the crumpled paper tight in my fist. I meant to go straight into a stall and flush the paper away.

Instead I cross the room and slide down onto the floor next to Sarah.

She turns to face me with a dull, tired look.

"What is it now?" she says.

I swallow over the lump in my throat. I try to think of something smart to say.

Instead I say, "I think I hate my father."

Sarah's eyes go wide. I can't believe I said that.

I don't hate my father. Do I?

My father is a very important, very respected man.

And I hate him. Maybe. A little.

"Why?" Sarah finally says.

I start to tell her I should never have said such a thing, and she can never repeat it.

Instead I tell her the story.

"When I was ten," I say, "before I got sick, we went to a protest, the whole family, out at Kiskiack Lake. Do you remember when they were having all those protests?"

Sarah shakes her head. That's right. She only moved to Davisburg from the North a few years ago. I don't know how I could ever have forgotten that with the way she talks.

"Well," I say, "some agitators were talking about integrating the lake, and we were protesting it. It was the first time anybody had really targeted Davisburg that way. We were all shocked they'd come after us, since this is such a nice, quiet town. Anyway, we won, of course—I mean, surely even you wouldn't support integrated *swimming*, right?"

Sarah just stares at me, so I keep going.

"At the end of the day they made the announcement, that the integrators had lost, and the protest turned into a victory rally. It was—well, I can't even tell you how much fun it was. Everyone was jumping up and down and cheering. My mom was crying, she was so happy. Even my big brothers were happy, and usually you couldn't get them to act excited about *anything*. They were grinning, and Daddy was slapping them on their backs, and *Daddy* was grinning. And then he picked me up and put me on his shoulders and gave me a sign to hold, and everyone could see me over the huge crowd, and they all smiled and waved. And even though I knew the real reason everyone was happy was because we'd won, right then, it felt like they were all cheering for *me*. Does that make sense?"

Sarah nods slowly.

"And Daddy walked all around the rally with me still up on his shoulders, and everyone was smiling at him, and Daddy seemed so proud to have me with him. Finally, when people started to leave, he put me down, but he still looked so, so happy. I'd hardly ever seen him look happy up until then."

Sarah's eyes are fixed on mine. That used to feel unnerving. It doesn't anymore.

"You know what?" I say. "I think that was the last time my father ever smiled at me."

I'd meant to tell Sarah that story so she'd see I didn't really hate my father, but remembering that day has only made me sad. I can't remember the last time I saw my whole family, together, happy.

"What did you mean, 'before you got sick'?" Sarah says. "Were you sick?"

I nod. I'd forgotten I mentioned that. "Well, when I was little, I used to get sick all the time. I was always in and out of the hospital. I had pneumonia a couple of times. And I had scarlet fever. But then in fifth grade I got *really* sick. They were afraid it was polio."

Sarah sucks in a breath.

"It turned out it was just diphtheria," I say. She nods. For a second I think she looks relieved, but I must have imagined it. "But when it started out, my leg was acting weird, and then I fainted in school one day. So the first thing the doctor told my parents was that they had to rule out polio. The way my father acted when the doctor said that—I think he lost half his hair that day. But after I'd been in the hospital a couple of days they got the real diagnosis. By then it was obvious it wasn't anything like polio. My neck was all swollen. I was a revolting mess, coughing and drooling all over the place, and I had these sores all over—" I swallow again. Sarah's still watching me closely. I don't want her to picture me covered in sores and drool. "And Daddy was angry because the hospital bills were stacking up even though there wasn't anything wrong with me that couldn't be cured. He thought I'd pretended to have polio just to get attention. Then when they let me out of the hospital, I was still coughing and crying all the time. It used to give Daddy headaches. He'd go around yelling for me to be quiet. After I got better and I stopped getting sick so much, he started—"

I stop. I'd almost told Sarah he hit me.

But why shouldn't I? All fathers hit their children. It's called discipline. Mom's been telling me so all my life.

Usually Daddy would hit me because I'd done something wrong and needed to learn my lesson. It would happen if I got a bad grade on a test, or forgot to do my chores or talked back to him at dinner. He'd hit my brothers since before they could walk, but when I came along, he let me be. He was so happy to finally have a girl he'd spoiled me rotten. At first.

"After that I decided I wasn't going to cry anymore," I say quietly. "But it didn't work. I thought it would make Daddy treat me the way he had before. Instead he just ignores me. It's like I'm invisible in my own house."

We sit in silence for a long time. Sarah probably thinks I'm a crybaby. A spoiled white girl who doesn't know how good she has it.

"I feel that way too, sometimes." Sarah's voice is so low I have to turn toward her to hear. "Invisible. My parents—they're different from yours, but they don't listen to me. They don't ask me what I want. They just tell me what to do. And I say, 'Yes, ma'am' and 'Yes, sir,' and I don't talk back, and I don't ask questions. That's what good daughters do. Being good means being invisible."

I think about sitting on Daddy's shoulders at that rally out at Kiskiack Lake. I try to remember what my sign said. Race Mixing is Communism! maybe.

I think about Sarah and her sister and the rest of their group walking into school on that first day. Everyone was shouting and striking out at them.

What was the difference, really, between Sarah and me?

Sarah's parents weren't with her that day, but her parents and their friends were the ones who filed the court case.

"What's that?" Sarah asks, pointing to my hand.

I look down. I'd forgotten all about my editorial.

Sarah meets my eyes. Neither of us moves. At first I think that expression on her face is pity, but soon I'm certain it's something else.

Sarah reaches toward my lap. For a flickering moment I think she's going to try to hold my hand.

I want her to.

Oh, God, I want her to.

This is happening. This is real.

I didn't want it to be real. I didn't want to even think it.

It's *wrong.*

But I can't keep lying to myself.

I want Sarah the way I'm supposed to want Jack.

But she's a *girl,* and a *Negro,* and a *girl,* and it's wrong, it's wrong, it's wrong—

Sarah doesn't try to hold my hand. Instead she takes the crumpled paper and spreads it out across her knees.

I let her.

She reads my scribblings, turning the paper this way and that to see through the parts I crossed out. I try to keep my face completely still. I can't let her see what I'm thinking. If she knew, she'd run out of here so fast you'd miss her if you blinked.

Then she looks back up at me. She's smiling. It's been a long time since I last saw her smile.

"We should go," she says after another minute. "I have to watch my brother this afternoon."

She stands up and brushes off her skirt. I stand, too. I was expecting her to say something about what I'd written. To argue with me, or call me a liar, or a hypocrite or *something*. Instead she moves toward the door. I duck into a stall and drown the paper before I turn to follow her.

"There's something I've always wanted to ask you," Sarah says as she pushes the bathroom door open. "That day, in the hall, with my sister. Why did you—"

She stops short. I turn to follow her gaze. Donna and Nancy are staring right at us.

Donna looks puzzled. Nancy's face is curled into a smirk. I can't tell if it's meant for Sarah or for me.

My heart is beating so fast it's a battle just to keep standing. I say the first thing I think of.

"So you see," I say, turning toward Sarah, "your people don't belong in this school. You have your own. You should be grateful we gave you that privilege. You should thank us, not fight us."

Nancy and Donna nod along. I could keep talking this way all afternoon—these sorts of words come as easily as breathing—but the look on Sarah's face makes me stop.

"Let's get out of here, Linda." Nancy links one arm through mine and the other through Donna's. "I can't handle the smell around these parts."

I try to laugh, but it comes out like a shriek.

Nancy marches us toward the front door. I glance back. Sarah is walking down the empty hall toward the side exit, her shoulders sagging under her faded yellow blouse.

She hates me. She *must*.

Well, but it's not as if I have any reason to care what she thinks. She's an agitator and probably a Communist and a...

My shoulders sag, too.

My friends chatter as we walk outside into the brilliant April sunshine, but I don't hear them.

I do care what Sarah Dunbar thinks of me. I care much, much more than I should.

That's why I've made such a terrible mess of things. And I don't even know where to start cleaning it up.

LIE #14

I hate her.

STUDY HALL IS packed today. Mr. Farrell is out and they couldn't find a substitute, so all his classes are being put into Study Halls. We have twice as many juniors and seniors as usual stuffed into one classroom, and two Negroes—Sarah and the junior boy. They're sitting in the front row the way they always do, with empty chairs on all sides of them, even though the room is so full people are sitting on top of desks and on the low bookcases at the back of the room.

Mrs. Gruber doesn't look happy about the crowd. She sighs more than usual and snaps at anyone who talks above a whisper, but she doesn't stop Bo's gang from throwing balls of paper at Sarah and the boy. It bothers me more today than it does on regular Study Hall days, when the junior boy is the only colored student in the room.

The boys throwing the paper are enjoying themselves, though. Bo and the others from Mr. Farrell's class especially.

Ten minutes into class the boys start taking bets.

"Ten cents I hit the girl," Eddie whispers, letting his wad of paper fly from the back of the room. Sarah doesn't flinch. The paper soars past her.

The boys laugh. "You can't throw to save your life, Ed," one of them says.

"I've got a quarter I get the coon in the ear." Kenneth fires off a spitball. It lands on the colored boy's shoulder. He doesn't brush it off. The boys howl with laughter.

"None of you know how to aim right." Bo stretches his arms over his head. His skin is so dark from working in the sun he's almost as brown as Sarah. "Tell you what. Fifty cents I clock that nigger in his big black head."

"I'll bet you," another boy says.

They've stopped laughing now. The whole room is watching Bo.

He's holding a baseball.

I could say something.

I stay quiet.

"I'm in, too," another boy says. There's a jingle of coins.

Sarah and the colored boy are still sitting straight up in their seats, looking at the board. They don't know what's happening.

I should say something.

"All right," Bo says. "Watch this."

He throws the baseball, hard.

It sails to the front of the room. It smashes into the back of the boy's neck. He falls forward and we all hear the crack as his forehead hits the desk.

The boys let out peals of laughter.

I want to throw up.

Sarah runs over to the colored boy. After a second, Mrs. Gruber gets up, too.

"Paulie? Are you all right?" Sarah says.

The class keeps laughing.

I could get up. I could stand up and go get help.

I stay where I am.

The colored boy is sitting up now, waving Sarah off, saying something too low for me to hear.

"He looks all right," Mrs. Gruber says.

Sarah gapes at her. Then her expression goes smooth again.

"He ought to go to the nurse, ma'am," Sarah says. "I'll walk with him."

"No!" the boy says. He sounds awful. The way Daddy sounded the night after he came back from visiting Senator Byrd and drank two glasses of whiskey at dinner. "I'll be fine."

He stands up, legs wobbling. Then he sits back down.

The laughter from Bo and the other boys only grows.

Sarah looks straight at Mrs. Gruber. They stand, staring at each other, for a long moment. Finally Mrs. Gruber rolls her eyes and says, "All right, who threw that ball?"

No one speaks. The boys are still laughing, but they're doing it behind their hands now.

"It was Bo," Sarah tells her. "Ma'am."

"Shut up, you didn't see nothing," one of the boys says. "You were facing front the whole time."

"I heard him say he was going to do it," Sarah says.

"Nobody threw it on purpose," Brenda says. "I didn't see who did it, but I could tell it was an accident."

"Yeah," Kenneth says. "If it wasn't they woulda hit him smack in his big black face."

Now they're back to laughing out loud.

Mrs. Gruber sighs and goes back to her desk.

"Wait." Sarah hasn't moved from her spot at the front of the room. "He could've really hurt Paulie! We have to tell someone. There's that rule about fighting."

Mrs. Gruber gives Sarah a withering look. "Well, if we can't determine who was involved, I don't know what you expect me to do."

"It was Bo!" Sarah's getting louder. Talking faster. "Everyone heard him! He said he was going to hit Paulie! He was taking bets on it!"

"Lost those damn quarters, too," another boy mutters. Sarah glares at him. He snickers.

"You have two choices right now," Mrs. Gruber says to Sarah. "You can sit down, or you can go to the principal's office and tell him exactly why you insist on acting out in my class."

Sarah stands quietly for a moment, looking right at Mrs. Gruber. They're the same height.

Then Sarah says, "Thank you, ma'am."

She turns on her heel and walks out the door.

Brenda gasps. So do I.

I think about going after her.

I think about telling the principal I saw Bo throw the ball. Mr. Cole might not believe Sarah, but he'd believe me.

But if I go, everyone will know I'm the one who tattled.

They'll say Linda Hairston—good little Linda Hairston, the newspaper editor's daughter—has turned into a nigger-lover.

Everyone will hear about it. All my friends. Jack.

And when the gossip's that good, there's no way it won't reach Daddy's ears.

I shrink into my seat. The colored boy is still sitting in the front row. A knot is already forming under his shirt collar. The boys are balling up more wads of paper to throw at him.

I wonder what it would be like to have that colored boy's nerve.

"Is the boy all right?"

Sarah's just arrived in the back room at Bailey's. I'm on my feet and the question is out of my mouth before she's even closed the door.

She slides it shut and turns around to face me. Her eyes are blazing.

Judy looks back and forth between us, biting her thumbnail

and clutching a cigarette so hard the paper's crumpling. I told Judy what Bo did. I left out the part about what I didn't do.

"Is who all right?" Sarah says.

"Who?" I can't believe her. "The boy! From Study Hall!"

She frowns, her eyes crinkling. "Paulie? How do you know about that?"

"What do you mean, 'how do I know?' I was right there!"

"Oh. You were in that class?"

She didn't even notice me?

"Yes!" It's all I can do not to stomp my foot. "Is he hurt badly?"

"He says he's fine." Sarah sits down and shrugs, but she's talking even faster than usual. "I called Mrs. Mullins and told her about it. She's trying to get him to see a doctor."

She's talking about Helen Mullins. The ringleader of the local NAACP. The most ardent integrationist in Davisburg. Daddy says Helen Mullins represents everything that's wrong with the modern Negro.

I shake my head. I don't have time to think about Helen Mullins.

"He *has* to see a doctor," I say. "Bo hit him really hard!"

"I know."

"But it's important! Tell him it's important he sees a doctor!"

"He knows," Sarah says. "He'll do what he wants. This isn't the first time Paulie's gotten hit this year."

There's patience on her face.

I thought she'd be angry with me for not helping. For not doing anything at all.

She's not. She never expected me to help in the first place.

"Tell me something, Linda." Sarah gives me that look again. The one that makes me feel about six inches tall. "What do you think it is we do every day? You think a few people call us names? You think no one ever gets knocked down the stairs? You think no one ever gets hit with a rock, or a stick or a dictionary?"

"Shoot, Mr. McDonald is here early," Judy says, peering out the cracked door. "I have to go up front."

Sarah and I ignore her.

"Do you even know how frustrating it is, talking to you about this?" Sarah crosses her arms in front of her chest, staring me down. "You think it's not your fault because you aren't the one throwing baseballs, but I read the things you print in the school paper. You're as bad as your father, egging the others on."

"Don't talk about my father!"

"I have to go," Judy says again. She slips out, closing the door behind her.

"I read the one you didn't print, too," Sarah goes on. "The one you threw in the toilet. For a second I believed that was what you really thought. Not that what you wrote yesterday was so great, mind you, but it was a step above your usual thoughtless claptrap about—what do you call it?—*Southern pride*."

Her words leave a hole in my chest. It's like she's peeling me open.

I told her so much yesterday. Soon I'll be laid completely bare in front of her. She'll know every thought I've ever had. Every weakness I've tried to hide.

"What happened to the boy today wasn't my fault," I say, my voice trembling.

Even though we both know I could've done something.

I could've walked up to Bo and snatched that baseball out of his hand.

So much has happened this year that I could've stopped, if I'd tried.

"Paulie," Sarah says. "The boy's name is Paulie."

I nod, but I'm shaking.

"You're worse than Bo. Worse than all of them." Sarah's shaking, too. "You make me so *angry*. They're all too dumb to know why they're wrong, but you understand it. Or you could, if you'd bother trying."

I want to answer her, but there aren't any words.

"I get so furious every time I think about you." She looks like she might cry. "You're nothing but a spoiled girl who's too busy worrying about what everybody thinks of you to actually *think* about anything. So you just do what your daddy tells you. Your daddy who you say you hate so much. I keep thinking I see this other part of you, this part that knows better, but then every time I do you turn around and say something stupid, and it just makes me so *angry,* Linda. You make me *so...*" *She tilts her head down, closes her eyes and pinches the bridge of her nose with her fingers. Her voice drops to a whisper.* "*Angry!*"

So Sarah does think about me.

I wonder how much. I wonder if she thinks about me at night when she can't fall asleep.

My thoughts are spinning around too fast for me to understand them.

"It's all I can think about anymore." She looks up. Her arms are stiff at her sides. She stares straight into my eyes. "Sometimes at night I can't even sleep because all I can think about is how frustrating you are."

That wasn't what I meant.

"Tell me one thing." Her voice is low. I have to lean in to hear her. "You said in your editorial, the one you threw away, that you'll never stop being a segregationist. I want you to tell me why."

That's an easy question. I don't even have to think.

"It's tradition," I say. My voice cracks. "It's protecting our heritage."

Sarah nods. "And why do you want to protect your heritage so badly? Because it makes you better than us?"

"Nobody's better than anybody else." I sound desperate even to my own ears. "It's about maintaining our Southern way of life."

"Your way of life is keeping other people down." Her chin

quivers. "You saw what they did to Paulie today. Do you want to know the things they've done to me?"

No. I don't.

I want to hurt anyone who ever did anything to Sarah.

I think about the first day of school. About moving my seat away from hers in Math class.

I bite my cheek. I will *not* cry. Not in front of her.

"That's why you're so much worse than the others." Her voice shakes. "Because you could do something about this if you tried. Instead you say the same thing over and over again. Even though it doesn't make any sense. And you *know* it doesn't make sense, Linda. I *know* you know better. I can see it in you. You're so close to understanding it, if you'd only try."

She's lying. She doesn't know me.

She's trying to confuse me. It's all part of her scheme.

"You don't know anything about me," I whisper.

I *hate* Sarah. I *hate* her.

"But instead you go on, publishing your little articles and giving your little speeches." She shakes her head. "You're such a hypocrite."

"Stop it!" She's looking right at me. I try to turn my head to avoid her gaze, the frightening look in her eyes, but she's everywhere. "Leave me alone!"

I try to push past her but she steps into my way. Our faces are only inches apart.

"Why were you so eager to know how Paulie was doing?" A tear slides down her cheek, leaving a shiny brown path behind it. "You were just sitting there. Would you have just sat there if it had been me instead of Paulie?"

She did know I was there.

She *does* pay attention to me.

"No." My face feels hot. "I mean, I don't know. Please, just leave me alone."

"No. I won't. I've had enough of doing what people like you tell me."

I swallow. My throat feels like it's closing up.

"Why do you have to be this way?" I say. "Why do you have to get inside my head and mix everything up?"

"Why do *you* have to be this way?" She scrubs at her cheek with her hand, wiping the tear away. The patch of skin there looks red and raw. I want to run my fingers over it. I want to stop her from hurting. "Every time I start to hope you might—every time I let myself think—*every time,* you turn around and do something even more *hateful* than the time before."

She hates me.

I knew it. I'd hate me, too.

The door to the back room is still cracked open. Far off at the front of the store I can hear Judy laughing with Mr. McDonald, coffee cups tinkling on saucers, Mr. Fairfax ringing up an order at the register.

But the whole world might as well be me and Sarah.

"Please don't feel like that," I whisper.

"I can't help it," she whispers back. "I've tried and tried. I can't make it stop."

And then she kisses me.

And the whole world goes black.

I'm dreaming.

I've had this dream before.

When the light fades back in, I don't know how much time has passed, but I'm kissing her back. Something is dancing in my chest. Sizzling. Sarah feels soft, and light, like silk. She tastes like fresh, clear water, the kind that only runs in the springtime.

Then I remember.

This is wrong.

It doesn't matter if it feels right. It's *wrong.*

I break away from Sarah and step backward.

I half hope she'll come with me. I half hope we'll keep kissing and kissing, the way boys and girls do in the movies. That a sunset backdrop will fall down behind us and carry us off to happily ever after.

Even though she's a girl. Even though she's colored.

I want to keep kissing Sarah forever.

Sarah steps back, too. She's clapped her hand over her face. Tears are streaming down her cheeks.

She knows this is wrong as well as I do.

"Sarah—" I start to say. Then I stop.

Just behind her, the door to the back room is open.

Judy's in the door frame.

I start to ask how long she's been there, but I can tell from the look on her face.

Sarah's out the door before Judy's even started to scream.

part 3

The Old Rugged Cross

Sarah

LIE #15

Pretending will make
this go away.

MY HOUSE IS ten blocks from Bailey's. I run the whole way.

When I get there I'm sweating under my jacket. I'm still chanting the same prayer I've been saying ever since I made it out into the crisp April air.

Please, God. Please, please, please, God. Let this be a dream. Let me wake up and have it be morning.

A lot of horrible things have happened since we came to Jefferson, but this is the worst.

I fumble to open the front door. Mama is on the couch working on her lesson plan. I run upstairs without saying hello and fling open the door to my room.

Ruth is there.

"What's wrong with you?" she says.

I turn around and rush down the hall to the bathroom. I lock the door behind me and stare at my face in the mirror.

I know what's wrong with me. I've known for years.

I thought if I ignored it, it would go away.

I should've known that's not how the Devil works. Sin doesn't go away simply because you wish it gone.

I'm just as bad as the white people say I am. Dirty. Low. Unnatural.

I've never even *imagined* doing anything like that. I never let myself.

But I know why I did it.

It's been going on for months now. The more I saw of her, the more I lost my head.

I've been thinking the worst kind of sinful thoughts. About her. About what it would be like to be *with* her. In the sinful way boys want to be with girls.

I lost control. I can *never* lose control.

I let myself get carried away imagining who she really was. I listened to everything she said, and I still told myself she wasn't really like that. I thought about how she saved Ruth in the hall, and about that confused look in her eyes every time I challenged her, and I built it up into something that wasn't really there. I refused to see what was right in front of me.

I thought I'd finally met someone I could talk to. Someone who might understand.

I'd started looking forward to those afternoons. Even when we argued, there was something there. Some spark under my skin that made me want to keep arguing.

I'd rather have been with her than at home, or school or anywhere else. Without her, I'd just be alone again.

I thought she was different from the others. But it was all a trick. A sick joke.

She's a true segregationist all right. And she figured out the truth about me, too. She even has proof.

Plus, Judy saw it. She knows everything, too.

Maybe Judy's not the only one. There were other people in Bailey's this afternoon. Anyone could've—

Wait.

Can people see it on me just from looking? Is that what Ruth meant when she asked what was wrong with me?

I take cautious steps down the hall and push open the door to my room.

Ruth hasn't moved. She's lying on her bed doing her homework. There's a Frankie Avalon song playing on the radio. I hate Frankie Avalon.

Ruth glances up at me, then looks back down, a bored expression on her face.

I wait to see if she'll do something else. She keeps writing, then finally drops her pencil and lifts her head. "What? I can't concentrate with you squinting at me like that."

I step inside the room and close the door.

"Is everything—all right?" My voice comes out high-pitched. Unnatural. Like the rest of me.

"What are you talking about?" She looks back at her homework.

"You know. Everything."

"No, I don't know. You're the one who's acting strange."

I leave, closing the door behind me. I ignore Ruth's call of "Okay, *now* what?" and go back into the bathroom. The phone rings in the downstairs hallway, but it's a faraway sound, like the audience's laughter on a television show.

Ruth can't see it.

I shut my eyes and send a quick prayer of thanks. Then I remember it isn't right to pray about something like this.

It's only a matter of time before they all figure out the truth. Something this huge can't stay a secret.

I get down on my knees to pray, but this time the prayers won't come.

I should've stayed with Alvin. Then this wouldn't have happened. I'd still be the same girl who walked around the park with him, listening to him drone on about his elocution instructor.

Maybe I can still get Alvin back. Or some other boy.

Maybe this is fixable.

Yes. Of course it is. I'll just pretend this never happened. I can just—

I sit down on the toilet lid and sob.

It's the first time I've cried since that day at school, in the bathroom. The first time I really talked to *her*.

I wonder when she figured it out. I bet it was that very first day, in the auditorium. I bet she saw it on me right away.

All she needed was concrete evidence. And now she has that, too.

I should go to a doctor. There's got to be something they can do to make sure this doesn't happen to me again. Some sort of treatment program.

But I can't go to see Dr. Augustus. I'd have to ask Mama to make the appointment for me. What would I tell her? That her daughter is a—

Mama and Daddy can't know. Not ever.

I bend over and let the tears fall onto my knees.

Aren't things hard enough already? Why did *this* have to happen to me? Of all things? What kind of plan does God have for me?

But God doesn't do things like this. He doesn't make people this way.

This is the Devil's doing.

There's a knock on the bathroom door.

"Not now!" I call.

"Sarah?" comes a small voice. Bobby. "Sarah, I have to go."

I want to tell him to wait, but Bobby can't wait. If you make Bobby wait he'll wet his pants. And guess whose job it'll be to wash them.

I dry my eyes on the hem of my skirt and stand up. I will the tears to stop.

I open the door. Bobby rushes in past me, slamming it closed behind him.

God will show me the way out of this. I have to pray harder, that's all.

I'll pray at home. At school. Every second I don't absolutely have to be doing something else, I'll pray for God to fix me.

I'll work at it, too. I'll dress more femininely. Mama is always after me to get one of those flowered dresses the pretty white girls show off in *Seventeen*'s Easter issue every year.

I'll get her to take me shopping. We can get all the flowered dresses she wants.

Jewelry, too. I don't like wearing jewelry because I don't like the way it rubs against my skin, but I'll get used to it. Daddy gave me a pearl necklace last Christmas to wear on special occasions. Maybe Mama will let me wear it on Sundays from now on.

But the most important thing—more than the clothes or the jewelry, more important even than the praying—is that I can't see *her* ever again.

We're almost finished with the French project. I can do the rest of the pages by myself and give them to Judy. Judy's not going to want to be seen talking to me ever again—who would?—but I can stick them in her locker before school when no one's around.

In class, I won't look at her. At lunch I'll sit with my back to her table. And in the halls I'll just have to watch out for—

I lean back against the bathroom door, my head thumping against the hard wood. *Another* reason to keep a watch out in the halls.

But I don't have a choice. This is important. I can't risk anything like this ever happening again. I can't risk being anywhere near her.

It almost makes me sad.

There was something about talking to her. Something that lit a fire inside me.

And it wasn't all anger. Talking to her made me feel like something was buzzing in my veins. Even if I'd spent the whole day up until then feeling empty and dull.

With her I didn't have to be polite. I didn't have to think everything through before I said it. At the end of a long day of not talking back to anyone, I looked forward to the incredible feeling of saying whatever I wanted out loud.

I thought someday, I might even have a real friend at this school.

Tears prick at my eyes again.

The bathroom door swings open. Bobby peers up at me. "Sarah? What are you doing?"

"Nothing." I blink the tears away. I pick Bobby up and set him on my hip, even though he's getting too big for that now. "What are *you* doing, silly?"

I tickle his belly. He giggles and squeals.

Usually I don't bother talking to Bobby much. I have a lot on my mind. Too much for little brothers.

But maybe spending more time with him will remind me how important it is to get married and have children of my own. I'm almost eighteen. It's time I started thinking about those sorts of things.

Past time, really. My friend Frances has had a hope chest since freshman year. Every Christmas her parents give her a new piece of silver for it. Her pattern is Chantilly.

I need a silver pattern. I need a hope chest.

I need to get Mama to teach me some more recipes, too. How can I expect to cook for my husband if all I can make is fried okra and pot roast?

And I need a new boyfriend. Alvin won't do. He's barely taller than I am. When we went to the Harvest Dance last year and I wore high heels, I had to keep slumping down.

"Sarah?" Mama's voice on the stairs makes me jump. Bobby

shrieks in my arms, thinking this is a new game. "Your father and I need to talk to you. Bobby, go play in your room."

Bobby wriggles out of my grip. My heart thumps in my ears. How did they find out?

That phone call.

Oh, *God.*

Did *she* call?

Or was it someone else? Judy, maybe? It could've been anyone. The door was cracked open and—

No. The *how* doesn't matter. What matters is what I'll say to Mama and Daddy about it.

It was all a big misunderstanding. The two of us were talking, and it only looked like we were doing *that,* because we were—there was—

No. It'll sound like I'm making excuses. I'll say she forced me to—

No. That would be just as bad.

I'll say—

"Well, come on," Mama says.

I bow my head and follow her down.

"What's Daddy doing home this time of day?" I ask to distract myself. I'm afraid I'll fall down the stairs if I'm not careful.

"He's only working three nights a week at the *Gazette* from now on."

"Why? So he can have more time for the *Free Press?*"

Mama only says, "Mmm."

It's too late to think of an excuse. Daddy is sitting in his chair in the living room, looking the same way he did when Ruth got a C in Math on her sixth-grade report card.

Mama sits on the sofa and points me toward the love seat at the far end of the room. I sit down and smooth invisible wrinkles in my skirt, trying to keep my hands from shaking.

"I only have one question, Sarah," Daddy says after a long minute. His jaw is twitching.

I close my eyes and pray, in a final flicker of hope, that this will all turn out to be a dream.

"Why did you disobey me?" Daddy says.

I open my eyes. Disobey? He's never told me not to—I mean, not that he would've *needed* to, but—

"My instructions were very clear," he says. "So were Mrs. Mullins's."

Mrs. Mullins? I've certainly never talked to Mrs. Mullins about—

"We said no extracurricular activities," he says. "None. Did you think being my daughter made you an exception to that rule?"

Oh. *Oh.*

He's talking about the choir. They must've found out about it somehow.

They don't know what happened today.

I almost laugh, I'm so relieved. Mama and Daddy are still giving me that hard look, though, and I'm still sitting in the punishment seat.

"I'm sorry, sir." This is easy. I know how to play the good child. I've been playing the good child all my life. "You're absolutely right. I shouldn't have disobeyed you. It was wrong to join the choir without your permission. I'll go right in tomorrow and tell Mr. Lewis I'm quitting. You should give me whatever punishment you think is right. I could do all the dishes and the laundry for the next two weeks."

Mama sits back in her seat, satisfied. Daddy is still watching me, though.

"You didn't answer my question," he says. "I asked you why."

Oh.

I try to remember what I was thinking when I walked into Mr. Lewis's office and asked him for the sign-up sheet.

It was a terrible idea. I'm glad Mama and Daddy found out

about it because now I can drop out easily enough. Then I won't have to see *her* at practices anymore.

It was her fault I signed up in the first place. I decided to do it that day we listened to the Édith Piaf record. When I sang, I could tell *she* thought I was good.

Her thinking I was good made me feel like I could do it. Like I could do anything.

Plus I couldn't shake the thought that one of us ought to join *something*. Ruth wants to join the cheerleading squad next year. I don't want her to have to be the first.

Of course I can't say any of that to Daddy. So I think quickly.

"I thought it would be good for the movement," I say. "For the white people at school to see a Negro can sing as well as they can."

Daddy rubs his chin. I wait for Mama to say something about pride being a sin, but she's quiet, too.

I answered Daddy too well for my own good. He's got the look in his eyes now that he gets when he's working on a good story.

"Well, you might be right," he says. "If they put you on that stage and you sing better than the white girls, they can't help but take notice."

"Robert," Mama says, a warning in her voice.

Mama and Daddy lock eyes for a minute. Then Daddy turns back toward me.

"Sarah, go to your room," he says. "We'll call you back down to tell you your punishment."

I nod.

Then I go sit on the top of the stairs, where Ruth and I always sit when we want to listen in on Mama and Daddy.

"They probably won't give it to her to begin with," Mama's saying when I press my ear to the wall. "If we let her audition she's only going to get her heart broken."

Audition? For what? I've been in the Girls' Ensemble for weeks. There was no audition, just a sign-up sheet. It said the

Girls' and Boys' Ensembles are "open to all juniors and seniors with a love of music." Freshmen and sophomores are stuck joining the Glee Club. The only group that requires an audition is the Balladeers.

Everyone in Davisburg knows about the Jefferson Balladeers. They sing at the pageant at city hall every Christmas. They won the state choir contest last year for the white schools.

She's in the Balladeers.

But I wasn't about to ask Mr. Lewis about the Balladeers. The white parents in this town would just as soon elect a Negro mayor as see a black face standing among their best and brightest on a competition platform.

"That teacher who called, that Mr. Lewis, said they only pick one soloist from her ensemble group," Daddy tells her. "Plus one from the Glee Club and one from the fancy one."

"The Balladeers," Mama says.

"Right. How many dang choirs does one school need, anyway?"

"You know how these white parents are. Everybody thinks their child's got the voice of an angel."

Daddy scoffs. "Well, Sarah's probably better than all those Balladeers put together. She's bound to beat out every last one of them, if this Lewis is as honest a man as he purports to be."

I feel a tiny flicker of happiness. That's just about the nicest thing I've heard Daddy say about me.

"If Sarah gets a solo in this spring show, well then, that'll show them all, won't it?" Daddy says. "They can argue about color all they want, but there's no arguing with talent. Maybe this is the sort of thing we need to beat Jim Crow."

The spring show? That's what that phone call was? Mr. Lewis wants me to audition for a solo in the *Jefferson High spring concert?*

I'd have to audition in front of the whole choir. The girls who drop nasty notes in my purse. The boys who try to trip me every time I walk through the door. I won't be able to make it through the first verse of my audition song before they shout me down.

She'll see the whole thing. She'll laugh at me with her friends. If they haven't killed me first.

"You're losing sight of what matters here, Robert," Mama says. "Sarah knew what the rules were, and she ignored them. And she deceived us to do it. Besides, we all agreed we should wait to integrate the extracurriculars until next year. Helen Mullins thought so, too. Let folks get used to black faces in their classrooms first. Put them in their clubs and teams second."

"Well, after the first set of growing pains this integration has gone better than we expected," Daddy says. "There's been no violence. No one's been expelled. It's time we reassessed the plan. Let's call Helen and see what she thinks."

Daddy doesn't think there's been any violence?

He thinks the integration has gone *well?*

Doesn't he remember—

No. He wouldn't.

He doesn't know what happened to Paulie today. Because I didn't tell him.

And he doesn't know about the boy who grabbed me in the hallway. I didn't tell him about that, either. I didn't tell anyone about that.

But Daddy *does* know about the people throwing rocks and spitballs and pencils. I guess he chalked that up to "growing pains."

My head throbs. I climb the rest of the stairs and sit in my room, ignoring Ruth when she tries to talk to me. I try to start my homework, but I can only stare at the closed cover of my History book.

It was stupid to think she might've called the house.

She'll call her friends instead. And they'll call *their* friends.

Tomorrow, when I get to school, everyone will already know.

She'll tell them I attacked her. That I'm unnatural. Wicked. They'll all believe her.

They'll come at me in the parking lot. Or sooner. I close my eyes and see a horde of white people mobbing our station wagon. The others will get hurt, and it'll be me that brought this upon us.

I can't control it. It's like it isn't a part of me. It's something foreign that's taken over. Ever since *she* stepped in between Ruth and those boys in the hall. Ever since she watched me sing that day, with a smile on her face that looked like the sun was shining right through her eyes.

Seeing her like that—it felt like I'd found a place where I belonged.

Before I met her, I never knew it was possible to feel that way. That just being near someone could make your whole body light up. That having her look at you could make you lose your head.

It was enough to make me think there was another girl hiding inside her, buried beneath the part of her that spouted the usual segregationist claptrap. A girl who understood what was really going on. A girl who understood *me*.

But it's not right. Not any of it.

I've gone to church every Sunday since I was born. I always try to do exactly what God wants of me. Not to stray into the path of temptation and sin.

I didn't want to do what I did today. I didn't want to feel any of these things.

I only ever wanted to be like everyone else.

I'm about to start crying again when Mama calls me back downstairs.

"You will be responsible for the family's laundry for the next month," Mama says before I've even sat back down. I nod fast so they won't notice my chin quivering. "And you'll continue to do the dishes after dinner. Your sister will continue to do the breakfast dishes. It wouldn't be fair to take away her chores just because you're being punished."

I keep nodding. A whole month of washing everyone's underwear, all by myself. It's less than I deserve.

"Your mother and I have also made a decision," Daddy says. He glances at Mama. She nods. "You should go ahead with the audition for this concert."

"I really don't need to," I say quickly. "I should quit the choir altogether. It isn't right for me to stay after I disobeyed you."

"We'll decide what's right," Daddy says. "You're being punished for what you did, but it'll be good for the white people to see some of you making contributions to the school. Tomorrow afternoon you'll all meet at Mrs. Mullins's house and she'll tell you more about the new rules for extracurriculars. And when you audition on Friday you'll do your very best."

"I'll help you rehearse," Mama adds. "We can use the piano at church."

I nod, but my face feels strained. Mama must notice because she adds, "Don't be nervous, sweetie. You always loved singing with your friends in the concerts at Johns."

Right. My friends. The people I've barely seen since I started at Jefferson.

Singing in the Johns choir feels like something from another lifetime.

Maybe if I sing badly enough in the audition on Friday, Mr. Lewis will decide to kick me out of the Girls' Ensemble altogether. It would mean seeing that much less of *her*.

But Daddy said I should do my very best. And I can't imagine humiliating myself in front of a roomful of white people on purpose.

"Now go on up to your room and finish your homework," Mama says. "Then come back down. There's a load of laundry that'll need hanging."

I nod and leave without another word.

There is no punishment that would be enough for me.
Even prayer can't help me anymore.
I'm going to Hell, and there's nothing I can do about it.

LIE #16

I can do this alone.

THE NEXT MORNING, I step onto the curb and wait for the shouts to start.

I don't even know what names you call someone like me. I wonder if they'll sound worse than the usual names. On the first day of school being called "nigger" felt alien. I thought I'd get used to it eventually, but I haven't yet.

I wonder if I'll get used to the new ones. Then I wonder if I'll even have time to hear them before the beatings start.

I shiver. It's not cold today, but I barely slept last night. The edges of my vision are blurry. I'd think I was still dreaming if I couldn't feel the wads of parking lot gum sticking to the bottoms of my loafers.

Chuck walks out in front of the group. Lately he's started smiling and waving at the crowd like he's Miss America, even though it makes the white boys shout and throw things at him more than ever.

I walk behind him with Ruth and Yvonne. I wonder what Ruth

will think when she hears what they'll say about me. Just like on that first day, I want to put my hands over her ears.

The shouts begin.

"Niggers! Coons! Burrheads!"

I wait for the words to change. For the white people to see me in the group and charge at me. For them to pull me away from my friends and lay into me with kicks and punches.

My heart thuds. I should've warned the others. I don't want anyone getting beaten on account of my sin.

I'm still waiting for it to start when we're halfway across the parking lot.

But no one's paid me any special notice. I might as well be any other Negro.

"Go back to the jungle!" a girl shouts from the middle of the crowd. Then she turns her back on us and goes on talking to her friends.

I recognize two of them. They're in the Delta Tri-Hi-Y group. They must have heard the news by now.

But the Delta girls don't even look at me. Everyone's acting like it's any other day.

Then I see *her*.

She's standing with three girls I don't know at the far edge of the crowd. Her back is turned. All I can see is the curl of her red hair and the slope of her chin as she leans down to say something to her friend.

Why isn't she looking at me?

"Hey." Someone's pulling on my wrist. "Sarah! Wake up. We've got to keep going."

I blink. I must've been staring at her for half a minute.

Ruth is gripping my arm, glaring. "Will you move, please?"

"Sorry." I wrench my arm out of my sister's grasp. We speed up to catch Chuck and Yvonne.

I can't believe I let myself lose focus. None of us can afford to take risks like that. Anything could happen if we aren't paying attention.

But I don't understand. Why isn't anyone coming at me?

Is it possible she didn't tell them? That she wasn't pulling a trick?

Is it possible she's like me?

No. *She* is a perfectly normal girl. I'm the only freak.

She's probably biding her time. Waiting until the right moment. I'll have to stay on guard.

And I do. All day long I keep vigilant. Ready to deny it all. To pretend better than I've ever pretended.

But no one gives me a second look. Not even *her*.

I see her twice during the day. The first time is when she walks past my desk in French. I try to avert my eyes, but I'm too slow.

She doesn't look at me.

She never used to miss an opportunity to narrow her eyes at me, but today I might as well be invisible.

She isn't in the cafeteria when I arrive for lunch. I sit in my usual seat and try to join in the boys' conversation about what happened on the last episode of *Gunsmoke*.

Then I realize Judy's looking at me.

I start to panic. Any minute, she's bound to stand up and tell the whole school what she saw.

But all she does is fix her eyes on my face.

She stares at me through the whole lunch period. I'm too nervous to eat. Ennis tries to give me his green beans but I shake my head and mumble that I'm worried about my English test.

I wasn't really worried about my test, but I should've been. I didn't study, and it's only because I read the story we're studying two years ago that I don't fail altogether.

Nothing unusual has happened by the end of the day, but I'm so tired from all the worrying, I can't even muster the energy to hold my head up when the white people chant "Nigger!" at me as I climb into the carpool to Mrs. Mullins's house.

I catch my second glimpse of *her* in the parking lot as we pull away. She isn't talking to anyone. She's just standing there. At first I think she's watching me, but she turns her head so fast I'm sure I imagined it.

I wonder why she isn't with her regular group of friends. Maybe that's part of the trick somehow.

The meeting at Mrs. Mullins's goes on for hours. I sit on the floor next to Ennis, trying to keep my eyes open while she drones on about the new extracurricular activity policy.

It's been nineteen hours since *it* happened. I haven't been able to concentrate on anything since.

"Now then, if you'd like to join an activity, raise your hand," Mrs. Mullins finally says.

I blink at her. So does everyone else.

No hands go up.

Mrs. Mullins just finished explaining that from now on, if we want to sign up for any clubs or teams, we can, as long as we talk to her and our parents about it first. To make sure it won't be something that'll bother the white people *too* much. (She didn't actually say that last part.)

Mrs. Mullins frowns at us, her perfectly curled hairdo looking cockeyed as she tilts her head. "We thought you'd be happy to have this opportunity."

"I'm not about to sign up for anything," one of the sophomore boys says. "I don't want to spend any more time with the white people than I have to."

"I'm always so happy at the end of the school day because I know I'm leaving soon," Yvonne says. "I don't want to stay at that place any longer."

"There's no point," Ruth says. "They don't want us in their clubs. Why should we bother?"

I frown at her. "What about cheerleading?"

Ruth rolls her eyes. "As if anyone could even hear my cheers over the white people. They'd all be too busy shouting *at* me."

My heart dips in my chest.

"Well I'm glad Sarah doesn't feel the same way all of you do," Mrs. Mullins says. "I'm sure she'll do us proud at her audition tomorrow."

Ruth and her friends glare at me.

I can't believe I ever thought joining the choir was a good idea.

I lower my eyes and brush carpet fluff off my skirt. It's old, gray and woolen, longer than the style is now. I've had this skirt since junior high.

It used to bother me that I couldn't wear my nice clothes to school. Now I can't imagine caring about something like that.

Ennis nudges my arm. "Don't worry about them. You're going to be great."

I try to smile at him, but I don't have the energy for that, either.

"Hey, listen," Ennis whispers after a minute has passed. Mrs. Mullins has moved on to talking about class schedules. Chuck is still trying to get transferred into advanced Physics, even though the principal has already said twice that it's impossible, no matter how many extra Science classes he took back at Johns. Mrs. Mullins is telling Chuck there's nothing more to be done, but Chuck's shoulders are clenched tight.

"Are you doing anything Saturday?" Ennis whispers.

I shake my head. The white people's spring dance is this Saturday. I wonder if *she* will be there. With her fiancé.

"How about going to a movie with me?" Ennis whispers. "There's a new one with Tony Curtis."

I blink.

A movie? With Ennis?

I turn to face him. He ducks his head.

Ennis just asked me on a *date*. A normal, Christian, boy-girl *date*.

"Yes!" I say too loudly. The others turn and look at me again, but I don't care this time.

Ennis beams. "Pick you up at six-thirty?"

I nod. I even manage a smile of my own.

This will all be all right.

I can forget about what happened yesterday. I can learn to be normal.

I just have to make sure I do everything right.

I try to smile at Ennis again, but he isn't watching me anymore. So I look him over, considering.

Ennis is a nice boy. He's polite. His clothes are always clean and pressed. He doesn't have a car, but he can borrow his father's. He makes good grades and he's from a good family. My parents will like him.

I've never really thought of him in that way before, but what does that matter? Anyway, it's only because I haven't had time to think about very much at all since school started. Any normal girl would be happy to be with Ennis.

I wonder how soon I can get him to ask me to go steady.

He's tapping his right hand against his knee. He's wearing his class ring, the one we all got last year at Johns. I picture how his ring will look on a chain around my neck.

Once *she* sees me wearing it she'll know I'm not really like that. There won't be any point to her spreading stories about me. All of this will be behind me.

Not that I want *her* to ever look at me again.

"Mrs. Mullins? Could I say something, please?" Paulie's raising his hand.

Mrs. Mullins takes off her glasses, wipes them with a cloth and nods. Her eyes are fixed on the floor. Paulie stands up and takes a breath.

"I wanted to let you all know today was my last day at Jefferson," he finally says. "I'm transferring back to Johns for the rest of the year."

I gasp. I'm wide-awake now.

"Noooo," Ruth whispers. She clasps Yvonne's hand.

"What?" Ennis stands up, his smile long gone. "You're not serious."

"You can't give up, Paul," Chuck says, his voice breaking.

But Paulie's already given up. It's clear from his face.

I can't blame him.

He kept saying he was all right after what happened in Study Hall yesterday.

He wasn't. No one would be.

It wasn't only the injury. The doctor looked him over and said he was lucky. He's got a knot on his neck and a bruise on his forehead but nothing more.

If the baseball yesterday was the only thing that had happened, Paulie could've kept going. I'm sure of it. But there was the baseball, and the rocks, and the spitballs and the pencils. And the shouts, the notes, the whispers. The footsteps behind you everywhere you go. Looking over your shoulder all the time to make sure no one's followed you.

I'm not the least bit angry with Paulie. I wish I *were* Paulie.

"I'm sorry to hear that, Paul," Mrs. Mullins says. "After your mother called me last night I'd hoped you might reconsider."

"No," Paulie says. "I've had as much as I can handle."

The adults are shaking their heads. Behind me Miss Freeman mutters something to Mr. Stern about "setting back the movement."

I have to stop myself from snorting. What business is it of Miss Freeman's, or any of theirs? They weren't in that room with Paulie when it happened. They didn't get detention from the principal for trying to help their friend, like I did yesterday. They aren't getting called names all day by angry white people, like all of us are.

It's hard to think about the good of the movement when you can't hear yourself think for the shouting.

The grown-ups always act like they're the ones who have

it hard. None of them knows the first thing about what this is like for us.

We're pawns in their game. The Negro parents versus the white parents. Bo and Eddie and their friends, they're pawns the same as us. The same as *her*.

I wonder how many of the grown-ups on either side would sacrifice us pawns if that's what it took to win.

Paulie is still standing above us, his expression fixed.

If I were at Johns I'd be having a normal senior year. Taking college prep classes. Getting ready for prom. Rehearsing for my guaranteed solo in the spring concert. Instead I'm studying junior-high algebra and steering clear of white people's spit.

If I'd stayed at Johns I wouldn't have met *her*. None of *that* would have ever happened.

I want to go with Paulie. I want to be the girl I used to be.

It takes all my strength to keep the tears from falling.

"We'll miss you, buddy," Chuck says, shaking Paulie's hand.

Everyone goes over to say goodbye.

We'll still see Paulie. There will still be church picnics and neighborhood dances. Dates and parties and ice-cream socials.

But when we see him again, he won't be one of us. He's leaving us that much more alone.

Yet even when I try, I can't be angry with him.

Ennis walks out with me when the meeting is over. Ruth goes down the hill to Mama, who's talking to Miss Freeman by the car.

"So I'll see you on Saturday," Ennis says.

Right. Our date. I force another smile. "Of course."

"We might have the movies to ourselves," he says. "There's a dance all the white people will be at."

I nod. I'm just glad I don't have to worry about seeing *her* there.

Paulie comes through the door behind us. Ennis shakes his hand.

I wonder how long it'll take Paulie to forget Jefferson. If he'll keep dreaming about being followed for months to come, or if it will all go away once he's living a normal life again.

I want to ask him, but I don't know how. I still don't know how to talk about this, even with my friends. Ruth and I don't talk about it, either, not anymore. We feel it so much we don't want to talk about it. Talking about it means feeling it all over again.

"Did your daddy give you a whupping when you told him?" Ennis asks Paulie.

Even though Ennis was joking, Paulie doesn't smile.

"My father didn't say much," he says. "He said it was my decision. Then he went out to the garage and worked on the car. He was banging on it for the rest of the night so loud I could hardly get to sleep. My mother cried when I told her, though. She said it was because she was so happy. It'd been making her sick, me going to that school every day."

I swallow.

"They never wanted me at Jefferson in the first place," Paulie goes on. "I'm the one who signed up. I didn't know it would be like—well. It doesn't matter now."

Ennis and Paulie start talking about their community baseball league. I stop listening and watch Ennis's face as he talks. I wonder if he'll try to kiss me on Saturday.

It's wrong to French-kiss on a first date, but if he tries I won't stop him. I need to erase what happened.

Ennis is still talking about baseball. "My father is always after me to quit because they won't let us play against the white teams, but I told him if I can't play ball I'll just about lose my mind, and he said— Hey, Sarah, are you all right? You look funny."

That's because I'm still thinking about kissing him.

"I'm fine," I tell him. "I have to go. My mother's waiting for me."

"All right. See you Saturday. Oh, and tomorrow, too, at school, of course."

He smiles at me again. I don't know how he can muster up smiles so easily. I couldn't do that even before *it* happened.

I say goodbye and join Mama and Ruth at the curb. Mama is looking from me to Ennis and back with a smile. That should make me happy. Instead it makes me want to cry again.

This should be the easiest, most natural thing in the world. Going on a date with a boy.

Maybe if I try hard enough it will be.

Mr. Lewis told me to come to the Music room during lunch for my audition.

After I slide the last few pages of our French assignment into Judy's locker, I spend the rest of the morning going over my audition song in my head. It's one I've sung countless times before. I practiced it five times last night after dinner, with Mama playing the piano and reminding me to stand up straight.

I've sung solos in rooms full of people plenty of times, but never in a room full of white people.

I wonder if they'll scream names at me during my audition. If they'll throw things. If they'll shove me into the piano in the middle of a verse.

If my audition had been last week I'd have kept singing no matter what. Even if it was with the last breath I took. I wouldn't have given the white people the satisfaction of seeing me do otherwise.

I'm not sure I'm strong enough for that today.

But when I get to the Music room it's empty.

There are no choir members crowded on the risers. No lines of people waiting to take their turn at the piano. Just a huge vacant room full of crumpled sheet music and the smell of teenagers' sweat.

The desk lamp is shining under Mr. Lewis's office door. I knock.

"Come in," he calls.

I open the door and stand in the threshold, wondering if I misunderstood him about the audition time. Or if I misunderstood altogether and this was all just another trick.

"Ah, Miss Dunbar." Mr. Lewis nods and comes out into the Music room. "Ready for your audition?"

"Yes." I look around at the empty room. "Where are—"

"I decided to hold individual auditions this year. Takes the pressure off some, doesn't it?"

The relief is so strong I want to cry again.

"Do you mind singing along with a recording?" Mr. Lewis moves toward an ancient record player and gestures for me to go to the front of the room. "Normally we'd have a student accompany you on the piano, but everyone's at lunch right now."

"That's fine."

"'Amazing Grace,' right?"

"Yes, sir. That's right."

I clasp my hands in front of my face, close my eyes and say a quick prayer. Then I open my eyes and smile, the way Mama told me to.

The familiar opening notes chime on the record. I take a breath. And I start to sing.

It's strange, singing alone in this big room with no one but Mr. Lewis in front of me. I've never sung here like this, with my full voice. During choir practices I'm always too busy looking around for the people whispering at me or throwing things, but today I let my voice ring out the way I do when I sing in church. Mr. Lewis watches, his chin resting on his hand, his lips pressed together tightly.

When I finish I hold my place and keep smiling, the way you're supposed to when you're waiting for applause, but Mr. Lewis is still making that strange face. I shift my stance and glance behind me.

I nearly jump out of my skin. Three white girls are standing just outside the door, gawking at me.

Then the one in front steps aside, revealing a fourth girl.
Her.

She's fiddling with a gold chain around her neck. She sees me looking and bites her lip, but she doesn't turn away.

Is she here to sabotage my audition? Surely it's too late. Surely Mr. Lewis won't let her do anything. Surely—

The girl at the front of the group turns and runs away, clutching her books to her chest. The other two run after her. Their chattering voices echo down the hall.

I can only make out a few words. One of them is *uppity.*

She goes last after her friends' footsteps are already far down the hall. She's still chewing on her lip as she walks away. As if there's something she wants to say.

Did she tell the others? Is that what they're giggling about?

Why is she acting this way? What's she thinking?

I hate not knowing. Before *it* happened I used to be able to tell what she was thinking just by the look on her face.

"Don't you worry about those girls," Mr. Lewis says. "Curiosity is only to be expected."

Mr. Lewis is either a liar or too naive for his own good.

He rifles through a stack of papers on the piano, pulls out a few pages and passes them to me. It's the sheet music with the vocal melody for "Amazing Grace."

"I'm glad we invited you to audition," he says. "I spoke to Mrs. Pinkard over at Johns, and she told me you were the best singer she'd taught in years. She said I'd be out of my mind if I didn't give you a solo in our spring concert. I see now what she meant."

A solo? In the spring concert? The white people will have my head.

But I remember what Daddy said. I can't let him down.

"Thank you, sir," I say.

He nods and scribbles something onto a notepad.

"We'll have you reprise that performance. With a pianist accompanying you, of course."

I nod. It's done.

The night of the concert may well be my last night at this school.

If I even make it until then. Once word gets out that I've been assigned a solo, the white people will never leave me alone. I'll have to be constantly looking out for baseballs and worse.

I turn to go. Mr. Lewis calls after me when I've got my hand on the door.

"By the way, Miss Dunbar? You should be very proud. It took a lot of courage for you to do this."

I drop my eyes to the ground and thank him. Then I hurry down the hall.

Mr. Lewis doesn't know the first thing about me.

I can't ever be proud of myself again.

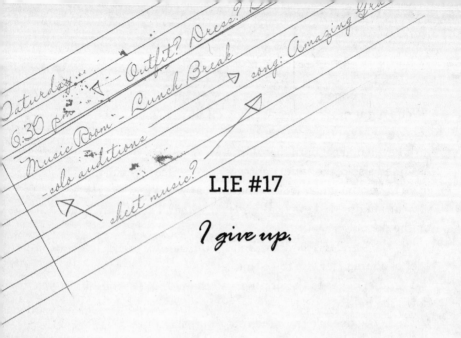

LIE #17

I give up.

"I DON'T KNOW why you keep your hair so long." Mama jerks at my scalp with the curling iron. "Let me take you down to see Estelle. She'll give you one of those pretty shorter styles like your friend Frances has."

"I like it this way." I grit my teeth for another yank.

"It's so old-fashioned." Ruth pats her own short hair. She's sitting at the kitchen table, eavesdropping when she's supposed to be doing her homework. Mama always does our hair in the kitchen so she can heat the combs on the stove. "You've got the longest hair of anyone in school."

"I said, I like it this way."

Mama frowns but doesn't say anything more. Ruth rolls her eyes at me when Mama's back is turned.

The truth is, before *it* happened, I'd been thinking about cutting my hair. It's getting down past my shoulders now. It takes forever to set it. And Ruth is right: it's old-fashioned. None of the other girls at Jefferson have hair past their chins.

But long hair is feminine. Everyone knows that. Until I've fixed this problem I need to be as feminine as I can.

Tonight is my first date with Ennis. My one chance to do this right. I can't take any more risks.

"Yee-haw!" Bobby screams, running through the kitchen in his cowboy hat. All three of us jump, and Mama nearly drops the curling iron on my head.

"Quiet, you!" I call after him.

"Aw, Sarah, let him have some fun," Daddy says, following after Bobby with a toy gun tucked under his arm. Daddy took Bobby to see the Western matinee this afternoon. Before the movie starts, all the boys Bobby's age line up outside the theater in their cowboy outfits and bandannas and toy horses and pretend they're real cowboys. Bobby usually isn't allowed to go, since we have chores on Saturdays, but Mama and Daddy have started letting us out of chores more often these past few months. Except me, with my month's worth of laundry.

"Can I go out this afternoon, Mama?" Ruth says. She's noticed our lack of chores, too. "Yvonne and I want to look at the new purses."

"Which new purses?" I say.

"With the round handles."

I know the kind she's talking about. They're all over school. Square pocketbooks with cloth covers and round wooden handles. You can buy different colors and prints to match your outfit.

She has one. All the popular white girls do.

Since when does my little sister want to look like a popular white girl?

"Don't you think you spend enough time with Yvonne as it is?" I say.

"I wasn't asking *you.*" Ruth glares.

"Of course you can go out shopping, honey," Mama says. "Do you have enough money left from your allowance?"

"I think so."

Now Mama's ignoring me, too.

I'm tired of my family.

I'm tired of having to lie to everyone.

"Did Ruth tell you what she did at school yesterday?" I ask Mama. Ruth's chin jerks up. She shakes her head for me to stop. Maybe now she'll think twice about talking back to me. "She went right up to a gang of girls who were picking on Yvonne and said they were white trash."

Mama bites her lip.

Ruth glares at me, but she should know better than to do stupid things like that. Bo's gang went after her on the second day of school, just because she talked to a white girl in the locker room. That time Ruth wasn't even being rude—all she did was tap the girl on the shoulder and tell her that her slip was showing, but the girl didn't even listen. After class she told her boyfriend Ruth had come up to her. That boy told his friends, and the next thing we knew, it was all over school that Ruth had told a white girl she "smelled like cow shit." I don't think Ruth has ever said the word *shit* in her life.

Lord knows what could've happened to Ruth in the hall that day if *she* hadn't stepped in.

And Lord knows what *she* even did that for. I used to think it meant so much. No matter how many awful things she said, I always remembered what she'd done that day. I was so convinced that day was proof that she wasn't what she seemed to be. When it must've all been part of the same game she'd been playing the whole time.

"Well?" I ask Mama. "Aren't you going to punish Ruth?"

"Ruthie, you know better than to use terms like that," Mama says. "You should ask forgiveness when you say your prayers tonight."

"That's it?" If I wasn't sitting at the end of a hot iron right now I'd jump out of my seat. "Think what could've happened if those girls had turned around and fought back! We aren't supposed to talk back to the white people, it's rule number one!"

"Stop being such a know-it-all," Ruth says. "I can think for myself."

"No you can't. Not if you don't see why that was a stupid thing to do. You're just too immature and spoiled to understand it."

"Quiet, both of you," Mama says. "I can barely hear myself think. Now keep it down while I go get the hairpins."

We nod as Mama goes up the stairs.

"You think Yvonne's not good enough to be my friend," Ruth whispers. "Bet it's because she lives in New Town."

"I didn't say that!" I struggle to keep my voice down. "Look, you need to be more careful. You can't always be watching out for Yvonne. You have to take care of yourself."

"So I'm supposed to just sit there when people say things like that about my best friend?" Ruth bites her lip. "You should've heard. It was awful. About her father and her mother and how under her clothes she was probably covered in—I can't say it. It was horrible."

I sigh. I try my hardest not to listen when the white people at school talk about us, but I know the kinds of things they say. How we don't bathe. How we have hooves. How we bleed dirty black blood.

"You should pray for her," I say. "That's the best help you can give."

"That's not enough. She's my friend and I'm going to do what's right. You'd do the same thing. Or the old you would have, anyway."

I sit back, stunned. She doesn't think I'd stand up for my friends anymore?

That's not true. I tried to help Paulie in Study Hall that day, even though I got detention for it.

I suppose she's partly right. Last year I wouldn't have kept walking if I'd heard people saying nasty things about my friend.

I wouldn't have called them white trash, either, but I'd have tried to help.

Now it takes all the energy I have to keep walking in the first place. When it would be so much easier to just sit down on the floor and give up altogether.

Last week Bo and his gang finally figured out the routes I was taking to see Ruth between classes. Now, wherever I go, at least three of them are always in my way. They stand shoulder to shoulder, blocking the hall when I approach. If I try to go around them they'll shuffle over to that side of the hall. If I try to go back they shuffle behind me.

They always keep straight faces at first, but before long one of them will snicker. Then the others will join in. Then people watching us will start laughing, too. Soon the whole hall is full of white people laughing at me.

Twice that first day I didn't make it back to my own classes before the tardy bell. When I brought the detention slips to Mama and Daddy to sign I got a lecture about how I was setting a shameful example for the rest of the group.

I'm used to detention now. It's only one more hour to get through.

The first time I had detention it was me, Chuck, two of the younger Negro boys and a roomful of white greasers with sideburns and hair slicked back with Brylcreem. Those boys are too poor to be part of Bo and Eddie's gang, but just as mean. They spent the hour throwing bottle caps at us, trying to spin them at the right angle so the metal would slice into our skin. When we were finally dismissed, the teacher left first. Four of the greasers surrounded my desk before I could get up. One said, "Where you think you're going, coon?"

While I was still calculating what to do—whether I could escape by crawling under the desk or if that would only make it easier for the boys to catch me—Chuck pushed the smallest of the boys out of the way, grabbed my arm and hauled me out of

the room. We ran down the hall and were out of the building before we realized they hadn't even bothered to chase us.

After that day, the greasers didn't try to stop me from leaving. They settled for throwing things. Last time one of them lit
a ball of paper with a match and was about to let it fly when the
teacher saw and made him put it out.

My life doesn't feel like my life anymore. The girl I was last
year, when I went to Johns, might as well have been some other
person. A distant cousin. Or someone I saw in a movie once.

Mama comes back into the room with a fistful of hair pins.
She unwinds the last curl from the hot iron, pins my hair and
says, "Well you'll look pretty for your date, long hair or not. Go
look in the mirror."

I go, with Ruth trailing after me. We stand in front of the hall
mirror. Mama's done a good job. My hair is falling in soft curls
around my face.

"Want to borrow some lipstick?" Ruth whispers.

"What are you doing with lipstick?" Ruth and I aren't allowed
to wear makeup until we're eighteen.

"Shh! I don't want Mama to know."

"Well, where did you get it?"

"It's Yvonne's."

"I'm telling you, that girl's a bad influence."

"Oh, you're worse than Mama."

I roll my eyes. Ruth rolls hers back.

"What color is it?" I finally say.

Ruth laughs and leads me up to our room.

The lipstick is a dark, dark red. The kind Hollywood stars
wear. Not a shade good girls in Davisburg wear to the movies.
I try it on anyway and gaze at my reflection in the mirror.

I don't look sick. I certainly don't look like *that* kind of girl.

What does that kind of girl look like, anyway?

I wouldn't know. I've never seen another girl like me.

"Are you going to kiss Ennis?" Ruth asks, startling me into a blush.

"It isn't right to kiss on the first date," I say. Even though I'm planning to do exactly that.

"That's old-fashioned, too. Everyone does it now."

"Who's everyone? Yvonne?"

Ruth shrugs.

I turn around. "I certainly hope *you* haven't kissed anyone yet."

"No, but I would. If I was out with a boy I wanted to kiss. Besides, kissing isn't so bad, as long as you stop there. You remember what Great-Aunt Mabel always said—just keep your skirt down and your panties up."

I start to laugh, but I stop myself in time. Sometimes I can't believe Ruth and I are sisters. I would never have said anything like that when I was her age.

"*Is* there a boy you want to kiss?" I say.

Ruth shrugs again, but the corner of her lip curls up.

"Who is it?" I shouldn't encourage her by talking about it, but I can't help it. It's sweet to think of my little sister liking a boy.

She shrugs again. "It doesn't matter. He already has a girl."

"That's probably for the best. You're too young to date. Besides, people will talk about you if you go around kissing everyone. And boys won't treat you right, either."

"I didn't say I wanted to go around kissing everyone. Just that I don't see what's so bad about kissing *someone*. If he's a nice boy, and you like him."

"What's bad is you get a reputation. And your reputation sticks with you forever. Remember Minnie Moore?"

Ruth nods. Minnie was in my class back at Johns. Someone saw her kissing Bucky Robinson in a car after the Harvest Dance junior year. It might not have been so bad, except her date for the dance had been George King.

By the next day everyone at school knew Minnie was fast.

Now the only boys she can get dates with are the ones who've already left school and are working out on the tobacco farms. And everyone says those boys only date her for one reason.

"I know," Ruth says. "I just think if you like someone enough you shouldn't have to worry so much about what other people think. Shouldn't it be about you and him being happy with each other?"

I wipe off my lipstick and send Ruth back downstairs.

When she's gone I put on my garter belt and hose, my dark blue dress, and the one-and-a-half-inch heels I only wear on special occasions. After dinner Daddy gives me a dollar, the way he always does before dates "in case the young man needs gas money." I've told him a hundred times no decent boy would ever take money from a girl on a date, even if it meant hitchhiking to the theater.

At six-thirty on the dot the doorbell rings. Mama shoos Ruth and Bobby upstairs and Daddy lets Ennis in the front door. Ennis says hello to Daddy, then smiles at me. He's wearing his plaid button-down, creased brown pants and just-shined shoes.

It's awkward, the way it always is on a first date. Even though Mama and Daddy have met Ennis dozens of times before, and even though they've known his parents for years, Daddy still looks Ennis up and down like he's a stranger.

Finally Mama steps in. "I made some lemonade. Would you like a glass?"

"That sounds wonderful, thank you, Mrs. Dunbar, ma'am."

Mama smiles at Ennis's politeness. Even Daddy stops frowning. I knew this was a good idea.

We sit in the living room. Mama goes to the kitchen to get the lemonade.

"So, Ennis, how are things going at Jefferson?" Daddy asks.

Ugh. I wish we could talk about anything but school.

I can tell from the way Ennis hesitates that he doesn't want to talk about it, either. Finally he says, "We're getting by. I have to say, sir, your daughters are examples to us all. They've been handling it so well. And with Sarah singing in the spring concert, everyone is just so proud."

I cringe. That was too much. I try to signal Ennis with my eyes to cut it out.

Daddy smiles at him. "Well, we're awfully proud of her, too."

"Now, Robert," Mama says, coming in with a pitcher. "Can't you see you're embarrassing poor Sarah."

Mama asks Ennis a question about his mother's flower beds. Soon they're talking about daffodils and Daddy is taking out his newspaper.

I cough and nod toward the clock over the mantel. Mama nods back and everyone stands up to say goodbye. Daddy shakes Ennis's hand. Ennis helps me with my coat, and suddenly we're outside. Alone.

Ennis opens the car door for me and gives me that same smile he's been smiling ever since school started.

I can do this. I can make myself like Ennis as much as he seems to like me.

When we get to the theater, it's clear Ennis was right. None of the white people from school are here. Instead there are white kids from the high school over in Fairfield, where they don't have a movie theater. Some kids from Johns are here, too.

Girls always stand off to the side while their dates line up for tickets, so I go join the others while I wait for Ennis. Three girls from my old school are already there.

They say hello to me. I say hello back. Then they go back to gossiping, and I twist my hands together and hope Ennis hurries up. I haven't seen these girls in months, and I have no idea what to say to them. Their lives are still the same as always. They barely even see white people most days. They might as well live on a different planet.

While two of them are talking, the other girl, Cookie—her name is Bobbie Jean Cook, but everyone calls her Cookie—keeps looking at me out of the corner of her eye. I pretend not to notice. Then she comes and stands right in front of me.

Cookie is known for picking fights. She's the sort of girl who thinks everyone is looking at her funny, and who isn't afraid to say so. I've always gotten along with her, though. I've always gotten along with everyone.

Not anymore.

"Why are you standing over here in the corner by your lonesome?" Cookie says. "You think you're too good for us now, Sarah Dunbar?"

The other two girls look down, but neither of them argues with Cookie.

"Is that why you never call any of us, or come to our parties or talk to us after church?" Cookie goes on. "Do you think you're white now that you're up at that school?"

"Aw, come on, Cookie," one of the other girls says. "Leave her be."

I want to answer Cookie. The old me would have.

I don't know what to say.

I certainly don't think I'm better than anyone. Not after what I did.

I don't know how to tell her I just don't have the energy to keep up with my old friends anymore. That my life isn't big enough to deal with all the awful things and still fit in everything that used to be important to me, too.

So I just shake my head at Cookie, trying to tell her she's wrong without words. Until Ennis's hand on my elbow saves me.

Ennis greets the girls warmly, and they smile flirty smiles back at him. I smile up at him, too. Now I don't have to make excuses.

Ennis and I say goodbye to Cookie and the others and climb the stairs to the hard wooden seats in the balcony, the Negro section. There's plenty of space available on the main level below us, where the seats have soft upholstery and the ushers sweep the popcorn off the floor after every show, but neither of us says anything about that.

For this one night, I want to forget about color and all the rest of it.

While the movie's running, I almost do. Forget about color, that is. I can't forget about the rest.

The movie is a comedy, and everyone in the theater but me laughs the whole way through. Even Ennis keeps chuckling. Sometimes he'll glance over at me to see if I'm enjoying it, and I try to smile a little. It's a silly movie, about two men who dress up like women and play in a band with Marilyn Monroe, and I don't see what's supposed to be so funny about that. It isn't natural. It isn't Christian.

So I grip the large Coke Ennis bought me and drink it down as fast as I can. The Coke is full of ice and my fingers are freezing, but I don't put down the cup. If I did, Ennis might try to hold my hand. The idea makes me jitter.

I look over at him from time to time. His eyes crinkle when he laughs.

This is what it will be like when we go steady. Every week we'll come to the movies and sit in the balcony drinking Cokes. He'll come over to my house for dinner sometimes, and he and Daddy will talk about the news. This summer we'll go swimming at the creek and sit together at the church barbecues.

Next year, when we're at college together, he'll take me out to dinner at fancy restaurants in Washington. And later, when we're married, he'll—

Married.

Married.

Well, yes, of course. I'm supposed to be thinking more about marriage and children. My future.

But thinking about it alone in my bedroom is a different thing altogether from thinking about it next to a boy with a very nice smile in a very dark movie theater.

I like Ennis well enough, but marriage? What do I even know about marriage?

Marriage is being a good wife. Being there to support your husband. Having dinner on the table when he comes home from work. Raising respectful children. Keeping a pleasant home.

It's what Mama does. When one of us has a problem, Mama always has the answer. When Daddy gets frustrated with work or with the government, Mama's there to calm him down.

That's what marriage is. Being responsible. Always knowing what to do.

I never know what to do anymore. I don't think I ever will.

Marriage means other things, too. Kissing. And other things that come after kissing.

Ennis is a nice boy. I like it when he smiles at me. But the idea of kissing him doesn't make my heart race in my chest, the way the magazines and novels say is supposed to happen.

And to think about other—things—I—

I don't want to think about *things* with Ennis.

I close my eyes, trying to steady myself. Before I realize it, I'm thinking about *her*. I'm thinking about the slope of her neck above her blouse collar. I'm thinking about the way her hips swing when she walks. I'm thinking about the way she looked at me that day right before I—

Maybe I don't have to marry Ennis. Maybe I don't have to marry anyone. Maybe I'll just—

What? What future is there without a husband and children? Nothing. There's nothing.

Normal girls don't think this way. Normal girls hold their dates' hands and smile back at them and—

Her face floats before my eyes again.

I bolt out of my seat.

Ennis stands up, too. Behind us someone whispers, "Out of the way!"

"I'll be right back," I whisper to Ennis, willing my voice not to tremble along with the rest of me. He nods and sits back down, laughing at something Marilyn Monroe said.

I edge out of the row. I need to be away from these cramped seats. And I need to go to the bathroom, thanks to all that Coke.

As I'm closing the door to the theater behind me I hear one of the men on-screen saying, "Now and then Mother Nature throws somebody a dirty curve. Something goes wrong inside." Everyone laughs.

I wonder if that's what happened to me.

Mama and Daddy don't like us to use colored bathrooms. They say we should come home and use the bathroom there instead, but it's not as if I can run home in the middle of a date.

I push open the door to the colored women's room. The first thing I notice is the smell. No one has cleaned this bathroom in a long time. The trash can is overflowing. And when I get into a stall, the toilet paper is the same rough kind we had at my old school. I hadn't even realized I'd gotten used to the softer stuff.

When I come out to wash my hands I watch the other women lined up in front of the mirror, fixing their hair and talking to their friends. Gossiping, like the girls outside.

I wonder what it is about me that makes me care about things like having a dirty bathroom or sitting in those hard wooden balcony seats. None of these women by the sink seem to care much. They're busy. Thinking about their families. Their jobs. Their real lives.

They all look a lot happier than I feel right now.

Why do I think I deserve anything different than anyone else? What am I doing going to Jefferson, getting yelled at in the halls, having to worry about my little sister's safety all day long?

What's the *point* of it all?

I envy these women. I bet none of them ever doubted whether they should get married. I'm sure none of *them* ever had any unnatural feelings.

For the rest of the movie I sit with my arms folded tightly

across my chest. When Ennis offers me his popcorn I shake my head without looking at him.

Even the movie seems determined to make me feel worse. At the very end one of the men kisses Marilyn Monroe in front of everyone while he's still dressed as a woman. Everyone in the movie gasps and screams, and everyone in the theater gasps and screams and laughs harder than ever. I bite my thumbnail so hard I nearly rip it off.

Gasping. Screaming. Laughing. That's how you're supposed to react to things like *that*.

"Did you like the movie?" Ennis asks as we're waiting to leave the theater.

"I thought it was ridiculous," I say. "As if anyone would let two men go around dressed like that. It's not right. They should've thrown them both in jail."

Ennis raises his eyebrows. "I think it was meant to be a joke."

"It's not a very good joke, then."

He shakes his head. "All right. Next time we'll see a Western."

I nod, and Ennis laughs again.

I should be glad he's not angry at me for disagreeing with him. I should be happy he's mentioned going on another date.

I can't feel any of the things I'm supposed to feel.

Ennis asks if I'm hungry. I say yes because boys only ask you that if *they're* hungry. He drives us to Stud's Diner in Davis Heights.

We all used to go to Stud's every day after school, but I haven't been there since school started this year.

Walking in the door feels like stepping back in time. Before we've made it three feet, there are people all around us. Ennis smiles and says hello and shakes the boys' hands.

I gaze around. Cookie isn't here, thank the Lord, but I still recognize every face I see. They're all from another world.

Frances, my best friend from Johns, is here with Bucky Robinson. She's wearing his class ring. I didn't know they were going steady.

I wanted to stay in touch with my old friends. I really did. But Cookie's right. I haven't done much more than say hello in the church hallways. After my first week at Jefferson I tried to call Frances and some of the others a few times. I even went over to Frances's house once with some other girls to listen to records after school.

But it was nothing like last year. They only wanted to ask me what Jefferson was like. And I didn't want to tell them. My friends were nice about it, but I didn't want to relive it all again just to satisfy their curiosity.

Since then I've only talked to Frances a couple of times. After my first few weeks at Jefferson I just couldn't bear the thought of picking up the phone and facing a million questions from my friends. After another few weeks had gone by, they stopped calling me, too.

Frances smiles and says hello. I say hello back. I can barely hear myself over the noise in my head.

"Hi there, Sarah," a boy says. I blink in surprise. It's Alvin, my old boyfriend, smiling up at me. I murmur hello.

Frances pulls me to one side. "You're going with Ennis now? That's wonderful. He's a doll."

I shake my head. "This is our first date."

"Well, good luck. You know he went out with Rose Marie for two months last year and never asked her to go steady. You've got to be careful."

Frances and Bucky lead Ennis and me to a group of tables at the back. Everyone's in couples. There are no groups of girls sitting together, the way we used to do when we were juniors. Everything is so much more serious now.

I wonder if Frances will marry Bucky Robinson. Isn't that what going steady is for? That's what all this is about, isn't it?

A few years from now everyone sitting here will be married.

The girls will have babies they'll push around in carriages. The boys will wear neckties or work shirts every day and grill hot dogs every summer.

That's how it's always been. It's what I've always wanted. Until this week it never occurred to me to question it.

Ennis and I sit down at the only empty table and order milk shakes. Then we look at each other, each of us biting our lips in turn. Ennis coughs and pulls a paper napkin out of the dispenser, crumpling it into a ball.

It's funny. At school Ennis and I talk every day, but now I have no idea what to say to him.

I never used to have this problem with *her*. We always had plenty to say, even if we were shouting it. Even when she was wrong, there was a certain pleasure in correcting her. In seeing the way her face creased when she tried to think of how to answer me.

Talking to her came naturally. Like breathing.

Except nothing about my time with *her* was natural. Besides, I shouldn't be thinking about it now. I should be focusing on Ennis. I have to make sure he really likes me. I should talk about things he's interested in.

"Have you seen a lot of movies with Tony Curtis?" I ask him.

Ennis smiles and drops his napkin ball. "A few. *The Defiant Ones* was my favorite. Have you seen it?"

I shake my head, and Ennis launches into the story of the movie. His face gets more animated the longer he goes on.

I could love him. I think.

"Who are these two strangers?" another familiar voice says.

"Paulie!" I jump out of my seat. It's only been a day since I saw him last, but it feels like years. Ennis gets up, too. "How are you liking it back at Johns?"

"It's great." Paulie is smiling bigger than I've seen him smile all year. "It's really, really great."

"It's as if he never left," says the junior girl with him, Shirley

Battle. "Except all anyone talks about anymore is what a hero he is, for all of us."

Paulie grins and drops his head.

Cookie and her friends didn't seem to think I was any sort of hero.

"I wish Chuck were here, too," I say. "Then it would be a real reunion."

Paulie catches Ennis's eye and snickers. Ennis starts to smile, then bites his cheek. I hate it when boys have private jokes.

"I don't think we'll be seeing Chuck," Ennis says. "He doesn't come to Stud's on Saturday nights much anymore."

"Not when he's got something better to do," Paulie says, chuckling. "With somebody he can't bring down to old Stud's."

Ennis smacks Paulie's arm, but he's laughing, too. I roll my eyes and sip my milk shake.

Ennis notices I'm bored and changes the subject. "Have try-outs started?" he asks Paulie.

"Next week," Paulie says. "We'll miss you this year. With you gone, everybody's saying Alvin will wind up pitching."

Ennis grits his teeth. Alvin was the relief pitcher last year. Every time he went in for Ennis we could count on the other team scoring at least two runs.

Jefferson's baseball tryouts were last week. Bo Nash is the pitcher again this year. None of the Negro boys tried out. They didn't want a beating.

Paulie and Shirley say goodbye and go to sit with Frances and Bucky. Ennis keeps talking about movies, but he doesn't seem to care as much as he did before Paulie came around.

Ennis walks me to my door at the end of the night. I'm so nervous I have to clasp my hands together to keep them from shaking.

This is it. This is when I should let him kiss me.

But when we get to that top step, I know inside it's already over.

I can't do it. Not because of the no-kissing-on-the-first-date rule—that's silly, like Ruth said—but because it's just not right.

Ennis is a nice boy, but I'm not a nice girl.

I can't let him get mixed up with someone like me. Not until I've fixed this.

So I stand as far away from him as I can and say, in my best church voice, "Thank you for the evening. I had a lovely time."

Ennis takes a step back. "You're welcome. So did I."

I swallow. "I do hope you have a safe drive home."

"Thank you." He swallows, too.

This is when he'll ask me for a second date. If he wants to.

"Do you, ah—" He stops, looking at me.

I look back at him with my best church smile.

"I suppose I'll see you on Monday," he says instead.

My heart flips with relief. Disappointment. Fear.

What if I never get another chance like this? What if I spend years looking back on this moment, wishing I'd fixed everything the one time I could?

I can't let that time with *her* be the last time I ever kiss someone.

I can't let her win.

But Ennis is already turning back toward the street.

"Wait!" I say.

He turns back.

"I, ah—"

I don't know how to get a boy to kiss me. I try to think of how it goes in the romance stories I steal off Ruth's bookshelf, but I can't remember any of them now. Ennis looks at me queerly, as if I have food on my nose.

So I stand up as high as I can on my tiptoes, and I kiss *him*.

It's wrong. It's all wrong. It's not how things are supposed to go.

Girls don't kiss boys.

But that's not why this doesn't feel right.

Ennis is as shocked as I am. He stumbles on the step before he bends down to kiss me back. For a moment we just stand there with our lips pressed together. My neck hurts from straining up so far.

Aside from that, I don't feel...anything.

It didn't work.

I'm still thinking about *her*.

I'm not fixable.

I step back, putting a full foot of space between us. I want to wipe my mouth off.

"Next Friday," Ennis says in a rush. "Do you want to go out next Friday?"

"Yes!" I say.

I can't believe he hasn't noticed I'm not normal yet. It might as well be written all over my face in bright red paint.

"All right." He pinches the bridge of his nose. "That's good. I'll, ah, see you at school."

He walks back down the steps, shaking his head as though he's dizzy.

I squeeze my eyes shut to keep from crying.

I can try harder. I can spend the rest of my life trying.

I'll only be fooling myself.

I'll never be able to do this right.

LIE #18

I hate her.

REVEREND TILLMAN TALKS a lot about Hell.

He says Hell is a prison of endless misery. Universal damnation. Hissing, burning torment that never ends, where infidels and sinners suffer for all eternity.

He says the wickedest sinners go into the deepest belly of Hell, to a lake of fire and brimstone. Just standing on the rim of that lake, looking down on the burning and the screaming and the torment, would be enough to drive a sane man to madness.

He says none of us on Earth can fathom the true torments of Hell.

I don't know as much about Hell as Reverend Tillman, but I know Reverend Tillman has never been inside Jefferson High School.

Because surely Hell must be worse than this. Something has to be.

It's been nearly four months since we first came to Jefferson. Still, every day, when I walk out of that school building, my heart pounds and my hands tremble. Every day, there's a roaring in my ears no voice can penetrate.

Maybe God placed me at Jefferson to show me the wages of my sin. But that doesn't explain why the others are here, too.

Ruth doesn't deserve to be here. She hates it all as much as I do, but she's better at pretending. When we step into the parking lot each morning and wait for that first round of shouts, Ruth smiles her broadest smile at the white people, daring them to make her stop. She keeps smiling until we get inside. Then she links arms with Yvonne and sets off for their Homeroom, strutting down the hall in their matching cardigans, pleated skirts and knee socks, just like the matched sets all the popular white girls wear. They ignore the shouts of "nigger" that follow everywhere they go.

Ruth begged and begged me to stop following her around all day, and I finally gave in. None of us has actually been hurt since Paulie left, but the name-calling is still as bad as ever, and I still look over my shoulder constantly to see who's following me.

The problem is, looking over my shoulder makes me that much more likely to catch *her* eye by accident.

It's been five weeks since that afternoon. Sometimes I'll go hours at a stretch without thinking about what happened. One Saturday I almost went the whole afternoon before *her* face popped into my mind.

Nighttime is always the worst. Because she's there when I dream.

Sitting on a crate in the back room at Bailey's. Tossing her hair in French class. Bending over a book, her lip twitching as she thinks of something funny. In the dreams there's always a light beaming down that makes her hair shine, her cheeks glow, her eyes twinkle.

The worst part—the part that makes me want to cry from the shame—is that in my sleep, when I see her, I'm *happy*.

When I first start to wake up, in that strange in-between place where I'm still half dreaming, she'll still be there, smiling at me.

And I'll be smiling back at her.

Then I shake myself awake and remember that *she* doesn't make me happy. She's the worst thing that's ever happened to me.

I can't smile at her. Even when I'm dreaming.

Then I get out of bed, go out into the world and play the part of a normal girl. Even though sooner or later, someone is bound to see me for the imposter I really am.

I can make all this go away. I just need to try harder.

So on our second date I let Ennis kiss me again. We did it in the car that time, so we wouldn't have to worry about my parents seeing through the window.

It was all right, I guess. It didn't feel all swooshy-stomach, fancy-music, swirly-backdrop, like when the boy and the girl kiss at the end of the movie. It felt awkward, and a little boring. I couldn't tell how long we ought to sit there with our lips pressed together, so after a minute I pulled away and said I had to go inside. He didn't look especially disappointed, so maybe that's how kissing between boys and girls is supposed to go. If that's so, then I don't see what all the fuss is about.

Ennis and I have gone out a few other times since then, and we've kissed every time. Usually only for a second, to say goodnight. That's fine with me. I think kissing could just be for special occasions, really.

Ennis walks me to most of my classes now, and carries my books in the halls. He hasn't asked me to go steady yet. I don't really mind that, either.

But I feel terrible for lying to him. If Ennis knew what I was really like he'd want nothing to do with me.

Some days at school I'll catch a glimpse of *her* by accident. That only makes it worse.

I still listen for the whispers in the hall that would mean she's told them about me, but so far, there's been nothing. Just the usual taunts of "nigger" and spittle on my clothes.

She must be biding her time. Trying to catch me off guard. Whatever she's got in mind, it won't work.

I wish I knew what she was thinking, though. I miss knowing what's going on in her head.

When I glance in her direction in the halls, she always turns away. But sometimes she'll look back again after a minute. As if she's trying to catch my eye. Trying to say—something. I don't know what.

Choir practice is the worst of all. She's always right in the front row, where I can't help but look at her.

During our last practice, Mr. Lewis asked her to sing a solo verse so the other girls could hear it done properly. It was the first time I'd heard her sing. She's good. As good as I am. Maybe better.

What's strange is, even though the other girls in the choir pick on me all through rehearsal, *she* never says a thing. It's as though she doesn't even know I'm there.

The others try to trip me on my way to the risers. Girls whisper hateful things in my ear when Mr. Lewis isn't paying attention and stick torn-up bits of paper in my hair. When I climb down after practice, trash falls from my hair like confetti.

Some of the girls leave me alone. They just stare at me. Their looks range from curiosity to disgust to loathing.

But *she* never looks my way at all.

Sometimes, I wish she'd look.

Only for a second. Just so I'd know she remembers, too. That I didn't imagine the whole thing.

She'll have to look at me before long, though.

Mr. Lewis announced the lineup for our spring concert two weeks ago. All three sections of the choir will be performing with the band. There will be three soloists, one from each section. A sophomore girl will solo for the Glee Club, I'll solo for the

Girls' Ensemble and *she* will solo for the Balladeers. Then the three of us will lead the full choir in the last song of the show.

After that announcement the other girls stopped giving me curious looks. Instead all their looks were murderous.

Except hers. She acted as though she hadn't even heard.

Sometimes I think the girl I see at school now can't possibly be the same one I sat with every afternoon at Bailey's. That girl wouldn't have ignored me during the announcement. She'd have been shooting me the angriest look of all. Then she'd have written an editorial calling it the greatest travesty of our time.

Her editorial that week called for better-quality napkins in the cafeteria.

I wish there were someone I could talk to about this. Not *that* part, of course, but the rest of it. The hateful looks from the choir. The way it felt when I got to school the day after the announcement about the solos and saw the word *Nigger* scrawled across my locker in bright red lipstick. But there's no one.

I still talk to Ennis at lunch, but things are different between us now that we've been going on dates. He doesn't tell me what he really thinks about things anymore. He says what he thinks I want to hear. Whenever I manage a smile for him, he gives me a wide grin back, like he's won a prize at a county fair.

I can't talk to Mama, either. Whenever I say anything about school, she looks so worried and upset it makes me worried and upset, too, and I finally give up and go stare at my homework.

I could talk to Ruth, but Ruth hates talking about school. She's forbidden us from asking her about it at the dinner table. When she's on the phone with Yvonne they only talk about which boys they think are nice and who might be at Stud's Diner that weekend and what dress they liked most in the latest *Seventeen*.

And now it's too late. The concert is tomorrow.

Our last practice will be after school today, with the full choir and the band. The three soloists will be singing in front of the whole group for the first time.

I need to be ready. I need to sing better than these people have ever heard anyone sing before, white or Negro.

But I can't focus. I can't think at all. Because I'm in Math class, keeping my head tilted so I won't see *her,* and trying to ignore the tiny balls of paper bouncing off my back. Mrs. Gruber is passing back our tests from Tuesday and pretending not to see the trash sailing past her from the boys' desks.

"See me after class," she says when she passes me, not bothering to give me my test. I nod. It hurts to be polite to Mrs. Gruber now that Paulie's gone.

I go up to her desk after class. She waits until everyone else is gone before she slams my test paper down on the tabletop.

"Maybe at your old school this was considered acceptable," she says. "Here you won't get away with it."

I blink. "Pardon? Ma'am?"

She stabs the paper with her fingernail. "This is algebra. If you don't solve the problems you can't get the answers."

Oh. We're supposed to show our work on these tests. I only wrote the solutions.

But the test was so easy. I learned all of this two years ago.

And I was so tired that day. I'd been up half the night, slipping in and out of dreams.

Besides, the morning of the test we'd had an air raid drill during Homeroom. When we'd filed into the hall and crouched down to duck and cover against the wall, someone shoved me into a locker so hard I slammed my head against the combination lock. For the rest of the morning I saw stars every time I closed my eyes. It left me in no mood to do any more work than I had to.

I'm about to explain and apologize when Mrs. Gruber says, "Now tell me who you copied."

I gape at her.

She can't be serious. How could I have copied anyone's test? *Why* would I?

"I didn't copy anyone," I say.

"I've been teaching for twenty-five years. I've seen dozens of students cheat. Just tell me whose paper you looked at."

"I didn't look at anyone's!" I take a deep breath. If I lose my temper this will only get worse. "I swear it's the truth, ma'am."

She sniffs. "I saw you looking at Linda Hairston."

"I didn't look at *her!* I would never!" I swallow. Was *this* her plan? How? Why? "Did she say something about me?"

Mrs. Gruber sniffs again. "She didn't need to. I know what I saw. And the two of you got exactly the same grade on the test."

She means we both got a *perfect* grade.

Then I remember. On Tuesday morning I did glance back at her seat. She'd been resting her chin on her hand, tugging on a lock of hair, her eyes falling closed as she bent her head over her paper. She looked as if she'd been up half the night, too.

"I didn't copy anyone," I tell Mrs. Gruber. "I knew the solutions to the problems. Anyway, she sits on the other side of the room from me, so I couldn't have seen her paper in the first place. Please, let me retake the test. I'll write out all the steps this time."

She sighs. Probably planning to send me to the principal again.

Instead she rolls her eyes. "Fine. You get one chance. Today, after school."

I'm so surprised it takes me a minute to realize the problem.

"Could I do it at lunch instead?" I ask. "Today after school is our last choir practice before the concert, and—"

"One chance," she repeats. "Or you'll get a zero on the test, and you can tell the principal why you failed."

Cheating would get me expelled for sure. A white student might get away with a few days' suspension, since there's no proof, but I'm not a white student.

So I nod and swallow hard before I can say what I'm thinking.

I find Mr. Lewis at lunch and tell him about the test. He frowns at me, but he nods. He says he'll move the solo rehearsals until the end of the practice period so I have time to make it. He frowns again as I'm leaving, like he's about to say something else, but he just turns away.

I still think Mr. Lewis might be all right, but it's so hard to tell with anyone at this school.

After school I race through the test, which is all kids' stuff anyway, and wait while Mrs. Gruber grades it. She takes her time, comparing each question to the teacher's manual and complaining that my handwriting isn't neat enough on the equations. Finally she sighs again and tells me that I passed, and I should leave now.

I got another perfect score on that test. And she knows it.

Jesus taught us to love our enemies, but I don't think I'll ever be able to love Mrs. Gruber.

I'm forty minutes late to rehearsal. When I get there the Boys' Ensemble is finishing the run-through of their last song, "Night and Day." The room is sweltering and packed with people. The students look tired and annoyed. Mr. Lewis's hair is frazzled as he conducts the final notes.

"Lovely, lovely!" he calls as the song ends and the boys step down from their risers. "That'll do it, except for—" He sees me in the doorway. "Miss Dunbar! Good to see you. All right, everyone, we'll run through the solos and 'And Now Another Day Is Gone' and that'll be the end."

Everyone who didn't glare at me as soon as I showed up in the doorway is glaring now.

Mr. Lewis gestures for me to stand next to the piano at the front of the room. I move forward through the crowd, pretending I have blinders on either side of my face, trying not to think about all those eyes on me. Judy is watching from the horn section of the band, shaking her head at me the way she always does now.

She is already up front, in the spot right next to mine. She's the only person in the room who isn't looking at me.

When I reach the front and turn to face the room, row after

row of white faces stares back at me. All I see is a wave of anger. I keep my eyes straight ahead so I can't see *her*.

The sophomore soloist, Patricia Saunders, comes to stand on my other side. I can tell she's nervous from the way she's clasping her elbows. I smile at her. She blinks wide in surprise, then smiles back.

"Tomorrow night we'll begin with Miss Hairston's solo, since the Balladeers will still be onstage," Mr. Lewis says. "Then Miss Dunbar will perform, then Miss Saunders and then we'll bring all three choirs back out. For today we'll have the two piano pieces first. Mr. Russell, let's start with 'Come Thou Fount,' please."

I gulp when I recognize Gary Russell, the boy playing the piano. He's in Bo and Eddie's gang of friends. He's the one who lost fifty cents when Bo hit Paulie with the baseball.

Gary starts playing, and Patricia sings her solo. She's very good, and she sounds even better when she relaxes after the first verse. After she's done everyone in the room claps, and a few boys whistle in approval. I clap and smile at her again. This time, her smile back looks real.

"That was marvelous, Patricia," Mr. Lewis says. "Gary, let's move straight to 'Amazing Grace.'"

Gary checks to make sure Mr. Lewis can't see his face. Then he crosses his eyes and sticks out his tongue at me before he drops his hands to the piano keys.

He's so childish. They all are.

Maybe if I tell myself that enough times, this sort of thing will stop bothering me so much.

I close my eyes to center myself, then open them and smile as I sing the opening notes.

I watch the white faces watching me. They're all staring as hatefully as ever. Except Mr. Lewis. He's wearing his broadest smile.

I can feel *her* standing next to me, but I don't look at her. I couldn't stand to see her ignoring me again.

I finish the song, still smiling. A few seconds pass. Mr. Lewis starts to clap. Everyone else just stands there.

"All right, everyone!" Mr. Lewis finally says. "Miss Dunbar did a very good job! Let's hear it for her!"

He turns to face the rest of the group. The look on his face must be awfully stern because a few people in the front rows clap halfheartedly. I wish Mr. Lewis hadn't done that.

"Now for Miss Hairston's solo," he says. "Everyone, take your positions."

I watch in surprise as the other three girls and four boys in the Balladeers climb back up onto the risers on the other side of the piano. I thought we were all singing solos with only the piano for accompaniment, but the Balladeers have their songbooks out. Some of the other band members are picking up their instruments, too.

Gary and the band members start to play. The Balladeers start to hum. And *she* starts to sing "Ave Maria."

She's good. She's really, really good. She's not quite as good as the visiting choir who performed this song at our church Christmas service two years ago, but when she sings with the rest of the Balladeers in harmony behind her and the band backing her up, she sounds amazing.

She's going to make me look ridiculous at the concert tomorrow. She'll be out on the stage singing the showiest song of the night with a full band and seven of her friends on backup. Then I'll have to follow her, alone, with Gary at the piano making faces at me. Singing a song everyone in that audience will have heard sung a thousand times before. I wonder if she planned it this way.

They finish the song. The room thunders applause. Next to me Patricia has her face in her hands.

We muddle through the closing song with the full choir, and Mr. Lewis dismisses us. I can't wait to get away from everyone. Away from *her* most of all.

But the band members are closer to the door than I am, shoving past me with their instrument cases. Most of them don't say anything to me, but I hear them grumbling about how I was allowed to come late to rehearsal. How it's not fair that first I got a solo and now I'm getting special treatment.

"Nice song, nigger," Eddie Lowe whispers to me on his way down from the Boys' Ensemble risers. Gary is with him, snickering. "I bet they think you sing real good down at the zoo with the other monkeys."

I turn to collect my books, pretending not to hear them.

The room is almost empty when someone taps my shoulder. I jump and start moving fast toward the other side of the room. Every time someone touches my back, I remember lunch on that first day, the milk dripping down my shoulders.

Then a very familiar voice says, "Wait," and I can't help it. I turn around.

It's her.

We're the only two people left in the room. Mr. Lewis is in his office with the door closed. Everyone else is gone, their laughter echoing down the hall.

I don't want to be alone with her. What if it happens again? What if I can't control it?

I turn and walk faster. My hand is on the door when she says, "No, wait, please. It's important, Sarah."

It's so strange to hear her say my name.

I turn around. There are at least twenty feet between us. Surely it should be safe. No one would see us and think—anything.

What could *she* possibly have to say to me? Is she just going to tell me yet again why she hates me? Why I shouldn't be allowed to go to her school, sit at her lunch counter, breathe the same air she does?

Or worse—what if she's here to tell me I'm a freak, and everyone is about to know it?

I can't be in this room with her. I'm risking too much. Just seeing her standing there with her cheeks flushed and her books clasped against her chest feels—it feels—

I want to stay. I want to talk to her.

"I can't," I say, and open the door.

She shakes her head. "This is important. You should know. I heard some of the others talking about tomorrow night. They're going to—"

I shake my head back at her. "I don't want anything to do with any of *them*. Or you. You most of all."

She bites her lip. "But—"

I can't stand this. I can't stand to hear her voice. "Stop it! Leave me alone!"

"Sarah, please—"

I can't.

I slam the door behind me.

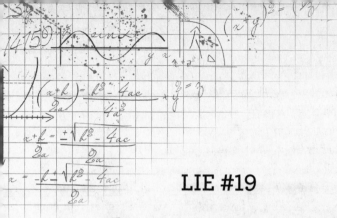

LIE #19

There's no use fighting.

"WILL YOU SIT already?" Ruth says. "You're making me crazy pacing like that."

I sit on my bed. The concert is in an hour. I should be practicing, but I can't bring myself to leave my bedroom. "I'm not pacing."

"You're pacing." Ruth glances up from the diary she's writing in. "And tell me that's not what you're wearing?"

I smooth out my long white dress. We'll wear our choir robes for most of the concert, but Mr. Lewis said the soloists should wear dresses during our songs. I've spent all afternoon starching the dress I wore for last year's Christmas pageant. "Why?"

"This isn't church. No one else is going to be dressed like that. All the other girls will be in high heels and lipstick. You look like you're going to the junior high dance."

I bite my thumb. "How do you know?"

"Trust me." Ruth goes to the closet and rustles through the dresses on my side. She shakes her head as she passes each straight skirt, each solid-colored high-necked collar. "Why are all your clothes so boring?"

"It's called being *mature*," I tell her.

Ruth rolls her eyes. Then she tugs at a piece of purple fabric. "What's this?"

"Oh." I forgot about that dress. After *it* first happened I asked Mama to let me send away for a dress I saw in *Seventeen*. It cost fourteen ninety-five. Mama's mouth dropped open when she saw the price, but when I told her I needed it, that it was *important*, she looked at me for a long time, then nodded.

When it arrived two weeks later, I stuffed the dress in the back of the closet and forgot about it. By then I'd lost my appetite for fancy jewelry and colorful dresses. I didn't want to wear something that would make people look at me. All I wanted was to disappear.

"Here," Ruth says. "You can wear this with Mama's green church shoes."

"I don't know," I say.

Ruth is already unbuttoning the back of my white dress. "If you're going to stand up on a stage in front of a crowd full of angry white people you might as well look pretty while you do it. Here, put on another slip, the neckline on this dress is too low for that one."

It turns out I don't have a slip with a neckline low enough for the *Seventeen* dress. I have to wear an old half-slip under my crinoline petticoat, with my garter belt and hose underneath and only my bra on top. I feel almost naked as Ruth helps me pull the dress over my head.

It's worth it.

The dress is short-sleeved with a flowery spring print—purple, white and green. Much brighter colors than I normally wear. It has a high waist, which Ruth assures me is the latest trend, and a row of tiny buttons running from the collar to the waist. The V-neck shows a full two inches of skin below my collarbone.

With the crinoline the skirt flounced out so far I'm worried my choir robe will look bunchy, but Ruth says the robe is so heavy it'll hang straight down. I'll probably be hot from wearing all that fabric under the stage lights, but at least I won't be shivering from the cold as well as my nerves.

Not that I've had much time to think about my nerves in the flurry of getting dressed. I wonder if Ruth did that on purpose.

"Oh, Sarah," Mama says when I come down the stairs. Daddy's standing off to the side, his eyes on Mama, who's got one hand clenched on the knob of the banister. They must've been in the middle of a conversation. "You look so pretty. Doesn't she, honey?"

Daddy drags his eyes away from Mama, turns to me and smiles. "You do look very pretty, Sarah. Very grown-up indeed."

I smile back at him. Maybe tonight won't be so bad.

Then Daddy squints. "Wait. Are you wearing lipstick?"

I cover my mouth with my hand. It isn't the dark red color Ruth gave me before. Just a light, pretty shade, like the kind Mama wears. I didn't think they'd notice.

"Go wash it off," Daddy says. "You know the rules. No makeup until you've graduated."

I turn to go. I should've known better than to try this. Mama and Daddy are still upset with me for joining choir in the first place, and for all the detentions, and—

"Oh, Robert," Mama says. "It's a special occasion."

I turn back, cautious, in case Daddy contradicts her.

But neither of them is looking at me anymore. They've got their heads bent together.

I back up the stairs and duck behind a corner so they'll think I've gone back to my room.

"It'll be all right," Mama whispers. "We can make it a few more months."

"But a few more months after that, the savings run out," Daddy says. "If Hairston keeps cutting my hours at this rate."

Mama sighs. "If you'd left your name off some of those articles maybe he'd leave your hours alone. It's bad enough that we're on those state NAACP lists. You really think he's going to stop punishing you?"

"I can't let him think I'm afraid of him, Irene."

"Well, Sarah can work this summer. That'll help. And we'll figure something out for the fall."

Work? This summer? Me?

I go to the bathroom and shut the door.

I've heard Mama and Daddy talk this way before. They never stop worrying about money. We paid too much for the house, Mama always says. We live beyond our means. The *Free Press* is one advertiser boycott away from going out of business. The *Gazette* doesn't pay Daddy enough for the work he does.

Now his hours are being cut. By *her* father.

I hunt around for a cloth to take off the lipstick.

I've never had a job before. I'll get one, of course, if Mama and Daddy need me to. Maybe Judy could get me work at Bailey's. I could be a stock girl.

I don't want to work for a man who threw a glass in his trash can because he thought my lips had touched it, but I'm sure Daddy doesn't want to work for a man who writes editorials about how Negroes are scientifically inferior, either. You don't always have a choice.

I pause with the cloth halfway to my lips.

I *like* how I look right now.

I look serious. I look like I matter.

And Daddy was right. I look grown-up.

I put the cloth away and go downstairs.

I'm ready.

The concert is going well so far.

Too well. It's making me anxious.

The topmost rows of the auditorium are packed with brown

faces. From the stage I can see Mama, Daddy, Ruth and Bobby sitting with Chuck and Ennis and their parents. Reverend Tillman, Mr. and Mrs. Mullins and Miss Freeman, our neighbors Mr. and Mrs. Jackson, Mr. and Mrs. Muse, and what looks like half my church choir, plus Frances and her sisters and their parents, plus some other Negroes I don't even know, are all gathered with them. Every last one of them beams down at me as I finish singing with the Girls' Ensemble.

When we're done singing, the Negroes clap harder than anyone else.

I smile at them as we step down from the risers and let the Glee Club climb up for their big song. After this the Balladeers will perform. The solos will be next. First hers, then mine.

I take deep breaths as I step into the wings and pull off my choir robe. I'd like to watch the Glee Club, but I'm too nervous to stand still. Soon, the concert will be over, and we'll all go to a party Frances's parents are throwing at her house to celebrate. I try to think about how much fun it will be, but I can't think about anything but the next five minutes.

Backstage everyone's in clusters, whispering. *She's* in the center of a group of girls wearing deep green Balladeers robes. The Balladeers get the nicest costumes on top of everything else.

I wish I'd waited to see what she was going to tell me at rehearsal yesterday.

But I can't talk to her. I can't be in a room with her. It's too risky.

I have to work to remind myself of that sometimes.

In my dream last night we were in the back room at Bailey's. She smiled at me. It was the same smile I saw her give Coach Pollard one day as he dropped her off.

In the dream I smiled back at her and we touched hands. That was all—just our fingertips stroking each other. I couldn't believe how electric that simple touch felt.

When I woke up this morning my face was burning. I had to

pray harder than I've ever prayed before I could get out of bed. Even then my legs were shaking.

Because the dream didn't feel wrong. It felt the opposite of wrong.

The song ends and the Balladeers take the stage. Six members of the band climb up to play along as the eight singers harmonize.

I imagine what it would be like to be out there with them. To have the best music, the best costumes. To be part of the best school singing group in the state.

But I wouldn't be soloing tonight if I'd been put in the Balladeers. That's something.

"What?" Mr. Lewis says behind me. His voice is sharp with anger. "Where is he? What happened?"

I turn around, but Mr. Lewis is talking to a boy I don't know. The boy shrugs.

"Fine," Mr. Lewis says, lowering his voice. "I'll play it myself. Where's the sheet music?"

The boy shrugs again. Mr. Lewis throws up his hands and storms out the side door.

The Balladeers are almost finished with their song. We'll have to go out onstage in less than a minute.

Patricia, the Glee Club soloist, comes to stand beside me. She looks even more nervous than I feel.

"Don't worry." I smile, trying to forget what I just heard. I can't afford to think about anything but the performance now. "You'll be terrific. You were wonderful in rehearsal yesterday."

She smiles back. "Thank you. So were you."

That's the first time any of the white students have said anything good about my singing. Well, except Judy. And *her*. But they don't count.

The Balladeers are on their last line. They're good, but I don't think they're that much better than my church choir.

She is in the front row, smiling a fake smile. Her voice shines out of the group. She's the best of them all. Mr. Lewis was right to pick her as the soloist.

I recognize her father in the second row of the audience. He isn't smiling. I'm not even sure he's awake.

The group finishes. It's time for Patricia and me to join her onstage, but there's no one at the piano.

Suddenly I know what Mr. Lewis and the boy were arguing about.

"Gary's not here," I whisper.

"What?" Patricia's head jerks up. She hasn't figured out what I have. That Gary didn't want to play the piano onstage with a "nigger" singer. "Who's going to play with us?"

"Mr. Lewis said he'd do it. He went to go get the sheet music."

"Go where?" Patricia is shaking. We're both thinking the same thing. If Mr. Lewis went back to the Music room, that's all the way on the other end of the school.

The Balladeers and band members onstage are looking for us in the wings. *She* has taken off her choir robe and stepped back out in her black dress and pearls. They don't need the piano for her performance—not when there are so many other instruments onstage—but they aren't supposed to start her solo until Patricia and I are out there.

The audience is rustling, looking at their watches. Until now the show has flowed seamlessly from one song to the next. If we don't start soon they'll think the concert is over.

"Girls, get out there!" hisses Miss Jones, who's backstage helping with the robes.

"There's no one to play the piano," I whisper.

"Get out there anyway. Linda's up first, and you've got the band."

But the band doesn't know my song or Patricia's. They're only here to play with *her*.

Patricia is breathing fast. "I can't sing a cappella," she says. "I *can't*."

"You won't have to," I say. "Mr. Lewis will be back before you need to—"

"Go!" Miss Jones shoves us forward, none too gently. "Or they'll all leave and the PTA will raise a firestorm!"

There's no time to argue. There's no time to even take a breath.

We're out on the stage.

The rustling stops. The room is completely silent now. Everyone is looking at me. No one's smiling.

My family is staring, too, their mouths in fixed straight lines.

I step to my mark and glance toward Patricia, willing her forward. She meets my eyes and steps up next to me.

That's the band's cue. The opening notes of "Ave Maria" rise up.

Her voice is even better than it was in rehearsal. I try to relax and lose myself in the music, since that's the best way to prepare for my own performance, but I can't. Instead I watch her face as she sings.

She looks beautiful, but she doesn't look happy.

She doesn't look nearly as confident as she did in rehearsals. She keeps shooting anxious looks down into the audience. At her father.

Mr. Hairston is definitely awake now. Awake, and frowning.

Next to him is a pretty dark-haired woman who must be her mother. On his other side is a bald man who looks familiar. Mr. Hairston leans over to whisper something to the bald man, who whispers something back. Mr. Hairston looks at his watch.

Onstage, she keeps singing, but her hands are clasped too tight in front of her.

They finish the song, and the Balladeers and band members file off the stage while the audience applauds. I want to clap, too—she sounded wonderful—but it wouldn't be professional, so I glance back toward Patricia with a smile.

Patricia isn't looking at me. Her eyes are fixed on the floor.

She shifts her weight from one foot to the other. She's so pale I'm afraid she's going to be sick.

We still don't have an accompanist. The band members are all gone. It's just her, Patricia and me on the stage.

And it's my turn to sing.

Well, there's nothing to be done about it. I'm not going to give up before I've begun.

I've sung a cappella before, but never in front of a crowd like this. Never on a stage with a spotlight shining on me and a girl I've kissed three feet away. Never in front of two hundred people who want nothing more than to see me fail.

I'm not going to let these people see my fear.

I move to the center of the stage. *She* takes my place next to Patricia. She's looking toward the piano stool, her brow creased in confusion.

I inhale. If I wait any longer, the "Nigger!" shouts will start. The only reason they haven't already is that everyone's still wondering why I'm standing here.

So I clasp my hands behind my back and sing "Amazing Grace."

I sing it the way I used to sing at picnics in Chicago, when all the families on our block would gather for old-fashioned Alabama-style cornbread and fried chicken and collard greens.

I gaze out into this audience of shocked, stony-faced white people and imagine they're the friendly black faces of my childhood, calling for me to sing a pretty Gospel song on a lazy afternoon.

After the first few lines the crowd is rustling again. The shouts will come any second, but I'll keep singing no matter what. I'll finish the song even if they shout me off the stage.

'Twas Grace that taught my heart to fear
And Grace my fears relieved.
How precious did that Grace appear
The hour I first believed.

It's a beautiful song. It's about God's love. God's love isn't going to be stopped just because some angry white people want it to be.

I keep singing.

The shouts don't come.

I raise my voice, singing to the very back of the room.

To *her*, too.

I want her to hear me. I want her to hear how without backup, without instruments, without even a single piano to accompany me, I can sing just as well as she can.

I want her to know I don't care what she thinks of me. What rumors she tries to spread. I have more important things on my mind than any trick she could ever pull.

Through many dangers, toils and snares
I have already come.
'Twas Grace that brought me safe thus far
And Grace will lead me home.

On the last verse, when the catcalls still haven't begun, I bring my hands out from behind me and I stop holding back. I sing the way I sing this song in church every Easter, my hands in front of me in praise to the Lord, my voice echoing across the room.

I'm not thinking anymore about what I look like in my new low-necked dress. Or who's watching, or what they think of me. All I'm thinking about are the words I'm singing and the Lord I'm singing them to.

The Lord has promised good to me.
His word my hope secures.
He will my shield and portion be
As long as life endures.

When I finish, the room is as silent as when I first walked out. I wait for the shouts. They'll come any second now.

Instead, someone's clapping.

It starts in the back of the room, with Mr. Muse. Then Mrs. Jackson joins in. Half a second later there's Daddy, on his feet in the very back row, clapping harder than anyone. Ruth leaps up beside him.

Then all the Negroes have joined in. Ennis stands up with Daddy. The other Negro students and their families, sitting in the back rows, are clapping, too.

There are even some white people clapping. And *smiling*.

There are white people in this room, total strangers, smiling and clapping for me.

But most of the white people aren't doing either. A lot of them look angrier than ever.

Her father is one of them. His hands are folded in front of him, his eyes fixed on my face. He's looking more closely at me than he ever did at her.

Mr. Lewis steps out onto the side of the stage, setting sheet music on the piano and clapping along with the others. He smiles at me. I smile back.

I glance at *her*, expecting her to be just as angry as her father. I stole her spotlight. They'd all be talking about her performance now if I hadn't come along and distracted everyone. If she hasn't already told everyone the truth about me she's bound to do it now.

But Linda's smiling at me.

And clapping. People are looking right at her, but she's clapping for me anyway.

Something swells in my chest. It's both completely unfamiliar and completely right.

I must be imagining things. She couldn't possibly—

Does this mean she's forgiven me?

No. No one in their right mind would forgive me, not for—

Then, from Linda's side, comes a wail.

It's Patricia. Her face is buried in her hands. She's heaving with sobs.

I should have said something to reassure Patricia before I went out. I shouldn't have shown off so much.

Mr. Lewis sits down at the piano in a hurry and plays the opening notes of Patricia's song, "Come Thou Fount of Every Blessing."

It's too late. She's already running off the stage.

LIE #20

I don't want to be this way.

THE AUDITORIUM IS silent.

Mr. Lewis has stopped playing. He's staring offstage after Patricia.

I look back and forth from him to the audience to Linda. Everyone looks as lost as I feel.

Finally Mr. Lewis gestures to Miss Jones to send the rest of the choir back onstage. He plays the opening notes to the last song of the show, "And Now Another Day Is Gone."

I start singing automatically. So does Linda.

For the first verse of the song, while the rest of the choir hurries onto the risers, straightening their robes and looking back for Patricia, Linda and I sing alone, together.

It feels strange.

It feels wrong.

It feels right, too.

I can't help noticing our voices go together very well indeed.

With cheerful heart I close my eyes,
Since Thou wilt not remove;
And in the morning let me rise
Rejoicing in Thy love.

We finish the song with the rest of the choir. The crowd applauds, much harder than it did for me, but the applause isn't as loud as it was for the first part of the show. No one knows what to think of what just happened.

When the show ends I stumble offstage with everyone else, trying not to trip in my too-high shoes, and look for Patricia.

But everyone else already found her.

She's in a far corner surrounded by a group of girls from the band. Before I can get through, half the Glee Club and the Girls' Ensemble are around her, too. Even the Balladeers join in. Five girls throw their arms around Patricia while she sobs.

I want to tell her it's all right, that everyone gets nervous, but I can't penetrate that circle of white girls.

Before I can figure out a way to try, one of the Balladeers—a crooked-nosed friend of Linda's whose name I've never learned—separates herself from the others and takes a step toward me.

"Why couldn't you leave her alone?" she says.

"What?" I sputter. "I only tried to help!"

"You *had* to show off, didn't you? Couldn't you tell she was already nervous enough?"

"I didn't have any choice," I say, even though the girl is partly right. It was prideful, the way I sang out there. Pride is a sin.

The girl ignores me and goes back to the circle. I catch Patricia's eye, hoping she'll defend me. Instead she scowls.

She detests me just as much as the rest of them.

Backstage is nothing but hateful faces. Soon the parents will come in and it'll be even worse. I have to get away.

There's a girls' bathroom to my left. I duck inside before I can think of a better plan.

The room is empty. Everyone else is still too interested in gossiping. I lock myself in a stall and climb on the toilet seat so anyone looking underneath won't see my dark ankles.

Only a second goes by before the first wave arrives.

"Can't believe she would do that," one girl is saying. "Patricia's so sweet. She didn't deserve to be treated that way."

The door swings open again. More voices, more giggles. The bathroom is full. I recognize Linda's voice in the crowd, and Judy's, but they aren't talking to each other.

"Well, I can believe it," another girl says. "They're a nasty people, all of them."

"Maybe the Nigra didn't do it to be nasty," an unfamiliar voice says. "We don't know if—"

The other girls talk over her.

"Oh, she meant to do it, all right," the first girl says. "My mother says there's nothing wrong with *most* colored people, but these integrators all take after their parents and the NAACP. All they want is to stir up trouble."

"They're Soviet infiltrators, that's what I heard," another girl says. "Like the Rosenbergs."

"I thought the Rosenbergs were white?" someone asks.

"I can't even keep track of what they're after," another one says. "I'm just angry they ruined our senior year."

Then everyone is talking at once, about me and my friends, and how integration will be the end of their town, and how it's ruined their whole year, until I can't understand the words anymore. At first it's a relief. Then one voice rises above the rest.

"Why, whatever do you mean, Donna?" Linda says. She sounds light and good-humored. It's strange—I've only ever heard her arguing. She sounds like she's acting in a play. "I'd hardly say the integration has ruined *your* senior year. When you and Leonard were out at Bailey's the other night, it looked to me like you were enjoying yourselves just fine. I bet you weren't thinking about integration *then*."

Everyone laughs. Donna says, "Well, no. That night, I had other things on my mind."

Another girl says, "I bet you weren't talking about integration in his car later, either."

Donna protests, and everyone breaks into scandalized giggles. I'm glad they can't see me roll my eyes.

Still giggling, the girls splash in the sinks, fix their makeup and pat their hair. The door opens and closes again and the sounds fade until there are only two sets of feet left in the room. I recognize those feet.

I peek through the gap between the stall doors. Judy is leaning into the mirror, compact in hand, sliding on her makeup with painstaking strokes as Linda watches.

"You can go," Judy says. "I told you, I don't need your help anymore."

Linda tugs at her hair. "I miss talking to you. That's all."

"I wish you'd leave me alone," Judy says. "I told you, I don't like it. If people find out we're in here together—"

"No one cares." Linda tosses her hands up. "No one else knows about that, all right? No one's going to say a word if they see you with me."

"Well, *I* know what you did. And it's wrong."

"I know," Linda says. "You've told me a thousand times already."

I can't believe it.

They're talking about *that*.

It's the first time I've heard anyone say it happened. That I didn't just dream it.

There's no way I can come out of this stall now.

"You've got to be careful," Judy says. "Everyone will talk about you."

"No one would've found out." Linda fiddles with the taps, turning them on and off again. "I'm not stupid enough to let that happen."

"*I* found out," Judy says. "I wish I hadn't. Don't bother asking me to forgive you, because I won't."

I don't understand. Why is Judy upset with her? What happened in the back room was my fault, not Linda's.

"I'm not asking that," Linda murmurs.

"Good. Now would you please leave? I don't want somebody finding us in here alone."

"You're being silly," Linda huffs.

There's a long pause where Linda watches Judy in the mirror. Judy doesn't say a word. She keeps her eyes fixed on her reflection and strokes her makeup into place.

Linda bites her lip. Then she's gone, the bathroom door swinging behind her, the click of her high heels on the tiles fading into silence.

I keep watching Judy in the mirror, waiting for her to leave so I can go, too. Then she turns around.

"You can come out, Sarah," Judy says. "I saw you looking through the door."

Oh.

I come out of the stall. Judy's makeup is done now. She watches me in the mirror, her eyes tracing my every movement.

At first I wasn't sure what to make of Judy, but once we started spending time together those afternoons at Bailey's, I got to like her quite a bit. She was sweet, and she could be very funny sometimes. It got so I could always relax around Judy.

That's long over now.

"I wanted to tell you I'm sorry about Linda," Judy says after a second. "I didn't know, or I'd have warned you. I mean, I wouldn't have been friends with her in the first place if I knew, of course, but—oh, you know what I mean."

I blink, lost. "What?"

"It's all right. You don't have to pretend it didn't happen. I was there. And anyway, she told me all about it."

"She did?" I bite the inside of my cheek, hoping the pain will make me forget the sudden pounding in my chest, the ringing in my ears.

"Yes," Judy says. "I can't even imagine how awful it must have been for you. I mean, that sort of thing isn't normal. It isn't *natural*."

Wait.

Linda told her all about it?

All about *what*?

Because it sounds like Linda might have said—

Like maybe, just maybe—

But I can't ask. Not without giving something away. I have to play along.

That's easy. I don't even have to lie.

"I know," I say. "Of course it isn't natural. It's not Christian."

"That's right." Judy snaps her compact closed. Her frizzy brown hair falls across her thickly made-up cheek. "Ugh, I can't even stand to talk about it. It's revolting."

"Yes, it is," I say. "It's just plain wrong."

"I don't know how you even endured it." Judy fiddles with her compact. Her hands are shaking. "I swear, I had no idea Linda was like that. Please, you have to believe me."

She meets my eyes. Her lip is quivering.

"Of course I believe you," I say.

"You'd think if you knew someone long enough, you'd—well." She shakes her head. She looks about to cry. "But she promised me she'd leave you alone from now on. You should be safe."

I don't understand Linda's trick at all.

Why would she lie to Judy? Say it was *her* fault?

What could Linda possibly stand to gain from that? She lost her best friend. She may well lose her reputation.

"Did you tell anyone?" I ask. "About Linda, I mean."

"No." Judy laughs without humor. "Are you kidding? Ugh. I don't want anyone thinking I'd be friends with someone like that."

I'm safe.

I'm *safe*.

I'm so relieved I could hug her, but when I reach for the tap on the sink to wash my hands, Judy edges her arm away from mine.

She never used to do that before. She was one of the only white girls who didn't shy away when I passed her in the hall.

She didn't mind when I was only colored, but now that I'm tainted with something else, Judy's not taking any risks. Whether it was my fault or not.

I can't blame her. I'd do exactly the same thing.

"Thank you," I say. "For telling me, I mean."

"You're welcome." She turns on the tap two sinks down from mine and sticks her hands under it, even though she washed them before she did her makeup. "I also wanted to say, it wasn't right what they were planning tonight. That's why I got rid of Gary. I'm sorry about how it turned out, though. I didn't know Mr. Lewis didn't have the music."

"*You* got rid of Gary? I thought he got rid of himself. Wasn't that what Linda meant yesterday when she tried to—"

I stop talking when I see Judy cringe. I shouldn't have mentioned Linda. Now Judy thinks we were up to more of that unnaturalness yesterday.

"I thought you would've heard," she says. "Everyone was talking about it. Gary's plan. It wasn't even his idea, it was his girlfriend, Carolyn's. She told Gary to play your song wrong. Move the notes on the piano up until they were so high you couldn't sing them. So you'd sound bad. They were talking about it all through rehearsal before you got there."

Oh. *That's* what Linda was trying to tell me.

I wonder what would've happened if Carolyn and Gary's plan had worked. Maybe I would've broken down onstage like Patricia. I shiver.

Why did Linda try to warn me? Why did she lie to Judy about what happened?

What in Heaven's name has Linda been *thinking* all this time? I've missed her so much.

Those long afternoons arguing with her. Laughing at her frustration as she tried so hard to make an argument she didn't even seem to believe.

I told Linda things. Things I don't tell my other friends.

I've always kept to myself. I never really talked much with the girls at Johns about what I was thinking or feeling. We just talked about school, and television shows, and what we'd do that weekend. I never talked about much more than that with my friends back in Chicago, either.

I talk to Ruth the most of everyone. And Mama. But they're family. I worry too much about disappointing them to tell them what I'm really feeling.

I thought it had to be that way. That I had no choice but to stay quiet, with only my own thoughts to keep me company. I never thought there was any other way to live.

Until I met Linda.

Of all people, I had to pick *her*.

Except I didn't pick her. I didn't plan any of this. It just... happened.

There's so much I don't like about her. She's absurdly stubborn. She'll say anything it takes to make her point. She's determined to prove herself right, no matter the consequences. She's far too opinionated for a girl.

But...I'm all those things, too.

That's why Linda and I argued so much. That's why I liked it.

It was *fun,* in a strange way. It distracted me from everything else. From all the hard parts.

With Linda I didn't have to put on a brave face and pretend none of it bothered me. I didn't have to play the nice girl or the big sister. I didn't have to be anyone but me.

I miss that. Even though it was wrong, I miss spending time with her.

But what if it *wasn't* wrong?

No. That's foolish to even think. It's wrong because God says it's wrong. Who do I think I am, questioning the will of God?

But thinking about Linda doesn't hurt the way it used to. There's none of that wrenching feeling that used to come every time I remembered that afternoon. I wonder what that means.

Judy is looking at me in the mirror, her eyebrows raised. I struggle to remember what we were talking about.

"So where was Gary tonight?" I ask.

"I, uh." Judy smiles, but only for a second. Then her face goes cold again. "He lives in my neighborhood. So I told Mom about how Gary put ants in Miss Whitson's soup last week. Mom told Gary's mother, and she grounded him for two weeks."

"Oh." That almost makes me laugh. I hadn't heard about the ants in Miss Whitson's soup. "Won't he know you're the one who told?"

Judy shrugs. "Maybe. But someone had to. It isn't right, the way they treat you and the others."

I want to hug her again.

I wish I could still be friends with Judy, but that's over now. All because of one mistake.

"Thank you," I say. "That was really, really nice of you."

"Tonight," she says. "You sounded—good."

"Thank you."

I want to tell her I'll miss her, but there's no point.

She won't miss me back.

LIE #21

I'm not brave enough for this.

WHEN I GET backstage, they're all there.

Mama, wrapping me in a tight hug. Bobby, wanting me to pick him up. Frances, smiling awkwardly. Ennis, squeezing my hand and telling me I sounded beautiful. Ruth, looking over her shoulder to make sure no one is sneaking up behind us.

They're so happy, and I'm so lost, and all of them are talking at the same time, and there's so much noise and confusion I almost don't hear the man off to the side saying, "Bunch of Communists."

Daddy hears, though. He stiffens and turns toward the man. It's the father of one of the girls in the ensemble, Brenda Green. Brenda is cowering next to him. At first I think it's because she's embarrassed for her father. Then I realize she's just scared of Daddy.

"Robert, don't," Mama murmurs.

"I'll have you know my family are all God-fearing Christians," Daddy says to the man.

The man looks less sure of himself now that he's face-to-face with Daddy, but he shakes his head. "I know who you are, boy. I read what you wrote in the *Pilot*. Sounded socialist to me."

"What I wrote about in the *Pilot* was equality," Daddy says. "Equality is an American principle. It's what our nation was founded on."

Mr. Green scoffs.

"It's the truth, sir," Ruth says. "It's in the Declaration of Independence. 'All men are created equal.' Thomas Jefferson wrote that, and he was as American as American can be."

Mr. Green stares down at Ruth, speechless.

"Ruthie, honey, hush," Daddy says, putting his hand on top of Ruth's head the way he used to do when she was little, crushing the pink bow she's tied into her hair.

The fight has gone out of Daddy's eyes. He just looks tired.

Mr. Green puts his arm around Brenda and they turn away. I let out a breath I hadn't realized I was holding.

"All right, it's time for us to go," Mama says as though none of that just happened. "We'll celebrate Sarah's success over at the Morrisons'. You ought to come, too, Ennis, and your parents of course."

No. Ennis can't come. I can't sit next to him on a sofa and pretend to feel something I don't. Not tonight.

"That's very nice of you to extend the invitation, Mrs. Dunbar," Ennis says. Out of the corner of my eye I see Linda and her parents walking toward Brenda and Mr. Green. I look away fast. "I'll have to speak with my mother, but I'm sure we'd be happy to."

No. Tonight isn't like all those other nights when I could play the part. Make Ennis think I was just as interested in him as any normal girl ought to be.

Up on that stage, when I saw her clapping for me, I felt the start of a change inside.

It's frightening. I don't know what it means.

I miss everything about her.

I don't miss her reciting her father's editorials, but I miss that look in her eyes. The one that said somewhere inside—maybe so deep she didn't even know it was there—she knew better than to believe her own words.

By the end I really do think she was starting to figure it out. Up until *it* happened.

"There she is!" a new voice says behind me. "The lady of the hour, the star of the show, Miss Sarah Dunbar!"

It's Chuck, wearing a pressed button-down shirt and a wide smile. I smile at him and gesture for him to lower his voice. Linda and her father are only a few feet away. I don't need Chuck drawing any more attention to me.

Chuck follows my gaze. He sees Linda, too. There's a nasty look in his eye.

"You know, Sarah, you were way better than that white girl," he says, too loud. Daddy tries to catch his eye, but Chuck ignores him. "Don't be fooled by all that applause she got. There wasn't a soul in that auditorium who didn't know you had her beat. They're just too scared to clap for a colored girl."

"Shush, Chuck," I say, but it's too late. It's clear from the hurt look on her face that Linda heard him. So did her father.

"You want to watch your tongue when you talk about white girls, nigger," Linda says. I've never heard her call anyone a nigger before. It sounds worse when she says it than when other people do. "Everyone knows what you did to Kathy Shepard."

Time stands still.

No one moves. No one speaks. Every eye in the room is fixed on Chuck.

I look from Linda, to Chuck, to Mama, to Linda's father. Every face is grave except Mr. Hairston's. He's smiling.

Chuck steps backward, as if Linda shoved him. Then everyone is talking at once.

Brenda Green shrieks. Linda turns, and from the surprised look on her face it's clear she'd forgotten Brenda was nearby.

She'd probably forgotten anyone was watching at all. Except her father. I'd bet a thousand dollars she only said what she did because he was there.

Not that it matters now.

The picture flashes in my head before I can stop it. Emmett Till. The fourteen-year-old colored boy in Mississippi who whistled at a white woman.

The men there beat him. Shot him. Gouged out his eye. Tossed him in the river.

Brenda runs over to a girl in a band uniform and whispers in her ear, looking over her shoulder at Chuck the whole time. The band girl shrieks, too. They turn and run toward another group, boys and girls both, clustered together near the exit doors. Soon all of them are whispering.

Everyone moves very fast after that.

Mr. Hairston is already gone. Linda and her mother are speeding out after him. The rest of the Negroes are headed toward the exit behind the stage, away from the white people. Ennis's head darts from side to side as he searches for his parents. Mama hefts Bobby up into her arms and says, "All right, girls, time to go. Quickly, now." Daddy puts one arm around Ruth and one around me and walks us fast toward the far exit, dodging through the crowd.

I don't see Chuck. I look back toward where he was before, but I can't catch a glimpse of him. All I see is the gang of white students by the main exit. They're looking around for someone, too.

"Come on now," Mama says when we get outside. "We'll go over to Frances's and have some cake and celebrate how wonderful Sarah was. Won't that be fun?"

No one answers her.

Frances's house isn't fun at all. Hardly anyone is there. Frances and I don't have any more to talk about than we did at Stud's. The adults bring out food and drinks and try to talk about the concert, but they keep ducking out to answer ringing phones and talking in hushed tones in the kitchen when they think we aren't looking.

There's so much going on that I manage to talk to Ennis quietly in the hall where the others can't hear us. I ask him where he thinks Chuck is.

"Oh, don't worry about him," he says. "I saw him go out the side door quick. He's probably hiding out until things die down. He'll be back at school on Monday and we'll all have a good laugh."

I can't tell if Ennis believes what he's saying.

"Is there any truth to it?" I ask. "Tell me, now. This is what you were talking about with Paulie that night at Stud's, wasn't it?"

Ennis nods slowly. "I told him he's a doggone fool, but he says they love each other."

I shake my head. I can't believe Chuck would be so thoughtless. This is the white people's worst fear. Their pretty white daughters running off with Negroes.

I think about that photo of the boy in Mississippi again. I wish I could scrub that picture from my brain.

Finally Daddy announces that it's time to go. Bobby has already been sleeping for half an hour on the Morrisons' love seat and Ruth is yawning up a storm. Mama looks like she'd just as soon stay at the party longer, though.

"Are you certain about this?" she says.

Daddy nods. "Sure as sure can be."

But he doesn't drive us straight home. Instead he takes us through Davis Heights, ten minutes out of our way. Ruth and Bobby are so sleepy they don't notice. Mama's sitting up straight in the front seat, shooting looks at Daddy that he's pretending not to see.

I don't like this. I don't know what it is, but I don't like it.

"There," Daddy says under his breath. He pulls the car over with a jerk. On the other side of the street there's a crowd gathered, but it's too dark to see what's going on. Bobby wakes up with a small sound of protest.

"Don't, Robert," Mama murmurs in the front seat.

Someone runs up to the car. I jump back, remembering the man who tried to open our car door on the first day of school, before I see that it's a Negro man. He glances at me and Ruth and Bobby in the backseat, then gestures silently to Daddy.

Daddy gets out of the car and goes across the street with the man, his long legs striding fast.

"Mama, what's going on?" Ruth says, panic in her voice. "Where's Daddy going?"

Bobby starts to cry.

"Hush, all of you," Mama says. "Be still."

Then she gets out of the car, too.

My heart thuds in my chest. They can't leave us here.

"Sarah, what's happening?" Ruth shrieks. Next to her, Bobby sobs.

The car door on my side opens. I'm about to shriek, too, but it's Mama. She gestures for me to get out.

I'm afraid to. I don't know what's going on out there, but I climb out anyway. Mama closes the door behind me and hands me her car key. Her hand is shaking, but just a little.

"I need you to be in charge now, Sarah," she whispers. "Just like at home when you're the babysitter, all right? I need you to do exactly as I say."

"Yes, ma'am." Over Mama's shoulder I can see people gathered in the front lawn of a house. Others are running from the house to the street and to the alley on the other side. The wind shifts. I smell smoke.

"You drive Ruth and Bobby home and put them straight to bed," Mama says. "Lock all the doors as soon as you get inside, and don't turn any lights on. Don't open the door for *anyone*, do you understand me?"

I recognize the house we're parked in front of. It looks different in the dark, but it's Chuck's house.

"I understand," I say.

"Your father and I will be home as soon as we can." Mama puts her hand on my cheek and meets my eyes. She bends down to press her hand against the car window, looking hard at Ruth and Bobby. Then she turns, gathers her skirt in her hand and runs toward where Daddy is standing on Chuck's front lawn with two other men.

I stare at the car key in my hand. I've never driven on the street before. Daddy has taken me for a few practice drives in the church parking lot after services but that's it. Mama said there was no use getting me my license before I turned eighteen. She said a young girl didn't need to be driving around where she could get into trouble.

I open the car door with shaking hands and get into Daddy's seat. It takes me two tries to start the engine.

"Sarah, what's going on?" Ruth asks from the backseat. She's crying. Her voice quivers the way it did when she was five and saw something scary on the television. Bobby wails even louder than before.

"Mama said for me to drive home," I say. "Can you make Bobby be quiet?"

There's a cross burning in Chuck's yard.

That's what Daddy and the others are doing. Making sure the fire's out. And trying to find the white men who set it.

I pray Daddy and Mama aren't the ones to find them.

I don't know how we make it home. There are hardly any streetlights in this neighborhood, and I don't know how to turn the headlights on, so we're driving in the dark. The car moves at a crawl as I squint to look for street signs and run over curbs with every turn. Each time we hit a bump, Bobby shrieks louder.

Ruth is sobbing next to him, no help at all. When we finally get to our neighborhood there are more lights to see by, but I'm just as frightened as I was before. It's only by luck that I find our street and pull into the driveway without hitting anything.

This is why we went to Frances's after the concert. Mama and Daddy knew something like this might happen tonight. Even before Linda said what she did about Chuck, they knew. They knew the white people wouldn't let us have even one night to be happy.

I'm shaking harder than ever when I get out of the car. When Ruth climbs out of the backseat I grab her by the shoulders and whisper, "I need you to get yourself together and help me. Can you do that?"

Ruth's eyes are wild in the dim light, but when she speaks she has enough sense to keep her voice down. "Where are Mama and Daddy? Why did they leave us?"

"They'll be home soon. We need to get Bobby in bed, but Mama said not to turn any lights on. Can you help?"

Ruth's eyes are still shiny, but she nods. I lock all the car doors while she lifts Bobby out, carrying him like a baby. He's fallen back asleep.

I use Mama's key to let us into the dark, silent house. I can't remember ever being this frightened.

It's worse than the first day of school. Then we were surrounded by people. Being alone is much scarier.

What if someone already broke in through the back and they're in here waiting for us? What if they're hiding upstairs? Would they hang us, even though we're only children?

I can't think this way. I can't let Ruth and Bobby see me afraid.

I lock the front door behind us and take Bobby out of Ruth's arms. Together, we climb the stairs. Bobby's much heavier than the last time I carried him. We creep up in the dark, the lights from outside casting in through the windows, making me want to jump. But I can't. I'm responsible for my brother and sister. I have to make sure we all stay safe.

Bobby's room is pitch-black except for the tiny square of moonlight coming through the gap in the window shade. Ruth starts to raise it, but I shake my head. We get him over to the bed and tuck him in. He groans in his sleep, but his eyes stay closed.

Ruth leaves without a word and goes to our room. I follow her, suddenly exhausted. She climbs into bed without getting undressed and pulls the blanket up over her head.

I lean against the door frame and gaze out the moonlit window. My limbs feel like lead, but I should stay up and wait for Mama and Daddy to get home. I should be awake in case the phone rings, or someone knocks on the door. Even though Mama said I shouldn't open the door for anyone. No matter what.

I change into a robe and go back down the dark stairs, feeling my way with the banister and trying not to flinch at the lights from passing cars. The dark, silent house is just as frightening as it was before, but I keep my head high, the same way I do at school.

The wait goes on for hours. Or that's what it feels like. Every set of headlights passing could be a driver slowing to throw a brick through the window. Every creak of the house settling could be an angry white fist thumping at the back door.

When I was Bobby's age, during the war, there used to be blackouts. I'm too little to really remember it, but Mama told me stories. I used to get so scared I'd cry for hours, walking around the dark house, bumping into things, thinking I saw monsters lurking in every corner.

But I'm not a little girl anymore. The monsters that lurk now are real. And I can't let them see that I'm afraid.

LIE #22

Adults always know what's best.

BOBBY COUGHS ALL through breakfast. I glare at him.

"Stop faking," I say as Ruth gathers up the dishes. I was up late, sitting on the couch waiting for Mama and Daddy and trying not to think about what might have happened to them. I have a Saturday full of laundry ahead of me. I don't have the patience for another of Bobby's imaginary sicknesses. "I'm onto you."

Bobby puts his head down on the table and coughs some more.

"I'm not faking," he mumbles.

"Don't you remember the boy who cried wolf, Bobby?" Daddy says. His face is hidden behind the morning *Gazette*. He's got to be even more exhausted than I am. When he and Mama finally got home, he made Mama and me go on upstairs to bed. Everything was all right, he said, but he was going to stay in the living room and keep a watch out, just in case. I don't know if he slept at all.

Bobby coughs again.

"He just needs a cough drop," Mama says. "Sarah, run on over to Bailey's and pick some up. We're all out."

I haven't been to Bailey's since that day.

"I have to do the laundry," I say. "It's going to take all day."

"You should've thought of that before you disobeyed, shouldn't you?" Mama says, sounding way too pleased with herself.

Ruth sets a stack of plates down on top of the newspaper, bending the front page back. Daddy yanks the paper out from underneath and shoves the page under the table.

But it's too late. I already saw.

Daddy shakes his head at me. He saw it, too.

I think fast. I don't want Ruth to know. Not until she has to.

I need to read it, though. I need to know everything.

I nod at Daddy to show I'll keep quiet. After a second he nods back and passes the paper to me under the table.

Mama sees. "Robert, do you really think that's a good—"

I ignore her and go outside to the back porch, the paper tucked under my arm.

My hands are shaking. As much as I want to know what it says, there's a big part of me that would just as soon stay ignorant, but it's too late for that.

I turn to the photo I saw before. It was taken at night, and it's hard to make out exactly what's happening, but it's definitely Chuck in the photo. His head is bowed. White policemen are on either side of him, holding his arms. One of the officers is bald and looks familiar.

The other policeman is younger. He's smiling at Chuck. The kind of smile that makes you shiver.

The story is only three paragraphs.

Negro Boy Questioned in Assault
By Gazette Staff

Charles Irving Tapscott of 16 Butterwood Lane
in Davis Heights was questioned last night by

police in connection with an assault on Miss
Katherine Shepard of New Town.

The Negro Tapscott and Miss Shepard are both
students at Jefferson High School. Tapscott is
among the nine Negro students integrating the
school.

Police are conducting a thorough investigation.
Tapscott is in police custody to ensure the public's safety. Charges are expected to be filed.

In police custody.

What does that mean? Is he in jail? Or is he locked up in some policeman's shed somewhere?

Ennis said Chuck had gone somewhere safe. He was only trying to make me feel better. I was a fool to believe him.

When Daddy was a boy his family lived in Alabama. The Thanksgiving he was six years old, people around town started saying one of Daddy's grown-up cousins had stolen a turkey. The white men who came to his house that night weren't police. They didn't file charges, and they didn't conduct any investigation, but after that night, Daddy's cousin never walked again.

Daddy told me that story three years ago. We were in the middle of another round of integration hearings and I was tired of going to court every day. It was summer, and I didn't want to sit in a hot, stuffy room listening to white people talk about us. I wanted to go swimming with my friends in the creek by Clayton Mill.

Daddy sat me down and told me about his cousin. He said that was why we had to keep fighting, even when it seemed like we'd never win. Because his cousin never got the chance to fight.

When Daddy first told me the story, I felt guilty. I nodded and apologized and promised I'd go back to court. I'd listen to every second of it, even when the thermometer reached eighty-five and the sweat dripped into my eyes.

Today that story means something different to me altogether. What if I never see Chuck again?

Things like what happened to Daddy's cousin aren't supposed to happen here. That's why my parents moved from Alabama to Chicago in the first place. They didn't want us to grow up the way they did. That's what they always say.

Then why did they bring us here? Why couldn't we stay in Chicago, where we could go weeks at a time without ever seeing a single white face? Where burning crosses are just in scary stories, no different from goblins and the boogeyman under the stairs?

I'm about to throw the paper down and go ask Daddy if he knows anything else about Chuck when Mama steps out onto the porch, shutting the door quietly behind her.

"Why did you try to hide this from me?" The anger is bubbling up inside me now. "You don't think I have a right to know?"

"It's not about that." Mama's face is calm. So calm it makes me even more anxious. "After everything you went through last night, we didn't want you to worry when there's nothing you could do to help."

"There's got to be something I can do. I could—"

I stop. I can't think of anything I can do.

"I spoke to Lucille Tapscott," Mama says. "She and Carl are staying at her sister's for now."

"Why?" Then I figure it out. "Oh. The paper printed their address."

Mama nods.

That will mean more than just a cross in their yard one night. It will mean shouts from the sidewalk all day long. Rocks through the windows. Gunshots, maybe.

"Do they know where he is?" I ask her.

"As best they can tell he's at the police station in a holding cell. They're trying to get the girl to make a statement so they can press charges."

"Kathy hasn't said anything yet?"

Mama shakes her head. "Do you know her from school?"

"No."

But Linda does.

I'd have thought Chuck would be too smart to go near a white girl, but he would've said the same about me.

"How can they put someone in jail for rumors?" I say.

Mama shakes her head. "Sometimes it just works this way, honey."

I know it does.

We're colored. The rules are different for us.

"Your father thinks William Hairston, the editor of his paper, might be involved," Mama goes on. "Apparently he has a daughter who goes to Jefferson. Friends on the police force, too."

I remember why I recognized the bald policeman in the photo with Chuck.

He was sitting next to Mr. Hairston at the concert last night. The two of them were whispering together during Linda's solo.

Did they plan this? Did *she?*

I rip the newspaper in half.

Mama flinches, then fixes me with a steady look.

I don't care.

I'm too tired for this. I'm too scared for Chuck.

I just want it all to go away.

"What's the point of all this?" I'm talking too loud. Almost shouting. "If they're only going to turn around and treat us this way? Why bother integrating the school? They'll never want us there. They'll never let us be like them. We might as well just stop now before it gets worse!"

Mama strides across the porch and grabs my arm, so hard my skin twists under her grip. She looks even angrier than me.

"Now you listen and you listen good." Her voice is so quiet it scares me. "Nobody's going to *let* us be anything. We have just as much right to this world as they have, and we are not going to wait around for them to give us permission. If we have to prove it to them, we will, but I don't ever want to hear you talk that way again."

I swallow. "Why did we move down here? Why couldn't we have stayed home where we didn't have to worry about all this?"

"Because this is the United States of America and we have the right to live anywhere we please, young lady." Mama closes her eyes and draws in a long breath. She lets go of my arm and takes a step back. When she looks at me again that calm from before is back. "And because your father and I want to be a part of what's happening in this part of the country. We wanted that for you children. You can understand that."

I used to think I understood. I used to trust Mama and Daddy to always know what was right.

I'm not sure anymore.

I don't know if coming here was the right thing to do. I don't know if this long, awful year at Jefferson is worth it. I don't know if it ever will be.

Chuck is in jail right now. Just for being one of us.

Mama and Daddy and their friends say the world is changing. Are they seeing something I'm not seeing?

Or are they just saying it because they want so badly for it to be true?

"I just want Chuck to be okay." My throat closes up over the words. I'm fighting so hard not to cry.

"I know, honey." Mama takes what's left of the newspaper out of my hand. I've crumpled the torn pages into a tiny ball. "I know you're worried about your friend, but there's nothing you can do for him. And sitting here hysterical won't help anyone. Your little brother needs you now."

She hands me a dollar.

"Let me give you some advice," she says. "When you're upset, and there's nothing you can do to make things better, it helps if you have something worthwhile to do. Sitting and stewing will only make you feel worse."

I nod.

I know Mama's only trying to help.

But she doesn't know everything about me.

And no matter how hard I try I can't make myself feel worthwhile as I begin the ten-block walk to Bailey's.

I'm unnatural. Degenerate. Sinful.

I wonder if it's possible to be those things and still be a good daughter. A good friend. A good sister. I don't see how it could be.

But I don't love Bobby any less than I did before it happened. I'm not any less worried about what's going to happen to Chuck than I would have been, either.

I still get good grades like I did before. I sing as well as ever. I'm still polite to people at church. And I'm taking even better care of my hair and my clothes than I did before. Especially now that I'm doing all the laundry.

I don't understand the rules of sinning. Is God testing me? What Chuck did—was it a sin, too? Is God punishing him? Why would He punish Chuck but not me?

Maybe if I atone enough, and I never do it again, I'll still be allowed to go to Heaven.

That idea should seem like such a blessing, but it only makes me more confused.

I'm getting closer to downtown. There are more people around. Some people from Jefferson are standing outside Bailey's, smoking cigarettes and gossiping the way they always do on Saturdays. Linda's there, smiling up at Bo Nash. I look away before they can see me.

Instead I wave to old Mrs. Jackson, who's on her way out of the Food Town with a sack of potatoes. She waves back and calls out that I sang beautifully last night.

God wouldn't have let her say that if He thought I didn't deserve it.

Would He?

I'm frowning to myself, thinking so hard I don't even see Chuck until I nearly walk into him.

He pulls himself to a stop slowly. He blinks at me. "Sarah?"

"Chuck!" I'm so happy to see him I can't believe it. "What are you doing here? Did they let you out?"

Chuck shrugs.

That's when I notice the smell. He's been drinking.

"They let me out," he says, slurring his words. I've never seen him like this. It's shameful. He's usually such a nice boy. "Said she wouldn't say nothing on the record."

"Of course she wouldn't." I try to sound soothing, the way Mama does when Daddy's been up all night working on a story. "My mother said they only brought you in because of the rumors."

"Rumors, Hell." Chuck shakes his head, then stumbles, trying to walk away from me.

"Chuck, please." This isn't the Chuck I know. I wonder if I should try to take him somewhere. His aunt's house? I'm sure he wouldn't want his parents to see him this way. And my house would be just as bad. "You know better than to use that kind of language."

He snorts. "You should hear how those police talk. Give you a right heart attack."

"Did they—" I don't want to ask. I don't see any bruises on him, but that doesn't necessarily mean anything. "Was it awful?"

He takes a swig out of a brown bottle I didn't notice he was carrying. "They walked around in circles and asked me questions about white girls all night long. Did I ever speak to a white girl. Did I ever call a white girl on the phone. When I saw a white girl on the street, did I look at her, and *how* did I look at her."

I shake my head. The police should've known Chuck isn't like that.

But they didn't know anything about him. All they knew was his color. And that was enough.

"I knew what to do," he goes on. "I knew to answer every question, 'No, sir,' and 'I'm sorry, sir,' and 'I would never, sir.' They kept me locked up all night and I had to keep no, sir-ing them until I thought my chin was about to fall off from nodding so much. All I could think about the whole time was that picture in *Jet*. I couldn't stop no, sir-ing, not unless I wanted to wind up like that, too."

He's talking about that same picture. The boy from Mississippi. None of us could ever forget that picture.

He shakes his head again. Then he looks at me. For a second, his eyes are clear. "Sarah, we don't deserve this bullshit."

His language is crass, but he's right.

"They think they can do whatever they want." He takes another swig from the bottle. "They think we won't do anything about it."

I don't like the look on his face. I try to think of what Mama would say.

"That's why we took them to court." I speak slowly to make sure he understands. "To prove they couldn't tell us what to do."

"It didn't work." He shakes his head.

"We have to be patient."

He throws the empty bottle over his shoulder. It misses the trash can by ten feet. "I'm done being goddamn patient."

"Chuck!" Even without the drinking, I can't believe he said that in front of me. I can't believe he said it at all.

"I'm sorry, Sarah," he says.

Then he turns and runs toward Bailey's, shouting. The white people hear him and look up.

I can just barely make out Bo Nash's face as he turns our way. He's grinning.

part 4

This Is the Day That the Lord Hath Made

LIE #23

I'm the same person
I was before.

Linda

WE HEAR THE colored boy before we see him.

At first I can't understand what he's saying. It's just garble, shouted in a colored boy's voice.

Then he appears around the corner. Every one of us, even Bo, shrinks back.

We're gathered outside Bailey's like we always do on Saturdays when the weather's nice. Everyone from our group of friends is here, even Judy. She's taking her cigarette break and standing as far away from me as she can get. She just finished doing her morning cleanup of the dining area, and she's left her mop and bucket propped up against the side of the building for the stock boy to take out back.

Eddie had been doing an impression of Mr. Lewis at the concert last night, the way he crossed his legs at the piano like a fairy. The laughter has only just died off.

The colored boy is getting closer. No one's laughing now.

It's the boy who was with Kathy. The one who caught me in the hall when I fell that day. The one who insulted my singing in front of Daddy. Chuck, his name is Chuck. It's clear from the way he's walking that he's drunk.

He crosses to our side of the street and stands at the curb, looking right at us.

I flinch. So do most of the other girls. Even the boys look shaky.

Bo gets his wits about him first.

"What're you doing out of jail, boy?" he calls. "You break out or something?"

The colored boy mutters something.

"Speak up, boy," Eddie yells. "We can't understand your coon jab."

"I've got to talk to somebody," the boy says. He's rubbing his knuckles and glancing around at us, like he's looking for someone.

Me. He's looking for me.

He remembers what I said last night.

I said it because he made me angry. And because Daddy was watching. But it doesn't matter why I said it. What matters is that I said it, and someone heard it, and they told someone, and then everyone knew. It was all anyone was talking about the rest of the night. This morning, Daddy said the boy was lucky the police caught him before anybody else could.

The boy takes another step toward us.

Most of the girls turn and run inside the store.

I stay where I am. So does Judy. She's got her hand clapped over her mouth. There's fear in her eyes.

I want to disappear. Make all this vanish away. Poof.

"He goes ape on us, we'll mess him up so bad he'll wish he was still in jail," Eddie mutters, too low for the colored boy to hear. "Stinking nigger."

Bo takes a step toward the boy. The boy steps over the curb and into the parking lot.

He's on Bo's turf now.

But he isn't looking at Bo.

"You did this." The colored boy points his finger at me. It might as well be a gun, I'm so frightened.

"Hey, now!" Eddie glances back and forth from me to the boy. His brow is furrowed. He must not have heard I'm the one who started this whole mess. "That's our girl Linda. You best not be thinking of messin' with her."

"That's right," Bo says. He doesn't bother to look at me. "You want to talk to somebody, you talk to us."

Daddy didn't say one word to me after the concert last night. Nothing about how well I sang. Nothing about the colored boy.

But when we got home he went straight into his office and locked the door. He was on the phone for the rest of the night.

I know exactly who he was calling. Whenever he gets hold of an especially juicy piece of information about a Negro, the first thing he does is call his police beat reporter. Then he calls his buddy at the station.

The only thing I can't figure out is how the boy got away from the police so fast. I don't see any bruises on him. Not that it'd be easy to tell, since his skin is so dark. I'm not sure if Negroes even get bruises, come to think of it.

Well, if they do, this boy will have plenty of them soon enough.

Bo swings first, but the boy turns away in time. Bo's fist bounces off his jaw. The boy reaches back to take a swing.

That's as far as he gets. The boys are on him before he's moved another muscle.

I blink. A second later all I see is a pile of bodies on the ground, fists flying, legs swinging.

I don't see the colored boy at all. He must be at the very bottom of the pile. With at least fifteen guys on top of him, punching, kicking.

"Stop it!" I yell, but no one's paying attention.

Judy runs into the store, screaming, "Mr. Bailey! Mr. Bailey, come out here, now!"

"Stop it!" I yell again.

I move toward the pile of boys, but I don't know what to do. Even if I could pull one of them off he'd only fling himself back on again.

I can see the colored boy's leg. Blue jeans with an inch of brown skin peeking out above the shoe. The rest of him is blocked from view by the boys who are still crouched over him, punching.

I can't tell if it's getting better or worse. The boy's leg isn't moving much.

I tug at the buttons on my blouse cuffs until they pop off.

This boy—Chuck—he caught me when I fell that day. He didn't have to do that.

Bo breaks away from the pack and goes to grab Judy's mop and bucket from where they're leaning against the wall. He hands the bucket to Eddie and takes the mop, gesturing for the rest of the group to back away. I can only see part of Chuck's side this time. He's not moving. Eddie turns the bucket upside down, dumping the filthy water out all over Chuck, making the boys laugh. Then he flips the bucket back over and slams it down into Chuck's chest. I hear the crunch of ribs breaking.

The group converges back over Chuck, punching and kicking. Bo joins in, thrusting the handle of the mop down with all his strength. I can't see Chuck anymore, and I'm glad for it.

Even God will never forgive me for this.

That's when I see Sarah.

She's standing on the sidewalk, her eyes fixed on Bo's gang. She's out of breath. She must have run here.

In spite of everything, the feeling flares up inside me. The same one that's come every time I've seen Sarah since that day. I ignore it and wave my arms desperately at her for help.

The boys are standing up now, to better aim their kicks. Bo is slamming the mop handle down again and again. He pauses to wipe his brow, then looks up and sees Sarah watching. He grins at her, too wide, baring his teeth. Then he shifts the mop handle under his arm and cups his hands in the air like he's squeezing melons.

Sarah crosses her arms over her chest and backs away.

The boys wouldn't hurt Sarah, would they? She didn't do anything. Besides, she's a girl.

The other boys are noticing her, too. Bo's not the only one grinning.

The door to Bailey's bangs open. "What the Devil?" Mr. Bailey shouts.

At the sound of his voice the others stand up. The colored boy is still on the ground, lying on his back with his eyes shut, clutching his side. His nose is broken. Blood drips down his chin.

"Call the police!" I tell Mr. Bailey.

"Yeah, she's right, call 'em," Gary calls out. "Tell them this here nigger belongs back in jail."

Mr. Bailey surveys the group of boys. "All right, you've had your fun. Now scram."

Bo and his friends shuffle away, leaving the colored boy on the ground. Kenneth delivers one last kick to his side, but the boy doesn't seem to feel it. His shadow is spread out wide under him, even though the sun is directly overhead.

Mr. Bailey glances my way, then turns and goes back inside. It's obvious he's not going to call the police. Maybe I should do it myself.

But Eddie might be right. The police might punish the colored boy instead of Bo and the others.

I should ask Sarah. She'll know what to do.

But Sarah and I haven't talked since—

Never mind. That doesn't matter at a time like this.

"Sarah?" I say, embarrassed at how small my voice sounds.

Sarah isn't looking at me. She's kneeling on the ground next to the boy.

Oh, no. I hadn't even thought—what if he's hurt badly?

What if he dies? Will it be my fault?

I go to the boy's other side. Sarah glances at me, but her face is blank. She turns back to him. "Can you talk?"

He grunts something I can't understand. Sarah frowns. "What was that, Chuck?"

This time he doesn't grunt at all. His shadow is growing longer.

Then I realize it isn't a shadow. It's blood. There's an open wound running down the side of his head. Blood flows out of it in streams.

Oh, *God*.

"We have to call the hospital!" I cry.

Sarah ignores me. She's murmuring to Chuck in a voice so low I can't make out the words.

"I'll go inside and call them," I say.

Sarah shakes her head. She doesn't look at me. "Mr. Bailey won't let you use the phone for that."

She's right, of course.

"Then I'll—" I don't know what to say. I can't think of anything. "I'll—"

"You stay here with him." I can't believe how calm Sarah sounds. "I'll go across to Mrs. Muse's and call from there."

"Yes, all right, yes, I'll stay here with—"

But Sarah is already running across the street.

I kneel down onto the pavement next to the colored boy.

The blood isn't just coming from the cut on his head. It's seeping through his shirt, too. I remember in Health class they said to put pressure on the wound, so I reach for his chest and press down lightly with my fingers. His face seizes up in pain, and I snatch my hand back.

I did this.

I said something stupid, and now a boy is bleeding on the pavement in front of me.

I climb to my feet. My whole body is shaking. I rub my hand on my skirt absently. When I look down my skirt is bloody, too.

He looks so awful. I can't see how he'll possibly live.

Footsteps behind me. I turn around. Sarah is approaching us, her eyes on Chuck.

"They're coming," she says. She kneels down again. Her skirt is stained with blood, too.

"Will he be all right?" I ask her.

She shakes her head. She doesn't know.

We sit in silence. Sarah takes a white handkerchief out of her purse and presses it against Chuck's head gently. Soon the handkerchief is sopping red.

After a few long minutes the ambulance pulls into the parking lot, moving too slowly. Customers spill out of Bailey's, attracted by the siren. I recognize some of them, and I see them recognize me back, but the siren is too loud to hear what they're saying to each other. Probably starting a fresh round of gossip about William Hairston's daughter associating with colored people. *By choice,* mind you.

The paramedics tell Sarah and me to move away. They lift Chuck onto a stretcher. His face flinches again as they lift him. It's the only way I can tell he's alive.

They load him in the ambulance and pull out of the parking lot, the siren still blaring. No one asked us what happened to him. No one seems to care.

"He'll be at the hospital, right?" I ask Sarah once the sirens have died down and the crowd has drifted away. "Can I go see him?"

Sarah turns to me. It's strange, being face-to-face with her after all this time avoiding her gaze. Her eyes are as bright as ever. Brighter, maybe. Sharper.

"He won't want to see you." She's speaking slowly, deliberately, the way she used to when I first knew her. She's being careful around me again.

My heart sinks. "Of course."

Sarah looks off to the side, as if she's turning something over in her head. "I won't be able to see him, either. Mama and Daddy would never let me go."

"Why not?"

She shakes her head. "They'll be upset enough I was here when it happened. They won't want me anywhere else there could be trouble."

"Maybe they shouldn't let you come to school, then."

As soon as I've said it, I wish I could take it back.

I wish I could take back everything I've ever said to her.

Sarah meets my eyes. It's the first time we've really looked at each other since that day.

"My brother's sick," she says. "I don't want to see that man again. That Mr. Bailey. Will you go in the store and get a pack of cough drops?"

She holds out a dollar bill.

I stare at her.

She's asking me for help?

Sarah?

"Look, if you don't want to do it, I'll find somewhere else—" She starts to snatch the dollar away.

"No, no, no. I mean, of course I'll do it." I take the dollar. "Sarah, I—"

She cuts me off. "Mama and Daddy will hear about what happened soon enough, and they'll spend the rest of the day on the phone with Mrs. Mullins and the others. If you really want to hear how Chuck's doing, you can come home with me."

I'm already nodding before I've realized what this means.

She asked me to go to her house. To a house where colored people live.

William Hairston's daughter.

Anyone could see me.

They could tell my father. I can only guess what would happen then.

And I don't care.

Sarah's mother pours me another iced tea. I take a sip. It tastes exactly like the iced tea at home.

I thought you'd be able to tell from looking at a house that colored people lived there, but Sarah's living room could just as easily be ours, with its matching sofa and love seat, its woven beige rug, its television propped in the corner across from the big soft chair. Sarah's father must sit there to watch the news. The same way Daddy does.

"Are you sure you don't want to call your mother, Linda?" Mrs. Dunbar asks me again. She's stirring her tea too fast. The spoon keeps rattling against the glass. "She must be worried you aren't home yet."

"That's all right, thank you." I remember to add, "Ma'am."

Mom won't be home for hours yet. Daddy was in one of his good moods this morning, working in his garden with his shirt-sleeves rolled up and a Winston stuck behind his ear. He even waved at me and wished me a good morning as I left for Bailey's. Mom goes to the shopping mall in Chesterfield every Saturday, though, and she stays there until it closes. Even if Daddy's in a good mood in the morning there's no way to know how long it'll stay that way.

I don't tell Sarah's mother that, of course.

Mrs. Dunbar has been superpolite to me all afternoon. She's been talking nonstop, asking me about myself and my family, rushing around to fetch more food and telling Sarah to fluff the cushions to make sure I'm comfortable. She even gave me an apron to wear so the bloodstains on my skirt wouldn't show. She's being far more polite than she really ought to be. If Sarah came over to *my* house, my mother would—

Well, Sarah would never make it through our front door, so it wouldn't matter.

Sarah's mother didn't smile when she first saw Sarah and me coming up the driveway. She looked like she'd have been happier if we'd turned around and left altogether. By the time we'd reached the porch, though, she was smiling up a storm, saying, "Sarah, I'm so glad to finally meet one of your new friends from school."

As soon as we went into the house, though, Mrs. Dunbar went straight to the living room and drew the curtains closed. Then she turned around and beamed that same big smile at me. I was confused, because it was still bright and sunny out.

Then I realized Mrs. Dunbar was closing the curtains because she didn't want to risk anyone seeing the family visiting with a white person.

Sarah introduced me as Linda, leaving out my last name. Mr. Dunbar isn't here—he works another job at a colored paper on the weekends, I heard—but Sarah must not have wanted her mother to know who my father was.

I was glad. I wish Sarah didn't know, either.

Sarah tried to introduce me to her little brother, but he ran up the stairs as soon as he saw me and hasn't come down since. Mrs. Dunbar gave him a cough drop from the bag we'd brought and murmured something about him not feeling well. I think he was afraid of me.

Sarah's sister is here, too. I recognized her from school. She recognized me back. I could tell from the way she tried to trip me when I got up to go to the bathroom. The little brat. I haven't seen her since then, either.

Mrs. Dunbar has spent most of the day on the phone, trying to find out more about Chuck, just as Sarah predicted. There was no answer at his house or his aunt's. One of his neighbors heard his family had gone to meet him at the hospital. That's all we know so far.

Despite her polite smile I can tell Sarah's mother is anxious for me to leave. That's why she keeps talking so much. I do the same thing when I'm nervous.

But I need to stay until they find out if Chuck is all right. I need to know how badly I hurt him.

I've tried to tell myself that's the whole reason I'm here, but the truth is, I'm here because I want to be near Sarah.

Since her mother has been with us the whole time, Sarah and I haven't been able to talk much. It's just as well. I don't know what to say.

For a month all I've thought about is what I'd say to Sarah if we ever spoke again.

I never thought we would. I never thought she'd want to.

I wish I knew what she was thinking.

The phone rings. Sarah's mother hurries into the hallway. She says hello, and Sarah and I strain to hear more, but Mrs. Dunbar drops her voice to a murmur.

Sarah stands up. "I'm getting a lemon bar from the kitchen. Want one?"

"Yes," I say. "Please. Thank you."

Sarah shakes her head. "Stop acting so polite. It's not like you. You're making me nervous."

I want to tell her I *am* polite.

It's just that I was never polite to *her*. Not before.

Before what, though? Before today?

Or before what happened last month in the back room?

That day, she told me I was worse than Bo. Worse than all the others.

She told me I was as bad as my father.

My father is a brilliant man. Everyone says so. I used to accept everything he told me as the absolute truth.

He used to tell me I wasn't as smart as the other girls. Wasn't as pretty. Wasn't as good.

Then he stopped talking to me altogether.

Except to tell me about the colored people. For years now he's hardly talked about anything else.

He said colored people weren't as good as we were. That was why they lived in different neighborhoods, went to different schools, worked at easier jobs for less money.

I believed him. Everyone did.

But that doesn't mean what happened to Chuck is right. Or what happened to that colored boy down in Mississippi a few years back, either. The one that sassed a white woman.

Daddy wrote about that boy after the trial. He said there wasn't enough evidence to convict those two white men, and the courts had done their job. The day after his editorial was printed I found a letter he'd written to one of his friends. The letter said the colored boy was a fool who should've known better than to talk about white women in Mississippi.

Sarah thinks I'm no different from Daddy. I don't know if she's wrong or right.

I'm the one who's responsible for what happened to Chuck, though.

And what did I do when the boys went after him?

Nothing. That's what I did. Just like I did nothing when Bo threw the ball at Paulie. Or when my friends were talking about Sarah in the hall that day.

But white people and colored people are different. They just *are*. Everyone knows that. If we were all the same we wouldn't look different, or act different.

God made the world the way it is for a reason. He chose to separate the races. Who are we to question Him?

The problem is, all of this makes sense when I'm just thinking about the principle of the thing. When I start to think about Sarah, though, everything gets mixed up in my head.

Because I'm white, and she's colored. I'm supposed to be better.

But she's smarter than me. She's prettier than me. She's a better singer than me. She's *better,* period.

And how is that possible? How could God have let that happen?

If Chuck had just stayed in his rightful place—if the colored people hadn't come to our school—if the NAACP hadn't filed their lawsuit—he'd be all right now. Paulie, too. No one would spit on Sarah and her sister on their way to class.

If they had just done what they were supposed to do. If they'd just listened to Daddy. Just listened to me.

But who am I to tell someone like Sarah what to do? I'm nothing next to her.

She walks back in carrying a tray of lemon bars and sets them down on the coffee table. I gaze at the brown skin of her outstretched arm as she arranges the napkins on the table. All I can think about is how badly I want to touch her.

I know it means there's something wrong with me.

Sarah knows it, too. She saw right through me. Right to my worst, most secret sin.

I don't know why Sarah brought me here. I don't know how she can stand to be around me.

Sarah's mother hangs up the phone and comes back to the living room. She sits down and takes a sip of tea.

"No news," she says. "Mrs. Muse was calling to see if we'd heard anything."

I nod. All day the Dunbars have talked about Mr. or Mrs. This-or-That as though I know who these people are.

"So, Linda, are you a senior, too?" Mrs. Dunbar asks.

I can't believe she's bothering to make small talk. From her politeness and her lilting *Gone with the Wind* accent, so different from Sarah's clipped Northern one, I'd have thought Mrs. Dunbar was one of what Mom calls the "gentlewomen of the Deep South" that she and her friends admire so much. Except I don't think the gentlewomen Mom and her friends are talking about are colored.

"Yes, ma'am," I say.

"Have you decided where you're going to college?" Mrs. Dunbar says.

"I—"

I mean to say I won't be going to college since I'm getting married after graduation, but that future—moving into a little apartment with Jack and picking out flatware and bedspreads—seems further away than it did at the start of the school year.

I stuff a lemon bar in my mouth so I won't have to finish my sentence.

"I've had enough waiting," Sarah says after a moment. "I want to go see him."

"You most certainly will not. After all, we have company." Mrs. Dunbar gestures to me.

Sarah and her mother argue, still in those polite tones.

I watch the fire rising in Sarah's eyes and remember how she looked that day in the back room. As though she'd have shot me dead on the spot if she could.

Then I think of how she looked last night at the concert. Standing on the center of the stage in her pretty purple dress, her eyes shining and a smile on her face. She looked happier than I've ever seen her.

Before last night, I'd never seen her look happy at all.

I wonder what Sarah would ask for if she could have anything she wanted. A better world, probably. One where color didn't matter.

What else? What would she want for herself? What are the things that make *her* happy?

After that day, Sarah never looked at me at school. If I caught her eye by accident she always covered her face and turned away.

I knew what that meant. I knew shame when I saw it.

At first I wondered if she'd told anyone, but then I saw how her eyes darted away from mine and I was sure it was a secret. She wouldn't go around talking about something like that.

A thud on the front door makes all three of us jump.

Is something wrong? Does someone know I'm here?

Is it Daddy?

Sarah's mother smooths her dress and pats her hair. If I hadn't seen Sarah do the same thing every morning before she came into class I'd never have known Mrs. Dunbar was nervous.

"You girls stay here." Mrs. Dunbar goes to the entryway.

Sarah moves to the chair nearest the door. She leans in far enough that when her mother opens it I'm sure whoever's out there will see her. I want to hiss at her to move, to pull her back myself if that's what it takes. Before I can, she leaps up and runs to the door.

"Ennis!" she cries. "Have you heard anything?"

It's the other colored boy. The one who sits with Sarah and Chuck at lunch every day. He was talking to Sarah last night after the concert, too.

"I'll tell you what I know," Ennis says. "Can I come in?"

Sarah leans in to whisper something to him. That's awfully familiar of her.

Ennis comes into the living room. His eyes narrow when he sees me, but there's no surprise on his face. I must have been what Sarah was whispering about.

"Of course, come in, Ennis," Mrs. Dunbar says. "You know Linda from school, I'm sure? She's paying us a call. Please, come in and tell us how Chuck is doing."

There's a thundering sound on the stairs. Sarah's little sister runs down. "Did someone say something about Chuck? Is he all right?"

Ennis's eyes soften. "He's hurt pretty bad, Ruthie."

I close my eyes. For the second time today I want to make everything vanish. Undo all the damage I've done and wipe it back to a blank slate.

All five of us sit in the living room. Ennis positions himself close to Sarah on the sofa. Mrs. Dunbar makes Ennis take a lemon bar. I wring my hands in my lap. It's as if the Dunbars and Ennis are used to talking about things like this.

"They let me see him in the hospital," Ennis finally says. "He's lost a lot of blood, and he has some broken bones, but the real problem is, he took a blow to the head. They're not sure when he'll wake up."

When? Or if?

I can tell Ennis is watching what he says in front of Sarah's little sister, and probably me, too. So I try to look in between his words.

Chuck is alive. But maybe not for long.

"He'll wake up soon, I know it," Ruth says. "He's too tough for anybody."

Ennis smiles at her. "Of course he is."

Sarah and her mother are both clasping their hands in their laps so hard their knuckles are turning pale.

"Did you learn anything else?" Mrs. Dunbar asks after a minute.

Ennis glances at Ruth, then at me. His eyes narrow again.

"It's all right," Sarah says. "Tell us."

Ennis frowns, then shrugs. "Well, it'll be in the paper tomorrow anyway. Jefferson expelled him."

At first I think I heard him wrong.

People don't get expelled for—

He isn't even *conscious*—

He didn't *do* anything—

Ruth is on her feet before I can find the words.

"They *can't!*" She swings her head with the force of her words. "They can't *expel* him. It's not his fault what happened. He's hurt! They wouldn't expel a boy who's in the hospital! It's not *right!*"

"They said he broke the no-fighting rule," Ennis says. "Hugh Bailey called the principal and told him what happened. He said he didn't catch any of the white boys' faces, but he could identify Chuck for sure. The rule is it doesn't matter who started the fight. Anyone involved is automatically expelled."

I shake my head. This is absurd. Not a single one of those boys will be punished for what they did—but *Chuck* will? Chuck who very well might *die?*

"I was there," I say. "I can tell them who the other boys were. It was Bo and Eddie and Kenneth and—"

"It won't matter," Sarah says softly. She looks just like Ennis. Resigned. "It only counts if there's an adult witness."

Ruth shakes her head, her face crumpling. Mrs. Dunbar holds out her hand.

"It's not *right*," Ruth says. She takes her mother's hand and squeezes it hard.

I look back and forth between the four of them.

I don't belong here.

Ennis is sitting on the Dunbars' couch as if he's sat there a million times before, his knees apart, his shirt rumpled, his eyes on Sarah.

I'm in a stiff chair with my back straight, my ankles crossed and my hands folded in my lap. The way they taught us to sit at cotillion when calling on our neighbors.

They all knew this would happen. Even Ruth doesn't look surprised. Just desperate.

This isn't my world. It's theirs.

I stand up. "I should be getting home. Thank you for the—"

How do I thank them for telling me their friend is in the hospital, and that he's being punished for it? What are the words for that? What's the etiquette?

"For the tea," I say instead, wishing again I could disappear.

"It was very nice to meet you, Linda," Mrs. Dunbar says over Ruth's head. "Sarah will show you out."

I don't want Sarah to show me out. I don't want to see that

look on her face again. The one that says she never expected anything better from me than this.

But when she moves toward the door, I follow. Sarah leads me out onto the porch and closes the door behind us.

"If he wakes up, will he still get to graduate?" I ask. There are only four weeks of school left.

She shrugs. "Mrs. Mullins will figure something out. Maybe he'll go back to Johns for the rest of the year."

"How are you so calm? This is awful."

Then Sarah gives me the worst look of all. Her head is tilted, her lips pursed in a half frown.

She *pities* me.

"You really think I'm calm?" she says.

"Oh. I don't know. You seemed so—" I'm stumbling over the words.

Something is different now. I want Sarah to understand that. I want her to see how I feel about all of it. About her. I want—

"I don't want to see anything like this happen again," she says. "Not to anyone else I care about."

I nod. "Of course not. How will you—"

"I'm getting out of here," she says. "I'm getting out of your school. And I'm getting my sister out, too. So none of us will have to go through this ever again."

LIE #24

She doesn't matter.

Sarah

I DON'T GO to sleep until after three that night. There's too much to do.

First I have to wait until everyone else has gone to bed, so I can write the letter to Mr. Deskins. The writing takes two hours by itself. I have to find the right words. The ones that make it sound like I have permission from Mama and Daddy, but that aren't outright lies. The ones that ask for a favor without sounding as though I really need help.

After I finish, I find an envelope and a stamp in Daddy's desk and the address in Mama's notebook, and I seal everything up. Then I stare at the envelope for the next thirty minutes, arguing with myself over whether to mail it.

I should. Of course I should. I even told Linda I should.

But what will Mama and Daddy say? And what about Ruth and Bobby?

Finally I change out of my nightgown into a pair of jeans, let myself out of the house without making a sound and start the eight-block walk to the post office.

No one else is out this late around here. Over in Davis Heights, Stud's Diner is still open. So are a few other places. Rough places someone like me wouldn't go. Here in Morningside everyone is tucked in, asleep, well behaved.

If he wakes up, Chuck and his family will have to move. Mama said they might try to find a school in Richmond where he can finish out his senior year. It's too dangerous for him to stay in Davisburg.

It doesn't matter that the rumors weren't true. The idiot white girl told the police Chuck didn't do anything, but the paper won't write about that, of course. Not as long as William Hairston has anything to say about it.

Daddy's been working all afternoon on a story about it for the *Davisburg Free Press*. Mama hasn't said anything, but I can tell it makes her nervous. The white people don't read the *Free Press* yet, but there's no way to know they won't start tomorrow.

I reach the post office and stare at the mailbox for five full minutes before I open the tray and drop my letter in.

There. It's done.

If I ever doubt this decision, I only have to remember the look on Bo Nash's face this morning. And what I said to Linda this afternoon.

She acted so strange today. I couldn't believe she actually said yes when I called her bluff and invited her over. Then she sat in my living room as prim and proper as if she were having tea with the Queen of England. After she left, Mama said she wished all my friends were such quiet, well-behaved girls. Then she took me aside and asked if Linda wasn't a little slow. Another day, that would've made me laugh.

I've put off thinking about Linda since she left. There was too much going on. Ennis visiting. The news about Chuck. Deciding to write the letter.

But I'm thinking about her now.

Maybe this isn't just about something being wrong with me. Maybe there's more to think about than that.

The Linda I met on the first day of school would never have come to my house. She wouldn't have yelled for the boys beating Chuck to stop.

She wouldn't have clapped for me at the concert. Certainly not in front of her father.

Maybe I was right about her all along.

Or maybe she's changed. Maybe we both have.

Thinking about Linda always makes me look over my shoulder, in case someone's watching, but I'm all alone on my deserted street.

And even if I wasn't, no one can see inside my head except me and God.

I used to think you could spot a sinner a mile away. People like Bo Nash and William Hairston and Nikita Khrushchev were bad. People like my parents and Mrs. Mullins and Reverend King were good. It was easy to tell the difference.

But now I don't think that's how it works. Whatever I think, whatever I feel—it isn't spelled out on my face.

No one is going to judge me for what I'm thinking and feeling except me and God. And I'm not sure I understand how God judges people anymore, either.

I don't understand why He would punish someone like Chuck. Or the boy in Mississippi. Or all of us Negroes. Being told we can't sit at a lunch counter isn't the same as being beaten, but it's a punishment, too.

I don't understand why He allows all of that to happen, but still hasn't punished me for what I did that day with Linda.

I searched through the Bible, trying to understand. There was something in Leviticus about men lying with men being an abomination, but nothing about women. All I could find was Paul's letter to the Romans, where it said, "For this cause God gave them up unto vile affections: for even their women did change the natural use into that which is against nature: And likewise also the men, leaving the natural use of the woman, burned in their lust one toward another; men with men working that which is unseemly, and receiving in themselves that recompense of their error which was meet."

Where's the recompense for *my* error?

I must've read those verses a hundred times over the past few weeks. I still don't understand what it was those women Paul knew did that was so wrong. Or how Paul knew so much about what those women were up to.

I don't know what the men's "natural use of the woman" means, either, but it doesn't sound like something any respectable woman ought to be used for.

In Paul's letter to the Ephesians he said, "Slaves, be obedient to them that are your masters according to the flesh, with fear and trembling, in singleness of your heart, as unto Christ."

The slaves who were my great-great-great-grandparents probably had fear and trembling to spare.

Daddy says since we're just lowly humans we can't expect to understand everything that's in the Bible, but we have to follow it anyway because it's the Word of God. But Daddy also says the white people interpret the Bible for their own ends when they want to. They use the curse of Ham in Genesis to say colored people are less than whites.

I don't know what I'm supposed to believe anymore. I want to follow the teachings of the Lord, but I don't know how. It's so complicated. Why would God give me these feelings if they're wrong?

How do I know if I'm living according to His plan if I don't know what His plan is?

When I used to talk to Linda I felt more alive than I ever had before.

I was better with her. Stronger. I knew what I was supposed to do.

Now I can't tell up from down or right from wrong.

If something—someone—makes me feel that way, how can that be against God's will?

It wasn't God who decided to make my great-great-great-grandparents slaves. It was white men who wanted to make money. They made up the rules everyone else had to follow.

What if this—this rule that says what I did in the back room that day is a terrible sin—what if that's just a rule some old white man made up, too?

Isn't it blasphemous to even think that?

I don't know. I don't understand how any of this works anymore.

I feel lost. Like my head is spinning around on my shoulders.

I can't shake the feeling someone's been lying to me all along. Because they don't think I'm smart enough to understand the truth.

I've had enough.

It's time I figured out the truth for myself.

"I don't want it." Ruth shoves the bag across the breakfast table Monday morning. "I'll tell the teacher it's still dirty."

"I ran it through the wash twice." The look on Mama's face means she's fresh out of patience. I bet she wishes I were still on my laundry punishment so she wouldn't be the one dealing with Ruth's Gym suit. "It's clean. Take it with you or you'll get another detention."

"I don't care," Ruth says. "They can give me as many detentions as they want."

"You get many more of those and you'll fail," I tell her. "You really want to repeat freshman phys ed?"

"I don't care," she repeats.

"Stop being so immature," I say.

"Leave me alone!" Ruth throws her fork down with a clatter, leaps out of her seat and thunders upstairs.

We all stare after her.

"Well," Mama says. "I suppose she's still upset about Chuck. Though that's no excuse to be rude at the table."

But she left two pieces of bacon untouched on her plate. That's not the Ruth I know.

"I'll bring her back down," I tell Mama. She nods distractedly. She's already moved on to clearing the plates.

"The carpool will be here any minute," I tell Ruth when I find her sulking on her bed. "We don't have time for temper tantrums."

She doesn't look up. "I'm not having a temper tantrum. I'm not a little kid, remember?"

"All right." I sit down on the bed next to her. "Look, it's only Gym class. Everyone hates it. You have to take it anyway. I did."

"You didn't take Gym at Jefferson."

Oh.

I'd been so busy thinking about how much I hated my own classes I hadn't given a thought to Ruth's.

Only the freshmen and sophomores take Gym. And Gym is the only class that requires taking your clothes off.

"Is it that bad?" I ask softly.

Ruth picks at a loose thread on her pillowcase. "Last week they turned the showers up on Yvonne as hot as they'd go. She got burned so bad she was crying."

"Did the teacher see?"

Ruth shakes her head. "The week before that they stole Delores's bra and hung it from the bulletin board in the boys' locker room."

I'd heard about that. I meant to check on Delores afterward, but I'd been busy getting ready for the concert.

"Do you think he'll wake up?" Ruth murmurs.

So this is about Chuck after all.

"Yes," I say, hoping I sound more certain than I feel.

"Will we ever get to see him again?"

"After he moves, you mean? Of course. Richmond isn't all that far away. He can come back for visits."

I don't think he would come back, though. Once I get out of here, I'm never coming back to Davisburg.

"He was my favorite," Ruth says. "He was always smiling, or saying something funny."

Ruth is talking about Chuck as if he's already dead.

"I know," I say. "When he moves, I'm going to miss him, too."

"You don't have to worry. You have Ennis."

I sit back on the bed and eye Ruth carefully.

"Did you have a crush on Chuck?" I say. She covers her face with her hand. I smile. "Was he the one you were thinking of that day we talked about kissing? Ruthie, you know he's way too old for you."

"Oh, what do you know." Ruth doesn't look sad anymore. Just tired. "Daddy's five years older than Mama."

"Yes, but neither of them is fifteen."

"Don't you even talk. That white girl you had over here the other day is going with Coach Pollard. Do you know how old *he* is?"

"You shouldn't listen to idle gossip," I say to cover up how alarmed I am. I'd forgotten all about Linda and Mr. Pollard.

Ruth stands up and grabs her books off her dresser. She's back to her normal self. Annoyed at her big sister. "Let's go. I've had enough of you telling me what to do for one morning."

I roll my eyes and follow her downstairs.

Mama is waiting for us at the door just as Mrs. Mullins pulls up. Ruth takes her Gym suit from Mama, who whispers a quick "Thank you" to me low enough that Ruth can't hear.

But when we slide into the backseat of the car Ruth throws her Gym suit to the floor in a ball, then stabs it with her loafers until it's squashed down flat. Then she kicks it again. And again.

If I had any doubts left, they're gone.

I need to get us out of this. Ruth most of all.

By dinnertime, I'm even more determined.

School today was a nightmare. We were supposed to be reviewing for our end-of-year exams, but no one even pretended to pay any attention to their schoolwork.

Word about Chuck's expulsion had gotten around before we got there. Signs were posted all over the school written in thick pencil saying Two Down, Eight to Go. The teachers took them down when they saw them, but the white students must have made dozens, because whenever one vanished another went up in its place. Everywhere I went the white people jostled me more than ever, knocking my books out of my arms, throwing balls of paper at my back. Shouting, "The big nigger got what was coming to him" and "Ain't you learned your lesson yet, girl? Don't none of y'all belong at this school."

It still makes me angry, but now that I know what real fear feels like, these hallway shouts don't upset me as much as they used to.

This all just seems so *silly*.

It's as though I've grown a shell around myself. Something for the shouts to bounce off of. Something the spitballs can't penetrate.

I'm better than all this.

These people can do what they want, but they can't hurt me. I'm stronger than all of them put together.

It's a strange feeling, but once it came it didn't go away. Not when Bo leered at me in the lunch line. Not even when someone left a crude drawing in my locker of a girl hanging from a tree with a note that said "You're up next."

At the end of the day, another strange thing happened.

It was after seventh period. I was walking toward the side exit with Ennis, both of us getting hit from all sides with balled-up pieces of paper. What was odd was that paper was flying all over the hallway—and not all of it was aimed at us. Everyone was talking about it, too. I couldn't understand it all, but I caught a "bunch of lies" here, a "Coach Pollard" there and one "acting weird at Bailey's" on the way out.

"What the Devil?" Ennis muttered, looking at all the trash.

He caught the next paper that flew our way and uncrumpled it. It was a copy of today's school newspaper.

Ennis shrugged and passed it to me. There wasn't a garbage can nearby and I didn't want to throw trash around the school like everyone else, so I tucked it into my purse.

Then I forgot about it. Until now.

As we're finishing our peach cobbler Daddy turns to Ruth and me and says, "So tell me, girls. Do either of you know this Linda Hairston? Bill Hairston's daughter? Next time you see her at school, you tell her I said to keep it up, all right?"

Then he sits back, smiles and takes a long puff on his cigarette.

I look at Ruth for an explanation. She shrugs. "She's your friend, not mine."

"Oh, is she a friend of yours, Sarah?" The gleam is still in Daddy's eyes. "Guess the apple fell far from the tree."

"Is this the Linda who was over here on Saturday?" Mama looks at me sharply. "You didn't tell me she was William Hairston's daughter."

"I didn't—" My face flushes. Why is everyone talking about *her?* "Daddy, what do you mean, 'the apple fell far from the tree'?"

"Didn't you read your school paper today?" Daddy says. "Honey, I'm disappointed in you. It's important to keep up with the news. Especially when the news is this good. I tell you, the story I'm writing about it for the *Free Press* is going to make Hairston sit up and take notice."

Now Mama's sharp look is pointed at Daddy. "You're going to

write an article about William Hairston's daughter? She's only a child, Robert."

Daddy smiles again. "The girl went to the printer herself, on a Sunday, and told them it was a last-minute change. The school administration didn't even know she'd done it until she started passing out copies at the end of the school day. It was all anyone was talking about at the meeting this afternoon. I'm telling you, Irene, if we don't write on this we're passing up the only positive story to come out of this entire ordeal. If it gets Hairston's goat, well, that's icing on the cake."

Mama is still glaring. "Children, you're excused."

As soon as I get upstairs I take the crumpled newspaper out of my purse. When I turn to the editorial page I understand why everyone was so excited.

```
JEFFERSON HIGH CLARION
Monday, May 25, 1959
First, Do No Harm
By Linda Hairston, Editorial Page Editor


I never thought I would say this, but this week,
I witnessed something that made me ashamed to
call myself a Southerner.
    I saw a gang of more than fifteen boys attack
another boy. This boy was alone. He couldn't de-
fend himself against such a large group. He is
in the hospital now, still unconscious. He has
been unfairly expelled from school.
    Why did the gang attack this boy, you ask?
    The answer is simple: it was because the boy
was a Negro.
    Like my fellow students, I was upset when the
courts forced the integration of Jefferson. I
believed it was wrong. I believed it would hurt
```

the integrity and traditions of our school and our state. I still hold those beliefs today.

But the brutality I witnessed this week hurts our integrity more than the courts and the NAACP ever could.

We all must stand up for what we know is right. It is up to us, as Americans and as the generation who will someday lead this country, to set the right path for those who will come after us.

I am still proud to be a Southerner, but I am not proud of the people who commit acts like this in the South's name.

The South is better than that.

I put the newspaper down and rub my forehead.

Oh, *Linda*. Linda, Linda, Linda.

You'll be lucky if you live through tomorrow.

LIE #25

I'm ready.

Linda

THEY'RE ALL STARING at me.

I pretend everything's normal. I pretend I don't mind.

I'm sort of used to it, after all. I'm popular. When you're popular, people stare at you.

But no one's ever stared at me like this. Like I'm a creature from a horror movie. The kind you don't really want to look at because it's disgusting, but then you look anyway because you want to see what it'll do next.

They're talking about me, too. I see it in their faces, but I don't hear it. Whenever I turn a corner, everyone shuts up and stares.

When I get to my regular table in the cafeteria, everyone goes quiet at once. That's how I know my friends are talking about me, too. I'm not surprised, but it hurts all the same.

Most of them won't even look at me. They're glancing back and forth among each other.

Judy is sitting as far away from my seat as she can get, as

usual, but she nods in greeting when I sit down. She hasn't done that since that day in the back room.

"Sorry I missed your party Saturday," I tell Donna. "I got home late and Mom wouldn't let me go. Was it a fun time?"

Donna and the others just go on staring.

Finally Nancy says, "Yes, it was a fun time. Except half the boys there were limping. Some of them were hurt, you know."

"Well, maybe they should think twice before they do something like that again," I say.

Nancy rolls her eyes.

"I liked Linda's article," Judy says.

Now everyone's staring at *her*.

"Well, I did." Judy cups her hand over her cheek, but she doesn't look down.

I've never seen her act this way.

She must know what she's risking. Judy lives in New Town, and she wears a pound of makeup every day on top of the bright red blotch that covers half her face. The only reason Nancy and the others put up with her is because she's my best friend. Or used to be.

But she keeps going.

"I don't think it's right," Judy says. "The way they all went after that Nigra boy when he was by himself. It wasn't a fair fight."

"What Linda wrote, though?" Nancy says. "About the boys we've gone to school with all our lives? Who were defending girls like us against a dangerous colored man? I don't want people to think I'd go around saying things like that about the nicest boys at this school. I don't want them to think I'd be friends with someone who would, either."

I shake my head at Nancy. Is this really all it takes to have someone turn on you? All because she wants so desperately to go steady with *Bo Nash?*

"Coach Pollard is bound to be upset when he sees it," Donna

says. "A lot of those boys are on the team. Linda, if you don't do something about this soon it could ruin your whole life."

"And over that colored boy," Brenda says. "After what he did to Kathy. It could've been any of us!"

"He didn't do anything to Kathy," I say. "She said so herself. That's why the police let him go."

"Do you know what people are saying about you?" Donna shakes her head. "What they're *calling* you?"

"Let me guess," I say. "Nigger-lover?"

Everyone gasps, shocked I said it out loud.

The truth is, I'm shocked, too.

That's not what I am. I'm not an agitator or a Communist or an integrationist. I still don't think it's right for the NAACP to tell us what to do in our own school.

But no one asked me what I really believe. They've already decided.

"You *do* know?" Donna says. "Then, Linda, please, let's go to the newspaper and have them print an apology. You can say you were sick or something. Or that it was a joke, or—"

I stand up. I don't know what I'm doing. I just know I don't want to listen to this anymore.

I grab my lunch tray. I haven't eaten, but I'm not hungry. I turn to leave.

Then I remember that only a short time ago I didn't think about these things any more than my friends did. I turn back around.

"Go home and think about it," I tell them. "Really think about whether what happened on Saturday is right. That boy, Chuck, is in the hospital. He might not ever wake up. Please, just think it through. Then we can talk again."

Nancy shakes her head sadly. The rest of them act as if they didn't even hear me.

That's all right. I'm done now.

I go to dump my uneaten food. My heart is still pounding.

When I wrote the editorial I wasn't thinking about this part. About how it would look to my friends, or Jack or everyone at school.

I thought about how it would look to Sarah, though.

I thought it might make her start to forgive me.

I thought it might make her see that I'm not the girl she thinks I am. That there's more to me than that girl.

But even more than that, I thought about how it would look to Daddy.

I thought about him reading it in his office over his morning coffee. How his mouth would turn down. How his brow would furrow. How he'd throw the paper down and reach for his phone to order every copy rounded up and burned.

I was up all night. Terrified of what Daddy would say, what he'd do, when he saw it.

Terrified. And hopeful.

The truth was, I *wanted* to make Daddy angry. I wanted to make him *something*.

But that still hasn't happened. Because he hasn't read it yet.

It's been a full day since the article came out, but he doesn't even know about it. Daddy hasn't read anything I've written in years.

Before long, someone will tell him. "Hey, Bill, your daughter playing a prank on you? Don't tell us you've got one in your own family. You better whup some sense into that girl."

After that, something will happen.

The waiting is almost worse than the *something* will be.

Someone shoves a lunch tray in my back roughly. I have to grab on to the counter to avoid falling into the trash can. "Hey!"

"Hey, nothing."

I turn around. It's Bo Nash.

"Or should I say, 'Hey, nigger-lover.'" He tilts his head to the side.

"Leave me alone, Bo." I dump my tray and slide it onto the counter, trying to act as though I'm not afraid.

But I am. After what I saw on Saturday, anyone would be afraid of Bo.

He won't do anything to me. Not here. He knows everyone would see. He wouldn't hurt me.

Right?

"You best not go around spreading lies," he says. "We hear one word about you telling tales to the principal, trying to make trouble—"

"If I did it wouldn't be a lie," I say. "I was there. I saw it."

Bo steps closer to me. Too close. I step back. My spine is up against the counter.

"Don't think we won't come at you," he says, his voice low and rough. "I'm not scared of your little boyfriend. I'm done playing football for this school. And I'm not the only one."

All right. Now I'm afraid.

"I have a question for you, Bo," says a sharp voice behind him.

It's Sarah.

I will her to stop. To leave.

Bo might not hurt me in front of everyone, but that won't help her.

She doesn't stop.

"Do you ever fight fair?" she says. "Or are you always going after girls? Or twenty against one? Is it that you're too scared for a real fight?"

I don't think Bo is scared of any kind of fight, but Sarah's certainly got his attention.

"Hey there, nigger bitch." He turns to her and raises his voice so the tables nearby can hear. "Been singing any more of that coon music for your nigger friends? Or, wait, you've hardly got any nigger friends left, have you? They're all getting beat out of town. Guess you and that shrimpy little sister of yours'll be next."

Sarah flinches at the mention of Ruth. Not enough for Bo to notice, though.

"You know what you are?" Sarah puts her books on the counter and stands facing him, her hands on her hips. She looks just like her mother. "You're nothing but a coward."

"Oh, yeah?" Bo's still smiling, moving closer to her. Waiting for her to back away, like I did. "How you figure that?"

Sarah stays put. "You only go after people you think are weaker than you. People you think you can scare into not fighting back."

Half the cafeteria is watching now. Sarah's talking just as loudly as Bo. They're only inches apart. I grip the counter, wondering if I should run for a teacher. If it would be safe to leave them here.

"You know you'll never make it out of this town," Sarah tells Bo. "You'll never be anybody. So try to make everybody else feel bad. I bet *you* feel so bad you cry yourself to sleep every night."

A couple of the boys watching from the next table snicker. Bo glances at them.

"What have you ever done that's been good for anyone else?" Sarah says. "Or are you just taking up space at this school? Trying to have some fun while you wait until you're old enough to be the town drunk, slumped over on a bench in front of the hardware store at ten o'clock in the morning?"

More snickers. No one in the cafeteria is talking now. They're all watching Sarah and Bo.

I can tell from the way she's tapping her heel that Sarah's nervous, but she doesn't let Bo see. She keeps her chin high, her expression fixed.

Bo glances around at the people watching. After a long moment, he sneers at Sarah.

"Well at least I'm not a doggone ugly nigger," he says.

Sarah looks at him.

Then she starts to giggle.

Bo's eyes narrow. "Stop laughing, nigger."

That only makes her laugh harder.

Then I'm laughing, too. So are some of the girls at a table two rows down.

They're not laughing with Sarah and me. They wouldn't dare openly laugh at Bo.

But they're laughing all the same. And Bo isn't.

Sarah turns away from him, still giggling, and retrieves her books from the counter. She glances my way. Our eyes meet. I nod, and in the same moment, we turn on our heels and walk out of the cafeteria as the laughter spreads from table to table.

Not a single person tries to trip us on the way out.

For half a second, it feels like we might have won.

Then I look back and see Bo watching us. This isn't over.

Even so I can't help smiling when the cafeteria door closes behind us and Sarah and I are alone in the hallway.

I try not to think about what everyone must be saying about me back there. It doesn't work, but I keep smiling anyway.

"I can't believe you did that," I say.

Sarah smiles at me, but her smile is shaky. So are her hands.

"Listen," I say, talking fast before I can change my mind. "My dad works late and my mom will be at her bridge club until dinner. Can you come over after school? We could—talk."

I don't expect her to say yes. I don't expect her to even think about it. She'll probably just get that same pitying look she gave me at her house on Saturday.

Instead, she nods, slowly.

Maybe something really is about to change.

LIE #26

*I don't know how
to do this.*

Sarah

LINDA'S HOUSE LOOKS exactly like mine.

It's obvious that it's a white house, of course. It's in Ridge-wood, for one thing. And for another, there's a Negro woman in a uniform cleaning the kitchen when we arrive.

When we first walk in the door the Negro woman looks as though she expects me to pick up a rag and join her. Then her eyes go wide and she offers us iced tea, as polite as you please. Linda says no and looks embarrassed as she leads me down the hall to her room.

Other than that I could just as easily have been in any of the houses in my neighborhood. Linda's house and mine even have the same carpet in the front hallway. Hers is older, though. "More established," Mama would say.

Her room is the same size as mine, but since she doesn't have to share it she's covered all the walls with photos torn from magazines. Girls in pretty dresses from *Seventeen*. Handsome actors in ads for movies I watched from the balcony.

On her dresser there's a framed photo of Coach Pollard. It's from the Jefferson yearbook from a few years ago, when he was a student. I go over for a closer look.

"Are you really going to marry Mr. Pollard?" I blurt out before I can think better of it.

Linda closes the door behind her. We stand facing each other with her dresser, and the photo, between us.

"Of course I am." She sits on the desk chair, crossing her ankles and folding her hands on her knee. "We can't announce the engagement while I'm still in school, that's all. Jack is a gentleman. He always thinks about propriety."

My throat feels dry. I wish I'd taken the drink her maid offered.

"Are you going to marry that boy?" she says. "Ennis?"

I try to laugh, as though such a thought has never crossed my mind.

"You're going steady, aren't you?" she says.

I shake my head. "He hasn't asked me. Anyway, we're far too young to think about marriage."

Linda nods. "It's much easier with an older man."

This isn't what I'd hoped we'd talk about this afternoon.

I'm curious about Linda and her fiancé, of course. I have been ever since Judy first told me. At the beginning I thought it couldn't possibly be true. Linda wore a pin on her collar every day, but she and Mr. Pollard didn't act the way going-steady couples do. When Kenneth Cox and Brenda Green walk down the hall together he keeps his finger threaded through the cloth loop at the back of the neck of her Villager blouse, as though she's about to make a break for it.

Then I saw Linda and Mr. Pollard talking next to his car in the Bailey's parking lot one day. The looks they were giving each other were serious. Very serious.

"How did you start up with him?" I sit on the edge of her bed. There's nowhere else in the room to sit.

"It was last summer, out at Kiskiack," she says. "He works there, and I went up every day in July. We got to talking. It was simply one of those things."

I nod. You always hear about scandalous things that happen at Kiskiack Lake in the summer. I've never been there—colored people aren't allowed to go anywhere white people swim, not in the South—but everyone hears the stories.

"When's the wedding?" I ask.

"After graduation."

"But when?" Graduation is only three weeks away.

"Oh." Linda shrugs. "Jack's difficult to pin down. You know how men are. He says he'd just as soon whisk me away somewhere. Elope, you know."

I don't like the way Linda's talking, as though she's reciting dialogue from some romance novel. I like the way she usually talks better. Especially now that she's stopped trying to convince me Negroes are inferior.

Come to think of it, I still don't know why she stopped doing that.

"What happened to you?" I say. "Why did you print that article? You must've known what people would say."

She shrugs. "I've never worried too much about anything Bo Nash might think."

"This isn't about Bo. You know that."

She shrugs again and leans over the back of her desk chair. Her pleated skirt bunches as she tucks one leg under the other. A few inches of bare skin peek out above her knee sock. I stare at it for a moment before I catch myself and look away.

"I don't know." She tucks her head into her arm. I can't see her face. Can't see what she's thinking. "I—I don't know. Once I started thinking about it, I got to a place where I couldn't think myself back out again."

I knew it. I *knew* Linda was too smart to believe all those things she said.

"What place was that?" I say.

"Ah." For a long time, she doesn't say anything. Finally, she looks back up. "It was after what happened in the office that day. With Miss Jones. When she wouldn't let you go get your brother when he was sick."

"Oh." I'd forgotten all about that. "Bobby was fine. He was only faking."

"Well I didn't know that then. I thought he was really sick, the same way I used to get sick when I was little, and he was only going to wind up sicker because Miss Jones was treating you that way. And she was only doing that because you were colored. Your little brother never did anything to anyone. And what the boys did outside Bailey's on Saturday—well, it was kind of the same thing, wasn't it?"

Miss Jones.

Seriously? Miss *Jones?*

Everything I've ever said to Linda about the movement didn't make an impact at all. She just needed to see Miss Jones being a pain.

"I just knew it wasn't right, what they did to that boy." Linda's eyes are fixed on the wall. "And it was my fault. Because of what I said."

I don't argue with her. It *was* her fault what happened to Chuck. Partly. But if she hadn't said what she did, someone else would have sooner or later. It was bound to happen once Chuck took up with Kathy Shepard.

But if what Ennis said is true—if Chuck and the Shepard girl love each other—why shouldn't they be together? Why do they have to care about what Bo Nash thinks?

"It's like what Bo did to that other boy in Study Hall," Linda says. "Everybody knew that was wrong, but nobody wanted to say it."

"So did you write that editorial to say beating people up was wrong?" I say. "Or to say segregation was wrong?"

Linda shakes her head. "You know I'd never speak out against segregation."

Of course.

I should've known she didn't *really* understand.

But I want her to. More than anything.

"When they canceled the prom, and that boy's parents held a private dance just for the white students, you knew that was wrong, didn't you?" I ask her. "I could tell you did. I saw it in your face."

Linda meets my eyes. Hers are steely. "You make it sound so simple. It's not."

"You don't think I should be allowed to go to the same dance as you?"

"Of course I think *you* should, but you're different. You're Sarah."

That should bother me, her saying something like that. It does bother me, but part of me wants to smile, too.

She thinks I'm different.

She really feels something for me. Like I do for her.

And even if she still supports segregation, she won't go on that way forever. She's still hanging on to that last thread of who she used to be. It's got to be hard to let go, but before long, she'll come to understand the truth. I'll help her.

"It seemed to make sense, at first," she says. "I always thought the school was right to cancel the prom. Colored people and white people dancing together? Everyone knows that isn't right."

She looks up as if she expects me to argue. I don't.

Everyone does know that. Even I know it.

But I'm sitting in Linda's room anyway.

"But then," she goes on, "when I kept thinking about it, it made me wonder. Why does *everything* have to be about color?"

"I don't know," I say. "But it is."

"Yes," she agrees. "It is."

She looks at me with those steely eyes again. For a long time we just gaze at each other, neither of us speaking.

Linda's changed. She's changed more than I ever could've imagined when we first met.

I try to imagine what that would be like. To think about something so hard you realize you've been wrong your whole life. To go out in front of everyone you know and tell them you've changed your mind. It's no wonder she's still holding on to some of her old beliefs, but it's still incredible what she's done.

I try to imagine being that strong. Then I realize I *am* that strong.

Why have I always been so afraid to believe that?

"At the beginning," I tell her, "I wanted to die. When we first came to Jefferson, all I wanted to do was take Ruth and get us both out of that place. I wanted to go someplace far away where I could go to sleep and never wake up."

I've never told anyone that. I've never had anyone I could tell.

I never admitted it to myself, either.

"I don't feel like that anymore, though," I add. "Everything's different now. I mean, in a lot of ways it's just as bad as before, but I guess *I'm* different now."

"You wanted to—what?" Linda's smile is gone. "I mean, I guess I knew it was bad, but I didn't know it was *that* bad. And it was us that did that to you."

I start to say that it wasn't her, it was the others—but that would be a lie, too.

"I'm sorry," Linda says. She's staring at her hands. "You must hate me."

"I don't hate you. I never really did. Well, maybe those first few days." I smile at her again. She smiles back, but her chin wobbles. "After that I tried to keep on hating you, but it never worked. I kept seeing these little things you did or said. I could tell there was something different about you. Even though you were William Hairston's daughter."

Linda lowers her eyes again.

"You know my father works for your father, right?"

She nods. "Daddy didn't even know he had an NAACP worker on his staff."

I chuckle. "Your father needs to open his eyes."

Linda doesn't answer. Did I say something wrong?

"Sorry," I say quickly. "I shouldn't talk about your father that way."

"You can talk about my father however you want." She's still looking at the ground. "Believe me, I've heard enough people singing his praises for a lifetime."

I think again about how Linda looked at her father at the concert. How he looked back at her. How he frowned.

I wonder what it's like living in a house with William Hairston. I wouldn't want to spend another day here either if I were her.

"Is that why you want to get married so soon?" I ask, softening my voice so she won't get angry. "Because you want to get away from him?"

"Of course." Then she sits up straight and adds, "But really it's because I want to be with Jack. Jack is wonderful. He'll make a perfect husband."

"You don't have to get married to leave," I say. "What about college?"

She laughs.

"I'm serious," I say. "I'm going to college this fall. You could, too."

"College isn't for people like me," she says. "College is for girls who haven't already met the right man. And haven't learned how to type and take shorthand."

I know she's only parroting something she's heard people say, so I try not to let that hurt my feelings. It still does, though.

"If you get married right away, you won't ever get to be on your own," I say. "You'll go straight from your father to your husband. Don't you want to have any time to yourself?"

"What for?" She blinks at me.

"To think about if marriage is what you really want." I pronounce the words slowly. I never thought I'd say something like this out loud. I've barely said it in my own head. "Or if you want something else."

"What else is there?" Her eyes are clear and steady.

"I don't know," I say, because I don't. "But maybe there's something."

"There isn't." Her voice is flat. "Trust me. I checked."

"What do you mean, you checked?"

"I went to the library." She reaches into the gap between her desk and the wall and pulls out a paperback, an ancient tattered thing with pages falling out. "This was stuck behind a shelf."

The book's torn cover shows two white girls, one with blond hair, one with brown. They're both wearing slips that are cut down low. They're sitting on a bed together. One girl is looking off to the side, ashamed.

"Where was this in the library?" I flip the inside cover open, trying to keep it from falling off. The cover makes it look like— but no. Surely there aren't books about—

"I was looking for a book I found in the card catalog. It was by a doctor, Kingsley something. Only his book wasn't on the shelf. Someone must have stuck this one there instead. It doesn't have library tags."

I read the first few sentences of the book. It seems normal enough, but that cover—

"The book talks about it," Linda says. "It's about two girls at college who—well. Anyway, it ends horribly."

So it *is* a book about that.

Now that I know, the cover seems different. It makes me feel— something. Something I shouldn't feel.

I squeeze my eyes shut.

"There's no other way the book could've ended," Linda says. "When something's unnatural it can't go on too long before somebody gets punished for it."

My thoughts are racing. I can't stop looking at the book cover.

"I'm not sure that's true," I tell Linda. "I think maybe it's us who do that to ourselves. The punishment."

Linda takes the book out of my hand and waves it over her head. "The girl in this book almost gets expelled from college."

Expelled? Really? I suppose that's why it's so important to keep it a secret.

But that's only a story. It's not real. I don't know how this works in the real world.

"Why were you looking for this in the library?" I ask.

She looks down. "I wanted to understand why it happened. What it meant. There was no one I could ask."

It. She's talking about *it.*

"What do *you* think it meant?" My fear grows with each word. We're crossing a line now. Talking about *it.*

Linda shakes her head. "I guess it means there's something wrong with me. That's all it could mean, right?"

I shrug. When I answer her, I speak slowly, figuring out each word as I go. "Well. I don't know what it means. I've thought and thought and thought about it, but I can't figure it out. I don't think it's so simple as a book like that would say, though. I don't think anything's as simple as it looks from the outside."

Linda stares at me for a long time.

"You've thought and thought and thought about it?" she says softly.

I'm trembling, but I nod.

"Me, too," she says.

I flush. I'm still trying to think of what to say next when a door slams in the front hall.

"Is that your maid?" I say.

Linda doesn't answer. She's gone stiff.

A man's voice rumbles toward us from the front hall.

"Is she here?" he bellows.

Linda bolts out of her chair, her eyes fixed on the door, her face stark white.

I've been afraid of my father before. When I'd broken a rule and was about to be punished for it. I've never been *that* afraid, though.

Something here isn't right.

Then Linda's running to the window. If her father finds me here—

I scramble toward her and together we push up the seam. I gather my skirt in one hand and hoist myself over the frame without even checking to see how high the drop is.

Fortunately, it's only three feet. I land in a crouch, one of my loafers coming off. As I pull it back on I wonder how I'll explain the grass stain on my sock to Mama.

Then Linda tumbles out the window after me, landing on her backside.

Is she crazy? Her father must know she's home.

But I help her pull the window back down. And when Linda starts off running around the side of the house, I follow her.

"What are you doing?" I whisper, looking from one side to the other. Surely her father will come out to look for her when he finds her missing.

"We have to get away from here," she says. "He's seen the article. He has to have. There's no other reason he'd be looking for me."

She takes my hand and tugs me after her.

We dart between houses and through yards. A few of Linda's neighbors are outside. A woman weeding her garden. Two old men smoking pipes in rocking chairs on a porch. A few others we pass in a blur. We're moving too fast to get a good look at any of them, but I'm sure they notice us. A colored girl and a white girl—and William Hairston's daughter at that—running through the fanciest white neighborhood in Davisburg? Who *wouldn't* notice?

Linda stops to catch her breath when we're half a block away. We're safe from the neighbors now, in an alley between an old empty house and a corner store, hidden from the street by a row of Dumpsters. Even Linda's father won't think to look for us here.

"He didn't know you wrote that article?" I ask.

"No. He didn't see it yesterday, but now—" She rubs her eye. "I shouldn't have done it. I don't know what I was thinking."

"Yes you do. You told me. It's about right and wrong, remember? That's all any of this is about."

"No it's not," she says. "It can't be. Because *this* is wrong, remember?"

She lifts our hands. They're still clasped tightly. Even though we aren't running anymore.

"I don't think right and wrong is always that simple," I say.

She stares at me for a long minute. Then she kisses me.

Her lips on mine are warm and sweet and wonderful.

It's so different from that day at Bailey's I can't believe it.

There's none of the fear. None of the anger.

It just feels...good.

But how can it? Isn't this supposed to feel the *opposite* of good?

How could God let something so wrong feel like this?

Why is it all right for me to kiss Ennis, when that doesn't feel like anything at all, but not Linda, when kissing Linda feels like *this?*

Kissing Linda is the only thing all year—except for singing on that stage—that I've actually wanted to do. Wanted for me. Not for my family, or for the movement or for anybody else but me.

This is who I am. And I like me this way.

And I think God just might like me this way, too.

part 5

Amazing Grace

TRUTH #1

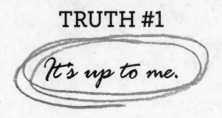

It's up to me.

Linda

I DON'T WANT to go home.

We hide in the alley for half an hour, and then Sarah has to go. She's worried for me—she asks if I want to come to her house instead—but I tell her it's all right. I'll have to face him sooner or later.

He knows it, too. He's been waiting for me.

He brought his chair into the hallway and set it up facing the door. He's already sitting there when I push it open, looking right at me from six feet away, a cigarette in his left hand and a drink in his right.

How long has he been waiting?

It doesn't matter. Somehow or another I'm going to have to pay him back for every second.

For a while he watches me, not speaking. So I don't speak, either. I close the door behind me and try to listen for Mom.

Is she home yet? Is she in the house somewhere, hiding from Daddy's mood?

I couldn't blame her. I've been hiding from Daddy's moods all my life. I just hid in an alley from Daddy's mood.

But I wasn't hiding alone. Not anymore.

Daddy takes another puff on his cigarette, his eyes still fixed on me. He hasn't look at me this hard in years.

I wonder if he can tell what I've been doing. That I had a colored girl in my room. That I kissed her. That I liked it.

I'm not ashamed of it. Not when there are so many other things to be ashamed of.

Sarah's right. We punish ourselves so much in our own imaginations. We convince ourselves everything we do, everything we think, is wrong.

For eighteen years I've believed what other people told me about what was right and what was wrong. From now on, I'm deciding.

I trust myself a lot more than I trust Daddy.

I cross my arms and lean back against the door. I'm terrified, but I try to look defiant.

"Did you think you were being clever?" Daddy stubs out his cigarette. "Lying to everyone? Claiming you had permission to write a piece of trash and insert it at the last minute when you had no such thing? When no editor, no teacher, no *parent,* had so much as seen it?"

I don't say anything. I don't take my eyes off him.

He's different now than he was when we first heard him shouting through the door.

I'm good at picking out the levels of Daddy's anger. When he first got home today, he was furious. He'd have come straight after me with his belt if he'd found me. He hasn't done that in years, but this would've been enough to set him off.

When he couldn't find me his rage would've simmered, fumed, into righteous indignation. If he'd found me then, he'd have shouted before he did anything else. Shouted what a disgrace I was, how I'd shamed the family, how I didn't deserve to bear his name.

Now, though, that surge of anger has cooled. And this is as bad as he gets. Because now he's had time to think it through. To decide exactly how hard I've made things for him. He's thought about what they'll write about him in the other papers. The jokes the newspapermen will make when they gather for their evening drinks.

The look on his face isn't anger anymore. It's disgust.

"I would like you to tell me," he says, speaking so slowly I can tell he's already written the lines in his head, already rehearsed them, "why you felt compelled to sign your name to that piece of garbage. To sign *my* name."

Oh.

He doesn't care that I wrote it. That I believe it. He only cares that I put my name on it.

"I knew my byline would draw attention," I say. His eyebrows leap up. He wasn't expecting an answer. "I wanted to show people I'd changed my mind. I wanted them to think maybe they could change theirs, too."

Daddy's hand tightens around his glass.

"Changed your mind, did you." His eyes narrow, but his gaze is steady as ever. He half smiles as he stands up, taking the time to set down his drink so it doesn't spill. Daddy always towers over me, but when we're standing so close together it's even more disorienting than usual. "And you thought that was worth sharing with the world, then? That everyone would care what *you* thought of things? I'm curious—how has that gone for you so far?"

I think of Bo's face in the cafeteria. And the fear that came with it. Wondering what he would do to me. If anyone would even care enough to help.

No one did. Except Sarah.

I don't have to listen to Daddy. I don't have to believe him.

He would never do what I did. He'd never write something that would turn people against him.

I'm stronger than he is.

It's up to me to decide what I do next.

"I hate you, Daddy," I say.

I reach behind me for the doorknob. Slow, so he won't see.

"You've always been a useless, ungrateful child." He steps toward me. His breath smells like liquor and venom. "You're too spoiled to ever be worth anything to anyone. That was our fault, your mother's and mine. We worried so much when you were ill that we got carried away. But you're grown now, and you don't want to go around saying things you'll regret."

"I will never regret this." I have the doorknob in my grip. "As long as I live."

"You will take that back." He's not smiling anymore. "It's already going to be bad for you. You're only making it worse."

"It's only as bad for me as I make it."

I wrench the door open.

I've caught him off guard, but he lunges forward anyway. Years ago, he'd have caught me. I'm faster now.

I have been for a long time. I just never noticed.

By the time I'm halfway down the front walk I know I'm safe. He won't come after me, not where the neighbors could see.

I'm safe.

I'm safe.

I'm *safe*.

"I don't feel right about this, Linda." Judy's mother stirs my chocolate milk. Mrs. Campbell always keeps cocoa in the house, even though it's expensive. It was Judy's and my favorite when we were little. "I think I should call your mother first."

"It's all right, I promise." I take a drink. I can't remember the last time something tasted this good. "She's not home yet anyway."

I'm not sure if that's actually true. I never did find out whether Mom was home when all that was happening before. I suppose it doesn't really matter.

"I know he's from a nice family, but all the same, people do talk when girls go out driving with older men." Mrs. Campbell peers out the window, looking for Jack's car. "Why don't you wait until Judy gets home from work and then you can all go for a drive together?"

I picture the look on Jack's face if I showed up at the curb with Judy in tow. It almost makes me smile.

"I promise we won't be out for long." I take another sip. "Thanks for this. It's good."

Mrs. Campbell smiles. "Judy won't let me make it for her anymore. She says she wants to reduce. I try to tell her she's too young for that, but she won't listen."

I wonder what Judy will say when she comes home and finds me here, given how "unnatural" and "sinful" she's always telling me I am. I picture her throwing a tantrum, the way Sarah's little sister did when we found out about Chuck being expelled.

But there's nowhere else I can go.

"Mrs. Campbell? Would it be all right if I stayed here tonight?"

She frowns. "I'm sure your mother wouldn't allow a sleepover on a school night. Judy isn't allowed to have them."

I decide to take a chance.

"I can't go home," I say. "I can't be around him."

Mrs. Campbell starts to say something, then stops. After a moment, she nods.

She knows about my father. She's known all along.

Mrs. Campbell has always understood more than she let on. Judy's the same way.

"Is your mother—" Mrs. Campbell cuts herself off when Jack's car pulls up out front.

"I'm sure she knows I'd come here," I say. "She'll know I'm all right. Please don't call my house? Please?"

Mrs. Campbell glances out at Jack. Then she nods again.

"Thank you." I finish the chocolate milk in one gulp. "I promise, I'll only be out for a few minutes."

Jack watches me closely as I come down Judy's front walk. I've never done this before. Called him up and asked him to come meet me. That's not the sort of thing the girl normally does. There's nothing normal about today, though.

He doesn't say anything about it when I climb into the car. He only smiles at me and asks, "Where to?"

"Anywhere but Ridgewood."

He pulls away from the curb, cursing as gravel spews from his tires. Judy's street isn't paved yet. Neither are half the roads in New Town. The houses here are tiny, and white and colored people live on the same streets. Sometimes even the same blocks.

People like Jack don't come to New Town if they can help it. Once I was old enough to understand that, I stopped coming here for visits. I made Judy take the bus to my neighborhood instead.

"So what's the emergency?" Jack says. "You sounded upset on the phone. Are some of the kids after you because of what you wrote in the paper? Need me to give them a good scare?"

I shake my head, even though his loyalty nearly breaks my heart.

"Can you pull over up here?" I point to a row of trees ahead.

"Sure." Jack pulls over and cuts the engine. He probably thinks I want to park. I used to like parking with him. It made me feel like we loved each other. Now I know that wasn't what I felt.

I don't know what love is, but I know it isn't what I have with Jack.

I told myself I needed him. That marrying Jack was my one way out.

Now I know there's never only one way.

Jack is a good man, but he isn't the man for me.

Maybe no man is. I don't know. I don't have to know all the answers yet. I just have to do what's right.

"I can't marry you, Jack," I say. "I'm sorry."

He looks at me for a long moment. Then he turns toward the windshield, his face stony. "I knew you'd change your mind."

"It isn't like that. I just don't think I'm ready to get married, not yet."

He grips the steering wheel. "Is it one of those boys at school? Someone on the team?"

"No. It's got nothing to do with anyone but me." I reach for his hand. He swats me away. "I'm too young to get married. I can't even make a decent soufflé yet."

That gets him to crack a smile. "You ought to pay more attention in Home Ec."

"There are only three weeks of school left. It's too late now."

He's still smiling.

That's how I know he doesn't really want to marry me, either. He knows I'm just a kid.

He didn't really understand that, not at first. By the time he realized he'd made a mistake, he'd already promised me. He gave me that ring because he knew how much I wanted it.

Jack is a good man. He didn't want to let me down. Today I've done him a favor.

Then why does this hurt so much?

I scoot into the middle of the seat and lean my head on his shoulder. He loosens his grip on the steering wheel and takes my hand.

I take a good long look at our clasped hands lying on the seat between us. It's so different from holding Sarah's hand. Jack's is big and callused with hair on his knuckles. White skin, of course. A little tanned from playing ball in the sun, but not so different from my own.

I like how Sarah's hand looks in mine. They're different colors, but they match. They look like they belong together.

Jack and I talk some more. About my cooking. About the new curtains his mother wants to make him. About who should captain next year's football team.

We don't talk about how much we'll miss each other.

I will miss Jack, but not in the way I used to think I would.

When we pull up in front of Judy's house, I take his ring out of my pocket, unfasten his pin from my collar and fold them both into his hand. He kisses me on the forehead.

Jack and I will never kiss again.

That's all right. It's better than only kissing one person for the rest of my life.

The rest of my life seems so much bigger than it did before.

Judy is in the house when I open the door. I expect her to yell for me to get out, but instead she just nods at me.

"I made up the sofa for you in the living room," she says. She looks sad and tired. She gives me a wrapped plate of fried chicken left over from the Bailey's dinner rush and one of her old nightgowns.

I used to stay in Judy's room when I slept over, but we were kids then. And different people, too.

I lie awake for hours that night on the Campbells' lumpy couch, watching a spider spin her web in a corner of the ceiling.

I thought my father knew everything about everyone. Especially me. I thought he could see deep inside me, to the darkest place. The sick place.

I thought that was why he hated me.

I didn't know I thought that until now.

But that's where it came from. The fear. The years of my life I wasted trying to show him I believed him. Trying to show everyone I was normal and perfect. Trying to fool them all.

I was wrong. My father doesn't know anything about me.

He doesn't hate me because of anything I am or anything I

did. When he started hitting me, it didn't have anything to do with me being sick, either the real sickness or the mental kind.

He hit me because he wanted to. Because that's the sort of person he is. He hates me for the same reason he hates my brothers, and my mother and the Negroes.

He hates us because he's a hateful man.

He's the one who's sick.

He's the one who did something wrong. Not me.

I don't realize I'm crying until I taste the salt on my lips.

In two days, I've changed everything. I destroyed the girl everyone thought I was.

I lost all my friends. My fiancé.

I walked out on my father.

I can't keep living the way I have been. Ending things with Jack was only one piece of it. What will happen to me when I go back home? What will I say to Daddy?

I don't want to go back there.

But what other choice do I have? I can't live with Judy and her mother forever. Mrs. Campbell's war widow pension is barely enough to cover their mortgage. She already works full-time at the real estate agency and takes in laundry, too. She's still hoping Mr. Pinkett, who owns Kiskiack Lake, will marry her one of these days, but in the meantime the money her parents left her is running out fast. And Judy's tips at Bailey's only add up to fistfuls of nickels and dimes.

I suppose I'll have to find work, too, if I don't want to go back home. Is that my only choice? To be lonely and fighting for pennies in Davisburg, like Mrs. Campbell?

As long as I stay in this town, I won't ever be able to forget Daddy's here. I won't ever be able to pick up a newspaper without seeing his name.

I thought marrying Jack, getting out of my house, would make everything better, but it wouldn't have worked that way.

It would've been pasting a Band-Aid on top of things and pretending that was enough to turn me into somebody else.

I have to do something more. Something just for me.

I can't sit back and let everyone else decide. I've been doing that long enough.

I have to take care of myself from now on.

And I'll have to trust myself to do it right.

TRUTH #2

None of them can touch me.

Sarah

OUR PRESIDENT ESSAYS are due today in History. We could write about any president we wanted as long as he was from Virginia. I wrote about Zachary Taylor, because everyone else was writing about George Washington or Thomas Jefferson and I thought Zachary Taylor was an interesting name. It turns out Zachary Taylor was a slave-owning plantation aristocrat. Same as George Washington and Thomas Jefferson.

At the end of the period Mrs. Johnson asks us to leave our essays on her desk. I reach into the homework folder in my notebook, but my essay isn't there.

I look everywhere. My purse. My other folders. It's gone.

"It was here this morning," I tell Mrs. Johnson. She raises a tired eyebrow. "I wrote about Zachary Taylor. I had it *right here.*"

"Then where is it now?" Mrs. Johnson says.

"It's— I don't know. Someone must've taken it when I got up to get a drink of water—"

Mrs. Johnson sighs. "Bring it in tomorrow and I'll only take off one letter grade."

All that work, gone. I'll have to rewrite the essay tonight and get a lower grade for doing twice as much work.

This isn't the first thing that's happened today. There was the ink sprayed in my locker this morning. And the wad of spitballs that landed on my skirt in Math.

It's Bo's doing. He's gotten all his friends, and all *their* friends, to gang up on me. Payback, for yesterday.

I should be angry. I'm upset about having to rewrite my essay, that's for sure, but there's no point being afraid.

Bo and his friends are going to do what they're going to do. Because they're children. They don't know any better. They aren't capable of learning new things. They simply need to be ignored until they get tired and go find something else to do. Like Bobby when he's playing the "Why?" game.

I do worry about Ruth, though. She shouldn't have to suffer just because I did something reckless.

I don't regret what I said to Bo yesterday, but if anything happened to Ruth my regrets would pile up faster than I want to think about.

I've gone back to my old habit of meeting her in the halls between classes. The first time she saw me there, she said hello. The second time, she rolled her eyes. The third time, she said, "Do I need to remind you I'm not six years old anymore?"

I smiled at her. I'm not letting Ruth get to me, either.

I don't think she really minds it, anyway. She knows we won't be in school together much longer. Three weeks from now, I'll have graduated and she'll be on her own.

But she won't be on her own at Jefferson. Not if I can help it.

I'm on alert the rest of the day, ready to head off any more childish pranks, but none of my other homework goes missing. There are only a few more taunts in the halls and pencils thrown at me in class than usual.

In Home Ec someone passes me the salt instead of the sugar when we're making pie dough. I notice right before I dump it into my bowl.

I start to relax. I start to think this is as bad as it will get.

I'm wrong.

It happens in Study Hall. When I arrive in the doorway everyone is already sitting quietly, but there's still half a minute to the bell and the teacher isn't there yet. Every seat is taken except mine, even though there are usually at least three or four empty seats around me. Someone must've moved the extra desks out of the room.

They've been planning this. Whatever this is.

The girls are smiling and whispering behind cupped hands as I walk by. I accidentally brush one girl's hand with my own when I pass her desk, and she jerks away with a gasp.

For a second the old anxiety comes back. The fear that she knows my secret.

Then I remember: none of these people know anything about who I really am. They've never even tried to.

I'm three feet from my desk when I see it.

My chair isn't empty after all. There's a clear liquid on it.

No. Not clear. Yellow.

I can smell it, too.

Urine. There is urine on my seat.

The others see me see it. And then the laughter starts.

I step back, wondering how they can stand to sit here with that smell. They're all rocking with laughter.

A few of them look disappointed. Probably wishing I'd sat down before I noticed.

The door swings open and the teacher, Mr. Dabney, comes in. The laughs die down to snickers. He strides over to his desk on the far side of the room as though nothing's amiss.

"Well, Sarah?" he says when the bell rings. "Will you be joining us for class today, or are you on your way somewhere more interesting?"

"I'm not sitting in that seat," I say. "I'll go get a chair from another class."

"The bell has rung," he says. "Sit down."

He can't be serious. "Sir, there's—"

Most of the boys, and a few of the girls, are laughing now. Mr. Dabney either hasn't figured out what happened or he doesn't care.

"Look," he says. "Either sit down or go see the principal."

Not the principal again. "But, *sir*—"

"Do you really think it's wise to keep talking back to me?"

So I leave.

I rewrite my Zachary Taylor essay while I wait in the principal's office. It's much easier here than in Study Hall where I'd be distracted by all the spitballs. By the time I get called in to see Principal Cole, Mr. Dabney has surely seen what happened, but he hasn't sent anyone to call me back to class.

The principal doesn't look at me when I come in. He's flipping through a stack of papers on his desk. I stand awkwardly by the door, since he hasn't told me to sit. The only other time I've been in his office was when I came to report what happened to Paulie. That time I didn't sit down, either. The principal just gave me a detention slip and sent me on my way.

"Sarah Dunbar," Principal Cole says, still looking at his papers. "Here you are again."

"Yes, sir."

"How many times have you been in my office this year?"

"This is the second time, sir."

He still hasn't looked up. "Seems like more than that."

He gestures with his papers to a hard plastic chair across from his desk. I sit.

"What is it this time?" he says.

I try to find a polite way to say it, but there isn't one. "Sir, Mr.

Dabney told me to come see you, because I wouldn't sit down in Study Hall, because someone had put urine on my seat."

The principal finally looks at me. He's about ten years older than Daddy, with thinning brown hair and wire-rimmed glasses perched on the end of his nose. "Are you trying to be funny, Sarah?"

"No, sir."

"My office is not the place for jokes."

"No, sir. I know, sir. I'm telling the truth, sir."

He leans back in his desk chair and meets my eyes. Last week I would've looked down demurely at my hands. Today I hold his gaze.

"Close the door," he says.

Startled, I stand up and reach for the door leading to the outer office. Miss Jones is looking right at me. I get a little relish out of closing the door in her face before I sit back down.

"I'm going to be frank with you, Sarah, because I sense a certain maturity in you," Principal Cole says. "This school year has been very difficult for all of us, but these problems were not unforeseen. I'm sure you're aware that the school board and administrators asked for more time to prepare before integration began, but those requests were denied by the courts. As a result, there's been some unpleasantness that could've been avoided. Like this nonsense in Mr. Dabney's class today."

I wonder if Principal Cole even listens to himself.

"Unpleasantness?" The words are coming out of me too fast. I can't stop them. "Is that what you call Paulie getting hit with a baseball? Yvonne getting run down in the hallway? Is unpleasantness what you call Chuck nearly getting *killed?*"

I stop to take a breath. Principal Cole is staring at me. He looks as surprised at my outburst as I am.

"I apologize, sir," I say quickly. "I—"

But I can't think of what to apologize for. I suppose I was being disrespectful, but there's nothing I said that I want to take back. Finally, I say, "I shouldn't have spoken out of turn."

"No, you shouldn't," the principal says. "Tell me, Sarah, how often *do* you speak out of turn?"

"Not often," I admit. The only times I can remember speaking out of turn all year have been with Linda.

"The school board anticipated that the Negro students entering white schools would have emotional difficulties," Principal Cole says. He isn't looking at me anymore. His eyes are hazy. "That was their chief argument for delaying integration. At the time, I questioned their position. I thought any supposed emotional problems would pale in comparison to the academic issues. The Negro schools are known to be inferior, so naturally, we worried that the white students would be impeded in their studies by teachers having to accommodate the Negroes in their classes. We've largely avoided that problem at Jefferson by tracking the Negro students into less challenging courses. But as for the emotional difficulties experienced by you Negroes— I'm sure you'll agree that the school board was right on the money with that one."

I clamp my mouth shut so I won't let loose what I'm really thinking again.

That's why they put us in Remedial. So we wouldn't hold the white kids back. Since they're so much smarter than us.

But now Principal Cole thinks we're having "emotional difficulties"?

What about the "emotional difficulties" from being told you aren't qualified to go to school with white people? The same white people who urinated on my chair?

"Sir," I say, measuring my words carefully, "Paulie didn't transfer schools because he was having emotional difficulties. He left because he was attacked. Physically."

Principal Cole takes off his glasses and pinches his nose. "Sarah, I'm going to ask you a question, and I'd like you to answer honestly, please. Tell me. Do you think I like seeing children get hurt?"

This feels like a trick. "No, sir."

"Things like what happened to your friend Paul. Do you think I want them happening in my school?"

"Of course not, sir."

"Then why on earth would I support something that was bound to lead down this path? It was inevitable, from the day the Supreme Court ruled, that children would wind up getting hurt. The courts can issue all the verdicts they like, but those judges aren't the ones who have to see it with their own eyes every day. They issued their ruling and washed their hands and left it for people like me to clean up the mess. I'm not bothered by childish nonsense like what happened in Mr. Dabney's class today, Sarah. When the doors to Jefferson opened in February, my priority was making sure every student in my school survived through June."

I open my mouth, but there are no words.

"So yes, Sarah, I call what's happened so far this year unpleasantness. And if we make it through the graduation ceremony without encountering anything more extreme than what we've already endured, I'll call that a victory. Are you planning to attend graduation?"

It's an odd question. He must know I'm a senior. "Yes, sir."

He nods, but his forehead creases. "Well, then. I'd say the hard part is over, but that might not be true. I suppose we'll see."

He stands up. I do, too. I know when I'm being dismissed.

I've gone through the door and am about to close it behind me when the principal says, "And, Sarah?"

I turn around. "Sir?"

"You're excused from Study Hall today."

I nod. "Thank you, sir."

I ignore Miss Jones's glare as I leave the office.

As I walk toward the stairwell, my loafers squeaking in the empty hallway, I realize something.

I'm not angry.

When I first started at Jefferson, a day like today would've made me furious. If I'd been Ruth's age it might've even made me cry.

Now it all simply seems ridiculous.

Urine. On my *chair*.

And they say the white people are supposed to be the civilized ones.

Principal Cole said he doesn't know yet if the hard part is over, but I know.

All year, the white people have been trying to show they have power over me. Because they've already figured out they have none.

I have the power.

I know what it feels like now.

For years, this was how I felt when I was singing. Now it's always there. And it's up to me to choose what I do with it.

My parents brought us to Davisburg because they wanted us to be part of the movement. I'm glad they did. I'm glad I've done what I've done. But it nearly broke me.

Maybe someday I'll write about injustice, like Daddy. Or be a lawyer like Ennis's father. Or a leader like Mrs. Mullins.

Except I'll be a different kind of leader. I won't lie to my people.

I want to help the movement. I just don't know how yet.

But whatever I do, it's up to me to choose what my future looks like.

I can keep sitting quietly, like a good girl.

Or I can get out the letter that came yesterday and decide for myself what happens next.

Chuck is awake.

Daddy tells us the news as soon as we get home from school.

Chuck woke up in the hospital this morning. He's still groggy, and his injuries are still serious, but he's going to live.

Ruth and I throw our arms around each other and laugh and cry. I pick her up and try to spin her around the way I did when she was little, but I don't get far. I let her go and we both fall, laughing, to the floor. Daddy tells us to behave ourselves like proper young ladies, now, but he's laughing, too, as he sends us up to our room to do our homework.

For the hour before dinner I think about not telling them after all. Now that we know Chuck is all right, it's become a happy day, a wonderful day, and I don't want to ruin it. But this can't wait any longer. I can't believe I've waited this long.

So as we're finishing up dessert, I tell Mama and Daddy there's something I want to talk about. They both look tired, but Mama nods and sends Ruth and Bobby upstairs. She can see how serious I am.

I show them the letter I got back from Mr. Deskins first. That will be the easy part.

They set it on the table between them and read it at the same time. Mama's frown deepens with each line. Daddy just looks horrified from start to finish.

"How did this happen?" Mama says. "Did you write to Mr. Deskins without telling us? Sarah, this is serious."

"I'll say it's serious." Daddy shoves the letter back at me. "While you are still under my roof you will—"

"I don't want to be under your roof," I say.

The kitchen is silent. None of us can believe I interrupted Daddy. Me least of all.

I force myself to keep going.

"It has nothing to do with you, of course," I say as fast as I can. "But I don't want to be here in Davisburg any second I don't have to. Not after what happened to Chuck. *Please*, Daddy. Mama, *please*, I need to do this."

They look at each other for a long time.

If they say no, I'll—I don't know what I'll do. Maybe I can survive in this town all summer.

If I never leave this house. If I never have to see another white person. Well, except one.

Finally Daddy turns back to me and taps the letter. "You'd be living with Frank Deskins and his wife. They'd keep an eye on you."

"Yes, of course."

Mr. Deskins works in the dean's office at Howard. He's the one who arranged for me to get my scholarship, and who made sure the school wouldn't hold it against me when I got placed in Remedial this year. When I asked if he could get me a job on campus for the summer, he wrote back right away and said yes. As long as I came up straight after graduation, and as long as I helped his wife take care of their two-year-old twins.

"They live in a nice neighborhood right near Howard," I say. "I'd be working in his office for the summer. It'll be a good chance to practice my typing. I'll send the money I earn back home to help out here."

Mama and Daddy don't look any more convinced than they did before, so I add, "Mama, you always said Mr. Deskins was a nice man, right? He's friends with Uncle John, isn't he?"

"Yes, of course he is," she says. "Honey, this isn't about whether Mr. Deskins is a nice man."

I know it isn't.

"We know you're upset about what happened to Chuck," Daddy says. "We all are. But what you have to understand, honey, is things like that don't only happen in Davisburg. Anywhere you go, you'll see things that aren't right."

I nod. I know it's the truth.

I still can't stay here.

"There's more," I say. "There's something else I want to ask you."

"There's *more?*" Daddy says.

But Mama doesn't look surprised. So I keep my eyes on her when I say, "I want Ruth to go back to Johns next year."

Daddy sits back in his seat, studying me. Mama doesn't move.

"She's been through enough," I say. "She deserves to go to a normal school. When I think of her living another three years like this one—I can't let her do it by herself. No one should have to."

They still haven't said anything.

I know what they're thinking. I'm thinking it, too.

No one should have to do what we did this year, but *someone* has to. If we don't, nothing will ever change.

This is how it works. Someone has to sacrifice. Or nothing will get better for any of us.

I just don't want to sacrifice my own little sister.

Finally Mama says, "Go get Ruth and bring her down here."

Does that mean they're saying yes?

I bite down my smile and run upstairs. Ruth is lying on her bed, writing in her diary and listening to a terrible Guy Mitchell song on the radio.

"Mama and Daddy want you downstairs," I say.

Her eyes widen. "Am I in trouble?"

"No. It's good news. Well, maybe." I'm grinning so wide, she starts grinning, too.

"Are we getting a dog?" she says.

"Don't be silly."

She rolls her eyes, but she runs down the stairs ahead of me anyway.

Mama and Daddy are waiting for us at the kitchen table. When she sees their serious expressions, Ruth's smile fades. She glances back at me, but I don't know what they're going to say, either, so I gesture for her to sit across from them. She does. I sit beside her and wait.

"There's something we'd like to tell both you girls," Daddy begins.

I nod, my smile starting to slip.

"We're very proud of the way you've handled things this year," he says. "We know it hasn't been easy. Most of the time it's been as hard as it can possibly be."

Ruth and I nod, waiting for them to get to the point.

"Sarah is leaving for college," Mama says. "She wants to leave right after graduation to work in Washington for the summer. And, Sarah, if that's what you really want, then you have our permission."

I close my eyes and say a quick prayer of thanks. Then I open my eyes and smile at my parents. "Thank you so much, sir, ma'am."

"There will be none of this sending money home, either," Daddy adds. "You won't learn a thing about what it means to earn a living that way. You let us worry about us and you worry about you."

"You didn't tell me you were leaving so soon." Ruth frowns at me.

"You should be happy," I say. "You'll have the whole room to yourself."

"That's true." She brightens. "But I'm going to miss you."

"Aww, Ruthie." I reach over to hug her. She squirms away.

Mama smiles. Then Daddy gives us a look that shuts both of us up.

"Ever since your first day at Jefferson, we've been talking about what Ruth should do next year," he says.

Ruth and I both bolt upright.

"You have?" Ruth says.

"We've made a decision," Daddy says. "You've had a difficult year, and you've worked hard. What you've done has made a huge difference. Next year another fifteen Negroes will be starting at Jefferson, and there will be thirty more at other white schools in the district."

"You've done enough, Ruthie," Mama says. "But we don't want

to have you transfer back to Johns next year. That would look like we were giving up. Instead you can move back to Chicago. We've had it planned since March. You'll live with your aunt and uncle and go to your cousins' school."

Chicago.

Our old school in Chicago was ten times better than Johns.

I can't believe Mama and Daddy are giving me what I asked for. Something *better* than what I asked for, even.

It isn't about sacrificing us for the movement. It's about making hard decisions. Because somebody has to.

But Ruth shakes her head.

"I can't do that," she says. "Don't you see? It wouldn't be right."

My sister is insane.

"Right?" I say. "What's happening now isn't *right*."

She shakes her head again. "You know what I mean."

"No, I don't." I can't believe my sister. I'm trying to help her and she's just being her usual stubborn self. "You're saying you want to go through another three years at Jefferson? By yourself?"

"I won't be by myself," she says. "I have my friends. And you heard Daddy. Next year there will be fifteen more of us. Who knows how many the year after that."

"What about cheerleading?" I say. "Are you just going to give up on ever having a normal life in high school?"

"Who says I can't cheer? They let you sing a solo at the concert. Maybe I'll try out for the squad next year. Who knows what will happen?"

"You're being crazy," I say. "Mama, Daddy, tell her she's being crazy."

But Mama and Daddy are grinning. Even wider than Ruth grinned when she thought we were getting a dog.

"Don't you see, Sarah?" Ruth says. "Someone has to do this. If we give up, nothing will ever change."

Yes. I see.

"Well, you can always change your mind, sweetie," Mama says. "It'll be your decision."

"I've decided," Ruth says.

"All right, then." Daddy stands up. "I have to say, I am very pleased with both of my daughters today."

"And here you thought you were going to be in trouble." I poke Ruth in her side.

"Ow!" She twists away.

She's so little to be making such a grown-up decision.

But she's not, really. Not so much littler than me.

I suppose Mama's right. I suppose it's her decision to make.

I suppose we all have to figure out our own futures.

I call her at Judy's house and ask her to meet me in the school parking lot. I hate the school parking lot, but it's the only place I can think of to meet at seven in the morning where we won't be seen.

It's still dark out when I arrive. She's already there, sitting on a concrete barrier and wearing a faded striped dress I recognize as Judy's. It's strange to see her out of her usual fashion-conscious skirt-and-sweater outfits.

"Hi," I say when I reach her.

"Hi." She stands up and smooths her skirt. She bites her lip and looks off to the side. We haven't talked in person since that afternoon in the alley.

"I'm leaving," I tell her. I don't know how else to say it. "Right after graduation. I have a summer job in Washington. My parents said they'll let me go."

She glances back at me for a second. Then looks away again.

"All right." She swallows.

"You should leave, too," I say. "You don't like it here any more than I do."

She gazes around the parking lot. The three stories of red brick that look more like a prison than a school. The scraggly trees and trampled grass that line the edges of the pavement. The street that leads downtown to the center of Davisburg. Linda's entire world.

She's been kicked off the staff of the school newspaper. Yvonne heard it somewhere. Next week the paper will print an apology for Linda's column about Chuck, saying it wasn't authorized and that the *Clarion* has a policy of not commenting on student disciplinary matters.

I don't know if Linda's heard the news yet. With no one talking to her at school, I might be better informed than she is now.

"I don't have anywhere to go," she says, her voice cracking. "I thought I did, but it won't work. It was all a lie."

"Then come with me." I know I sound crazy, so I say the rest as fast as I can. "There are a lot of jobs in a city like Washington. The family I'm staying with, they live there. They must know people who could find you somewhere to stay. There are a lot of colleges there, too. You could find one that takes late applications, and then in the fall you could—"

"Stop," she says. "Just stop. You know I can't do all that. I'm not like you."

"That's not true. You're the same as me. Except it'll be easier for you because you're white. You can go to any college you want, you can—"

"You have to be more than just white to pick up and start a whole new life." She stares down at the pavement. "Your parents are the ones sending you to college. I bet that's how you got the summer job, too."

I don't know what to say. I got the job for myself, but it wouldn't have happened if Mr. Deskins hadn't been friends with Uncle John.

Then I recognize that look on Linda's face. It's the same one she used to get when we'd argue about integration.

She doesn't really know what she's saying. She's making excuses, the way she always does.

Because she's afraid.

Linda's never lived anywhere but Davisburg. She's never lived with anyone she didn't have to hide from.

She's never even thought about what she really wanted.

I never did, either. Until now.

"Well what are you going to do, then?" I pose it as a challenge, the same way I used to when we'd argue. "Sit back and wait for someone to hand you a future? Or are you going to decide for yourself?"

That gets her attention. She looks up at me with shiny eyes. "I don't know. I just don't know."

"I don't know, either," I say.

We're talking about more than jobs and college.

We're talking about that day in the alley.

We're talking about this strange thing between us that we don't know how to talk about.

I don't know the words for how I feel about Linda. I don't know if it's the same thing girls are supposed to feel about boys or if it's something different. I don't know if it's right or wrong or somewhere in between. All I know is I've never felt anything like it before. And I'd like to keep on feeling it.

Is that enough?

I don't know.

"If you don't want to come to Washington you can go somewhere else," I say. "You don't have to come with me, but—is there anything for you here? Anything worth staying for?"

She gazes around the parking lot again.

"No," she says softly. "I used to think there was. But no. There's not a single thing."

"Then isn't it time you did something about that?"

She finally meets my eyes. "It's past time."

I take her hand and squeeze it. She squeezes back.

And even though there's no one else here, it feels like I'm holding Linda's hand in front of the whole world.

EPILOGUE
TRUTH #3

We did it.

Ruth

"SARAH DUNBAR, WITH honors."

We all stop breathing when they call her name.

Mama and Daddy are sitting on either side of me, gripping my hands. They're squeezing so hard my palms are getting sweaty, but I don't let go.

Sarah walks across the stage, her high heels clicking in the silent auditorium. Her back is so straight I bet you could balance an egg on her graduation cap and it wouldn't even roll.

Principal Cole smiles when he gives her the diploma. Even from here I can tell that surprises Sarah, but she smiles back.

Sarah turns around to pose for the photo, holding her diploma against her shoulder. Mr. Mack, Ennis's father, is taking pictures from up front. We all knew Daddy would be too nervous to work the camera.

The reporters snap photos, too. A dozen flashbulbs pop in Sarah's face.

Then, we wait.

This is when the shouting will start.

This is when anything else that's going to happen will happen.

That's why Mama and Daddy are so nervous. They don't talk about it, not around me, but I know it's all they're thinking about. It's all I'm thinking about, too.

It could be an egg thrown on the stage. Or some spitballs shot from the audience.

Or it could be a gunshot.

Mama is praying under her breath with her eyes wide-open. The prayer bobs in and out of my head. Not the words, really. Just the rhythm. Like breathing.

Thy kingdom come.
Thy will be done.

Nothing is happening.

Sarah is walking down the steps.

Nothing is happening.

It's over.

Without thinking, I leap to my feet and clap.

Mama and Daddy hiss at me to get down, but when nothing happens to me, either, they start clapping, too.

So do the Ennis's parents down front and a few other Negro families sitting near us. Even Principal Cole claps at Sarah's departing back.

No one shouted at her. No one did *anything*.

My sister graduated from Jefferson High School. She's the first Negro to do that *ever*.

"That was my sister," I tell the white couple behind us. The man doesn't look up, but the woman smiles at me. "My sister, Sarah."

"All right now, honey," Mama says, tugging on my arm. "Now sit down so the rest of the audience can see."

I sit, but I don't stop grinning.

She did it.

We did it.

Fifteen minutes later, it's Ennis's turn to walk across the stage, and Mama and Daddy tense up again.

But the same thing happens. Nothing.

Ennis crosses the stage, gets a handful of claps, poses for a photo and walks down again.

And when the whole class is done, and everyone throws their caps in the air, there are two black hands in the crowd of whites reaching for the sky.

All along, I was sure this would be worth it.

I was right.

We go to the bus station straight from the ceremony. I told Sarah that was silly. They should wait until later. They should at least go to the graduation party to say goodbye to their friends. Sarah said this was the only bus leaving all day, and anyway, she'd be back to visit. Then she said I should stop being such a busybody about everyone else's plans.

So I'm still wearing my itchy new church dress when Daddy hefts Sarah's last suitcase into the bus's luggage compartment with a grunt.

"What've you got in these, girl?" he says. "Rocks?"

Sarah smiles, but her chin is quivering. Any minute now she'll start crying like a baby.

I *told* her she shouldn't leave so soon. Maybe from now on she'll listen to me.

"You have Mr. and Mrs. Deskins's address, don't you?" Mama asks Sarah again. "You make sure to go straight there as soon as the bus gets in."

"I remember, Mama."

Mama nods. She's blinking back tears, too. Soon our whole

family will be bawling all over the Greyhound station parking lot.

The place is almost empty. Everyone else is still over at Jefferson. It's the only high school in town, except for Johns—that private school the white parents were setting up, the Davisburg Academy, is still trying to raise money—so everyone in town goes to graduation. The only other people at the station with us are Ennis, those two white girls Sarah knows, and one of the white girls' mothers.

One of the white girls, Linda Hairston, is taking the same bus as Sarah. She's staying for the summer with her aunt in Alexandria, right outside Washington. I told Sarah I thought it was funny they were taking the same bus, and she told me they planned it that way. She said they're going to spend some time together this summer, since they'll both be in the city. I told her that was funny, too, the idea of a white girl and a colored girl acting like they were friends. She told me things were different in Washington and I should mind my own business.

Ennis is saying goodbye to Sarah over by the suitcases. I pretend to check the luggage tags so I can listen to them.

"Take care of yourself," Ennis says. "I'll see you when I get up there in September. Maybe we can catch another movie sometime."

I hear the smile in Sarah's voice. "I'd like that."

I'd thought by now Sarah and Ennis would be going steady for sure, but he never asked, and she said that was fine with her. I don't know what's wrong with my sister sometimes.

Linda says goodbye to the other white girl and her mother and goes over to Sarah. Sarah waves at the other girl, too. The other girl, the brown-haired one who wears too much makeup, is holding her cheek and frowning.

The attendant steps down from the bus to say we've got two minutes until departure. He's looking back and forth from us to the white girls, his brow furrowed. Wondering about these two girls of different colors getting on a bus together, probably. He doesn't say anything about it, though.

Bobby is sitting on the curb, pouting. Ennis goes over to talk to Mama and Daddy. Sarah and Linda are whispering together.

I feel left out, so I sit on the curb with Bobby, tucking my skirt and crinoline under me so they won't get mashed.

"Don't you worry," I tell Bobby. "She'll be back for a visit before you even notice she's gone."

Bobby sticks his lip out farther. He always does that. He thinks it makes people feel sorry for him. It mostly just makes us laugh.

Sarah and Linda are still whispering. What could they possibly have to talk about? Aren't they about to get on a bus where they can talk for hours?

Sarah leans down to move one of her suitcases over to the side. Linda puts her hand on Sarah's back to steady her. I'm surprised she'd touch a colored girl after those articles she wrote in the school paper against integration.

Over on the sidewalk the other white girl clasps her hand over her mouth and her face wrinkles up, like she's horrified to see them touching. That's funny. I thought Sarah said that girl was all right with colored people.

"One minute," the attendant calls.

Sarah hugs Mama and Daddy goodbye, then lifts Bobby to his feet and squeezes him tight.

She comes to me last. She's finally crying. I am, too, but at least I have the decency to pretend otherwise.

"Be *careful*," she tells me. "I don't want to hear any reports about you acting reckless. It's not worth it."

"I know, I know." I'll be as careful as I want to be. I'm not the same person Sarah is.

"Listen." She drops her voice. "There's something I want to tell you. It's important, so I need you to listen, all right?"

"I'm listening." I shift from foot to foot. Sarah can be so earnest sometimes. It's tiresome.

"Other people will always try to decide things for you," she says. "They'll try to tell you who you are. Remember, no matter what they say, *you're* the one who really decides."

I shift my feet again, playing that back in my head, trying to figure out what it means. "You're not going to major in philosophy in college, are you?"

She sighs. "Just don't forget it, all right?"

"All right, all right." I nod the way I do whenever an adult tells me something they think is really important.

Sarah rolls her eyes. I roll mine back. We laugh.

Sarah and Linda climb up the steps of the bus. They turn around and wave to us. They're both grinning, even though Sarah is still wiping tears from her eyes.

Then they turn around and wind their way into the bus. They sit together in the backseat. I can see them through the window.

They're not looking at us anymore. They're talking with their heads bent close together. Closer than a colored girl and a white girl really should if they know what's good for them.

Unless they know more about what's good for them than everybody else is supposed to.

I keep watching them together as the bus pulls off and rolls away from us. I keep watching them in my mind even when they're too far away to see.

I don't understand everything that's happening, but I think I might be starting to.

And I think I know what Sarah meant when she said I'm the one who really decides.

* * * * *

Author's Note

WHEN I TALK with people about this book, they sometimes ask, "Was desegregation really that bad?" I never know exactly what to say. Every state, every school, every student had a different story. There were schools in the South that integrated largely without incident. But there were also schools where the integration process was much worse than at the fictional school in *Lies We Tell Ourselves*. In Birmingham, Alabama, a black minister was beaten with chains and baseball bats when he tried to enroll his daughters in an all-white high school. In Norfolk, Virginia, a black high-school student was stabbed by a white man while walking up the steps to her newly integrated school. Fortunately, they both made full recoveries—but there's no doubt that the danger faced by those involved in the early school desegregation battles was very real.

I grew up in Virginia in the 1990s, only one generation removed from these events. My parents were teenagers when the white public schools they attended were first integrated through the token desegregation efforts that took place in much of Virginia in the 1960s. The Supreme Court's *Brown v. Board of Education* ruling mandating the end of segregation came down in 1954, but many school districts in the South would remain effectively segregated for another twenty years or more.

A lot of schools today are still struggling with similar issues to the ones they dealt with decades ago. Sadly, discrimination, inequality and hate violence are very much still with us.

In my day job as a nonprofit communications strategist, I've served at organizations focusing on educational equity, gay rights, women's rights and beyond. I've worked on issues ranging from affirmative action to fair pay for women to the military's old "Don't Ask, Don't Tell" policy on gay service members. Though the issues we deal with now are much narrower in scope than school desegregation, it's amazing how often we seem to be having the same conversations today that activists had at the peak of the civil rights movement.

Lies We Tell Ourselves was a difficult book to write. I wasn't there to witness the school integration battles, and I've certainly never experienced anything like what Sarah, Ruth and their friends do in these pages. So I did a lot of research, focusing on memoirs and oral histories from the people who were on the front lines. Those histories were painful to read, and this book was painful to write. But none of it compares to the pain, and the heroism, of the people who lived it.

When a student like Sarah signed up to be on the front lines of the desegregation battle, it meant every single day she was plunged into a situation that was uncertain at best and dangerous at worst. It meant saying goodbye to what you knew—to your friends, your community and often your safety. It meant surrendering your life as you knew it for a cause that was much bigger than you.

For white students at integrated schools, desegregation meant a major life change, too. Although some were as opposed to the integration movement as Linda and Bo, many white students had never given a thought to it until they found themselves facing closed schools or potential violence in the hallways.

Although the sources I drew from for this story focused on real desegregation battles in Virginia and in Little Rock, Arkansas, the setting, characters and situations in *Lies We Tell Ourselves* are entirely fictional. There is no actual town called "Davisburg, Virginia." Sarah, Linda and the other characters in this book are not based on real people.

However, under a set of policies known as Massive Resistance, several school districts in Virginia did close their schools to avoid integration in 1958, including in Norfolk, Front Royal and Charlottesville. Another Virginia school district, Prince Edward County, shut down its entire public school system in 1959 and didn't reopen its schools until 1964. For more on what really happened in those school integration battles, do a search on "Massive Resistance" or check out some of the other sources listed below.

Memoirs I read while working on *Lies We Tell Ourselves* included *The Norfolk 17: A Personal Narrative on Desegregation in Norfolk, Virginia in 1958–1962* by Andrew I. Heidelberg; *Students on Strike: Jim Crow, Civil Rights, Brown, and Me* by John A. Stokes, about Prince Edward County, Virginia; *Warriors Don't Cry: A Searing Memoir of the Battle to Integrate Little Rock's Central High* by Melba Pattillo Beals; *A Mighty Long Way: My Journey to Justice at Little Rock Central High School* by Carlotta Walls Lanier; *The Long Shadow of Little Rock* by Daisy Bates; and *Lessons from Little Rock* by Terrence Roberts. I also learned a lot from David Margolick's book *Elizabeth and Hazel: Two Women of Little Rock* and his article in *Vanity Fair,* "Through a Lens, Darkly."

I watched and listened to interviews with the pioneers who integrated schools in Virginia in the 1950s and 1960s, including several members of the Norfolk 17, as well as black students who integrated all-white schools in other districts. For those interested in learning more about the history of integration in Virginia, I recommend two videos: "The Norfolk 17," produced by WHRO in February 2009, and "It's Just Me... The Integration of the Arlington Public Schools," produced by Arlington Educational Television in 2001.

I also relied on many newspaper articles in my research, including clips from the 1950s and 1960s and recent retrospective pieces. I found a *Virginian-Pilot* series on the Norfolk 17 printed in 2008, "When the Wall Came Tumbling Down" by Denise Watson Batts, especially helpful. Other newspapers I consulted included the *Daily Press* of Hampton Roads, Virginia, the *Roanoke Times,* the *Washington Post* and the *Charlottesville Daily Progress.*

Also of help to me in my research was a series of oral histories in the Virginia Black History Archives, "African-American Richmond: Educational Segregation and Desegregation." I also relied on articles and papers by scholars including Carl Tobias, James McGrath Morris and James Andrew Nichols.

Other nonfiction books I recommend for those interested in learning more about this era include *The Race Beat: The Press, the Civil Rights Struggle, and the Awakening of a Nation* by Gene Roberts and Hank Klibanoff, *Freedom's Children* by Ellen Levine and *The Warmth of Other Suns: The Epic Story of America's Great Migration* by Isabel Wilkerson.

The values many of us take for granted today are the result of hard-fought battles that happened years, decades and centuries ago. Working alongside the civil rights leaders we revere today, like Rev. Martin Luther King, Jr., and Rosa Parks, there were hundreds, if not thousands, of now-forgotten activists who sacrificed everything they had so people today could live the way we do. Every generation needs to remember that—and to remember that it's up to us to make sacrifices of our own for the ones who will come next.

Acknowledgments

THIS BOOK NEVER could have been finished, let alone published, if I hadn't had a lot of help.

Many thanks to my agent, Jim McCarthy, who picked me out of the slush pile and didn't blink an eye when I sent him this book, even though it was completely unlike anything I'd written before.

Thanks to my editor, T. S. Ferguson, who believed in this book, fought for it and worked his editorial magic on it. Thanks also to Natashya Wilson, Tracy Sherrod, Lathea Williams, the amazing design team and everyone else at Harlequin Teen who helped make *Lies We Tell Ourselves* a reality.

Thanks to the librarians in the Virginia Room at the Arlington Central Library, who pulled newspaper files and video clips and copy after copy of vintage yearbooks for me, and who didn't seem to think it was weird at all that I kept taking pictures of every page with my iPhone.

Thanks to Jessica Spotswood and Caroline Richmond, the

very first people I told about this book idea, whose support was key to my getting started on that extremely intimidating first draft. Thanks also to all of my other awesome writer friends who read my early drafts of *Lies,* even the really terrible ones, and were kind enough to give me fantastic feedback despite said terribleness, including Andrea Colt, Jaclyn Dolamore, Kathleen Foucart, Amy Jurskis, Miranda Kenneally and Anna-Marie McLemore. Their help was essential to getting this book in print.

Thanks to all my writer-and-reader friends in the DC MafYA, the Fourteenery and beyond. With such a wonderful writerly community, this job doesn't feel nearly as solitary as it's probably supposed to.

Thanks to my parents, Ray and Jean Reed, and to my aunt Sheila Talley, who always supported my writing, and who shared with me their memories of Villager blouses, circle pins and growing up in 1950s Virginia under segregation. Thanks to Mary and Steven Smith, who listened to me talk about my writing for years and encouraged me to stick with it.

And finally, thanks to Julia, for understanding and believing in this book, and in me.

Questions for Discussion

Common Core aligned and suggested for book club use.

1. How does the theme of the title, *Lies We Tell Ourselves*, present itself through the course of the book?

2. How do the lies and truths that start each chapter relate to the story as it unfolds? How do they impact your understanding of the novel? Cite quotes and phrases from the book to support your answer.

3. What are some of the parallels you can draw between being black and being gay in 1959 Virginia? How are the two similar and different? Use evidence from the text to justify your response.

4. Sarah spends much of the book trying to protect her younger sister, Ruth, who is very strong in her own right. In what ways does Ruth exhibit her strength? Cite specific words, phrases, and actions from the book to defend your response.

5. Why do you think Judy is so much more accepting of the black students than Linda and the rest of their white classmates? Support your answer with specific character traits and quotes and phrases from the novel.

6. Why does Sarah fall for Linda, who spends much of her time speaking out against integration?

7. Sarah and Linda have grown up in very different worlds, but in what specific ways have their lives been similar?

8. Linda tells Sarah that she hates her father, but she is constantly reciting his beliefs. Why do you think that is?

9. Chuck becomes involved romantically with a white girl. How does what happens to him relate to Sarah's relationship with Linda?

10. How is our current problem with bullying and cyber bullying in America's schools similar and different to the racism and abuse experienced by the African American students of this era?

11. How does the shift in first person point of view from Sarah to Linda and finally to Ruth, impact the reader? Why do you think the author chose to do this? What does it accomplish?

12. How does the author use Linda's school newspaper editorials to help move along the plot and shed light on both her character, and the opinions of the white segregationists of Davisburg? Defend your analysis with quotes and phrases from the text.

13. There are a variety of themes in this novel. List a few of them. What parts of the text helped you identify these themes?